Catriona McPherson, formerly a linguistics lecturer at the University of Leeds, now divides her time between California and Scotland. She writes full-time.

Also by Catriona McPherson from Constable

Strangers at the Gate

Catriona McPherson

CONSTABLE

CONSTABLE

First published in Great Britain in 2019 by Constable
This paperback edition published in 2020 by Constable

Copyright © Catriona McPherson, 2019

1 3 5 7 9 10 8 6 4 2

The moral right of the author has been asserted.

*All characters and events in this publication, other than those clearly in the public domain,
are fictitious and any resemblance to real persons, living or dead, is purely coincidental.*

All rights reserved.
No part of this publication may be reproduced, stored in a retrieval system, or transmit-
ted, in any form, or by any means, without the prior permission in writing of the
publisher, nor be otherwise circulated in any form of binding or cover other than that in
which it is published and without a similar condition including this condition being
imposed on the subsequent purchaser.

A CIP catalogue record for this book is available from the British Library.

ISBN: 978-1-47212-781-5

Typeset in Minion Pro by SX Composing DTP, Rayleigh, Essex
Printed and bound in Great Britain by Clays Ltd., Elcograf S.p.A.

Papers used by Constable are from well-managed forests
and other responsible sources.

Constable
An imprint of
Little, Brown Book Group
Carmelite House
50 Victoria Embankment
London EC4Y 0DZ

An Hachette UK Company
www.hachette.co.uk

www.littlebrown.co.uk

This is for Leslie Budewitz,
in sisterhood

Before

Looking back, it's tempting to say I knew from the start, as soon as Paddy said the word for the first time. I can nearly convince myself I shivered at the sound of it. *Simmerton.*

But I'd be lying. Truth is, there was a while back then when everything seemed fine. Or even better than fine. Everything seemed golden. If there were worries they were the usual kind that everyone has and then remembers, laughing. If I had doubts, it was only because I was prone to be doubtful. And the odd little frights and freak-outs? They were just stories to tell the grandchildren, come the day.

One thing's for sure. It arrived in my life dressed up as a lottery win. Paddy came bursting in after work one night, brimming. He clattered round the flat looking for me. I was in the loo so he started telling me through the locked door, upping the volume to be heard over the flush and taps.

'Partner!' he said, when I came out. 'I'm not even forty!' He held up a hand. 'I'm trying not to get ahead of myself, before you say anything. I know I haven't even been for the first interview yet.'

'I wasn't going to say anything,' I told him. 'You were invited to apply. That's good. I didn't even know that *happened*.'

'Invited to apply.' He echoed it as if the words tasted sweeter every time he repeated them.

'And the commute won't be too much?' I asked him.

'The commute'll be a beast!' he said. Finally he was setting down his briefcase and shrugging off his suit jacket, sliding it onto its hanger. 'It'll be pretty dull stuff once I get there too. Country solicitors. A bit of conveyancing and a lot of wills.'

'But partner,' I said.

'Under forty!'

When he came home from the second interview, I was waiting at the big window in our living room, looking down along the street, and I couldn't tell anything from his walk or the top of his head, bowed against the cold wind. When he got up to the flat, he took my hands in his. His face was so solemn – his beautiful face that I was still learning, a year into our marriage – that my pulse began to bump. He's leaving me, I thought. He's busted me. What else would make him look like that?

'It's *not* boring, Finn,' he said. 'It's anything but. It's specialised work and I'm made for it. I get now why they chose me.'

'Oh?'

'And that's not all. Have you been checking online?'

I sighed. I was supposed to be looking for a full-time post instead of what I had, which was three mornings clocked on and seventy hours of unpaid overtime. But I was too knackered and I didn't believe the job was out there to be found. I'd been telling myself that Paddy's good fortune would have to do for us both. I was new at being half of a whole, but I'd got that bit off.

'Because look,' Paddy said, letting go of my hands to scroll through his phone. He showed me the page on the Church of Scotland website. 'And I've got you an appointment to go down and talk to them.'

'Why would a town like Simmerton need a full-time deacon?' I said, once I'd read the job advert through twice and couldn't find any catches.

'Will you go?' was all the answer I got.

'Of course, but there's going to be a stampede. I've got no chance.'

I was wrong. One stormy night in November, with the windscreen wipers smearing and squeaking and the wind rocking the car, Paddy drove me down to Simmerton Parish Church where I met the minister and some of the elders. The job offer came pinging through as soon as we got to good phone reception on the drive home. A year guaranteed and maybe more, depending on funds raised.

Like winning the lottery. Golden.

Then, three weeks ago, more. Paddy came in from work so flushed and bright-eyed I thought he'd been at the pub. He had found someone who wanted to rent the flat for a year, he told me, at a price that would cover the mortgage every month with five hundred smackers to spare.

'This could be our chance to get started,' he said. 'On the—'

He didn't say 'housing ladder'. He knew I'd laugh at him. But that was what he meant. As far as I could see, we were already on the housing ladder. We owned our flat, with its high ceilings and deep skirtings. We owned our car outright. He had no student debt. This mysterious tenant was the solution to a problem we didn't have.

'And where would *we* live?' I said. I put a bookmark in my paperback and set it on the arm of my chair. We had an armchair in the kitchen. That's how already started we were.

'Simmerton,' Paddy said. 'Where else?'

'I don't want to be so far from my mum,' I said. 'In case there's a crisis.'

'That's what *I* thought,' said Paddy. 'But then I did it on the satnav.' He was digging his phone out of his pocket, as if I wouldn't believe him unless he showed me. 'It takes no more time to get up from Simmerton to your mum and dad's than it does to get all the way out there from here through the traffic. It's not closer, but it's quicker.'

I could see the point of that. If I was racing to my mum in an emergency, I'd rather be belting along quiet roads than crawling behind four buses. 'But *where* would we live?' I said. 'Even if it makes sense, it would mean house-hunting while we're getting settled in our jobs, and all the expense.'

'Well, this is the funny thing,' Paddy said. 'Lovatt's wife came out for lunch with us and she said they've got a gate lodge at their place. And we were welcome to it.'

'A *gate* lodge? Do they live in a stately home, like? Wait a minute, when was this?'

Paddy shrugged. 'Just a country house, I think. Widdershins.'

Widdershins. I'm not looking back through cracked glasses this time. 'That's an unlucky name to give a house,' I said.

'Probably old,' said Paddy. 'Not their choice.' He shucked off his jacket and threw it through the kitchen door towards the coat pegs. It slid to the floor, crumpled on top of my shoes.

'And *when* was this?' I said, trying to make sense of it.

'When I went down to sign things. Couple of weeks back. Want a cuppa?'

'Couple of weeks back, your boss's wife offered you a house,' I said. 'And you said to her we were keeping our flat in Edinburgh?'

'The conversation moved on before I had a chance.' He was facing the other way, filling the kettle. I stared at his back. 'I didn't want to be rude so I sort of just said that was very kind and I'd let her know.'

I watched him carefully when he turned round to face me again. 'Right,' I said eventually. 'Lovatt Dudgeon's wife offered you cheap digs in the arse end of nowhere and you left it hanging and then someone just happened to ask if they could rent our flat?'

'That's pretty much the size of it.'

If one of my repeat clients at work was telling me all this, in that voice, not meeting my eye, I'd know what to think: he had accepted the offer of the lodge and scouted round for a tenant without telling me.

'It's like something from a fairytale, Finnie,' he said. 'A little cottage in a wood. Latticed windows and crooked chimneys. '

'So you've been to see it, then?'

Paddy cleared his throat. 'We drove past it on the way to the house for lunch, like I said.'

'Actually, you said you'd gone "out for lunch" and you said you "thought" Lovatt Dudgeon had a country house.'

He was watching me now, chewing at the inside of his cheek. 'You're always telling me I don't take charge,' he said. 'Make your mind up.'

After one beat, I laughed. It was true. I loved Paddy, had loved him – or fancied him at least – from the moment I first clapped eyes on him across a crowded pub, but he did drive me nuts, with the watchfulness and the careful planning before any step, big or small. Once I'd met his mum it wasn't a mystery any more, but it was still annoying.

'Tell me this,' I said. 'Have you signed anything?'

'No way. Not without your say-so. If you want to stay here, driving two hours a day, that's what we'll do. But if you want to have a house practically free and be right there where you need to be, for your job . . .'

'My job's only for a year,' I said.

'So's the lease,' said Paddy. 'So's the tenant. It's perfect.'

'It is,' I said. 'It all fits. It's golden.'

'Golden,' Paddy repeated, and he laughed. I'd never heard him laugh like that before. He laughed at jokes and mean little videos online, but that was the first time I heard him laugh like a child, from delight. It was irresistible.

The day we moved in, he was as high as a kite. He loved the place. *Loved* it. I'd had no idea this waxed-jacket, black-Labrador stranger was lurking inside the taxi-taker I'd married. He didn't seem to notice I wasn't as giddy as him and I was glad of that. I didn't like being the drag suddenly.

Maybe if we'd driven down together, I'd have caught his excitement or he'd have caught my apprehension and we'd have settled in the middle. But Paddy had driven the hire van – half full of a fraction of our furniture, since the gate lodge had only two rooms – and I followed in the car with the back seats flat, clothes and bedding piled so high I couldn't use the mirror. Our pal Tony brought up the rear in his Jeep, ferrying the patio set that was a combined leaving and house-warming present from both our old jobs.

And so, as I crossed the bypass and the road went down to two lanes, as I passed a permanent car-boot-sale site, a steading development, and a flipping farm-machinery showroom for crying out loud, my mood darkened and darkened.

As I draw nearer to Simmerton, the hills rose on either side and crept close. I turned my headlights on. Pine trees loomed over me, dizzying when I looked up at their dwindling tips and black as death when I looked straight out at the solid bulk of their trunks in the deep shadow.

The town itself was tucked into the narrowest slit you could ever call a valley. Just one main street and a struggle of lanes on either side, clutching at the hills, soon enough giving up and petering out into those miles of pine trees.

'It's a bit gloomy,' I'd said on that first visit in November, in the rain.

'I think it's cosy,' Paddy had replied.

'Cosy,' I repeated to myself on moving day, when I was alone in the cottage for the first time. Paddy and Tony had gone into Lanark to return the van and scare up a pizza. I abandoned the two damp rooms full of boxes and went outside. Saturday night, I thought. And there wasn't a sound to be heard. There wasn't a prick of light to be seen. Just the black to either side, and the sliver of sky a denser shade of black between them. The gateposts were two smudges and the drive no more than a wet glint as it curled away and threaded into the forest. Not a forest, Paddy had said.

A *planting*. I didn't know the difference, but the company who leased the land for all those trees were his clients now.

I turned and looked at the gate lodge instead. It was squat and squint, with one bulbous bay window, like a toad's eye, lumpy harling the colour of mud. Cottages, I reckoned, should be whitewashed with thatched roofs and you should live in them for a week, then go home. Still, I'd agreed to a year of this so I tried to find a bright side.

We had a garden. There was that. I'd never had a garden before. I'd never dried washing anywhere except over radiators or on a clothes horse out on my mum and dad's balcony. I made my way round the side, the clenched side of the house without the bay window, round to the square of slabs where our house-warming present had been dumped. The cushion farted in its plastic wrapping as I threw myself down onto one of the steamer chairs, put my feet up on one of the little teak tables, and looked out across the drying green into the blackness, listening to the crackle of my eustachian tubes as I strained to hear something, anything. I stuffed my hands into my parka pockets and headbanged until my hood flopped over to cover my hair. I lit an imaginary cigarette and lay back. Actually, I hadn't smoked since the wedding, but I still found myself rolling up till receipts and dreaming, whenever I was alone. I even tapped to trim imaginary ash. Ironic if I gave myself cancer from fake-smoking receipts and inhaling the BPA.

One year, I told myself. I knew I could do a year. It wouldn't be the first time. I would get used to the quiet. And the trees. I would stop seeing them out of the corner of my eye and thinking someone was there. If only they looked a bit less like a silent army of strangers standing dead still and watching me. Or if only the ones at the edge didn't wave as the wind stirred them, looking as if they were shuffling their feet, just about to speak. If only there weren't faces etched into the swirl of the bark, knot-hole mouths wide open and black eyes weeping resin tears.

The first scream split the dark without warning. Starting pure and ending ragged, it echoed round the valley. I leaped up as a second came right on its heels, even longer and more piercing.

'Who's there?' I shouted. 'Are you okay?'

But it didn't sound like someone in trouble. It didn't sound anything like that girl in the underpass that time when I'd pelted forward to help her, only later thinking about what could have happened to me. This sounded like rage. Inhuman, maniacal rage.

My phone was in the house. I had nothing to use as a weapon. I couldn't even tell where the screams were coming from, couldn't plan where to lash out, if I'd had something to lash out with.

It was getting closer, though. I knew that much. I crouched behind the recliner, feeling my throat start to close. This couldn't be happening. It was the first night. The city was supposed to be dangerous, not the countryside.

Then I saw a sickly light sweep along the side of the house and rake across the trees, and I heard the Jeep engine. Paddy and Tony were coming back. I turned towards the drive just as a bundle of white tumbled out of the shadows and blew towards me. Ducked down with my arms over my head, I didn't even know I was screaming until I heard Paddy answering me.

'Finn?' He was charging towards me, skidding on moss

11

and leaves. 'What's wrong? Are you all right?' He was down beside me now, feeling my arms and shoulders all over as if I might be broken.

'Someone screamed in the trees and threw a carrier bag at me.'

'Threw a *carrier* bag?' Tony said. Paddy sat back on his heels and frowned. Tony had gone over to where the trees began and was squinting into the darkness.

'It could have been a pillow case,' I said. 'I shut my eyes.'

'Why would anyone—' Paddy had got out when a new scream came rolling down from the treetops.

'How's it so *high*?' I said. I knew I was whimpering, but the vision in my head was of someone scuttling away and scaling a tree, still screeching. 'I want to go home, Paddy. It's not safe here. Take me home.'

'It's a barn owl,' Tony said. 'It's high because it can fly. It flew at you because you frightened it.'

I opened my mouth to argue but the sense of it hit me in time.

'That's an owl?' I said. 'That noise is an *owl*? And aren't owls brown?'

'They're pale underneath,' said Tony. He was trying not to laugh at me. Not Paddy, though: his face was stark white, as if *he*'d had the shock and I should comfort him.

'Did you get a pizza?' I said.

They had but I was still too flooded with adrenalin to swallow and Paddy only picked at his too. Tony ate one slice and left.

Later, I stood at the bedroom window, looking out into that blackness again.

'It's not ideal, is it?' I said. Because the bedroom looked right out at the gateposts. In fact, because the window was bowed, it looked out at the lane on one side of the gateposts and the drive on the other. 'If anyone comes along, they'll see in. Same with the living room.'

'Well, duh,' Paddy said, 'it's a *gate* lodge. That's the whole point. The lodge-keeper was supposed to watch for carriages and go scampering out to open the gates and close them again.'

'They stay open all the time now, though, right?' I said. 'I mean we're not "scampering" instead of paying rent, are we?'

'Give it a chance, Finnie!'

'I'm giving it a chance. Look where I am. I've moved in, in case you haven't noticed. I ate that God-awful pizza, didn't I?'

'No, you didn't,' Paddy said.

'I didn't complain about it.'

'Till now.' He had a point. 'We can make our own pizza,' he said. 'Think about it: a partnership, a full-time deaconship and a free cottage? We've won the—'

'Lottery,' I said. 'Yeah. You do know, don't you, what the usual explanation is, when things look too good to be true?'

Monday

Chapter 1

We were walking up the dark drive to the big house. The fog was so thick it swallowed my torch beam a step ahead of me, so thick it dripped from the trees pressing in on both sides, so thick it turned my breath loud in my ears and cold in my mouth.

It was me that heard the footsteps because Paddy was sloshing through the puddle and I was edging round it.

'Hey!' I said, urgent but quiet. 'Someone's there.'

'*What?*' His voice was a squawk, and whoever it was up in the trees heard him and started plunging away from us, cracking twigs and kicking leaves.

'There!' I said. 'Listen.' But there was nothing to hear now. I played my torch back and forth, peering into the dazzle of lit-up fog.

'It was probably an echo.' Paddy was beside me now, his eyes screwed up and his chest rising and falling. 'Switch your torch off.'

I did. A second later another little bead of light snapped off too.

'My God,' I breathed. 'Did you see that?'

'Reflection,' Paddy said, but his voice was shaking. 'It's the fog. Playing tricks.'

'More fool us for letting it,' I said. 'Why didn't we *drive*?'

'We'd look like townies,' said Paddy. He was back to his normal voice. Me moaning meant him mocking, the seesaw of our marriage rocking steady on its base again.

'We *are* townies,' I said. Him putting on airs meant me puncturing them. Seesaw. 'A car would have given them warning we were on our way. Same as an entry-phone. This way, it's like we're ambushing them.'

'They invited us.'

'Actually, Paddington, they didn't invite us. Lady Bountiful just *informed* us.'

'One night,' he said. 'A welcome party.'

'And an office party on Friday to welcome us again. Then we'll need to have them over to ours. Before you know it, we'll be playing bridge.'

'I can think of worse things. Anyway, we need to sign the house papers.'

I said nothing. Typical lawyers, was what I was thinking. We were paying the council tax and bills in a free house off a colleague but God forbid we'd wing it. Anyway, it wasn't free at all, if this was in the small print. Paddy had never made me hang out with lawyers when we lived in Edinburgh. I loved that about him. 'We'll probably get run over,' I said, 'stumbling along a lane like something from Thomas Hardy.'

'They go in and out the other way,' Paddy said. 'She just came round by us today to say hello. And make your mind up. You can't get run over if it's too quiet. Do you like traffic or not? Eh? Finnie? Eh?'

The truth was I liked traffic that went past on the street, nothing to do with me. At teatime, when I'd heard a car, I was perfectly happy. It was when I realised the car was slowing and stopping right outside the gate lodge I felt my pulse quicken. I drew myself into the shadows at the back of the room where no one – Jehovah's Witness, broom-seller, serial-killer – would see me. When I heard the front-door handle rattling, I went through to the hall, keeping my right hand hidden behind my back.

The key turned, the door opened and Paddy put his head round it. 'Finn?' He'd squinted at me. 'Why's the door locked? Is that a *hammer*?'

'I'm hanging pictures,' I said. 'Was that a car?'

'Did you think it was an owl?' Paddy said.

But I wasn't ready to laugh about the owl yet. 'Who's there?' I said.

Paddy stood back and held the door wide for a tall, thin old lady in a belted mackintosh and buckled wellies. She had white hair brushed straight back and clenched up in a row of curls at her collar, like the Queen. A slash of red lipstick was the only colour on her pale, powdered face. Also like the Queen. She had better bones, though.

She was simpering up at Paddy. I'd seen it before. He could charm the birds from the trees. I used to watch him at church functions and marvel. One time he got out of a speeding ticket and the policeman even apologised for making us late.

'Tuft Dudgeon,' the woman said, dragging her eyes away from his face at last and marching up to stick out a hand. 'And you must be Finnie.' Her fingernails were red too and she wore a lot of rings. They dug into my palm as we shook. 'Welcome to Widdershins. I told Paddy here I wouldn't take no for an answer. You are having supper with us tonight. Seven for eight, dears.'

Then she turned round, wellies squeaking on the lino and marched off again.

'Tuft,' I said. 'Lovatt and Tuft Dudgeon.'

But Paddy didn't laugh with me. He laughed at me. 'I can't believe you're greeting guests with a hammer,' he said.

'I thought it had all changed,' I said, gazing after Tuft. 'Scampering out when they click their fingers.'

'What?' said Paddy.

'Never mind.' I went outside to make sure she had really gone and saw Paddy's racing bike sitting on its kickstand on the gravel. 'She gave you a lift home, then? That didn't last long.'

'She offered. I couldn't refuse.'

'Scamper, scamper,' I said, under my breath, as he wheeled his bike round to the shed.

Whether he heard me or not, he was smiling again when he came in at the kitchen door. 'It's Monday-night supper,' he said. 'We'll be back in time for the ten o'clock news.'

'That's not the point.' We had lived in our lovely flat for eighteen months and never crossed any of our neighbours' thresholds, except to feed a downstairs cat. And since when did he call it 'supper'? I went into the other room to where our so-called drinks collection was half unpacked. I thought we had a new bottle of sherry, but it turned out to be port and it was Tesco's own brand.

'What are you doing?' Paddy said.

'We can't go empty-handed.' I had my head in the fridge now, thinking maybe there was some posh pickle or something I could wrap in tissue paper. But we had cleared out all that crap before we moved.

20

'Ahem.' I looked up. He was holding a Christmas cactus, covered with flowers. 'I'm not a caveman, you know.'

'How did you get that home without her seeing it?'

'She didn't ask. People like the Dudgeons are masters of not noticing things.'

'People like the Dudgeons,' I echoed. 'Posh gits, you mean? Are you sure you want to take me along? What if they ask where I went to school?

'They won't,' said Paddy. 'They already know all about both of us.'

So there was that, too. Now, as I tramped up the drive in the pitch black, going for a meal I didn't want with a pair of old farts I didn't know, it hardly helped to wonder what they'd unearthed about me.

The drive had been tarmacked sometime in its life, but there were ridges and potholes, these days, and a deep ditch on both sides. Paddy had boots on and trudged straight through the bumps and puddles. I had put on a half-decent pair of wedges to go with my wrap dress and was picking my way a bit more carefully. When a giant sinkhole appeared in our torch beams, he went through it on one side, I round it on the other.

So we were far apart, right at either edge, when I saw the movement and Paddy said it was an echo, and then a reflection, and I didn't believe him. I don't know how long we stood there, the two of us. The *three* of us. It was long enough for my heart to stop banging and my fingers to stop tingling. Long enough for the slump after the rush to kick in. I felt my shoulders fall and turned to Paddy. I could see the glint of his wide-open eyes and the tiny white puffs of his panicky breathing. He wouldn't admit it, but he was as spooked as me.

'Hey,' I said, reaching out and squeezing his arm, before a cracked branch had me whipping my head back round again. Out there, in the trees, there was a flash of paleness, then the steady rustle of dead leaves as someone moved away up the hill. '*That*'s not an owl,' I said.

Paddy let go a long breath at last. 'No. It was a deer.'

'It had a torch. Deers don't have torches.'

'Deer don't have an *s* either,' said Paddy. 'It's like "sheep". And it wasn't a torch. It was a reflection. Let's ask Lovatt and Tuft if any of them are tagged.'

'Paddy,' I said. 'That was not a deer. A deer would run away. It wouldn't wait to see what we did, would it? *Would* it?'

'Maybe it was a dog. Maybe you saw its name tag glinting.'

I closed my eyes. Was that possible? What did I know about how light worked in fog? Or if deers' eyes – deer's eyes? – were like cats' eyes.

'Come on, Finn,' said Paddy, pulling at me. 'We'll be late.'

'Are there still poachers?' I said, when we were on our way again.

'Okay,' Paddy said, trying a laugh. 'We'll agree on poachers if it means so much to you.'

He slung the arm without the Christmas cactus round my neck as the drive ahead of us began to glow and we emerged into a clearing, where a lamplit house sat waiting.

It was a bigger version of the gate lodge, the same sludge-coloured walls and black timbers, the same latticed windows, squint in just the same way, bulging on one side of the door and clenched in the shadows on the other. It had more gables and chimneys, being so much bigger, and the ivy scrambling over it was clipped close, so you could see its stems clutching at the walls, like arthritic fingers.

22

'It's a nice house, isn't it?' Paddy said.

I looked at him to see if he was joking. 'Yeah, why not have fake beams if there's no neighbours to judge you?' I said. If I laughed at the place maybe I could pretend it hadn't unnerved me.

'Shh! It's not "fake",' Paddy said. 'It's Arts and Crafts. Come and see what it's like inside.'

I followed him up the steps. The porch was a circle of red bricks that made me think of a mouth. And inside the mouth the front door stood open, as if in welcome.

Chapter 2

'Poachers?' said Lovatt Dudgeon, taking our coats. 'Wouldn't that be marvellous! If I thought any of the local layabouts would trap a rabbit on my land instead of throwing chip papers out of the car window as they drive by, I'd take my hat off to them. Straight on, straight on.'

We'd entered a square hall with wood panelling and a real fire crackling away, but he was shooing us towards the smell of cooking at the end of a long corridor. There was a worn strip of faded carpet, prints just as faded on both walls.

'No, we haven't had a poacher here in living memory.' We arrived in a steamy kitchen. Tuft Dudgeon was basting something in a grill pan, holding a cigarette in the same hand as the basting spoon. 'They'd starve before they caught a fish and gutted it themselves, wouldn't they, Tuftie my love? If it doesn't come in freezer portions, they'd *starve*.'

'Says Raymond Blanc,' Tuft said, sliding the grill pan back in and slamming the door. 'Welcome, dears. Now, isn't that pretty? Put it in the middle of the table and we can feast our eyes on it over our *frozen* chicken breasts.'

The kitchen wasn't like the passageway. It was sleek, with brushed steel and granite. Very tidy too. Gleaming. I set the cactus down on a small table set for four beyond the island and turned to find Lovatt and Paddy already on their way out of the room.

'Gone to fetch drinkies,' Tuft said. 'Pull up a pew.' She bit her lip. 'That's not politically incorrect, is it?'

'Nope,' I said. I was used to people getting weird when they found out what I did for a living.

'Oh, good. I'd *crucify* myself if I thought I was being crass.' She winked.

I laughed as I settled onto one of the high stools. She shoved a bowl towards me. 'Rub that in, will you?' she said. 'Crumble-top. I've got some lovely early rhubarb.'

Silently thanking *Masterchef*, I rolled up my sleeves and got going.

'So,' said Tuft, smiling at me. She was scrubbing potatoes with a Brillo pad. I tried not to notice. 'Are you looking forward to getting stuck in? We're all very excited.'

'Uh,' I said.

'I'm a volunteer,' she added. 'Chair of the committee, actually.'

'The committee that . . .?'

'That fundraises,' said Tuft. 'For St Angela's and now for you.'

'Oh!' I said. 'You're my boss, then.'

'Not at all. You're the boss, dear. And you mustn't hesitate to bring your experience to bear. Your experience got you the job.'

'My experience,' I echoed. I'd been a deacon nearly ten years, but I'd never had a full-time gig anywhere. Maybe she

25

meant my hard-won skill-set. 'I was surprised, if I'm honest, that you needed me here. It seems so . . .'

I'd come to the interview expecting boarded-up shop fronts, with only the bookie and offy thriving, maybe miners' houses, sheltering refugees now that the mines were boarded up too. Instead I found a dress shop, an ironmonger's, three cafés and a family butcher. Snug little cottages. Trim gardens. Shiny cars.

'So smug?' said Tuft. 'So bubble-wrapped?'

'So settled,' I said. 'So steady. Paddy's job was a dream come true all on its own. Mine as well is like a fairytale.'

'You two, in a matched pair, are a dream come true for us!' Tuft said. 'Heaven-sent to lick Simmerton Kirk into shape.'

'Well, it'll be a listening brief for the first year, I expect. I've got a lot to learn from you all.'

'Very diplomatic. Although between you, me and the gatepost, the Reverend Robert Waugh is a bit of a chocolate teapot. Well, you did meet him, didn't you? When you came down to interview? I'm assuming you caught him between golf games.' She grinned at me, her eyes pinched against the smoke from the cigarette she held in her red lips. And maybe she saw me looking. 'Silly me,' she said. 'Would you care for a ciggie? I've stopped asking, to be honest.'

'I haven't had so much as a puff for over a year,' I said. She took it from her lips between finger and thumb, like a workie, and held it out to me.

I cocked an ear and heard Paddy laughing at something a good long way away from the kitchen. I grinned back.

It tasted a bit of Brillo pad against my bottom lip, but as I sucked a cool, harsh jet of smoke down into my lungs and felt the nicotine thwack me, I almost swooned.

'To be honest,' Tuft went on, 'I'm just as happy *not* to have a conscientious minister looking over my shoulder. Wouldn't you agree?'

A door opened somewhere else in the house and the men's voices grew louder. In one movement she took the fag from my hand and held out a bowl of olives.

'Stuffed with anchovies,' she said. 'They'll mask anything.'

She was asking me how Paddy and I had met when the kitchen door opened and they came back in with a drinks tray.

'We'd both spent time in Canada,' I said.

'Canada?' Lovatt's eyebrows shot up and bristled.

'But we met in Edinburgh after we were back again,' Paddy said. 'On St Patrick's Day. Finnie had a maple-leaf hat on.'

'Closest thing I could find to a shamrock,' I said, like I always do. It's a well-worn tale.

'And a year later we were married,' Paddy said.

'That's what I like to hear,' said Tuft. She was spiking the scrubbed potatoes all over with a fork. I thought I could still see traces of pink foam on them from the Brillo. 'Far too much shilly-shallying these days. It took Lovatt six weeks start to finish, from spying me across a crowded room to dropping on one knee. Met at Christmas, engaged by St Valentine's Day, married in time for Easter.' She threw the potatoes into the microwave and slammed the door.

'Thought I'd better snap you up while the going was good,' her husband said. 'Did you know, young Paddy, that there's a better answer than "yes" to a man's proposal?'

'Is there?' Paddy said. He was sucking down the large whisky Lovatt had provided, and had eaten two of the anchovy olives and a handful of crisps. Right at home.

27

'I said, "Will you marry me, my sweet?" and *she* said . . .'

They had their own well-worn tale.

'*I* said, "Yes, but only for ever",' said Tuft. 'None of this high-jinks-at-the-sailing-club nonsense for me.' She wriggled a pair of joined-together oven mitts onto her hands and reached into the grill for the chicken.

'I'd had a somewhat checkered past, you see,' said Lovatt, 'but I put it behind me from that day onward. And we've had a gay old time, haven't we?'

'Twenty-five happy years,' said Tuft. 'I wish you two the same and much more since you've started rather earlier. You're children still.' She pushed a bowl of pink glop towards me. I guessed I was supposed to sprinkle it with the crumble mix.

'And I'm no less romantic now than I was when I carried you over the threshold,' Lovatt said, in ringing tones. 'Age has not withered me.'

'Romantic?' said Tuft. 'When I was down in London seeing the Dutch masters for a few days, Finnie, he texted, "Have put your toothbrush in an egg-cup of Listerine for your return."'

'What could be more thoughtful than that?' said Lovatt, his eyebrows high on his bald brow again.

'This is beautifully *en pointe*,' said Tuft, prodding the chicken. 'I loathe overcooked meat. *À table*, children.'

I was a bit of a fan of no salmonella, but I didn't want to quibble.

'Most romantic gestures – teddy bears and whatnot – are so banal,' Lovatt began again, as we settled to our filled plates. The salmonella chicken tasted okay. Even the baked potatoes tasted okay, the Brillo soap zapped in the microwave.

'What I can't stand is home-made wedding vows,' said Tuft. 'Ugh. One squirms with embarrassment for them and it's all so terribly earnest.' She stopped with a fork-load of chicken halfway to her mouth. 'I hope I haven't dropped a brick.' We reassured her. 'We sat through one where the groom maundered on about loving his bride's sunny smile and her beautiful eyes. I mean to say: how many people have ugly eyes?'

I laughed and pressed my leg against Paddy's under the table, forgiving him for dragging me up the drive, for dragging me down to the lodge, for everything.

'The thing about Tuft that made me fall for her,' Lovatt was saying. 'Do you remember this, darling? It was Christmastime in Berwick. The last lovely family Christmas at Berwick, actually.'

'Such silliness,' Tuft said. 'Finnie, can you believe Lovatt's old empress of a mother was so horrified by Berwick station turning automatic – no more porters, no more ticket office – that she stopped spending Christmas with her dearest chum? It's like something from *Poirot*!'

'But, as I say, we were there *that* year,' Lovatt went on. 'Clambering through the demolition work on a perfectly fine Victorian railway building – you should see the place now, it would make you weep – and luckily you were there too, my sweet. And we were playing some silly parlour game. Stuff and Nonsense, it's called. The object is to ask the deepest, most soul-searching question one can and to give the silliest, shallowest answers imaginable. I asked Tuft – we had only just met – what she would wish for, had she but one wish.'

'Good question,' I said.

'And without a moment's hesitation Tuft said she would wish for an even number of days in the week. Six or eight.

Because then she could wash her hair every other day on the same days each time.'

Tuft put a hand to her collar and batted her lashes. 'I really meant it,' she said. 'I won on a fluke.' She took a slug of her wine. 'But that was all long ago now. Long, long—' She stopped speaking abruptly. Lovatt was glowering at her.

'Let's not be codgers, Tuft,' he said. 'The way to stay young is to live for the moment. What's the news of the day? Tell me more about these poachers.'

'Finnie isn't used to country life,' said Paddy, like he was. 'She thought she saw someone in the woods on our way up.'

'There's a pair of cottages down on the main road just beyond the lodge,' Tuft said, 'and both lots walk their dogs in our grounds. We don't mind, do we, Lovatt?'

'I rather like it. When I was a boy, a gardener lived in one and a housekeeper lived in the other. It's good to think the current residents still feel part of things.'

'That's a generous attitude to take about people bringing their dogs to . . . in your garden,' I said.

'I'd say *noblesse oblige*,' said Lovatt, 'if *noblesse oblige* were the sort of thing one could still say.'

'Oh, no,' said Tuft. 'That's gone the way of all flesh. Good grief, you'd get bopped on the nose for that. The world has changed.'

'For the better!' Lovatt announced.

'Yeah?' I said. 'That's not the usual view.'

'Oh, but, my dear!' said Tuft. 'It's true. I had my handbag stolen from a public lavatory last year in Florence. I had hung it on the hook on the back of the door, you know? And some rascal reached over the top, grabbed it and ran off.'

'How does that—' Paddy began. But Tuft spoke over him. Lovatt was laughing silently, his shoulders shaking.

'When I was a girl, I'd just have sat there in my modesty and lost all my traveller's cheques and my camera. But, these days, one can absolutely just leg it after the thief with knickers round the knees and pee running into one's shoes and no one turns a hair. That's got to be an improvement, wouldn't you say?'

I nodded, speechless.

'Although, speaking of knickers,' Tuft went on, 'I was trying to address a card to my godson the other day and I can never remember how to spell "Michael" so I thought I'd look at my label. And do you know? I wasn't wearing a single garment from Marks & Spencer. Not one. Bra, pants, warm vest, petticoat, thick tights. And not a St Michael label among the lot of them. I googled it instead, of course, but *what* a rude awakening.'

'That label's long gone, though, isn't it?' I said.

'Not as long as my knickers last me,' Tuft said.

Paddy was beaming at me and I couldn't help beaming back. Tuft Dudgeon was the dog's bollocks. I loved it here and I loved him for bringing me. I loved Tuft. I loved Lovatt too. Some of it was booze. Because this pair were drinking on a Monday night like my parents only drank at Christmas. But it was mostly love.

31

Chapter 3

'Are you making custard, darling?' Lovatt asked, pushing his empty dinner plate away. 'Do Paddy and I have time to go and sign a few boring papers?'

'More improvements,' said Tuft. 'Instant custard. Cup-a-Soup. Gravy granules.'

She curled back round to the topic of my job while she was whisking. 'The only thing about your appointment that troubles me, dear, is what you gave up to come to us. It struck me when the minister told me you'd accepted.'

'Can I do anything to help, by the way?'

'Hold my ciggie for me?' She winked as I lit one.

'I was only part-time in the last parish,' I said. 'This is actually a great move for the old CV.' I was starting to talk like her. 'Running a small deal single-handed is much better than being one cog in one wheel of a big one.'

'CV, eh?' said Tuft. 'We're but a stepping stone in your meteoric rise?'

'I wouldn't say that.' She was pretty savvy for a volunteer. 'I'm looking forward to it.'

'I hope you're looking forward to fundraising,' she said, 'because we've only got hard money for your post for a year and after that you're self-supporting.'

'Hard money?' I said, trying not to smile.

'I haven't always been a dotty old lady in pearls.' She took the cigarette and winked at me again. 'I'm slightly engaged in bottom-covering, though, if I'm perfectly honest. I pressed pretty hard to divert St Angela's money to you. You need to show a profit or it's egg on my face.'

'So . . . they're funding my job? St Angela's?' The name had come up in my interview and I'd assumed they were the nearest Catholics, till a quick google had put me right.

'They focus on the most difficult placements, the most challenging cases. Last-ditch efforts, you know. And it's not getting any easier.'

Finally something sounded like it needed a deacon. Cases and placements.

'I mean you *do* know,' said Tuft. 'Things are so tremendously much better these days in some respects, don't you think? Morning-after pills and medical abortions have helped a lot. You're not shocked to hear me cheering them, are you?'

I shrugged. She'd know better than me that the Church of Scotland took a practical view. I might have felt an ancestral twinge but I ignored it.

'Although I'll never approve – *never!* – of all the scans and genetic testing. Be that as it may, the pool . . . the available . . . I mean, the children who *are* still looking for homes need all the help they can get.'

'So it's not really Simmerton that needs a deacon,' I said.

'It's Simmerton that needs fresh blood on the team. Paddy

at Dudgeon and Dudgeon, and you at the kirk. Unstoppable! It eats money. As you can imagine. Simply devours it. Do you still have Canadian contacts you could squeeze?'

'So Dudgeon and Dudgeon are their lawyers?' I said, finally catching up. I had wondered how a country firm could specialise as much as Paddy seemed to think they did.

'Pro bono, case by case,' Tuft said. 'All of this is very dear to Lovatt's heart. Well, it would be.'

'Was he adopted? You know Paddy was, right?'

'That's what gave him the edge,' said Tuft. 'But not Lovatt. No, no, no.'

'*Did* he adopt?'

'Oh, my good gracious, no.'

I waited, but she just handed me an unwrapped dishwasher tablet and went back to whisking. 'That's the main reason I didn't just join the St Angela's board and do the fundraising direct. Too incestuous. Instead, I joined the church, joined the fundraising committee, rose to be its chair and carried out a coup. Simmerton Kirk is not only a major direct sponsor through its own efforts, but we act as the launderer of all sorts of cash from elsewhere. Oh, yes, the compounding potential of Church connections is not to be sniffed at.'

'Launderer?' I said.

'Clearing-house, if you prefer,' said Tuft, with another wink at me.

I didn't care that Paddy was crowing as we set off into the mouth of the drive again. The fog was even thicker and the temperature had plummeted. His torch app was picking up sparkles of frost on the ground but I was aglow.

'You've got a crush on her!' Paddy said. 'You want to ki-iss her. You want to mar-ry her.'

'Of course I do,' I said, loud enough to echo, even with the fog and the baffle of trees all around us. 'She's fantastic. Can you imagine her hobbling through Florence with her knickers down, spraying piss everywhere? I *adore* her. He's okay too.'

'He is,' Paddy said. He put an arm round me and cuddled in close for a bit of warmth. I couldn't return the favour because I was carrying the leftover crumble and a bottle of sloe gin.

'And she's not just comic relief,' I said. 'She's head of the church fundraising committee that's single-handedly keeping St Angela's afloat.'

'St Angela's,' said Paddy. 'It's pretty amazing, Finnie. This sleepy little town.'

'I thought I'd be able to swan in and wow everyone,' I said 'Turns out I'll have to paddle hard to keep up.'

'But that's good, isn't it?' Paddy said. 'It's going to work out okay.'

'It's going to be great. Owls, deers, dogs, poachers and all!'

'Drunken bum,' said Paddy, squeezing me and dropping a kiss on my parting.

'One thing bothers me,' I said. And waited.

'My mum,' said Paddy.

Paddy's mum. He'd warned me as we were walking up her path on my first visit. 'Don't mention adoption,' he'd said. 'We never talk about it.'

She didn't hide it from *him*, he told me, but she didn't discuss it with . . . 'Outsiders,' he said, screwing up his face at me. He knew how it sounded.

I shrugged.

Later, when we were engaged and I wasn't an outsider any more, I thought it would change. Paddy screwed up his face in just the same way again. 'She doesn't want you judging.'

'Judging what?' I said. 'That's crazy.' She'd hit the jackpot, as far as I could see. A single woman getting a healthy white infant in a closed placement. It's horrible, but Tuft was right. Adoption's a worse meat-market than dating. Those poor kids of fifteen and sixteen, smiling out so bravely from their photographs. Sibling groups, spina bifida, foetal alcohol syndrome. It would break your heart. *Did* break my heart when I was attached to a group home in the old parish and got to know them. Seven great kids, with their fat files and their care teams and their cautious progress plans.

'Judge *me*, maybe,' Paddy had said. 'Coming out of care. No way I'm descended from dukes and earls, is there?'

'Who cares?'

'My mum. And she's a bit scared of you. Because of the job. The Church. But you know that.'

I thought about it. I was used to 'the job' flummoxing people. The dog-collar especially. But it had never seemed like fear that got dished out to me in the neat little semi where Paddy's mum, Elayne, lived alone with her knitting machine and her thriving eBay business. It had always seemed more like disapproval. I was too old for him at thirty-five. Too old for her, she meant, thinking of grand-children. I wasn't a proper professional, probably after his money. My hair was too messy. I knew, from the way she looked at me, that she wondered where I'd got such tight corkscrew curls to go with my olive skin. And I smoked. She used to pull a tablecloth over the knitting machine and tuck it in tight underneath whenever I was there. 'I advertise my products as coming from a smoke- and pet-free home, you see.'

And it definitely wasn't fear she felt for my family.

But walking down the drive that Monday night, full of food and wine, still laughing about Tuft and her stories, Lovatt and his devotion, even Paddy's mum couldn't bring me down.

Then a thought struck me. 'Pad? Why did you put it in your CV that you were adopted, if you didn't find out about St Angela's till after?'

Paddy grunted. There's a grunt he makes, almost a laugh, when I've surprised him. 'Sobering up, are you?' he said. After a bit he went on, 'I think I just wanted to make a fresh start. Coming down here, the job – both jobs really, the house and everything. I wanted to be less . . .'

'Furtive?' I suggested.

'Jeez, you had that all ready and waiting! Less uptight, I was going to say.'

'Mission accomplished. Signing papers after all that whisky,' I said. 'Man, they can drink! Tell me you read them first. Because I didn't.'

I hadn't had the chance. Paddy had brought a cascade of them through, with just the signature lines showing, and said, 'Paw-print, Finn!' holding out a Bic.

'Have we met?' he said now. 'First I read them, then I signed them, and then I put them in your bag. Oh, wait! Dammit, I *meant* to put them in your ba— What?'

I had stopped walking. 'I've left it behind. I got distracted, with the crumble and gin to carry. I've left my bag in the kitchen.'

'It's only been five minutes,' Paddy said. 'They won't be in bed yet. Let's go back.'

'No choice. It's got the lodge key in it.'

I didn't think there was enough space between the banks of pine trees to let a wind blow through, but it got colder as we turned and retraced our steps. The glow faded until my face was stinging and my eyes watering.

'They're definitely still up, then,' said Paddy. Even more lights were on in the house now, upstairs as well as down. It shone out into the spangling fog, looking like an advent calendar with Christmas only days away.

'I still don't think it's a nice house,' I said. 'But it's got something.'

'Straight out of Agatha Christie,' said Paddy. 'Like Tuft said.'

I laughed. 'I know! *Porters*, for God's sake.'

'Shame they wrecked the kitchen, though.'

I glanced at him. It wasn't like Paddy to notice décor.

'Catch Tuft muddling through with a scrubbed table-top and a dresser!' I said. 'She had that dishwasher stacked and her cloths in bleach before we'd finished chewing. I reckon she only gave us the leftover crumble so it didn't clutter the fridge.'

'We'll definitely have to have a bit of a wipe round before we ask them back.' Paddy had dropped his voice since we were nearly on the doorstep.

The front door was still open and the vestibule light was on. And there sat my handbag on the letter-shelf of the hat stand.

'Bingo,' said Paddy. 'We won't need to disturb them.'

'They're a bit laid back security-wise,' I said, 'after what they said about the dog-walkers.'

'City slicker! Is everything still there? Phone? Wallet? No one's nicked your Tic-Tacs?'

'There's no papers, though,' I said, checking all the side pockets. 'Are you sure you put them in here?'

'No,' said Paddy. 'Like I said, I meant to. That's weird, though. Why wouldn't Lovatt have left them here too?'

'Typical lawyer,' I said. 'Handbags are one thing. But *papers*? He's probably put them in a safe.' I looked around, then pushed the bell that was half hidden by ivy at the side of the doorway.

'Finnie!'

'They're still up. Where's the harm?'

'Put the bag back. Quick. Pretend you haven't seen it. Pretend you rang to ask about it.'

'You're a partner,' I said. 'As per the papers. Stop acting like Bob Cratchit.' I rang the bell again.

'Maybe they're both in the loo,' said Paddy, after a minute. 'I hope Tuft doesn't do her Florence routine.'

I rang a third time. We looked at one another as the silence from inside the house seemed to grow and grow. 'Do you think they're okay?' I said at last.

'Maybe they're at it,' Paddy said, but neither of us managed a smile.

I stepped across the vestibule and knocked on the inner door. Then I put my ear to it. From inside the house I could hear the swish of the dishwasher, but nothing else. I tried the handle.

'Finnie! You can't just—'

It opened. 'Tuft?' I called. 'Lovatt?'

Paddy was standing beside me now. 'Maybe they went out the back to look at the . . . I was going to say stars.'

'They haven't got a dog, have they?' I stepped into the hall and looked around at the half-open doors, the long corridor towards the kitchen. The fire had died down to ashes but no one had put the guard over it. 'Or chickens or anything that needs to be shut up at night?'

'Lovatt!' Paddy shouted. 'It's us again. Is everything okay?'

The dishwasher stopped and there was absolute silence. I put my bag down on the carpet and began to walk towards the kitchen. My palms were sweating.

The kitchen door was half open too and all the lights were still on. The freshly wiped counter tops shone, clear and empty. Tuft didn't have so much as a fruit bowl messing the place up. The hob set into the island was white ceramic and chrome and it glittered under the light in the hood above it. There was just one dark mark towards the back. Gravy or pasta sauce or something. Except we hadn't had gravy or pasta sauce. We hadn't had anything that colour.

Paddy took another step into the room, moving past me. 'No,' he said.

I walked up to the island and looked over.

Tuft Dudgeon lay on her back on the floor, with Lovatt sprawled diagonally over her. Her eyes were open. Her mouth was open too and full of blood. It had stained her teeth in patches. And the lipstick that had seemed such a pure true scarlet looked nothing of the kind. Not now that so much real red was all around. I looked away from her face. Her arms were thrown wide and there was blood on her hands, seeping from deep gashes crisscrossed on her palms. There was blood underneath her, in a smear to one side and a splat to the other. It was creeping down her stockinged legs, revealed because her pleated blue skirt had kicked up in a cow-lick on the floor under her skinny hips.

Lovatt's face was hidden against her collarbone, as if he

was seeking comfort there. You might have thought that, if he was moving. If he was breathing. But the back of his tweedy jacket was stone still, and in the middle of it, right on the seam, a knife handle stood poking up out of a stain so dark it looked black, even in the bright lights beating down. Another knife, dull with blood, lay under his hand. He was still half gripping it. At least, his fingers were curled around the handle. As we watched, a single bead of blood ran the length of the blade and dropped, with a tiny shimmer, into the pool of red on the floor.

'My phone,' I said, surprised by the croak of my own voice. I patted my pockets, searching for its comforting weight. 'Nine nine nine.'

'No!' Paddy's voice was another toad's croak, just like mine. He turned and looked at me, his face so white I could see every little iron-filing speck of his stubble, so white his eyes looked yellow and his teeth grey, as he grimaced. 'No,' he said again. 'No police. I can't. We need to get out of here, Finn. I can explain everything. I *will* explain everything. But we need to get out of here *now*. We need to *go*.'

I felt as if I was floating up out of my body. There was a rushing sound in my ears, like the sea in a shell. It was deafening me. I saw Paddy's mouth move but couldn't hear the words. *Too good to be true.* I'd said that, hadn't I? There's a reason things look too good to be true.

'What?' I said at last, shaking the sea-sound and the memory out of my head.

'I should have told you,' Paddy was saying. 'I'm sorry. But we really, *really* need to get out of here.'

'Should have told me what?'

'Not now. We need to *go*. Trust me. I'll explain. I should

41

have told you before. I'll tell you now, I promise. But *please*, Finnie.'

'Should have told me before,' I repeated. I stared at him for a long moment, then plucked my cuff down over my knuckles and wiped where I had put my hand on the edge of the island.

'Thank God, thank God,' he said. He made it sound like one word, speaking on a massive breath he was letting go. *ThankGodthankGod*.

He took my arm and pulled me out of the kitchen, along the corridor, swiping up my bag from where it sat on the carpet, and out through the half-glass door.

'It doesn't change anything,' he said. His words were still tumbling over each other. 'I'm sorry. I should have told you.'

I wiped the door handle with the end of my scarf and we started walking.

'Tell me now,' I said. 'Start at least.'

'I've never been to Canada.'

I have no idea if the sound I made was a gasp or some kind of twisted laugh. 'Me neither,' I said.

We walked in silence the rest of the way.

Chapter 4

Paddy locked and bolted the front door while I checked the back. Then we met in the kitchen, where no one passing on the road would see the light. No one going up the drive would see it either. But anyone skulking out there in the trees – it *wasn't* a deer – would see everything: the unshaded bulb, the boxes and bubble wrap, the two of us stark-faced, standing staring at one another.

'Okay, explain everything,' I said. I had walked down the drive steadily enough, but as I spoke I started to shake. I leaned against the sink and covered my face with my hands but, no matter how hard I pressed, I couldn't get the image to disappear from behind my eyes. Tuft's open mouth. Her gashed hands. The jaunty swoop of her pleated skirt. The knife bisecting Lovatt's jacket on the seam.

When I took my hands away, tears were pouring down Paddy's face. 'I can't,' he said. 'I don't know where to start. I can't even think straight. What *happened*? How could that happen in the time it took us to . . . ?' He was staring at the floor as if he might find the answers there.

'I don't know,' I said. I'd seen domestic abuse before, of course. At work. I'd seen a woman's jaw dislocated so far she couldn't close her mouth, a man's back covered with bruises from his wife pinching him all night long as he lay turned away and curled up in their double bed, his hands pressed between his knees. And I knew it could start in a flash, especially at the end of a long night's drinking. I knew people put on a face in public. But, still, I couldn't believe those two people – those two old people – had done that to each other. If I hadn't just seen it with my own eyes, I'd swear it couldn't be.

'Maybe,' I said, at last, 'maybe one of them had early dementia. Lovatt. He was older, right? There can be violence with that. Maybe that's why he brought you into the firm. Maybe. And she was defending herself. The police will sort it out, Paddy.'

His head jerked up and his eyes flashed. 'I can't,' he said. 'I can't. I told you.'

'Shh,' I said, as if I was talking to a baby. 'Hush now. We have to. I know you panicked. I panicked too. They'll question us and they'll pull our records and there might be press. But what we need to do is tell each other everything and then it'll be okay. Won't it? No surprises. It'll be okay.'

Paddy said nothing, just kept staring at me. This was a new kind of seesaw. If he was going to fall apart I'd need to hold it together. Somehow. I went through to the living room and came back with that bottle of Tesco's port I'd been all set to take up there as a present, to share with them. Laughing and telling stories.

I slopped some into a mug and pushed it into Paddy's hands. He took it but didn't drink. I knocked mine back in two gulps.

'I'll go first,' I said. 'I got in the habit of saying I'd been in Canada to cover a hole in my employment history.' I checked my mug, but there wasn't a drop left in it. 'A decade back, I had a car crash. No one was badly hurt, but I got a year.'

'For dangerous driving?' Paddy said. Talking about the law had got through the wall of shock.

'I was over the limit.'

'That's six months.'

'I'm sorry,' I said. 'It's hard. I'm scared you'll hate me.' I waited for him to say that was impossible, and when he said nothing I went on: 'Drink-driving and failure to report.'

'You crashed when you were pissed and drove away?' Did he know how harsh it sounded when he put it like that? I couldn't look at him. 'But six months for each should have run concurrently.'

'Well, they didn't,' I said, still looking at my feet. 'I didn't *know* no one was badly hurt when I took off.'

'Bloody useless lawyer you had.'

I looked up and felt my eyes fill. He was still pale and his cheeks were still wet but he was smiling at me.

'It was the Church of Scotland prison chaplain that turned it round for me. It took longer than six months too,' I said. 'So the year was a blessing.'

'Who all knows?' he said, sounding as if he was shifting into a higher gear.

'My family,' I told him. 'My parents and my brothers, I mean, not the aunties and cousins.' They'd taken the crash, the court case and the prison sentence in their stride. But when it came to 'kicking the Pope in the nuts' – my dad's expression – I had finally managed to shock them. 'Work knows. They had to.' A shadow crossed Paddy's face. I thought

I understood it. 'Sorry!' I said. 'I know I should have told you too. Canada was a stupid lie I used for strangers. I've got an auntie over there. And then when you said you were a lawyer, I thought you'd run a mile. I knew I should tell you. I knew it would blow up in my face one day.'

'It doesn't matter,' Paddy said. 'It's all over and done with.'

'I take it your thing's nothing legal,' I said. 'Since you *are* a lawyer.' He said nothing. 'Aren't you?'

'Yep,' he came out with at last. A clipped little hitch of a sound. 'I am. Just. By the skin of my teeth.'

'So where were you when you weren't in Canada?' I said, when I realised he wasn't going to say any more.

'Brent Alpha.'

I echoed the sounds silently to myself. They didn't make any sense at first. Then: 'Oh! The oil rig? When was this?'

'Finished two years ago,' he said. 'The night we met I was celebrating getting back to work as a solicitor.'

I remembered my first impression of high spirits and a hard body, calloused hands. I knew he'd got softer round the middle in the time since, but then so had I. 'Why were you on an oil rig?'

'Because I needed the money. I had to pay off a loan.'

'But what kind of lo—' I began.

He cut me off. 'I made a mistake. With a client's assets. And I got burned.' It was as if every clipped little sentence took a whole breath to say. In between them he had to haul in another one. 'The client died. I had to come up with—' His breath ran out completely.

I pushed up off the sink and dragged myself across the few feet of floor as if I was scaling a cliff. I pulled his head down onto my shoulder. He slumped, a sandbag weight against me, and spoke into my neck. 'I had to come up with a shedload of cash or lose my job. I managed to get a loan, but the only way to pay it off in time was to leave my job anyway and work three years on the rigs.'

'Three years?'

'So now you see why partner before forty means so much to me. This chance. This new beginning.'

But that wasn't what I was thinking at all. What I was thinking was, how much money had he – what did he call it? – 'made a mistake' with, that it took three years' oil pay to clear it? And another little thought was wriggling away underneath that one that I couldn't face right now.

'Why didn't you tell me?' was what I said instead.

'I didn't tell anyone. "Canada," was what I always said. Like you. Everyone's got an auntie in Canada. And I avoided Canadians like yellow snow. I nearly didn't call *you* back after St Patrick's night.' He squeezed me. 'But I thought I'd chance a second date. Then a third. And you never talked about it. Then after, when you and me got serious, it never seemed like the right time to come clean. Like you said too.'

'Does your mum know?'

Paddy's breath was hot on my neck as he huffed out a bitter laugh. 'She chooses not to. For God's sake, don't say anything to her.'

'Does your work know? Does – did Lovatt know?'

'Yes,' said Paddy. 'I came clean about it to him and I still got the job. That's another reason it meant so much to me. It really was a completely new start. I can't believe it.' He pulled away from me and started pacing up and down the kitchen. 'New start! One bloody day and then this *nightmare*. This'll finish me, Finnie. This'll—'

'Wait, though,' I said. He stopped pacing and turned to face me. 'You managed to cover the "mistake", right? You made it good? With the loan? And you paid it off? So the police and the courts never got involved? Right?'

'Right,' said Paddy.

'So why did you panic about calling them? Up there.' I flashed on the scene again, the red drop splashing into the red pool, the colour of her teeth, nicotine and drying blood.

'There was talk,' Paddy said. He was back to those little bursts of speaking. 'It's a small place. Edinburgh. As far as lawyers go. I had friends who'd vouch. But there was talk.'

'Of what?' I said. I was thinking *here* was the reason he'd never dragged me to lawyers' parties. I'd thought they bored him too. But, really, he wasn't welcome. Because of the talk.

'What's going on in that head of yours?' he said. 'I'm sorry, Finnie. I really am sorry, you know.'

'Talk of what?' I asked again. 'Why would a financial "mistake" have anything to do with what's happened tonight?'

'I'd started to put it right off my own bat,' Paddy said.

'Good. That's good, isn't it?'

'Yes. But the timing was bad. I went to see the client. At home. She wasn't able to come to the office and she was far too set in her ways to have any truck with email. I went to see her, to work on her will. But I couldn't get in. She didn't answer the door. I went back to the office and . . . call it a hunch. I started clearing up the mess I'd made. I'd already cleared it up when the news came out.'

'That she'd died,' I said.

'In her sleep,' said Paddy. 'In her bed. Of natural causes.'

'But your colleagues thought . . .?'

'Bosses, in those days,' Paddy said. 'They didn't know for

sure, but they suspected I saw her dead, or even saw her die, and that was why I straightened everything out in time.'

'The mistake,' I said. 'The mistake you made.'

'Yeah,' said Paddy. 'I was trying to make her money work harder for her. I was trying to help her. I liked her. We hit it off together. She'd had a rough start. Like me.'

I nodded. I'd liked the look of Paddy that first night in the pub. But what kept me going back after we were both sober was that I trusted him. He was a straight arrow, a plain dealer, honest as the day is long at midsummer in Iceland. He told me what his hopes and dreams were, his fears and sorrows. He told me what embarrassed him and what annoyed him. He told me what he thought about religion, organised and personal, and never tried to spin it so he would seem like a better fit for a deacon.

'I thought you were the most truthful person I'd ever met in my life,' was all I said.

'I am,' said Paddy. 'And now you know why. Like I know why you're you.' Then he frowned. 'But, truthful or not, I'm going down anyway. I'll never survive another scandal.'

'You've forgotten something,' I said. He raised his eyebrows at me. 'You've got me now. You've got me rooting for you.'

Finally, he picked up the mug of port I'd given him and swigged it.

'You're right about calling the police,' he said. 'Of course we have to. So here's what we tell them: we moved here on Saturday. We went for dinner. You left your bag. We went back. We saw them. We phoned.'

'Except we didn't. We panicked. We came home.'

'Right. We came home, we locked the doors and we

phoned.' Paddy took his phone out. I watched him prod three times at the key pad. With his finger hovering over the call button he looked up at me. 'So we shouldn't say your bag was out on the hallstand, right? We should say we went into the kitchen to get it from where you'd left it hooked on your chair.'

'The kitchen chairs are the wrong shape for hooking,' I said. 'If you're going to give details they need to be right. Don't dial yet.'

He nodded and, very carefully, he put the phone down.

'Why did we come home?' I said. 'Why didn't we phone from up there?'

'We could tell them we only saw the bodies at a glance.' He was talking slowly. 'We didn't look long enough to work out what had happened. And we thought they'd both been attacked by someone else.'

'Right! And we were too scared to stay there. That's right. That's what we'll say. We left because we were too scared to stay in that house.'

'We walked back down the dark drive because we were scared?' he said. 'They'll never believe that.'

He swirled the dregs of his port in the bottom of the mug.

'No,' I said. 'They'll never believe that. So what will we say?'

Paddy shrugged, not meeting my eye.

'When you think about it,' I went on, after a while, 'there's no rush. They killed each other. They're both dead.' I waited, no idea what his answer would be.

'There's nothing for the police to investigate anyway,' he said eventually.

'No emergency,' I added.

For a long, still moment we stared at each other.

'No need to phone at all,' I said.

And I saw Paddy's shoulders drop. As if this was some huge relief. As if it had come out of nowhere. As if this wasn't on the cards from the moment I wiped my fingerprints off the edge of the hob and the inner door handle. From the moment we walked away.

Chapter 5

'So . . . did we go for dinner even?' Paddy said.

We had wandered through in the dark and were sitting side by side on the couch, not touching. We hadn't lit a fire since we'd moved in and the smell of the ashy grate made my stomach turn over. What century was this? Setting wood alight in the corner of your living room to keep warm. What were we *doing* here?

We were finding out we didn't know each other. How could Paddy not tell me about three years in the North Sea? Somewhere underneath the shock – her skirt kicked up and the blood pooling – that was nagging at me. But, then, I hadn't told him about my two times six months. And I knew how easy it had been. You just pushed it down so deep it was like it never happened. But I also knew what the pushing cost. So, even though this was the second worst night of my life, I felt the weight lift off me. No more secrets.

'Finnie?' Paddy was saying. 'Did we?'

'Depends. If anyone else heard we were going, we should say we went, right? *Did* anyone?'

'I don't know,' Paddy said. 'I don't think so. Lovatt never mentioned it when he left the office. It was only when Tuft offered me a lift home. She thought of it on the spur of the moment, I think. I don't know.'

'You'll soon be able to tell,' I said. 'When you go in in the morning. Won't someone ask you how it went? If they knew it was on.'

Paddy rested his head on the back of the couch and blew out a long, shaky breath. 'Right. When I go in in the morning.' I could tell he was running over the office staff in his mind. I had always been able to tell what Paddy was thinking, from about our third date onwards. Lovatt was the only other partner, but there was Abby the trainee, and Julie in the front office. 'I'll go in, and when he doesn't turn up we'll phone, and when he doesn't answer his phone, I'll offer to come back and see what's what. If anyone heard that we were going up for dinner they're bound to mention it by then, right?'

'Right.' I felt as if I had a lead blanket over me, pressing me into the couch, like for an X-ray.

'I'll have to take the car, though. So I can nip back. Okay?'

I thought about being here on my own with no car, knowing they were lying up there, chilling and stiffening. I shook my head. 'Better not do anything that looks different,' I said. 'If you don't want to cycle, I'll drop you off and then go in to work.'

'But that's something different,' said Paddy. 'You're not due to start till Wednesday.'

'I can't,' I said. 'I can't just sit here. I don't want to be here when the cops and ambulances come.'

'Okay, okay,' Paddy said. 'You go to work. I'll phone you

and say I'm taking the car for a bit. Will I park it at the office? Or will you park it at the church?'

'No,' I said. 'Don't phone me. There would be no need to tell me anything if you were just nipping out to check on them.'

'There's no way I'm going to make it believable.' Paddy's voice broke.

'You just need to try to forget what we know,' I said. 'Act as if we're starting our lovely new life.'

He said nothing.

'And soon it'll be over,' I said. 'We'll be back in Edinburgh. But can we get the tenant out? Will we have to stay with your mum? My lot?'

'I can't think about that,' Paddy said. 'I just need to get through tomorrow without blowing it. I'll go and check if they're okay. I'll find them. I'll call the cops. And then somehow they'll find out what happened. Maybe there's a history. Something to explain it.' He swallowed hard. 'Except I don't think I can do it, Finnie.'

'Okay,' I said. 'Okay. Have you got any meetings or appointments or anything?'

He gazed blankly at me. 'I was supposed to be meeting the factor from Blackshaw,' he said at last.

'You *are* meeting the factor from Blackshaw,' I corrected. 'That's the big agricultural conglomerate. Farm leases and contracting. Right?'

'And having a quick check-in with Abby to see how she's doing. I was taking over her training from Lovatt.'

'You *are* taking over Abby's training,' I said. 'Letting Lovatt take it a bit easy and concentrate on his pro-bono work for St Angela's. How old is he anyway?'

Paddy shrugged. 'Seventy.'

'Bloody lawyers,' I said, trying for a joke. 'Never know when to quit.' But it rang hollow and I saw a tear bulge up in Paddy's eye. It brimmed there until he blinked. Then it splashed down his cheek.

'It's going to be a long night,' I said. 'We should try to rest.' Then I burst into tears. I think it was the word 'rest'. Rest in peace. Eternal rest. There let the weary be at rest. That abomination on the kitchen floor was so busy, even in its stillness. So many colours of blood and so many different ways for it to spill, in smears and drips and blots. Leaking out of the gashes in her hands and seeping up into the tweed of his jacket.

'I really liked her,' I said, scrubbing at my eyes. 'I know I moaned on about moving to the sticks but tonight – for the first time – I thought I was going to be happy here, with a friend like Tuft Dudgeon. I thought we were going to be happy.'

'Maybe we will be,' Paddy said. 'Not tomorrow and not for a while, but when all of this is over. You'll make more friends. You've never had any trouble making friends.'

I nodded. I had never understood that difference between us – the way Paddy hung back. He'd pretend he couldn't go to a party even when he was free. He'd pay for someone's pictures ticket instead of asking them out for a pint. One time, just after we moved in together, I told him eight pals were coming round for pasta. I didn't know what I'd done, but I knew I'd done something. He bought twenty-quid wine we couldn't afford – I had been planning on a box each of red and white.

But Simmerton had been different, like a new Paddy to go with the new job and new house. He'd been up for this from the start. Even agreeing to go for dinner on the spur of the moment.

'I'm not going to lose my old friends,' I said. Paddy said nothing but he gave me a look I had to decipher. 'Hang on. You're not seriously thinking we might stay here, are you?'

'I'm not thinking anything,' he said, but I knew him and I knew that wasn't true.

'Won't the office close now? Won't you lose your job? We'll lose this place.'

'I signed the partnership papers, Finnie,' Paddy said. 'And I signed a lease on this cottage. Let's see what's what when the dust settles.'

When the blood dries, I thought. I shivered again. Not the port this time. Probably just the time of night and nothing but cold ash in the fireplace. January setting in.

'I don't think *I* can do it either,' I said. 'I want to phone the police now and get it over with. Get away from here. We can say we went back for my bag. Saw them, came here, locked our doors and phoned.'

'But they'll be able to tell they've been dead too long. What will we say we were doing?'

I tried to think about it. Five minutes to walk down the drive, two minutes to look for our key and realise we'd left it behind. Five minutes back up the drive. The bodies would still be warm when the cops got there. The blood would still be running.

'Or we say we used *your* keys to get back in here and I didn't realise I'd left my bag until . . . well, now. Then we went back.'

'On foot? At this time of night?'

'Or by car,' I said. 'I tell you what. Let's do it. Let's drive up there now and walk in, "find my bag" and then "see them" and then phone the cops. Eh? Why not? Then we'll tell them the God's honest truth.'

'Without phoning?'

I could feel a scream beginning to build in my chest.

'Phone, then!' I said. 'Phone them and get worried when they don't answer. Then drive up.'

Paddy hauled himself to his feet and went through to the kitchen.

'It's ringing,' he said. 'Oh, God, it's Lovatt's voice on the machine. Will I leave a message?'

'I don't know,' I said. 'No. Hang up, Paddy. I'm sorry.' I felt as if all my energy was draining out through the soles of my feet, but even as I had the thought, it made me picture the blood again. The spreading puddle of bright red under Tuft's body and the seeping black stain on the back of Lovatt's jacket.

Paddy was back beside me. He reached out and cupped my cheek, rubbing my temple with his thumb. It was usually comforting, but his hand was icy.

'I don't think we can go back now,' he said. 'We wouldn't, would we? If we phoned at this time of night and they were in their beds and didn't answer, we wouldn't go bothering them.'

'No,' I said. 'No, we wouldn't. It's crazy.' I grabbed his hand, pulling it away from my cheek and squeezing it. 'Look, we've done nothing really wrong, have we? Just a bit misguided. Let's call the cops and tell them everything. Tell them why we didn't phone. My prison sentence, your loan. Everything. How bad could it be, now that we're not keeping it from each other any more?'

Paddy didn't answer me. He changed the subject. 'Is that – the conviction – is that why you're only a deacon when women can be ministers?'

'Yeah,' I said. 'I'm waiting till the twelve years are up and it disappears off my record.'

'Not long to go.' He sat down on the arm of the couch and pulled me towards him. 'You'll make a great priest, Finnie.'

'I'm the lucky one,' I said. 'Twelve years and it's gone. Gossip lasts for ever.' I felt him flinch as it hit him again and we fell away from each other. 'I'm trying to say I know we can't phone the cops,' I said. 'I'm sorry.'

I double-checked the locks while he was in the bathroom. I'd been brought up on the seventeenth floor. The lifts were sometimes a slice of life but once we shut our front door we knew we were safe. Even the balconies had dividers that stuck away out, impossible to clamber round from one into another. And then Paddy and me's flat was at the top of a tenement – the penthouse, I called it, only half joking – with an entry-phone. This little gingerbread cottage felt about as safe as sleeping under a bridge. There was the bay window and a side window in the living room, the bowed bedroom window, one in the kitchen, one in the bathroom and two doors. Nothing to stop someone lobbing a brick through any of them and just climbing in.

At least they couldn't see us sleeping. Not unless they came right up and pressed their nose against the glass. Because the mattress was on the floor, the bedframe still in bits. The sight of Paddy lying down there with piles of clothes all around him made me feel better. It looked like a nest.

'Turn the light out,' I said, looking at the naked pane facing the drive. When he clicked the switch, the sheet of shining black glass glowed pale instead, from the fog pressing up against it.

'Sorry I never got the curtains up,' I said, shedding my dressing-gown and sliding in beside him. 'I was going to ask you to help with it tonight.'

'Right. If we hadn't gone out,' Paddy said. 'What did we do if we didn't go out, Finnie? Did we unpack?'

I leaned over him and switched the light on again. 'Come on, then,' I said. 'We'll sleep better for being tired out anyway.'

I started talking again, while I was holding the two sides of the bed and he was bent over the footboard, screwdriver in hand. His scalp was beginning to show through his hair at the crown. I wondered if he knew. I wondered if I should tell him, now we were done with secrets. Then the new secret, the one we were sharing, came screaming in again: her open mouth, the red underneath her blue pleated skirt, the black stain on his tweed jacket. So really I opened the subject to chase away that one.

'Pad?' I said. He grunted. 'I don't want you to tell your mum what you found out about me tonight.'

He sat back on his heels. 'Good call,' he said. 'She'd definitely judge you. She'd recategorise you. Stop resenting you for being perfect and start looking down on you. She'd love it.'

'Yeah,' I said. 'I know. Oh, God, maybe you should tell her. Maybe if people stopped hiding things and pretending life was better than it is, they wouldn't crack up so much. They wouldn't . . .'

As we both remembered why we were up after midnight putting our bed together, he bent his head again and picked up another one of the tiny screws.

'Are we doing the right thing?' he asked, just once.

'No,' I said. He froze until I went on: 'We missed the chance to do the right thing. But we're doing the best thing that's still an option.'

It was gone three o'clock before we were done. All the curtains were hung. The bed was up, the kitchen sorted. The boxes were flattened, tied with string and stored in the shed. It certainly looked like the house of someone who'd spent their evening unpacking. And when we fell back into bed after another shower, Paddy was asleep on his second breath. I started the Lord's Prayer and I was pretty sure I got as far as begging for forgiveness and promising to pay it forward before I drifted off. That was the bit that mattered right now anyway.

I dreamed of knives. Figures flitting between the dark trees throwing switch-blades that whistled through the air towards me. I caught them in my slick grip, gasping from the pain as they sliced into my palms, but knowing I couldn't turn my back or the knives would bisect me.

Tuesday

Chapter 6

Paddy woke from a nightmare of his own when the alarm went off. 'Too dark! Too dark!' His voice was ragged.

'I've changed my mind,' I said, over our first coffee. Paddy's eyes widened. 'I don't want to go in to work.'

'Jesus, Finnie,' he said. 'Give me heart failure, why don't you? Do you mean in case you can't act normal? You were quick enough to tell me it was a breeze.'

That was part of it. What if the news broke when I was standing chatting to the minister and I passed out? What if the sirens went past and everyone else belted out to see what was going on but my legs wouldn't carry me?

'Not just that,' I said. 'I want to stay close so they're not alone.'

'Who?'

'I know it's daft but I hate to think of them up there.'

Paddy shuddered as if I'd reminded him, as if he'd forgotten. Maybe he was doing a better job than me of blocking it out. Maybe his 'too dark' nightmare was just a bog-standard anxiety dream and nothing to do with this place. 'So will you give me a lift?' he said. 'Or should I cycle?'

'You can take the car,' I told him. 'It feels okay in daylight. I'll be fine here.'

'If you're sure,' Paddy said. 'And I'll phone you when—'

'And I'll see you tonight.'

'I'll say I was too tired to cycle. I'll say we were up late unpacking and—'

'No! Don't say anything. If anyone asks— No one's going to ask. You've got a parking space – but if anyone asks just say you need to get better waterproofs or a new back mudguard or something. And if they give you a slagging, just take it. Don't outline our busy night unpacking.'

'And you'll be okay?'

'I'll go out for a walk maybe. I'll be fine.'

'But be careful.'

'I can't be careful. I need to be care*free*. Just till they find them. Sometime today.'

It felt different once he had gone, though. When the noise of the car engine died and I stopped waving at the empty road, when there wasn't a single sound to be heard, except the wind clattering in the dead orange leaves of the hedge, I huffed out a huge sigh and watched the steam of my breath slowly fade. What kind of plant was it that hung on to its dead leaves all the way through till January? It wasn't right. It was like people lying cold and stiff on a kitchen floor with their eyes wide open and their mouths wide open, instead of tidy on their backs in the undertaker's, eyelids weighted with pennies and mouths tied shut. Of course, undertakers don't weight eyes with pennies any more or tie jaws shut with a mutch. They use little jagged contact lenses and bigger jagged gumshields. That's just one of the things I wish I didn't know. But I've visited more than one remembrance room, chumming along with someone who needed a restraining arm or a shoulder to cry on.

At least the wind had blown the fog away. In the ribbon of sky between the treetops in this slit of a valley, pale wisps of cloud scudded across dark banks of higher cloud, cloud so black the tips of the big trees disappeared against them.

I walked out across the paved bit of our front garden to the gateposts. The carving had softened and blunted over the years and there was moss in the dents. 'Widdershins,' I said, trying to trace the letters. But that wasn't what it said at all. It was two short words, one on each gatepost, not one long one repeated. The gates weren't in great shape either. They'd been propped open for years and now they were deep in weeds and rusted at the hinges. I gave one a bit of a tug but it didn't shift. Just as well. How would I explain closing the gates against the world for no reason?

'Get a grip, Finnie,' I muttered to myself.

About half one in the morning, Paddy had put our coat pegs up just inside the door and now I unhooked my warm jacket and pulled on my thick boots. I wished for a minute I had a dog to take with me. And the next minute I thought, Why not? I could get a dog. If we were really staying. And Paddy seemed to think we were. I'd never had anything bigger than a gerbil, but a great big dog with strong jaws sounded great right now. A docked tail too, so even if it was friendly no one would know.

I made sure I had my phone and my key and pulled the door shut behind me. I stood at the end of the drive and looked both ways, up the narrow gap in the trees towards the big house and out at the wider gap – not much wider, mind you – where the lane threaded through. The drive was more inviting, curving away into soft green darkness. If I didn't know what was up there, I'd be enchanted.

But if I hadn't met Tuft Dudgeon I wouldn't know we were allowed to go tramping all over their land, would I? So I turned away from the gateposts and went out onto the lane. There was no pavement, of course, just a single track and high verges of yellow grass and brown nettles on either side. If something big came round the corner I'd be in trouble. But I'd hear it and have time to scramble out of the way. I set off walking right in the middle, where the white line should be.

I thought what I was seeing, a minute later, was the fog coming back again or maybe some even paler, even lower cloud. Then the smell reached me and I knew it was billowing smoke. I quickened my steps. I could see the gable end of a house but the smoke was lower than the chimneys, belching out from behind a clipped hedge. I stepped up my pace a bit more until I reached open gates leading to a carport.

It was nothing to worry about, just a bonfire in the middle of a paved yard. I should have known. There were no kids lighting mattresses in skips round here. There was even a garden hose lying coiled up nearby in case of trouble. And there was a man looking on with a rake in his hand. I didn't know you were still allowed bonfires, what with the planet, but I wasn't sure enough to challenge him. I started walking again.

'Hello there!' He'd seen me. I heard a sound that might well be a rake hitting the ground as he chucked it down, then the walloping sound of someone hurrying in wellies. A dog, shut in somewhere, whined and scratched at the sound of his master's voice.

'Hello,' I said. 'Not much of a day for it.'

'Just burning some autumn leaves,' he said, a bit too heartily. Sounded like a guilty conscience. Maybe bonfires weren't allowed after all.

'Are you the new folk at the lodge?' he went on, coming and leaning over his gate. Add a straw in his mouth and he'd be Worzel Gummidge to the life, except that the hedge on either side of the gate was trimmed into perfect right-angles and flat on top, its tiny bottle-green leaves looking like something manufactured rather than anything that grew up out of the ground.

I smiled. 'Finnie Lamb,' I said, shaking his hand. 'Yes, we moved in on Saturday.'

'You'll excuse my wife,' he told me. 'She would have been up with a batch of scones but she's got a stomach bug. Running at both ends.'

'Oh,' I said, wishing I hadn't touched him. 'Sorry to hear that.'

'And where are you off to up that way?'

'Just getting a breath of fresh.'

'You've not started your work, then? I thought it was full-time for that money.'

'Oh. I— Well, I start on the fifteenth,' I told him, although I couldn't imagine why he needed to know. 'Are you on the committee?'

'No, that's incomers do that. I'm an elder. They don't come to the likes of me for committees. Same do when you were interviewed. I wasn't part of all that. *St Angela's.*' The scorn was thicker than the bonfire smoke.

'Mrs Dudgeon—' I started, knowing that Lovatt had been born here and was no incomer. Born here and died here, a voice in my head said.

'Aye, those and such as those,' said the man. 'If it was left to Simmerton folk we'd have been looking *after* Simmerton folk.'

'I'd have thought you'd be proud to have something like St Angela's in your town,' I said.

'It's not in our town,' said the man. 'It's up Stirling way.' As if Stirling was over the far horizon. But I'd met people just like him more times than I could remember: our street, our block, our landing.

'Stirling,' I repeated. That answered one niggling thought I'd been having. I'd wondered why, if it was a big enough deal to get us our jobs, I'd never heard of it.

'Nothing to do with us down here,' the man said.

'Well, I mustn't keep you,' I said, stirring myself.

He gave me a hard stare. 'There's nothing dragging you away. Next door's at work. He's the cowman over the Mains and she's a teaching assistant at the school. They've three weans all at the high school now.'

'Nice,' I said. 'Noisy for you, though.'

'Oh, we like it. Children playing. We never had any of our own, Myna and me.'

I tried again. 'Well, it was nice to meet you, Mr . . .'

'Sloan,' he said. 'I'll see you at Sunday service if not before.'

'Tell Mrs Sloan I hope she feels better soon.' This time I was firmer and started walking.

'Next door' was another cottage joined onto the Sloans'. Behind the high, panelled fence it had in place of a hedge, the front garden was full of dirt bikes and skateboards. I thought about the racket three teenagers would make through the connecting wall.

Why would anyone think I was out on a walk up a country

lane to meet people anyway? I asked myself. *Nature* was what this was all about. I picked up a couple of pine cones, to back myself up, but they were soft, rotten on one side.

When the panel fence ran out I was expecting the forest to press in again but, instead, the orange-stained boards gave way to another hedge. This one I recognised. It was holly. Six-foot-high bushes of it, full of birds tugging at the few wrinkled berries it still had left. I'd only ever seen it in florists' for a fiver a bunch, or sprigs stuck in wreaths and candle-holders.

There was a sign on the gate, a piece of driftwood painted like a rainbow, multi-coloured letters spelling out 'Bairnspairt'. I mouthed the unfamiliar word and looked back towards Mr Sloan, thinking it odd that he wouldn't mention another neighbour. Then I remembered Tuft – the flash of her face, her open mouth, her skirt swept up to the side. It came as swift and sharp as ever and it took an effort to drive my mind back to the thought I'd been chasing. She had definitely said, or Lovatt had said – the awkward slump of him over his wife and the horrible spike of the knife in the seam of his jacket – 'a pair of cottages'. The gardener lived in one and the housekeeper lived in the other and the people walked their dogs in the grounds of the house.

Taking that as a guide to country manners, I went over to the gate and peered in. This wasn't the neat boast of a garden tidied away for the winter and all the last leftovers burning. It wasn't the wasteland left by three teenagers with bikes and boards either. This place had vegetables growing in big boxes – misshapen stalks of Brussels sprouts looking like shillelaghs and lacy-leafed cabbages the size of car tyres – and seemed to have half a dozen blanket forts dotted around too. I leaned right over the gate to get a good look up the winding path to the house. It was definitely connected to Widdershins. It had the same latticed window panes as the gate lodge, and the paint peeling off the front door was the same liverish red as the paint peeling off our rusty gates, the same colour as the half-timbering, Paddy called it, on the Agatha Christie house. I gazed at it. Why would people pretend it didn't exist? The lights were on here too, glowing dimly. Maybe behind those windows was another—

'There's no one in.'

The voice made me jump and I turned to find a woman standing right behind me, smiling. She was stunning, white as a candle with black hair and red lips, eyes hidden behind sunglasses.

'Are you . . .' I began, but my voice sounded thin and far away and the next thing I knew my shoulder had banged against the rainbow name-sign and the woman was crouched down straightening my legs out from under me, cradling the back of my head in her mittened hand.

Chapter 7

'Did I just *faint*?' I said. I had never fainted in my life.

'You went down like a barrel of stout,' the woman said. She was crouched beside me in a deep squat, like women in India can do for hours, her knees round her ears pushing at the brim of her hat so it lifted off her head. 'I'm really sorry I startled you. Are you pregnant?'

'Bloody hope not,' I said. 'Does that actually happen in real life?'

'Nah, right enough,' she said. 'Did you hurt anything?'

'Pride,' I said. 'Jeans, maybe.'

The woman laughed and stood up again, holding her hands out. 'Try it,' she said. I took hold and she hauled me to my feet. She was strong even though she was a head shorter than me. 'How do you feel?'

'Fine,' I said. Her sunglasses were blue-tinted so it was hard to tell but my two little reflections looked fairly grim. 'I can't think what caused that.' It was a lie. I knew exactly what had caused it: the thought of the twelve hours gone by in the kitchen up at Widdershins, the changes taking place. Stiffening, softening again. Drying. Darkening.

'Whoa!' the woman said, grabbing me as I swayed. 'Look, come in and have a cup of tea, at least, hey?'

'This is your house?' I said. 'Sorry, I was just—'

'Oh, please,' she said. 'You didn't even go inside the gate. I've had a right old truffle round the gatehouse while it's been empty. Only natural.'

'That's right,' I said. 'I *am* from the gate lodge. Finnie Lamb.'

'Deacon of the kirk, solicitor's missus,' she told me. We were halfway to the cottage door now. 'I'm Shannon. Shannon Mack.'

I took a closer look but still couldn't fathom her. She could have been any age between twenty and fifty and she still looked as if she had a spotlight trained on her.

'I like your garden,' I said. The nearest blanket fort was made of an antique-looking patchwork quilt.

'Keeps the frost off the bananas,' she said, although I hadn't asked.

'Bananas,' I repeated. She opened the front door and ushered me in. The house smelt strongly of incense and curry powder, and the battered armchairs in the living room had Indian bedspreads thrown over them. There were even bookshelves made of bricks and planks. And the windows were draped with red, blue and purple scarves, turning the rooms cave-like in the winter light.

'Sit yourself,' she said, taking off her hat and unwinding a long scarf. 'Sweet tea coming up.' I shoved aside a heap of pillows and a duvet and settled on the couch.

The décor and incense went with camomile and a dollop of honey but when Shannon came back she brought a good big mug of strong builder's and my first sip was a hit of pure white sugar. 'Ooh, ta,' I said. 'I think I'm just tired. We moved in on Saturday and we've been at it pretty much full on.'

'Are you waiting on a call?' she said. I hadn't realised I was checking my phone. I laid it face down on the arm of my chair and wiped my hand on my jeans. If Paddy took ten minutes to get to work, then say twenty minutes to wonder where Lovatt was and discuss it with the rest of the staff, he'd be getting close to setting off again to check by now.

'Occupational hazard,' I said.

'What exactly does a deacon do?' said Shannon. 'If you don't mind me asking.'

'Not at all!' I was on safer ground now. 'We do outreach work, youth work, pastoral work, liaise with other agencies to arrange social care.'

'In Simmerton?' she said. 'That sounds like something for deprived areas.'

'Usually,' I said. She was echoing exactly what I'd thought on my first visit, except we didn't call them deprived any more. Of course, that trip had been in November, with late roses still blooming and fingers of light still filtering through the trees in the mid-afternoon. Now, in January, when Simmerton was battened down and bleak-looking, it was easier to believe it needed me.

'The only thing Simmerton's deprived of is sunshine,' Shannon said, as though she'd read my mind. 'Perfect for me. Is that what you were going to ask? Before you blacked out there, you said "Are you . . ."'

I shot her a look, because even in the lamplight, away from the fog, she really did have skin as white as snow, hair as black as pitch and lips as red as rubies.

73

'I was going to ask, "Are you real?" actually,' I said. 'You looked like something from a fairytale.'

'Ha!' she said. 'No, I'm not real. It's all fake. Hair, brows, lashes.'

'And coloured contacts?' Her eyes, now she'd taken off the sunglasses, were violet. Or at least they looked violet in the shaded light shining through the scarves.

'No, the peepers are mine, funky colour, failing eyesight and all. I'm an albino. As we're not supposed to say, these days. I'm a "person with albinism".'

'Oh!' I said. 'It sui— Would it be wrong to say it suits you?'

'In winter it does,' she said. 'But come summer I'll be slathered in fake tan. I get no end of snash on the albino boards for it. Well, sod them all. Did you know how Simmerton got its name?'

'Must be ironic,' I said. 'Bloody freezing in January.'

Shannon wrinkled her nose at me. 'I thought you'd be too holy to swear. No, it started out as "Summertown", because the sun only gets up above the sides of the valley from May to September.'

'Is that why you chose it? You're not from here, are you?'

'Glasgow,' she said.

'And what do you *do* down here?'

'I run a business. Well, a couple of businesses. Come and see.'

She brushed through a doorway under a garland of prayer flags and disappeared along a short corridor lined with more bookshelves. At its end, she threw open a door onto blinding whiteness. The walls and ceiling shone, and in the middle of the floor a trolley bed was covered with a white sheet. Above it, swinging on a mechanical arm, was a solid block of something electronic I couldn't understand.

'What is it?' I said, thinking of death chambers and shock treatments.

'It's a UV saturation unit,' she said. 'For people with SAD.'

'You sell sunlight?'

'By the hour,' she said. 'First session's free.'

'And are there enough SAD people in Simmerton to make a living?'

'I live cheap,' Shannon said. 'Peppercorn rent and a garden full of veg. I've got chickens round the back and I sell the excess.'

'Eggs?'

'And chicken,' she said, with a grin that had just a touch of relish in it, or so I thought anyway.

'I was going to say,' I said, veering away from the idea, 'you're lucky to have such a big patch. We've got ten feet and then a wall of pine trees. And Mr Sloan and the other cottage are right squeezed in at the side of the road. Your garden's massive.'

'It was the quarry,' Shannon said. 'All the stone to build Jerusalem was carved out of here.'

'To build *what*?'

Shannon laughed, closed the door on the white room and headed back to the armchairs by the stove, the mugs of tea. 'Jerusalem House. When the Dudgeon estate was intact, it was all over this valley. The main house was a big stone mansion up a cut on the *other* side. It's a shell now. Uninhabitable. All that's left is over in this cut: the dower house, this place, the two cottages and your gate lodge. And the trees, of course. Just the one or two pine trees. As you might have noticed.'

'Widdershins is a dower house?' I said.

'The Widow's Portion,' said Shannon.

'Ah,' I said. That was the gateposts deciphered. But I couldn't let myself think about a widow or a widower. One way or another, someone had lived a few moments of agony up there in that kitchen. Either Tuft, with her slashed hands thrown wide and her mouth filling with blood, or Lovatt with the knife in his jacket seam and the black butterfly unfurling its wings over his back.

'Of course, it doesn't matter so much now the family's died out,' Shannon said.

I put my mug down carefully on the edge of a bookshelf by my chair, shoving a couple of paperbacks further in to make room. 'Died?' I said, hoping she couldn't hear the dry catch of my voice. Was the news out already?

'There goes my Feminist of the Year award!' said Shannon. 'There might be a sister somewhere or an auntie. But no more Dudgeons. And Lovatt – have you met Lovatt? – isn't going to pull a Charlie Chaplin and produce any nippers now. Not with Tuft anyway. That would be a medical miracle to end all. Have you met Tuft?'

I tried to smile. 'You know them quite well, then?' I said, deflecting. I was wondering what had got Shannon her 'peppercorn rent', the way Paddy's partnership had got us ours.

'I know *about* them,' said Shannon. 'But I don't want to tell you the story on your first day getting to know your new home. It's not a very happy tale.'

I was sure – or I wished I was sure – she didn't mean their deaths. She couldn't possibly. She was just a nice woman who didn't gossip. She was friendly and funny. And yet I could feel – like a physical itch in my legs – a strong desire to get out of this cottage and away from her. Maybe it was the smell of curry powder and incense sticks. Maybe it was the syrupy sweet tea. I thought, the more I drank, that it had goat's milk in it. Maybe the heat of the woodstove was getting to me. Or maybe waiting and waiting for Paddy to call, for the news to break, was just more than I could stand. I muttered thanks, and stood up.

'That's not the right way,' Shannon said, when my hand was on the doorknob.

I blinked, then looked again at the door I was facing. She was right. This wasn't the way I had come in, but it looked like a solid front door, with a mortis lock and a pair of bolts.

'Sorry,' I said, pulling my hand back.

'No worries,' she said, waving a hand as she opened the door that did lead out to the garden. She was trying for airy now but she'd definitely said 'a couple of businesses', then only shown me one.

I made it back to the gateposts in minutes flat, keeping my head tucked down in case Mr Sloan saw me. It had to be my imagination that the temperature dropped as I passed between them. Had to be, although I couldn't help remembering that I'd thought the same thing last night: it was colder facing the house than it was facing away.

'Widow's Portion,' I mouthed to myself and my thoughts were spinning again. Had Tuft been a widow? Had she lain under her husband's slumped corpse, gasping for every wet breath, before she joined him?

I slid my phone out of my back pocket, checked the time, checked the volume, checked my message alert. It was after ten o'clock. What was Paddy doing? If I went back inside the cottage, how long was I going to have to sit there before he rang me?

'Why not go for a nice walk up the other way?' I said to

myself. 'Why live at the gate of a country estate and not go for lovely country walks? I'm sure the Dudgeons won't mind. We're neighbours and colleagues, after all.'

So I didn't go up the short path of chips towards my own front door. I set off up the drive to Widdershins again.

Chapter 8

It swallowed me like it swallowed the sunlight, deadening my footsteps and stilling the wind. A cut, Shannon had called it. Jerusalem House, derelict now, was up a cut on the other side of the Simmerton valley, and all that the Dudgeons owned now was here in this one. 'Five houses,' I said, 'and one or two pine trees.'

I had never seen them this way before, massed like an army, instead of standing in a bucket in the living room, twinkling and scented, or standing proud in the botanic gardens with a ring of needles, like a rug, on the wide velvet carpet of grass.

Those trees had no needles at all. They had no branches to speak of. Well, stunted little spindly things that made a cat's cradle between the trunks. I stopped walking, stood in the middle of the drive and looked up, no need to shade my eyes, at the dizzying dwindle of them, far above me. Up there was a suggestion of green, a sign of life, but down here not even the rain could penetrate. The drive and ditch were dark with damp, like all of Scotland in January, but two trees up the bank, the bark was pale and dusty, and cobwebs hung on those cat's-cradle twig tips, as if the trees had died down here.

But I needed to look where I was going, instead of gawping at the tree trunks, because surely the big puddle was coming soon. Yes, there it was, reflecting the white slit of sky above. And there at one edge were Paddy's boot prints. And there at the other edge were mine. My heart rose into the base of my throat, bulbous and soft like an egg, choking me. We had wiped our fingerprints from the door handle and the edge of the kitchen island and left *footprints* leading to a murder scene.

Whimpering under my breath, I scuffed over Paddy's first, leaving a churned mess of puddle mud and dead grass. You could still tell someone had been there, but not who. Then I splashed round the edge of the water, clouded and murky, reflecting nothing now, and started on my own.

I rinsed the soles of my boots in the puddle when I was done and checked I was leaving no new prints on the damp tarmac behind me as I went on my way. By the time the sinkhole was out of sight my breathing had calmed down and my heart had dropped back into its proper place.

What the hell was Paddy doing? Why wasn't he here already? He was usually so dependable. That was what had made me fall for him, dull as it sounds. Not at first sight. It was his looks and his laugh that St Patrick's night in the pub when I had my maple-leaf hat on and his hair was green with spray-on party dye. He was getting free drinks because of his name so he was hammered by the time we met. We were in the Doctor's, my friend and me, partly because it was just round the corner from the dosshouse where I was volunteering and partly because my pal reckoned we might meet junior medics there and be set for life. 'Drunk, confident, expensive shoes,' she'd said, pointing at Paddy as he tried an ill-advised Riverdance on the wet pub floor. 'He might well be a future surgeon and provider of *gîtes* and Beemers.'

He had caught sight of me at that moment and stopped dancing, wheeling back to face me. 'That's not a shamrock,' he said.

'No shillelagh, Sherlock,' I'd said. I was pretty drunk too, drunk enough to find myself hilarious.

'That's a maple leaf.'

'No kidding, Columbo.' I was really cracking myself up.

'Are you Canadian?' He was none too steady on his feet and another drunk passing behind him sent him stumbling into my arms.

'Am I Canadian?' I asked, turning to pull my friend into the wind-up, but she had melted away leaving him to me. She was a good pal that way.

'My name's Paddy Lamb.'

'My name's Ontaria Trudeau.'

'Really?'

'No,' I said. And finally he laughed too.

That was how it started, but soon enough it went deeper than a good time. He wasn't freaked out by my job. He wasn't put off by my family. He was nice. And good. And easy to love. He didn't deserve this mess. Neither of us did.

I had reached the top of the drive and there was the house. The Agatha Christie house, I had called it. Arts and Crafts, Paddy had told me. I shuddered. The colour of it sickened me and the way the weak, bleary lights shone now it was daytime. And there was another light I hadn't noticed last night, a carriage lamp above an archway leading round the side towards where the kitchen lay. Could I walk through that arch and, passing the kitchen window, happen to glance in?

A memory was nibbling at the back edges of my brain now. Tony was sitting in our flat in Edinburgh, with a decent pizza and the lullaby of traffic passing on the street below, and he was talking about . . . What was it? Public footpaths and rights of way and freedom to roam. I hadn't really been listening. I'd never imagined I'd need the information. I'd happily walk to a beach from a hotel or to the other end of George Street to see if John Lewis had the shoes in my size, but walking through empty countryside in stout boots and waterproofs wasn't me. Still, what I thought Tony had said – and not only because I wanted this to be true – was that England had all kinds of rules and regulations, but in Scotland you could go wherever you wanted. Within reason. And the only way to carry on up the Simmerton valley, without scraping yourself to shreds on those stunted pine branches, was to take a shortcut through Widdershins' garden, either up the far side in two tyre ruts that must lead to a garage, or through that arch and past the kitchen windows.

I didn't know anything about gardening, but I could tell as soon as I rounded the corner that the terrace beyond the archway was someone's pride and joy. Lovatt's, I reckoned, remembering Tuft's sharp red nails and all the rings. The urns and pots dotted about were bright with flowers, even in January. Pansies, I decided. Roses, neatly trained up the house walls, were a far cry from the scramble of dead twigs that was threatening the shed down at the gate lodge. And the strip of dark earth they rose up from was free of weeds.

It looked, crumbled and dark, like coffee grounds or caviar.

The first set of windows belonged to a living room. I saw ceiling beams and a dark green leather sofa-back, my own reflection tiny in a television screen. The next room was the dining room, long and thin – explaining the corridor we had taken to reach the kitchen doorway – with a table big enough to seat a dozen people and a sideboard with a crowd of bottles on a drinks tray. There I was again, in the mirror above the fireplace. And finally the kitchen. First came the small window above the sink. I remembered Tuft wrenching off half a dozen of her rings before she started rinsing the pudding plates to stack in the dishwasher. And there they still were, a little glittering heap on the sill.

My footsteps slowed as I came close to the big windows, a whole corner of windows where the little table sat. I was looking at my feet and felt my pulse begin to bang at the thought of seeing her face again. After another twelve hours, there would surely be some changes. The gashes would be scabbed over. The deep blood in its spreading pools wouldn't be shining. It would be as dull as the smears now. And her eyes wouldn't glint, after all this time. So perhaps looking now would be easier. Or perhaps from this new angle I would be able to see his face too. I took a deep breath, held it with my bottom lip caught in my teeth, and raised my head.

The curtains were closed. I was looking at the pale linings of a set of winter curtains blocking my view of everything except a row of little cacti in fancy pots that sat on the windowsill. Had the curtains been closed last night when we all sat down for dinner?

I couldn't remember and I didn't know what it meant even

if they hadn't been. Perhaps Lovatt and Tuft had closed them as part of tidying up and getting ready for bed. Only wasn't it more normal to close curtains for the evening and open them at bedtime, so they were ready for the morning? That was what Paddy's mum always did. She closed her curtains as soon as the lamps went on at dusk, but she pulled them back at lights out, so the dog-walking neighbours wouldn't see them at six o'clock and judge her, I always reckoned. It didn't matter so much on the seventeenth floor. My family only shut curtains when it was cold outside, for daytime naps, and when the sun shone on the telly.

I retraced my steps to where Tuft's rings sat, winking and glinting as my shadow passed over them. I leaned across the strip of dark earth and pressed my cheek to the glass.

The island hid everything. I could see the bare, clean kitchen and that single dark smear on the edge of the ceramic cooker-top. But I couldn't see the floor beyond. I couldn't see anything on the table side of the room at all, except one flash of pink. And that flash of pink made my blood stop. It was one of the blooms on the Christmas cactus. The Christmas cactus that someone in the Simmerton florist must have sold to Paddy yesterday. The Christmas cactus covered with my fingerprints. And I couldn't for the life of me remember if I'd admitted to Shannon that I'd ever met them, or if I'd denied it, or if I'd dodged answering.

I needed to go in there and get that plant. I needed to breathe through my mouth, so no smells reached my nose, and I needed to keep my gaze trained on the fleshy green leaves and soft pink flowers without looking down at the floor.

Except, if I did that, I might stumble over Lovatt's sprawled feet. Would he still be stiff? I had no idea. Maybe if I knocked against one of his brogues lying so awkwardly, toes down, on the floor, he would skitter out of place, jagged and brittle. Maybe some bit of him – a clawed hand – would snag on some bit of Tuft and they'd both clatter against the base of the island.

So I would look where I was going. I'd breathe deeply in and out and I'd step around their feet, grab the cactus and go. There was no need to look at their faces. I had a strong stomach anyway. I would be fine.

I made it to the front door. I was standing in the little vestibule, with my hand stretching out, my sleeve pulled down over it, when my phone rang in my back pocket, making me shriek and stumble, losing my footing as I fell backwards onto the gravel.

'Paddy?' I said. 'Oh, God, at last! What took so— Wait. Please tell me there's no one on the way to the house. I need to get out of here.'

He wasn't listening. 'Finnie,' he whispered. 'I'm coming home.'

'What's happening?' I said.

'I can't tell you.'

'Have you been out to the house?'

'I can't talk about it!' His voice sounded close to breaking. 'I'll be home soon and I'll tell you everything then. You can help me. You've got to help me. I don't know what to do.'

Chapter 9

'Jesus, Paddy,' I said, when he came in the front door. The shadows under his eyes were dark brown and the rest of his face was the colour of putty. 'What's going on?'

'Shh,' he said. 'Please, Finn.' He sat down carefully at one end of the couch and let his head drop back against the cushions. He closed his eyes, but they kept twitching.

'I hope you managed to look a bit more together than this in the office. What's happening?'

'I don't know and my head's killing me,' Paddy said, his voice a monotone.

'Migraine?'

He gave a thumbs-up instead of nodding. 'I didn't get to it quick enough. I wasn't thinking. I went in and they were all clustered round in the outside office. I thought the news had got out. Somehow. Then Julie said she hoped I was okay being tossed in at the deep end. And I asked what had happened and she said I was holding the fort for the next three weeks because Lovatt had gone off on holiday.'

'On *holiday*?' I wanted to shake him, make him open his eyes and look at me, at least.

'Shh,' said Paddy. 'He emailed last night. Late last night. Faxed through my signed papers and emailed saying Tuft and him were off on a jaunt and they'd be back in three weeks.'

'What time's late last night?' I asked. I sank down onto the armchair opposite him. 'We left at nine and he didn't email anyone after that, did he?'

'Shh,' said Paddy, again.

'What the hell's going on? They can't have faxed papers before you signed them. Anyway, if they'd planned a holiday before we got there, why didn't they mention it?'

'Please, Finnie.'

'Have you taken your pills?' I said. Six hundred milligrams of ibuprofen on top of his prescription painkiller usually worked, but it was a tight window.

'Yes,' he said. 'Too late, though. I need to lie down. Will you take my briefcase back into the office for me? I've got a folder Abby needs for the meeting with the Blackshaw factor.'

'Of course,' I said. I would have tried to think up an excuse to go in if he hadn't handed me one. I wanted to see if he'd managed to act even halfway normal or if he'd spooked both his colleagues, like he was spooking me. 'Look,' I said, 'we just need to sit tight. Someone will go into the house soon. The cleaner? Whoever waters the plants?'

Paddy stood up without opening his eyes and felt his way towards the bedroom.

By the time I got there with his sick bucket he was lying down flat with his shoes off, his tie loosened, his black-out mask and his noise-cancellers on. He was muttering to himself. 'Too dark. Too dark.' He must have heard me, though. Or maybe felt me moving beside the bed. The slightest noise, the slightest nudge is like torture when he's as bad as this. He put out a hand and I slipped mine into it. 'Thank you,' he said. 'I'm sorry. This on top of everything.'

I squeezed his fingers in reply. I never minded taking over when he was laid out. And 'on top of everything', dropping off a briefcase barely registered.

'Can I just ask you one thing?' I said, pulling one of the ear covers away from his head. 'Were the curtains shut?'

I was hardly even whispering, just breathing the words out, but Paddy moaned low in his throat and his frown deepened.

'You were facing the window while we ate. Were you looking at curtains or could you see your reflection?'

'Please,' Paddy said, and his face was getting that green tinge.

'Sorry. Forget it,' I breathed and left him.

Dudgeon, Dudgeon and Lamb had so many houses-for-sale displayed in their windows it was hard to tell what might be going on inside, but when I opened the shop door, flinching as an electronic buzzer announced my presence, it looked serene. There was a flatscreen with a slideshow of all the same houses rotating to the accompaniment of what sounded like the theme music to *Twin Peaks*. A middle-aged woman, scrawny from genes or diet, greeted me. Through a half-open door I could see another woman, younger, wearing a headset and talking very fast into the dangling microphone she held up to her chin.

'Mrs Roper?' the thin woman said. She had the drawstring

mouth of a lifelong smoker and her lipstick had bled into the lines, but her smile was warm.

'Finnie Lamb,' I said, shaking her hand. She was attractive or would have been with about ten pounds on her to get rid of the ropy look. But I guessed she was proud of the ropy look. At least, she had dressed in a pencil skirt and belted her clingy jumper to show it off. Through the open office door, the other woman waved, then made a face at the earpiece, apologising for whoever was keeping her on the line. 'I'm Paddy's wife. You must be either Abby or Julie, I'm guessing.'

'Julie.' She smiled wider. I had got a couple of early points with her for not assuming she was admin and the youngster in the bad suit and headset was the trainee solicitor. I smiled back.

'Thing is,' I said, 'Paddy's laid out with a migraine so I've brought his briefcase back. He said there were documents in it that someone needed?' I was well versed: I'd never admit he'd said a word about what the papers were, like he never admitted I said a word about any service-users.

'A migraine?' said Julie. 'I thought he was looking a bit peaky.'

'Not a great start,' I said.

'It's probably the stress of moving house and starting a new job,' Julie said. I knew women like her. If I was too concerned, or if Paddy acted sorry for himself, she'd scoff at the notion of migraines, but as long as we were apologetic, she would be kind.

'It's usually food,' I said. 'Cheese, chocolate and oranges. He can eat them all but not together. Two of that lot in combo and he's a goner.'

Julie tutted. 'I love a chocolate orange.'

'He'll be fine again by tomorrow,' I told her. 'But it's just one Dudgeon and no Lambs for today.'

Abby had finished her phone call and came out. God, though, that was a terrible suit, I thought, as I said hello. The wrong length for her wide hips, the wrong size for her narrow shoulders, the wrong colour – flat black – for her sallow skin.

'The other Dudgeon is Tuft,' she said. 'A sleeping partner. She hasn't practised law since long before they got married. Have you met her?'

I hesitated. Julie's eyes had gone back to her computer screen, but as the silence lengthened she quirked a look up at my face again. I knew I was changing colour. *Had* I met her? Had I met Tuft Dudgeon, fellow smoker, winner of parlour games, chaser of handbag thieves? How could I have forgotten to ask Paddy what he'd said to this pair about last night?

'Finnie?' Julie said.

Now they were both staring at me.

'I'm trying not to take it personally,' I said at last. 'Them disappearing off on holiday as soon as we get here. Was it a spur-of-the-moment thing, do you know?' I was trying to get them to say what time the messages came through. But they just shrugged. 'I mean, it can't be Paddy that's the problem or Mr Dudgeon wouldn't have given him the job. So I can't help thinking it must be me. Is she . . . very religious?'

'She's churchy,' Abby said. 'But more sort of flowers and fundraising than *God*. Why?'

'I'm a deacon,' I said. 'And sometimes people don't approve of woman deacons.'

'Oh, *you*'re the new girl,' Julie said.

'Not up here,' said Abby. 'We've had women ministers for decades. That's more an English problem, isn't it?' She was looking at me as if I was some kind of hysteric and I could hardly blame her. It was the first thing – the only thing – that had come into my mind but it was total codswallop.

'You'd be surprised,' I said. 'I've been spat at in the street when I've had my dog-collar on.'

Julie grimaced and tutted.

'Well, you don't need to worry about Tuft spitting on you,' Abby said. 'Or taking off for Brazil to get away from you.'

'*Brazil?*' Paddy hadn't said that, and I'd assumed Majorca or even Margate.

'She's a sweetheart,' Julie added. 'She'd kill me for calling her that, but she really is. She'd do anything for anyone. And she's a laugh and a half when you get a glass of wine down her. The stories of her misspent youth!'

Now both of them were smiling, sharing memories.

'And she can roll a joint that lasts for over an hour,' said Julie. 'You just wait till the Christmas party, Finnie.'

'Tchssh!' Abby said, flashing her eyes. 'Finnie's practically a priest. Shut up about joints, for God's sake.'

'Don't take the Lord's name in vain!' Julie shot back.

But the frozen look I knew was on my face was nothing to do with what they were saying. 'She sounds lovely,' I said. I blinked twice to stop the tears coming. It was all over: her tales, her kindness, her wild side. 'What's *he* like? I know about his interest in family law. But I'm not sure what it stems from.'

'Now that,' said Julie, hitching a buttock onto her desk and settling in, 'is another story. Twenty-five years ago when he married for the second time—'

Abby stepped in. 'But perhaps we should let Lovatt decide what he tells Finnie and when.' She gave me a brief smile. 'No

91

offence,' she said, 'but if he hasn't told Paddy maybe he doesn't want—'

'Of course, of course,' I said.

'Maybe he's decided to move on,' said Julie. Her voice throbbed with empathy. 'That would be wonderful. Imagine that, Finnie, if you and Paddy are the new start that lets poor Lovatt turn the corner at last and walk into a bright future.'

I nodded. I knew I should be nosier about whatever the hell she meant, but the picture was back behind my eyes again: Lovatt on the floor with the knife sticking up out of the seam of his jacket and the black stain, like a butterfly, spreading out over his shoulders. New start. Bright future.

'Well, I better be getting on,' I said. 'I'll see you again, I'm sure. Weren't we supposed to be having a bit of a thing on Friday? Or will you wait? Until.' I took a breath. 'The Dudgeons are back?'

'No chance!' said Julie. 'They can't troll off to a tropical paradise and expect us not to have a pie and a pint till they get back. Five o'clock on Friday, Finnie. Welcome to Simmerton. Ink it in. And forget what I said. Abby's right. I'm not one to pass on tales, anyway.'

The little flash in Abby's eyes told me exactly how true that was. I made my goodbyes and went out, flicking a glance up the street while I got back into the car.

I wasn't due at work until nine o'clock the next morning, for a welcome and orientation session with the minister, the elders and the chair of the fundraising committee. The chair of the fundraising committee who had allegedly swanned off on a tropical holiday without warning. If Simmerton was like every other parish I'd ever known, the delight and disgust over all that extravagance would be impossible to contain. Not even a new deacon to impress could plug their mouths. So I didn't need to wait for crumbs to fall from Julie's table. I'd find out Lovatt's sad story before the biscuits hit the tea tray.

Unless ... I thought, sitting with the engine running, staring up at the steps leading to the church door, where two toddlers were jumping about and two mums stood chatting and ignoring them. Unless the whole place was buzzing with it all today and they'd be finished by the time I got there, back to a united front again.

I'd just have to risk that. There was no reason for me to go in early and I didn't want that little kink in my behaviour to lodge in someone's mind. Anyway, I wasn't sure I could take any more questions right now. When my own colleagues asked if I'd ever met Tuft Dudgeon I needed to do a better job than I'd just managed for Paddy, so that when the bodies were found and people were picking over every detail, sucking every last shred of meat off the bones, the word wouldn't be going round Simmerton that something was up with me.

And something really was up with me. The two friendly women in the office, those two chatty mums at the church, even the two little girls running up the steps and jumping with their hair flying out behind them: everything was behind a kind of gauze that had fallen over my eyes. All I could see was Tuft's face and Lovatt's back. And all I could hear was the sound I imagined that drop of blood would have made if I'd crouched down close to listen.

Chapter 10

Paddy was deeply asleep when I got back to the gate lodge. His brow had smoothed, as far as I could tell above his mask, and the colour had come back to his cheeks and lips. I sat and watched him for a while, thinking, compiling a list of questions I needed to ask when he woke up. Had we gone up to Widdershins last night or not? Had I met Tuft Dudgeon? What time were the papers faxed through?

Maybe nine o'clock *was* 'late at night' here in the sticks. Life was pretty different in every other way I could think of. Especially the silence. When he was laid out in the flat, I would happily get on with making dinner or watching telly in another room. The walls were thick and the doors were good solid Victorian pine. But it wasn't that so much as the traffic, the neighbours' feet on the stairs, the slam of the street door. Paddy would never know if a noise worming its way past his noise-cancellers was down to me. Now I was stranded, shushing around the rooms in my socks, slowly turning the pages of a book, scared even to fill the kettle for a cup of tea in case the noise of the pipes woke him.

If there was something to do outside, I would happily have gone out and done it, even in the cheerless damp cold of this morning as it slid towards the murky afternoon.

I lifted the latch on the kitchen door and opened it silently. I put my wellies down on the slabs outside and stepped into them, then pulled the door over behind me. I took a few imaginary puffs of a non-existent cigarette, watching my breath plume out, like smoke, and trying to remember the surge of nicotine that had flooded me when Tuft handed over her fag the night before. Then I cast an eye around the few feet of garden, wondering what it would take to turn this dank patch into something like the terrace up at the big house. They had light. All we had was the dim barcode of tree trunks all around. But I remembered a courtyard garden in Andalucía with coloured bottles and painted bells hung from ropes in the dark corners. I stepped over the spongy grass – maybe it was moss – and stepped up onto the start of the bank towards the closest tree. I tugged at one of the bottom twigs to see if it was strong enough to dangle a painted— It snapped off and I lost my footing, scuffing up the top layer of fallen needles. It let out a strong smell of mould, like mushrooms, as the dark rot underneath came to the surface. I stood back on the moss with the twig in my hand, staring at the churned mess of my footsteps and trying not to think the thoughts that were crashing around in my brain. Mould. Rot. Stink.

I threw the twig onto the bank, but looking at it lying there just started another round. Dry. Brittle. Broken.

So I picked it up again and went round the side of the house to where the bin sat waiting. We had filled it to the brim last night but there was room for a twig. Lifting the lid raised my spirits too. There was a rash of Babybel rinds and a crumpled sweetie wrapper shoved in on top of all our stuff. I imagined the skateboarder kids from the middle cottage putting them in there as they mooched along the lane on their way to school. Or maybe Mr Sloan had found litter in the verge and picked it up, tutting. Either way, it was a sign of life. I turned back with a smile on my face and saw Paddy, his eye mask pushed up, standing at the bedroom window, watching me.

He opened the front door and wrapped his arms round me, kissing my neck.

'Thank God you're awake,' I said. 'I've been going kind of mental.'

'We've got a lot to talk about. I can't believe I sent you in there without telling you what to say. I didn't tell them in the office that we'd been to dinner.'

'Good,' I said. 'I managed not to say for definite one way or another, but I gave the impression I'd never met Tuft.'

'Right, right,' said Paddy.

We were in the living room now. 'I walked up there this morning and smooshed our footprints round that big puddle.'

His eyes opened very wide. He really had got rid of the migraine. He'd never be able to do that if it was still hanging around him. 'And I – don't kill me for this – but I went up round the house and looked in the kitchen window. The little one above the sink? You can't see them from there, but you know what you can see? That bloody cactus we took.'

'Jesus,' said Paddy. 'I bought it in the shop three doors down from the office. And they knew who I was. The girl behind the counter definitely did.'

'Will she remember that in three weeks?'

96

'Three weeks?' Paddy whispered. He swallowed and I knew he was thinking what I was thinking: what three weeks would do to both of them, lying there.

'I like your workmates,' I said, trying for cheerful. 'Julie's a laugh and Abby seems nice.' Too late, I realised saying that would put the thought of his other workmate – his partner – back into the middle of his brain.

'I've been trying to think it all through,' he said.

'Did you get anywhere?'

'First, I thought the internet might have been down so the messages didn't get through straight away. That would account for the "late" of "late last night".'

'So it would!'

'But they've got fantastic WiFi. Julie told me. So then I started trying to work out if the Brazil trip is significant.'

'Like how?' I said.

'Well, if one of them sprang it on the other and it started a fight.'

'That's insane,' I said. 'If – look, let's say Lovatt, for the sake of argument – if he had mental-health issues or some kind of degenerative condition, right, Tuft would know not to spring things on him.'

'Or if he booked the holiday in a manic phase, she'd know not to argue.'

'But the Brazil trip can't be real,' I said. 'We're being stupid, Paddy. Brazil's a blind. It's to stop people checking up on them.'

'Why?'

'Maybe . . . in case they took a long time to die,' I said.

Paddy's migraine hadn't got better enough for him to deal with that. He was turning green again.

'Sorry,' I said.

'You think they *planned* to do that to themselves? To each other?'

'Maybe they planned a more peaceful end,' I said, 'and one backed out. And that sparked the violence.'

'They *must* have,' Paddy said. 'No one would – no one *could* – plan that death for themselves. Could they? And, anyway, why would they want to die at all?'

'It doesn't have to be "they",' I said. 'It only had to be one of them. And Julie in your office did hint at some trouble in Lovatt's past. Abby shut it down pretty quickly but there's something.'

'But if you don't know what it is,' Paddy said, 'it could be anything.'

I nodded. 'And it's probably nothing. I just don't know which version is more insane, that's all. They went from lovey-dovey to bloodbath in minutes flat – no matter who started the stabbing. Or—'

'They planned it, set me up as partner to keep the firm going, sent an email about a holiday and then—'

'But *why*?' I said. 'What would the firm matter if they were going to be dead?'

'I don't know.'

'I wish to God I'd just phoned the police when we were standing up there in the kitchen,' I said. 'This is unbearable.'

'I wish you hadn't left your bag behind you,' Paddy said. 'Or you'd just picked it up from the vestibule when we went back for it.'

'I wish we'd said we were too busy to go for dinner last night,' I said. 'I wish I'd never met either of them.'

'Do you wish we'd never come?' said Paddy. 'Never taken the jobs? Never moved to this gate lodge?'

He sounded as if he was teasing me, mad as that would be. 'Of course,' I said. 'Of course I wish that. Don't you?'

'So you still want to leave? After it all dies down?'

'Of *course*,' I repeated. 'It's insane to think we'll weather this. Even if we don't slip up and get done for not reporting it, it's over, Paddy. Why can't you see that?'

Before he could answer, the landline rang out. It was too soon for junk calls, which meant it was either Paddy's mum or my dad, ringing up to see how our first few days were going.

'I can't,' Paddy said.

So I stretched over and lifted the whole thing off the sofa table, setting it in my lap. For one horrible moment, because we'd been talking about their phone line, their WiFi, I was convinced it was Lovatt on the other end. I shook that madness out of my head, sent up a quick prayer – 'God, give me strength' – and lifted it.

'Hiya!' I sang out. 'Lamb's House of Flattened Boxes. How can I help you?'

'If you're finished unpacking, I might bob down for a visit.' It was my dad. The sound of his voice made me want to sob. 'Unless you've started painting, that is.'

'Nah, you're good.' I managed to sound like my normal self somehow. 'We won't be doing any DIY yet awhile. We're both in at the deep end at work.'

'Bollocks you are!' My dad's voice pealed out with a deep chuckle behind it. 'You've landed a couple of cushy numbers down there, girl. Don't try coming the busy-busy with your mam and me any more.'

'Shows what you know,' I said. 'Paddy's partner's only buggered off on holiday for three weeks as soon as the ink's

99

dry on his—' Paddy was making frantic hand signals. I frowned at him and turned away. 'How *is* Mam?'

The sigh whistled down the line. 'Eh, she's sleeping a bit better. A run down to Simmerton would do her a power, Finnie.'

'Of course,' I said. 'I've got the smoking seats all set up in the garden. Solid teak with cushions. Saturday or Sunday. Take your pick.' Paddy was semaphoring 'No' at me. I turned further away.

'Sunday?' said my dad. 'You can't take Sunday off when you're still on the old one-day week, girl.'

'Call it Saturday, then,' I said. 'Come down for lunch.'

He cackled. He would never get used to me calling dinner 'lunch', like he'd never get used to me kicking the Pope in the nuts.

'Finnie, you've got to be joking,' Paddy said, when I'd put the phone down and rested my head against the back of the couch to calm my breathing. Performing for my dad had nearly done for me. I felt sick and faint again. 'Your parents? What if they find the bodies while your mum's here? It would wreck her for weeks.'

'Dad says she's been better. Sleeping well.' It was the insomnia that set her off on the wrong path again every time. She'd stay up on the internet and read things she shouldn't be reading. Then she'd be skipping pills. Then the writing started. Notebooks full of tiny scribbled lines. Then hospital. And then, eventually, it started all over again. 'Anyway,' I went on, 'if we're sitting tight until someone finds the bodies we need to do what we would do. That's what we would do. In fact . . .' I lifted the handset again.

'Finnie, no!'

100

'Elayne?' I said. She had answered after one ring as usual. 'How are you fixed this weekend? We were wondering if you wanted to come down for a little house-warmer. Just family. Saturday lunch?'

'What does Paddy say?' Elayne asked.

I knew she would. 'She wants to clear it with you,' I said, handing the phone over. Then I went into the kitchen to splash my face with cold water.

'You don't need to worry about buses,' Paddy was saying. 'Eric and Mary are coming right past your door. They'll pick you up ... They know that, Mum. They don't mind you sitting in the front seat. Mary's fine in the back. You're the only one that thinks that's a real thing.' There was a pause. 'We wouldn't have asked you if we didn't want you. We want to show you the house. And the office.' He took a deep breath. 'And the church.'

I was becalmed at the sink now, thinking. Elayne didn't actually go to church. But what Paddy had called 'fear' of my job had always come off like resentment. As if I'd laid claim to something I didn't deserve and made her look bad while I was at it. Because Elayne Lamb, abandoned wife, loving mother, beautiful knitter, sitting there in her neat little semi in her neat little suburb, was much more the sort of woman you'd expect to be 'churchy' than Finnie Lamb from the big flats, with her funny mum and her unemployed dad. Except it *was* a mum and a dad, still married. And somehow Elayne managed to resent that too.

'They don't smoke in the car,' Paddy was saying. 'No, I'm not coming up and driving back down again when Eric's going right past. Or the bus. It's up to you.'

I went back through and clicked my fingers at Paddy, asking for the phone.

'Elayne?' I said. 'Please come. If you're not busy. It won't feel like we've properly moved in till you've seen us here. I mean, my dad's great, but you know how my mum is and I want another woman to look at my cupboard space and that.'

She was silent.

'And I haven't got a bloody clue about the garden! We need a guiding hand there.'

'What a nice person you are,' Paddy said, when I had hung up. 'Have I told you that today?'

'I haven't deserved it today,' I said. 'I'm sorry for sniping.'

'Me too.'

'And don't worry about my mum. They won't find the bodies on a Saturday. It'll be a cleaner or an ironing lady when it happens. It'll be a weekday.'

That night, I dreamed it. Me in an overall with a big mop bucket on wheels, trundling it up the potholed drive, in at that round red porch, like a mouth, and through the vestibule door. Only I couldn't hold the mop-handle because it was a knife, so I shoved it, my shoulder against the flat of the blade, whimpering as I felt it cut into the seam of my overall arm, bisecting it, the dark stain spreading. As I curled my fingers around it to pull it free, at last I woke.

Wednesday

Chapter 11

To look at, Simmerton Parish Church was pretty typical early Victorian. Short steeple, double doors, stained glass. There's one in every town, left over from when the Church of Scotland was the biggest cheese around. Back in those days, the only competition was some wee St Joe's or Our Lady, half the size and none of the swagger. These days, Joe and Mary are doing fine, Muhammad too, peace be upon Him, and all those Protestant churches are feeling the chill. They hang on as places of worship in towns like this, or get turned into climbing gyms where gentrification sweeps through, carpet shops where it doesn't.

Sometime in the seventies, at a guess, Simmerton had bought up the plot next door and added an ugly brick hall. Then, within the last decade from the look of it, they had bought the plot on the other side and built a glass and steel extension for a charity shop and café.

When I came down for my interview the place had been deserted, shop and café closed, hall empty. Too late for Brownies and too early for AA. But it was humming with life this morning. It soothed me. I could hear voices in the vestry, the familiar sound of the minister talking someone down from misery or outrage. Music seeped out from the hall, loud and simple, made for babies to clap-a-handies to. And, in the café, there was my rich seam, at the table nearest the service area, with folders open and sheets of notebook paper ripped out and crumpled up. There was no mistaking a church committee. It was so ordinary and so familiar – so much part of life where things make sense and elderly devoted couples don't hack each other to shreds with knives – that my throat ached with swallowed howls.

'Finnie!' said the only man there, standing and coming towards me with his hand out. 'I recognise you from your mug shot.' The minister had asked for a close-up and I guessed he had put something in the parish letter or maybe even stuck me up on a notice-board.

'Here we were, thinking if you were late today we could have ourselves sorted before you came!' said a small woman, almost completely round except for her little legs and little short arms that looked as if she wouldn't be able to clasp them across her front.

'Are you elders?' I addressed the question to the last of the three, Shannon, my neighbour, who was sitting at the foot of the table, knitting something lumpy and porridge-coloured on a circular needle.

'Ho!' said the round woman. 'No, we're the volunteers, aren't we, Adam?'

'We are the volunteers,' the man agreed. 'I'm Adam Webb. This is my lady wife, Sonsie. And Shannon Mack.'

'Yes, I met Shannon yesterday.' I smiled and sat down in the empty chair opposite her. The head of the table, more or less. 'You're the committee who raised the funds to pay for my job for its first year? Shannon, yesterday you were asking me what a deacon does. Were you . . . Were you checking up on me?'

Sonsie – if that could actually be her name in a million years – started rumbling. But Shannon put down her knitting and laughed. 'I've only been on the committee for seven minutes,' she said. 'Adam and Sonsie weren't even sure if they could vote me on, just their two selves. I liked what you said yesterday. I didn't know there was anything like that going on here. But when you told me there was, I decided I wanted in.'

I could have wept. That was the quickest I'd ever recruited a volunteer in my puff and it was all for nothing. By the time the truth came out about Lovatt and Tuft, this parish would be in ruins.

'You've done a grand job for such a small committee,' I said, turning away from Shannon. Adam smoothed his moustache with the side of one index finger, but not in a villainous way. I thought he was comforting himself. His wife looked angry.

'We're not *that* small,' she said. 'There's someone missing. Mrs Dudgeon is the chair but she's . . . in the wind.'

'Dudgeon?' I said. 'The same Dudgeon as the lawyer? My husband told me *he*'d sloped off on a posh holiday.'

'I could kill the both of them!' Sonsie burst out.

I had done so well, keeping my mind from coiling up the drive and into Widdershins that morning. The vision of them was beginning to loosen its grip on me and, as long as I didn't think about it, I could almost forget they were up there. But Sonsie's words smashed through it all. I felt sweat prick at my lip and my brow, and I knew my hands, splayed on the table, were seeping a dark print onto its pale surface. I couldn't move them, but sitting there like I was at a séance wasn't much better. And Shannon was watching me, her knitting abandoned in her lap. If I fainted again, there was no chance of her believing I was okay.

'Sonia!' her husband said. At least the name made sense now.

'Ocht, I don't mean it,' Sonsie said. Shannon had started knitting again. I leaned forward, pretending to be fascinated by the pattern but really wiping away my handprints with my jacket sleeve. I was wearing my God suit, plain black with a dog-collar. It comforted me like Adam's trim moustache did him. 'I'm very fond of Tuft,' Sonsie went on. 'That's Mrs Dudgeon's name, Finnie. Tuft. She's been good to Simmerton. And she saved Lovatt's life, more or less.'

There it was. The story Shannon hadn't told me. The story Julie hadn't told me.

'Sonsie, there's no need—' Adam began.

'There's every need,' his wife said. 'Finnie needs to know what she's dealing with. If you don't want to hear it, you can go and do something else. There's three boxes to be sorted before the shop opens.'

Adam wasted no time getting out of the room. His crêpe-soled shoes squeaked across the café floor and we heard him speed up as he headed towards the other end of the annexe.

Sonsie laughed. 'Adam doesn't trust the shop volunteers. Three years ago someone took delivery of a box of coasters with a cracked one and they glued it instead of returning it. He nearly had a fit.'

'Army background?' I said. There was something about the little moustache and the twinkling short hair above his shirt and tie.

'Worse,' said Sonsie. 'Bank manager. I'm his second wife. We're just like Lovatt and Tuft that way. Except there's no heroics. Adam did a painting class at night school and I was the life model. Three years after his first wife ran off and left him. They didn't have children. But he's been a wonderful father to mine and he's born to be a grandpa. He's taught four of them to drive and they all passed first time.' She sat back and it turned out her arms *could* meet in the middle. She clasped her hands and said, 'So that's me.'

There was a wisp of emphasis on the last word. I took it and ran. 'What d'you mean by heroics?' I asked. I glanced at Shannon to see if she knew.

'Poor Lovatt,' Sonsie said, sitting forward again. 'We're nearly the same age, you know. Except I spend half my life in that dratted salon trying to hide the fact.' She waited for one of us to praise her. Shannon gave a low whistle and Sonsie patted her curls. 'Like I said, Tuft and Lovatt have no children. But Lovatt *had* children. He was a bachelor – oh, for years. Years and years. Then he came back with a wife and they settled at Jerusalem and had a little boy and a little girl. They'd be grown-up now, of course.'

Shannon was concentrating on a complicated bit of her pattern, tracing the instructions with a forefinger and murmuring to herself. Whatever was coming, she knew it already.

'Then Lovatt's wife was taken ill,' Sonsie said. 'His first wife. She was a beauty. Very different lines from Tuft. She was Amazonian, like a thoroughbred. English, of course. Peaches and cream. Clean-limbed. Yes, she was just like a thoroughbred racehorse. And I know it shouldn't make a difference, but it does.'

'What was it?' I said. 'Cancer?'

'Huntington's,' said Sonsie. 'She went from striding about the high street in her riding boots to walking with two sticks just like that.' Sonsie snapped her fingers. 'Her lovely hair. She had this chestnut hair all down her back in big curls. It went like straw at the end.'

'Poor Lovatt.'

'Poor Denise!' said Sonsie. 'That was her name. Denise. Not a very *smart* name, I always thought. It didn't really suit her. She was a very well-connected lady. Except she wasn't. Do you see what I'm getting at, Finnie? Do *you*, Shannon?'

We both shrugged.

'It's genetic, Huntington's is. Only her father had died very young in an accident so she didn't know it was in her family. But once she found out . . . Well, as I say, she was very well connected in one sense. She had lots of doctors in her social circle. And money. She had money. She had all the money, as it happened. Lovatt had the house and she had the cash.'

'So . . . the doctors gave her the best of care?' I said. I knew it was nothing so innocent. I had no idea where she was going, though. If I'd known I would have fled the room before I heard it.

'See, you're not allowed to be tested for it until you're eighteen,' Sonsie said. 'There's no cure anyway. And some people say, "Why find out? Why meet trouble halfway?" Well, Denise Dudgeon saw it differently. She didn't think she'd still be alive, or at least not *compos mentis*, when the children were eighteen. So she leaned on her doctor friends and she had the tests done.'

'No,' I said. 'Were they okay?'

Shannon's knitting had slipped off her lap onto the floor and she hadn't noticed.

'They weren't,' Sonsie said. She had tears in her eyes. 'They *both* had the gene.' I sucked my breath in over my teeth. 'So one night, when Lovatt was away from home, she gave them each some sleeping tablets and *she* took some sleeping tablets and then she lay down with them and set the bed alight with paraffin. She burned Jerusalem House back to the stone.'

I couldn't breathe.

'Wickedness,' said Shannon. 'They could have found a cure by the time the children showed symptoms. I mean, they haven't. But she wasn't to know that.'

I gulped at the air but my throat was closed. It made sense now – Lovatt's specialism, Tuft's fundraising. St Angela's. He had seen his own wife kill his children instead of letting someone stronger look after them. That would be enough to turn any man's life into a mission. It made sense of something Tuft had said too, about scans and genetic testing and how she loathed them.

'And because it was suicide,' Sonsie was saying, 'the insurance wouldn't even pay out on the house. That's why Lovatt and Tuft live up in the dower house by you, Finnie. Finnie? Are you okay?'

I balled my fist and used it to thump myself in the middle of my chest. The shock of it kick-started my breathing.

'Oh, that poor, poor woman,' I said.

'Tuft?' said Sonsie.

'Denise,' I said. 'She must have been in such torment.'

None of us had noticed the door opening. The minister made all three of us jump with his pulpit voice.

'Sonsie,' he thundered. 'I'm ashamed of you.'

Chapter 12

I *knew* I wasn't his first choice. The other candidates for the deacon's job were one man in his fifties who'd gone to the same Edinburgh school as Robert Waugh and one man in his forties who played golf as obsessively as Robert Waugh. The golf guy had pulled a couple of tees out of his pocket along with the loose change he was putting in the honesty box for his coffee and the pair of them spent the rest of the 'refreshment reception' practising swings and telling tall tales. I went to meet Paddy afterwards and gave him the thumbs-down from across the pub. When I got the job offer, in a text on the drive home, I couldn't believe the other two had turned it down so quickly. Now, though, sitting in Waugh's office getting scolded for gossiping, I found out different.

'We took a chance on you, Finnie,' he was saying. 'Tuft was very keen to see the church embrace a diversity of views.' I had no idea what that was supposed to mean, so I said nothing. 'I was concerned that someone from a city background wouldn't navigate small-town waters well. I was outvoted. And here I find you in the hen-house on your very first day.'

Hen-house?

'It must have *seemed* like gossip, Robert,' I said. He blinked at me. Maybe I was supposed to wait until I was invited to use his first name. Tough. 'But Sonsie was filling me in on something I think it's essential for me to know. The history behind the Dudgeons' close association with St Angela's. I mean, that's the explanation, isn't it? Lovatt Dudgeon has dedicated his professional life to securing good homes and bright futures for the most difficult-to-place children?'

I rubbed my hand over my brow, feeling a headache begin to settle there. That dedicated life was over, stopped by a knife lodged up to its hilt in his back. The strain of not letting the image flood my mind every minute was exhausting.

'In front of strangers, though,' Waugh said.

'Shannon?' I said. 'She's joined the volunteer committee.' And a bit of me resented even giving him that much. If he had a problem with what Sonsie said and whom she'd said it in front of, he should be taking it up with her. 'Would you like me to have a word with Sonsie on your behalf?'

He flushed, didn't like the implication that he needed my help. 'That young woman might have elected to sit in on a meeting,' he said, 'but I approve committee members. And I'll say anything that needs to be said.'

'That seems like the best idea,' I said. 'More straightforward.' I gave him a smile. He just about managed to give me one back. Then he pulled a thick file towards him and started, in clipped tones, filling me in on the other committees and working groups I was joining, giving me a set of notes to turn into a progress report on a mission twinning. I had suspected

114

he saw getting a deacon as a way to drop all the boring bits of his own job. As he kept talking, though – interfaith initiative, care-home-visiting schedule, youth group – I started to wonder what bit of his job he was actually keeping.

'We do the primary-school assembly every Thursday,' he said, 'and the high school on Mondays on a three-week rota along with Father Lymme and the Reverend Arthur Kayes, the Anglican. I wouldn't throw you in at the deep end tomorrow but . . .'

'Throw away,' I said. 'Is there a calendar of topics?'

'I'm sure you'll manage,' he said idly. 'Right, then.' He sounded as if he had finished.

'And then there's St Angela's.' I was surprised he hadn't mentioned it in his round-up.

'St Angela's is not under our remit,' he said. 'It's a separate entity, with its own board. It's not a Church concern.'

'But we're . . . Simmerton Kirk is partnering it, right?' I said. 'We're a major sponsor and we coordinate the fundraising efforts?' I knew my face creased with the sudden pain of remembering Tuft saying 'money-laundering' with a twinkle in her eye. The spark that was already dull when I saw her lying there and must be absolutely gone now.

'Right, then,' said Robert Waugh again. He didn't seem to notice that I was awash with strong emotions. As far as he was concerned, I had stopped talking and that was good. He stood up and came round his desk with an arm extended to shepherd me out. 'Let's get on with it all, shall we?'

'Let me at it,' I said. Maybe he was the sort of minister who did a lot of home visits, although offloading the care home to me suggested not. Or perhaps he was painstaking about his sermons. But it was hard to resist the idea, when I saw his little car belting off a few minutes later, that he was headed up out of the valley to the nearest nine-hole course.

Back in the café, Sonsie and Adam had disappeared. Shannon was wiping tables. I took my armload of folders to a quiet corner and sat down to study them. I had never had the time and space to read over paperwork before. At my last place, if I wasn't sitting in A and E with someone, trying to get them to calm down before the nurses called the cops, I was trawling round charity shops, trying to get five kids kitted out for school with the forty quid I'd nicked from the slush fund, or persuade some drama queen to unlock the function-room toilets and come out, or talk some kid who'd snapped into coming down off the roof, or sitting in on the interdepartmental case meetings when the nurses *had* called the cops, or the fire service had broken down the toilet door or the local newshounds had seen the kid on the roof and brought a camera.

What was I doing here? I thought again, with a budget report on the Holy Land trip fundraising. The kind of parish that could afford to send delegations to Palestine didn't need a deacon. If St Angela's had been funded for all these years without my help, what did Tuft Dudgeon think I could do that was so important?

Tuft.

It had been thirty-six hours now. I hadn't noticed whether the house was hot or cold on Monday night. Paddy's mum's was always frigid, windows open at the top, winter and summer the same, and the back door wide for hours after she'd cooked anything the least bit pungent, even though the extractor fan roaring away made sure there was no trace of dinner left anywhere. My mum and dad's flat was sealed tight against the draughts, plastic secondary 'glazing' put on every

October and not shifted till Easter. And every curry, every pair of my brothers' trainers, every brimming ashtray, every manky relaxation candle my aunties brought over to 'help' my mum, all of it was there in every breath.

But about the neat kitchen at Widdershins, I couldn't remember. If they were really going away to Brazil, they'd have turned the thermostat down. But if that was a blind, maybe the kitchen was snug and cosy – the heart of their home – and they were already beginning to swell and rot, lying there. I had no idea if flies would swarm in January. If there were no flies, there would be no maggots. Maybe, if the kitchen was cold, they would just dry out and mummify. Maybe in three weeks it would all be over and the remains – when someone finally broke in and found them – would be desiccated, mild.

I turned one of the plastic sleeves over, as if I was reading, in case Shannon was watching. Surely it wouldn't take the whole three weeks. Mr Sloan, walking his dog in the dark, would get suspicious of the lights blazing out night after night. Or walking his dog during the day, he'd wonder why they hadn't put them on a timer.

Someone would deliver a parcel or go to wash the windows. They couldn't see anything – I knew that – but they would stretch in to put the parcel on the hallstand in the vestibule, or they would knock on the inner door, then wrinkle their nose, lean in closer and sniff deeply.

Because, of course, Tuft and Lovatt wouldn't just politely desiccate and mummify. Of course they wouldn't be unobjectionable when they were found. Whether it was days away or if they made the whole three weeks, they would be what flesh is, what we all try so hard to pretend we're not.

'Penny for them?' Shannon was standing in front of me with her spray bottle and cloth. 'You're miles away.'

There was no point in pretending it wasn't true. I had jumped a foot in the air when she spoke. 'It's what Sonsie said. I can't get it out of my head.' God forgive me, I thought, for using that story as cover.

Shannon's face clouded and she sat down opposite, letting the bottle and cloth drop onto the floor beside her. She was definitely wearing contacts today, her eyes bright green instead of amethyst. Her black hair, white skin and red lips were the same though. I still thought of fairytales. 'She said more after you'd gone. They were just tiny, the kids.'

'I can't believe he didn't leave Simmerton,' I said. 'You wouldn't see me for dust.'

'Lovatt?' Shannon said. 'It's not even that he didn't leave. He came back. He didn't work here when it happened. He was in a great big practice in Edinburgh. And they had a posh flat in the New Town. Jerusalem was just for weekends and holidays. It was only after his wife and kids died that he started his one-man show down here and moved into Widdershins.'

'That is seriously weird,' I said. 'Why would he come back?'

'Maybe it was because everyone here knows his story. Maybe that makes it easier. He doesn't keep meeting new people who ask him the same painful questions over and over again.'

'Could be,' I agreed.

'Or maybe it's just that they're buried in the graveyard here,' Shannon said. 'The three of them. Maybe it's that.'

'Sonsie covered a lot of ground,' I said. I was thinking maybe Robert Waugh had a point about her gossiping.

'Is it morbid of him, if that's what it is?' Shannon said.

'Only natural,' I said. I felt my stomach move. The spray she had been using to clean the tables was some kind of summer-meadow scent, sweet and thick. It made me think of the air freshener they used in the chapel of rest at the undertaker's, so heavy and yet never quite managing to mask what lay beneath it.

'What does the Church say?' Shannon was asking. '*Is* it wrong to want to stay near the earthly remains? Is it you lot who've got all the rules about what to do with bodies?'

I could feel my vision start to soften at the edges. The bright shafts of sunlight beating in at the high windows were turning grey.

'"You lot"?' I said, forcing a laugh out of myself. '"Us lot", you mean. You're one of us now, Shannon. Oh, it starts with a committee and a couple of hours in the caff, and before you know where you are you'll end up with your collar on backwards.'

'Is that what happened to you?'

'Worse!' I said, trying to make a joke of it. 'I was a customer. Got a lot of help from a deacon in a parish in Sighthill when I was at a low ebb and that was that.' I seemed to be letting the Canada story go, I noticed. 'I'd never really had any plans before. Not after being a princess and an astronaut anyway.'

'Do you think you'll end up being a minister?' Shannon said.

'Nah, too much hassle. Do you think you'll always be a . . . What would you say you are?'

'White witch,' Shannon said. 'No, it's just a stopgap. I'm on a mission. No pun intended.'

'What sort of mission?' I said. 'Anything I can help with?'

'You my neighbour or you the deacon?' she asked.

'Me a friend, I was thinking really.'

'Maybe.'

'Come on, then,' I said. 'It's nearly lunchtime and I need the fresh air. Tell me.'

Chapter 13

But when we got out into the foyer, Shannon headed for the door into the church instead of the front door to the street.

'This air's fresher,' she said.

'That spray cleaner is bogging right enough,' I agreed.

'How soon do you think a brand-new volunteer can offer to make up some nice lemon and lavender without looking pushy?'

I said nothing. Mr Sloan at the cottages still resented Tuft after twenty-five years. Unless he was one of those who'd turn on a sixpence now she was dead and make out he was her best friend.

In here, it was easier to push away the thought of Tuft, dead. The cool dark of the church soothed me. I should have thought of it sooner. I sat down in one of the pews halfway back and bent my head. Guide my hand, Lord. Help me see the way forward from here. Help me see if I have lost my way.

Ten years I had been a member of the Church of Scotland. No mess, no fuss, as my dad said. Throwing it all away, was how my mum put it. 'Oh, Finnie!' she'd said. 'How *could* you?'

'It's different now, Mammy,' I'd told her. 'It's not us against them any more. It's all of us together against the void.'

'What *void*?' she'd said. 'And if we're all the same, why bother changing?'

There was no point trying to explain when I didn't understand myself. And Edinburgh was the wrong place to claim it was all over anyway. Hearts and Hibs fans still knocked lumps out of each other on derby days, apart from anything.

Maybe if Paddy and I had had a wedding mass. But how could we, when I worked for the opposition? So there we were, in my parish, with my boss at the altar and my granny and aunties scoffing under their breath in the front pews – *Well, if that's it, that's it. Like getting a dog licence.*

It rolled off me that day and most other days. I had no regrets. I even had a WWJD – What Would Jesus Do – tattoo. But I would have given anything to send up a Hail Mary for the souls of Lovatt and Tuft this morning. I shook the thought out of my head.

Shannon was up on the altar, having a look round. 'Do they actually use this big huge Bible? Or is it just for show?'

'I don't use the big one,' I said. 'It's usually a bequest and it feels cheeky to stick Post-it notes in it. I've got my own wee one that falls open at the good bits.'

She laughed and came back down to sit beside me. We were quiet for a minute. I think our breathing even got into sync. At least, I could see her sleeve rising and falling in time with mine. The air was dusty, like church air always is, motes in the coloured shafts shining through the stained glass.

'Can I ask a shit-ton of cheeky questions?' Shannon said, after another minute.

I nodded.

'Can I say "shit-ton" in a church?'

'Too late,' I said, laughing. 'Ask your cheeky questions.'

'Have you read it? The Bible, I mean. Cover to cover?'

'Once,' I said. 'It's like those budget box-sets you get in Asda. There's some great stuff and then there's stuff that you'd never actually choose if it didn't come free with the rest of it.'

'And you – stupid question, I suppose – you believe it all?'

'It's not really like that. I believe in gravity and evolution and climate change. Shoogle me awake at three in the morning and ask me about them, you'll always get the same answer. Faith is more like . . . moments. Glimpses, you know.'

'So you don't believe in, like, the burning bush and the virgin birth and all that?'

'I believe the stories help,' I said. 'Maybe those two wouldn't make the top ten.'

'And what do you think happens after you die?' Her voice had changed. This was the question she really wanted an answer for. Not a clever answer, or a cool answer that might change what she thought about 'churchy' people. She deserved the truth on this one.

'I think after we die we decompose.'

I heard her take in a breath so sharp it was almost a gasp.

'So what's the point of it all?' she said. 'If this is all there is?'

'This isn't so bad, is it?' I said, leaning over to the side and nudging her. 'Sitting here in this nice church in the quiet, having a bit of a chat. This'll do me. Family, sunsets, chocolate.'

'And then' – she snapped her fingers – 'gone?'

'Not as long as people remember you,' I said. 'That's what I think life after death really is. Other people's memories.

So that's why you live a good life. So a good load of people have got warm memories of you.'

'What about Heaven?'

'That's how we think of people who're dead,' I said. 'It harms no one.'

She said nothing for a while and I turned to see what was going on. Her white face couldn't have got any paler than it was already, and someone who wore contact lenses would always work quite hard not to cry, but she was definitely in some kind of turmoil.

'So,' she said, 'if someone's just dropped out of sight – if no one's grieved, or pictured them sitting on a cloud, if no one knows they're dead, that's like keeping them out of Heaven?'

I held my breath, while my heart thumped in the silence. 'I suppose so,' I said at last. 'Who is it you mean?'

She shook herself, as if coming out of a dream. 'Just generally. If someone's lost. And you don't know if they're alive or dead. So you can't picture them anywhere? Heaven or Hell or anywhere?'

'Now then, *Hell*,' I said. 'Hell's another whole deal altogether.'

She managed a short laugh to reward the joke. 'What about Purgatory? And Limbo?'

I blew my cheeks out and tried to think about it seriously, instead of getting angry, like I usually do. My mum's depression had begun with a late miscarriage in her forties. 'Last shake of the bag,' my dad had announced to my brothers and me, all of us mortified by this evidence of something we'd rather pretend didn't happen. It was a girl. It would have been a sister. But it was born dead at twenty-six weeks, my mum alone in the bathroom in the flat while my dad was at work and we were all out, my brother having a kick-about by the garages and me sitting on the wall by Khan's with my pals, taking turns to go in and buy single ciggies, cans of juice and chocolate snakes, making up more and more outrageous stories about what gorgeous Ijaz Khan had said to each of us. We were hysterical and obnoxious and as happy as clams.

Then I went up to the house to the toilet, found it locked, and listened to my mum telling me through the door to go and phone my dad at work and ask him to come home. Life before mobiles – it's hard to imagine now.

I reckon she could have recovered if she believed the wee mite had gone to Heaven. Or just been snuffed out. It was the Limbo of the infants, on the edge of Hell, that sent her on her downward spiral.

'D'you fancy some real fresh air?' I said to Shannon. 'A walk?'

'Yeah,' she said. 'That sounds good. Why don't we walk up the cut and take a look at the house? Unless you've already been?'

It seemed a weird idea to me, to look at the burned-out wreck of a house where three people had died, but, then, it was no different from looking at the ruins of ransacked castles really. Just more recent. 'Why not?' I said. 'No, I haven't been anywhere. And I need to get oriented.'

'Can you just take off from work, though?' Shannon said.

I could have told her she was more in need of pastoral attention than anyone else in sight so going for a walk with her was work. But we were sticking with the cover story of friendship. 'As long as you drive,' I said. 'Or if I'm back by five o'clock to pick up Paddy.'

125

'I can't drive. Albino people can't get driving licences.'

'Yeah? It really is more than pale skin, isn't it?'

'Just a bit,' Shannon said.

'Do you suffer from the cold?' I asked, as we walked back out into the foyer. 'Like arthritis. Because you could probably get a heating allowance.'

'What makes you say that?'

'The duvet on your couch,' I said.

She flushed, her white face turning so dark it was almost purple. 'Binging on Netflix,' she said. 'Busted!' Then she frowned at me. 'Why would we drive on a walk?'

'City girl,' I said. 'Drive to the start of the path and change into your mountain boots.'

'And download an app, right?'

She pulled on a hat and sunglasses as we descended the church steps and set off down the high street. Was it my imagination that a couple of the Simmerton townspeople gave us looks from the sides of their eyes as we passed by? It was a small enough town to make any newcomer stand out on a winter Wednesday morning, but still the memory was hanging round me of how Tuft and Lovatt, then Mr Sloan, had acted as if Shannon and her cottage didn't exist. Or maybe it was me, a woman in a dog-collar. I pulled my scarf over it and smiled at the next person we passed – a mum with a pushchair – who looked away, tight-faced and unbending.

'How long have you been here?' I said to Shannon. 'Is it a nice place for newcomers? Mr Sloan wasn't exactly friendly but Adam and Sonsie seem okay.'

We were passing the library now, a grey stone Carnegie job, solid and comforting. Except it looked like a coffee shop close up.

'The real library's out by the leisure centre,' Shannon said. 'Better handicapped access and all that.' She played a little tune, popping her lips. 'I'm not the best person to ask about how friendly Simmerton is,' she said at last. 'I'm not a good example.'

She had led me off the main street and up a lane that switched back and forth with little runs of steps where it was too steep even with handrails.

'Which way are we going?' I said, as the lane petered out into a track. 'How do you know where you are if you can't see the sun?' There were so many steps on this bit of path: maybe it was better to call it a staircase. Either way, I didn't have enough breath to keep talking until we got to the top where a viewing place was built out on an overhang.

We weren't above the treetops but there was light between the trunks in every direction, and we could see down through a gap in the planting to the Simmerton road snaking up the valley on one side and an even narrower valley with a narrower road on the other. A cut, as they called it.

'Is there prejudice?' I said, once I'd taken a couple of lungfuls of air and let them out again. Once I'd stopped panting. 'Is that what makes you a bad example?' I didn't think I had ever met an albino person before. There was a baddie in some thriller I half remembered.

'Nah,' said Shannon. 'Not here. Well, a few arseholes. But not really.'

'I wondered if that was why you dyed your hair.'

'Why do you dye yours?' she said.

I couldn't see her eyes behind the black lenses, but she was grinning in my direction. I put a hand up and ran it through my hair, overdue for a wash and needing the roots touched up. 'Fair point,' I said.

'Nah,' she said again. 'I reckon it's my businesses. The SAD light's bad enough. They think it draws attention to Simmerton's downside.'

I rolled my eyes. I had only been there a couple of days but up here, in the light, with a wedge of sky above me instead of a sliver, I felt as if I was close to floating.

'Plus it's making nancies out of everyone, pandering to imaginary problems. You know.'

'Oh, I know,' I said.

I waited to see if she was going to say more. But she turned away from the view and started down the far side of the hill. This path was just as steep. 'What's your other business?' I said at last. But I had left it too long. She hadn't heard me.

Chapter 14

'You coming?' Shannon shouted, from below me on the path. I went trotting down towards her. Descending was easier. Within minutes we were on the hard surface of a country road, emerging through a latched gate and slithering down a verge of dead nettles and brown bracken.

'This looks exactly the same as . . .' I said. 'Wait, this is *our* lane.'

'Right,' said Shannon.

'This is *our* lane,' I said again, stupidly.

'What do you think of the shortcut? When I saw your man setting off on a bike I wondered if he knew there was a quicker way on foot.'

A walk up the cut to look at the house, she had said. She meant the drive from our gate lodge to Widdershins. A walk up the drive was normal enough, surely. But to look at the house? To snoop at the house where our landlord and landlady lived, while they were away on holiday? I wished I could be more sure of why Shannon was thinking about souls in Limbo, stuck between the living and the dead.

'Did I tell you I looked in the windows before?' she said. 'I mean, not when there was anything to see.'

I couldn't speak. My mouth tasted sour with a sudden rush of adrenalin. We were passing the messy garden full of skateboards, passing the Sloans' neat patch, all the ash from yesterday's fire already cleared away. Mr Sloan's gates were open and the double doors were hooked back to show an empty garage. If they were out, there was no one within a mile of Shannon and me. Our footfall on the damp road was the only sound, as if even the birds had left in search of sunshine. I put my hands deep in my pockets, working my house key into my knuckle, and kept walking.

'Have I shocked you?' Shannon said. 'I was sure I had said. And I didn't mind you looking over the gate at my place.'

'Oh!' I said. 'You mean *my* house? Yes, you said you'd had a look at *my* house. Before we moved in. Like you said. Before there was anything to see.' I was babbling.

'Did you think I meant the Sloans'?'

'I thought you meant the big house,' I said. 'That's more worth gawping at than anything else.'

'Let's do it,' Shannon said. 'They're away, after all. Mind you, *you* don't need to press your nose to the window, do you? You and . . . Paddy, is it? You'll be invited round. You'll be on the guest list.'

'You're not?' I said. 'They don't—' I'd been going to say, 'They don't strike me as the snooty sort,' and I was even congratulating myself on saying 'don't' instead of 'didn't'. Then I remembered I wasn't supposed to know them. I was supposed to be walking up this drive for the first time. I wished I believed Paddy about that noise on Monday night being a deer. I wished I could be sure that this whole walk

130

thing wasn't a set-up, Shannon nudging me into lie after lie: I hadn't seen the house; I hadn't met the Dudgeons. Even the way she'd said *the* cut, *the* house struck me as careful and sneaky, like she was trying to wrong-foot me. Either that or my guilt was twisting everything. 'They don't still act like Lord and Lady Muck, do they?' I said. 'Even though they don't live in the *big* big house these days?'

'Maybe they hand out bowls of gruel and sixpences to the Sloans and the Manns,' said Shannon, 'but not to me. Although they've never threatened to sling me out, even if half of Simmerton thinks I'm on the game.'

'Right,' I said. 'Your other business.' But we had got to the puddle and Shannon was concentrating on picking her way round it. Remembering the way I had snapped that twig off and churned up the ground at the gate lodge this morning, I took the chance to have a good look off into the trees. I was sure I could see the pale ends of broken branches. More than one of them. Exactly the tell-tale signs there would be if someone – Shannon? – had been up there watching us and knew I was lying now. Maybe I should pay her back, just as sneaky.

'What you looking at?' Her voice came from right behind me and I flinched.

'I thought I saw a deer,' I said. 'Well, I thought I saw an animal and it's not going to be a wolf or a bear. Are there deer? It was too big to be anything else.'

'The trees are too close for deer,' Shannon said. 'They run up and down the firebreaks but they stay out of the plantings. It was probably a hare. Some of them are massive and what with them being up so high – I've jumped out my skin at hares more than once. Revenge of the ten-foot rabbit isn't in it.' She was quiet for a beat, then said: 'I can't hear anything.'

'It's not moving,' I said.

'Can't be a hare, then,' said Shannon. 'They're terrified of people. It would be offsky.'

'Maybe it's dead,' I said. I wished I hadn't said anything now. 'Do people hunt them?'

'They take them away for the pot if they catch them,' she said.

'Or trap them?' I only said that because why else would a hare sit still?

'That's a horrible thought.' Shannon chewed her lip for a moment or two. 'Give me a leg-up, Finnie,' she said, hopping over the drainage ditch and scrambling up the far side.

'What are you going to do?' I straddled the ditch and put the side of my arm against her bum, giving her a shove until she could grab on to a tree.

'Wring its neck,' said Shannon. 'Put it out of its misery.' She put a hand in front of her face to keep the twigs from snatching at her. 'But I can't see anything. Mind you – my eyesight. Here.' She was still hanging on to a trunk with one hand and she bent to the side and put a hand down to me. 'You have a look,' she said.

Her grip round my arm was firm and the upwards yank she gave me was strong.

'Wonder Woman,' I said, grabbing her to steady myself as the mouldy earth crumbled from under my feet. I peered into the trees, at the kicked-over earth and bent twigs I'd been sure I'd seen before. Spoor, they call it on the documentaries. I was right then.

'*Something*'s been here,' I said. 'Look.'

Shannon flipped the brim of her hat up and lifted her sunglasses. 'Can't see a thing,' she said. 'It's too bright without my shades and too dim with.'

Did I believe her? Was she claiming not to see the marks she'd left? Or was she being completely open about a disability while I trolled her? Why exactly did I suspect her anyway and not one of the Sloans or any of these Manns I'd never clapped eyes on? Teenagers mucking about in the woods made much more sense. And, now I knew about the shortcut of the path and steps, it could have been anyone.

'So your eyesight's really that bad?' I said, thinking that she'd be the last one to go blundering about a planting in the dark.

She turned her head. 'Nothing wrong with my ears, though.'

I heard it too. A car engine. Someone driving far too fast on these potholes.

'Hold tight,' Shannon said. 'We're okay up here.'

The car splashed past, racing away from the big house. It hit the sinkhole hard enough to make the struts thump. By the time Shannon had let go of me to put her glasses back on and pull her hat brim down it was out of sight.

'Delivery van,' I said, hoping my voice sounded steady because, near as I could tell as it flashed by, it was our car. It was Paddy. 'Poor old Lovatt and Tuft'll have to go to some Godforsaken depot somewhere to get something they probably don't want anyway. When they get back from holiday.'

'Hope he hasn't just left it on the step,' Shannon said, jumping down, then getting out of the way so I could jump down too without landing in the puddle. 'Well, we can check, can't we?'

I said nothing. How could I explain wanting to scrap the walk because of a delivery van? As we started up the drive again, her silence began to pulse, began to deafen me. Did she know that wasn't a van? Could she tell from the sound of its engine? Was she wondering why *I* was silent?

'So what's he like?' I said at last, trying to sound casual. 'Lovatt. Is he still . . . marked by his past or has he put it behind him?'

'It's like I was saying before,' said Shannon, as if a companionable lull had drifted naturally back towards some chat again, 'it *is* over for him. His wife killed his kids and herself. Brutal but final. It happened one day and every day after that takes him further from it. It's the not-knowing – never knowing whether or when – that doesn't disappear into the past. That sticks with you. There it is.'

I blinked. I had been looking at her as she spoke and hadn't noticed that we were round the last bend, facing Widdershins. It squatted there in the dull daylight, the stained-glass fanlights giving it a heavy-lidded look, as if it was watching me on the sly, hoping to catch me out. The skin on the back of my neck shrank and my hair prickled.

'They're not worried about break-ins, are they?' I said. 'They've gone off on their spur-of-the-moment trip and left the outside door open.' I had a vision of myself walking through that door and hearing it shut behind me. And it wasn't the slam of wood on wood I could hear, but the smack of lips.

'There's no crime round here,' Shannon said. 'I never lock my doors and windows either. What makes you think it was spur-of-the-moment?'

'I'm hoping it was, to be honest,' I said, after a moment's

wild scrabbling for an answer. I was no good at this. 'Otherwise they might have warned Paddy and saved him panicking.'

Shannon said nothing.

'It's a pretty house,' I added, thinking that was what I'd say if I was seeing it for the first time.

'Yeah?' said Shannon. 'I think it looks like a bullfrog. Those bay windows and that stuff it's covered in. Like a toad. It's nicer from round here, mind you.' She was walking towards the archway. 'There's a terrace.'

I followed her. 'I suppose it was the style back then,' I managed to say. 'It's like something from out of a black-and-white film. Greer Garson.' I was looking along the length of the terrace now, at the skeletons of the roses and the dark earth underneath them.

'And a colonel,' said Shannon.

'At a tennis party,' I agreed. I couldn't look at the house any more closely than an innocent visitor would, but something was worrying me about it. Something had changed.

'Plus the dead body lying in the library,' Shannon said.

Somehow I got a chuckle out. I even added a bit more to the scene we were painting. 'And there's someone who's got all the money, who's in a wheelchair. And he's got a secretary, and a trained nurse, but they're actually long-lost—'

'No!' said Shannon. 'He's the corpse. The one with all the money is lying in the library with a dent in his skull from a length of lead piping.'

I turned round and headed back the way we had come because suddenly it seemed to me that the difference was the light coming out of the house, and I had a horrible feeling that the kitchen curtains weren't closed any more, a horrible feeling that if we kept walking and glanced sideways we would see them lying there.

'Finnie?' Shannon's voice came from yards away. 'Oh, there you are.' She scurried back to catch up.

'I crapped out,' I said. 'I'd be dead embarrassed if someone saw me snooping.'

'Who?'

'Dog-walkers?' I said. 'I dunno. Farmers? Lumberjacks?'

'Lumberjacks are called foresters, these days. And they yomp around on quad bikes. They don't creep up on people.'

'Good to know,' I said. 'Let's go back down for a cup of tea. I'm cold.' It wasn't even lunchtime but the Simmerton valley was flexing its muscles. The strip of sky between the treetops was the colour of pewter and the still air was clammy as the chill came down.

'Yeah, the day's dead,' said Shannon. '"Each bright morning soon slain."'

'What?'

'It's a poem, translated from Norwegian, about long winter nights.'

'We should all have it on our fridge doors,' I said. 'They should sell it in the church gift-shop.'

'My mum gave me it on a little plaque when I moved here.'

'Is she Norwegian?' I was thinking about the lumpy knitting on the circular needle.

'No, she was English.'

'Was?' I said. 'I'm sorry.'

'She just believed in the power of poetry. A lot. She bought me a daily poetry delivery service for a whole year once.'

'Eesh,' I said.

'For my birthday.'

'Wow. She might at least have foisted it on some African village. Like those goats.'

'She meant well,' said Shannon.

And suddenly I had a flash of understanding. The combination of what she'd said about not knowing if someone was dead or alive, of being stuck because lost, and now suggesting that her mother had tried a bit too hard – even the fact that a woman with an English mother didn't have the slightest whisper of English in her voice. My Irish mammy had put a good few quirks in my accent even though I'd been born in Edinburgh and always lived there.

'Shannon,' I said, 'tell me to mind my own business, by all means, but can I ask you something?' She nodded. 'Are you adopted?'

'Yeah,' she said.

'And you're looking for your birth family?'

'Something like that. It's not going well.'

'You want to talk about it over a cheese toastie?'

I threaded my arm through hers and stepped up my pace towards comfort and home. This nightmare would end and I'd still be a deacon. I'd still need to reach out to strangers in trouble and help them. I'd had a life before this and I had to keep living it, for after.

Chapter 15

I opened the gate-lodge front door onto a burst of warmth.

'Finnie, thank God!' Paddy's voice came from the kitchen. 'Where the hell have you been? I came home to tell you—'

'I've got a friend with me, Pad-Thai,' I shouted back, in warning. The kitchen went quiet and Shannon and I gave each other a quick look.

'We can do it another time,' she began.

I shushed her. 'No, this is fine. Actually, this is perfect. Paddy's adopted too. Closed adoption out of the care system, which might not be anything like your situation, but he's bound to be more use to you than, well, me.'

He had come round the corner to the front door and was staring at me, listening to me tell a complete stranger intimate details about his life.

'Paddy, this is Shannon. She's one of the neighbours from just down the way there. We've been for a walk.'

'Maybe I should just—' Shannon tried again.

'I must have sounded like a right old Neanderthal there,' said Paddy, swinging into action in charmer mode. 'I don't usually demand to know why my wife left her kitchen, Shannon. Please stay and have some lunch. Give me your coat.'

'Paddy's worried about his city girl getting eaten by wolves in the woods,' I said, trying as hard as him to turn it harmless. Shannon was looking from one of us to the other with narrowed eyes, as she slipped out of her coat and handed it to me. 'Or hares, eh? Revenge of the ten-foot rabbit.' She kept her cap on and swapped her sunglasses for a lighter pair.

'Go through and sit,' Paddy said. 'I've got soup heating up. I'll make toast.'

I led Shannon to the living room. Paddy had laid a fire and lit a match and the flames were beginning to lick around the kindling sticks.

'Cosy,' Shannon said. 'And a kind man who cooks. You've hit the jackpot there, Finnie.'

I wrinkled my nose at her. I still didn't know how old she was, with her strange colouring and her face unmarked after a lifetime shaded from the sun. But she didn't seem cut out to be single – although, even as I thought it, I wondered what I meant by that. Maybe she'd had disappointments, if she really was forty, or maybe she'd scarcely started thinking about it yet, if she was closer to the twenty end. Or maybe – and this seemed a strong possibility – the search for her birth mother had got in the way of other searches.

'Otherwise we'd starve,' I said. 'I'm no cook. And my kebab-stand-finding skills are not much use to me down here. Thank God for Paddy.'

'Has *he* found his biological family?' she said, as I gestured her to sit.

But I couldn't think of a reply. On the coffee-table

– unmistakable, still with the upside-down mob cap of shiny paper it had come in – was a potted Christmas cactus. The same one. There was a wilted section where Paddy had crushed it, carrying it in the dark.

'Are you a vegetarian or anything?' I said. 'I'll check what he's making, this paragon of mine.'

'I eat chicken,' she said. 'You know, once I've wrung their necks.'

'Oh, yeah.' I went through to the kitchen, pulling the door closed at my back.

Paddy was stirring a bowl of soup, halfway through its microwave time. When he had re-covered it and put it back in, I took him in my arms and pulled his head down onto my shoulder.

'Jesus, that was close,' he said. 'I nearly shouted the news through the house.'

'The news that you went back?' I said. 'I saw the plant. Oh, my God, Paddy. How bad was it?'

He burrowed his head deep into me as if he was trying to scrub the memory off onto my skin. 'Don't ask,' he said. I could feel his words warming my neck. 'I want to forget before it gets its claws into me. If I blank it out all day and manage not to dream about it tonight, I might be lucky.'

The tomato soup was beginning to bubble in the microwave, seething and splatting as it turned. As if it was alive.

'Are there flies?' I whispered.

Paddy shuddered. 'Someone needs to get in there and officially "find" them,' he said. His close breath felt wet as well as hot now, making my neck prickle.

'Sorry, lovebirds!' said Shannon, suddenly in the doorway.

Paddy and I broke apart. 'I thought I should tell you I'm allergic to mushrooms.' She sniffed and smiled.

'All mushrooms?' Paddy said. 'Even just ordinary ones?'

'Even Campbell's ones.'

'I wouldn't eat *wild* mushrooms either,' I said. 'Death wish.' I pressed my lips closed.

'You eat wild mushrooms all the time,' Paddy said. 'I use three different kinds in that risotto you like.'

'He's a keeper,' said Shannon. 'It's a shame, too, because there's lovely trumpets and puffballs up in the woods and I can't eat any of them.'

'Up in the woods,' said Paddy. 'Right, right, up in the woods. Lovatt told me about everyone roaming in the grounds. Never mentioned the mushrooms.'

'Did he?' I said. 'That's a relief because that's where Shannon and me have just been. We came up over the shortcut from the back of the high street – I'll show you – and then took a tramp up the drive and back. It's a nice house. I'm looking forward to getting a neb inside it when they get back from their holidays.'

'That's what I wanted to tell you,' Paddy said. 'No, it's okay, Shannon.' She had started murmuring and edging towards the door. 'This is Simmerton gossip, not private business. Or it soon will be. And it's warmer through here till the fire gets properly away.' He paused. 'Julie reckons they're not *on* holiday.'

'What?' said Shannon. 'Who's Julie?'

I was cutting slices of bread and I kept going, concentrating on not slicing into my fingers. There was a jagged place in the loaf where my hand had jerked at his words.

'She's the office manager at DDL,' Paddy said. 'She filed

the partnership paperwork I signed and something about it caught her attention. She'd typed up the originals, you see.'

'Typed up?' I said. 'On an Olivetti?'

'Lovatt's pretty old-fashioned,' Paddy said. At least he was using the present tense, not hesitating and swallowing. 'Anyway, Julie noticed a couple of changes in the survivorship wording.'

That word stilled the breadknife in my hand. I laid it down and wiped my palm on my jeans.

'And she talked to Abby about it,' Paddy went on.

'Who's Abby?' Shannon said.

'Trainee solicitor,' said Paddy. 'So Abby had a quick shufti and she agrees.'

'About *what*?' I said, trying to make my strain into a joke, because there was no way on earth I could hide it. 'Spit it out, for God's sake, Paddy.'

'Abby and Julie reckon they've gone for good.'

For a moment no one spoke.

Shannon broke the silence. 'It did seem strange timing,' she said. 'Sonsie and Adam at the church said it seemed strange, Finnie, didn't they?'

But I still couldn't answer. I opened the fridge door, as the toast popped up, buying myself a moment. Then I didn't do anything. Just stood there.

'Telling you, Finnie, he's a keeper,' Shannon said, over my shoulder. 'Mushroom risottos *and* hot puddings.'

'Sorry?' I said.

'Rhubarb crumble,' she said. 'In the fridge. It's not every man would be making crumbles within days of moving house. You should hold on hard to this one.'

By the time I got the power of speech back, Paddy was

ferrying plates of soup through to the table in the living room. 'So what does Julie reckon they're up to?' I called after him. 'If it's not a straightforward holiday.'

'Reckons they've hooked it,' Paddy said, coming back, banging the tray against his legs, like a tambourine. 'Reckons they've done a runner. Abby too. Come through while it's still hot.'

I took the breadboard and butter dish and slid into my seat.

'Done a runner as in . . .?' I said.

'Where does that leave you two?' said Shannon.

'That's what made Julie suspicious,' Paddy said. 'They usually go to Norfolk, France at a push, so Brazil was weird to start with, you know. And then the partnership papers I signed have been amended to provide for me being left as sole partner if the other two partner positions are rendered derelict. Even the gate-lodge rent isn't a straightforward short-assured tenancy. It's got provision for five years with real rent, pegged to the rate of inflation, and an option to buy.'

I was stirring my soup slowly across and back. Paddy had whirled cream onto it and I was making trails in the spiral, turning the sharp lines into a pink blur across the surface of the bowl. I didn't understand why he was saying all this in front of a stranger.

'What does "rendered derelict" mean?' Shannon said.

'Oh, just vacated by death or disbarment,' said Paddy. 'It's pretty standard language. It's the fact of it being added that's so strange. I was supposed to serve a probationary period and then we'd revisit all that. And this house was definitely just a standard short-assured when we took it on. Right, Finnie?'

'Search me,' I said. 'But you told me you'd read the papers before you signed them. How could he change them?'

'I read PDFs,' Paddy said. 'It never occurred to me he'd change the draft. I just signed the lot.' I tried hard to keep my face neutral. I was sure Paddy had said he'd read the papers Lovatt showed him up at the house.

'Death or disbarment,' Shannon said. 'Not just taking off. Or do you get disbarred for leaving your practice?'

'Well, no,' Paddy said. 'But that's the other thing. Brazil, see? South America?'

'No,' Shannon said.

'The great train robbery,' I said.

'Right,' said Paddy. 'No extradition.'

'You reckon Lovatt and Tuft have run away to somewhere safe because they've done something?' I said. 'Something that makes it problematic to stay here? Something that'll get him disbarred?'

'But that's crazy,' Shannon said. 'They're paragons of virtue. They raise money and do thankless work that badly needs done. Why on earth would they need to go on the lam? It's ridiculous.'

I nodded. It was hard to see Lovatt Dudgeon as a desperado, but then it was just as hard to see him as a player in a murder-suicide. I knew it had happened because I'd seen it with my own eyes, but it still made no sense whatsoever. 'About the probation,' I said. 'Maybe you made a really good first impression. Maybe Lovatt decided to cut to the chase and miss out all the . . .' Even to my ears it sounded unlikely. 'But that doesn't explain the tenancy changing,' I added. I glanced at Shannon. She was sipping soup carefully from the edge of her spoon as if it was too hot to eat properly. Did people with

144

albinism have sensitive mouths as well as sensitive skin and eyes? I didn't know.

I was facing the window, and as I watched Shannon, wondering if she was all right, I saw movement out there. Mr Sloan was passing on his way up the drive. I couldn't see his feet, but I could tell by the way one arm was stretched out in front of him and the way he was walking in big steps leaning backwards, that he was being pulled along by a small dog. The first thought that crossed my mind was that I'd keep an eye on our wheelie-bin to see if he dropped his full bags in there, like those kids had dropped in their cheese rinds and sweetie wrappers.

"Scuse me,' I said, jumping up and heading out. I grabbed a cardie on my way past the coat pegs. I knew he walked up the drive all the time and there was no reason he'd suddenly go into the house but I had to make sure, or at least find out if he was the kind of man who could cope with a sight like that.

'Mr Sloan?' I said, as I pulled the door to. He had made good progress. There were *two* small dogs, as it happened, tugging at him from the end of a branching red lead.

He twisted round to see me. 'Oh, hello!' he said. 'Another day off, is it?'

I jogged to catch up with him, my hands driven down deep in my cardigan pockets.

'How's your wife?' I said. 'Still under the weather?' The two little dogs had stopped tugging him onwards and started tugging him back to see if I was interesting. They were some kind of terrier, I thought, with long silky coats and brown marks in the corners of their eyes. One of them bared its teeth at me.

'Tummy's better,' said Mr Sloan. 'Thanks for asking. But she's gone over on her ankle. It's up like a melon, so she's resting it.'

'Best thing,' I said. 'I'll pop in if you think she'd appreciate it. Doesn't have to be filed under a church visit,' I added, seeing his face fall. 'We could call it being neighbourly. I've already met Shannon.'

'Oh, have you?' he said sourly. 'Stop it, Sadie!' One of the little dogs had her lead in her teeth and was shaking her head and growling. The poo bags tied onto it near the handle rustled and she growled harder. 'Well, I would have spared you that.'

'Spared me what? Meeting Shannon?'

'She's no better than she should be. I can see into that back room from the top of my garden, unless she's got the curtains tight shut and pegged together.'

I would have dismissed it as gossip if it hadn't been for the way she'd shouted, '*No*,' when I put my hand on the door and the way she hadn't answered when I asked what her second business was.

'So why don't the Dudgeons just sling her out?'

Mr Sloan staggered to the side as the two dogs started pulling up the drive again. 'I'll walk with you,' I said, falling into step. 'Why don't they evict her?'

'It's not their way. They've shifted *us* onto a lifetime lease. We didn't even have to ask. It just came through the post to be signed. I like to think it's our reward for keeping the place up as nicely as we do. We've retiled all round the kitchen. Painted and papered upstairs.'

'When?' I asked.

'When what?' said Mr Sloan.

When did the Dudgeons hand over a new tenancy

agreement, was the answer but since he'd challenged me as boldly as all that there was no way I could keep digging. It was none of my business.

'Oh, I'm just thinking they were certainly busy before they went off on their holidays. Paddy was saying Lovatt had done a lot of overdue paperwork in one big go. I just wondered if yours was some of it.'

'Holiday?' Mr Sloan said. 'What holiday?'

'Haven't you heard?' I said. 'They've gone off on a trip to South America.'

'When was this?' he demanded.

I thought for a while before answering, unsure of how much I should know about their movements. I watched the rippling backs of the two little dogs. Their silk coats gleamed in the low light of the drive and their breath plumed out in front of them in quick puffs as they panted with the effort of dragging Mr Sloan at their pace.

'Monday or Tuesday, I think,' I said at last.

'Lovatt and Tuft Dudgeon have never gone off to South America,' he said. 'Someone's been having you on. Mrs Dudgeon stopped at my gate on Monday lunchtime while I was chipping my prunings and never said a word about any holiday.'

'Would it have come up?' I said. 'What were you talking about?'

'It did come up!' he said. 'She was saying for me to come and take some sacks of leaf mould for my beds. Her gardener makes more and more every year and they have no use for it now they've got their place so low-maintenance. But she said to mind and chap the door and she'd show me which ones were well-rotted and ready to go.'

'Maybe it was a surprise,' I said. My head was skirling with trying to keep the story afloat and the knowledge submerged. Still, I tucked away the titbit that there was a Widdershins gardener. Someone who might have a key to the kitchen door and might go in for a pee or a glass of water and end this waiting.

'No chance,' said Mr Sloan. 'Lovatt knew how busy she was with her committees. He'd never whisk her off like that and cause her a lot of bother when she got back again.'

'That's a good point,' I said. 'You never think of it when you see grand gestures on the films, do you? It's a lot of hassle for whoever's getting the surprise.'

'I'll knock when I get up there,' Mr Sloan said, setting my pulse bumping. 'Let Mrs Dudgeon know there's a silly tale going round. It's the least I can do. They've been good to Myna and me.'

'Right,' I said. I stole a glance at him from the side of my eye. He looked hale enough, although he had to be well into his seventies. But would the sight on the kitchen floor stop his heart? Would he get as far as the kitchen, though? If he saw the front door open and got no answer to his knocking, would he even go in?

'Hoo,' I said. 'I'm going to head back, Mr Sloan. I can't keep up with you. You're as fit as a flea!'

'Nothing wrong with me,' he said. 'I've done the same exercises every morning since my national service. My wife doesn't keep well, but there's nothing amiss at my end.'

That was as close to a guarantee as I was going to get so I left him to it and turned back, shivering and pulling my cardigan up around my ears.

Paddy was outside the lodge, hands on hips. Shannon

stood beside him, her coat back on but still wearing her indoor glasses.

'Where did you go rushing off to?' Paddy said. 'Aren't you freezing?'

'I saw Mr Sloan,' I said. 'I wanted to ask after his wife. And ask if anything funny had happened with his cottage.'

'And has it?' said Shannon.

'Yep,' I told them. I shuddered. Paddy took off the fleece he was wearing and draped it round my shoulders. 'They've been switched to a lifetime lease. I think Julie and Abby are right. I think the Dudgeons got you down here and signed up, got me installed to take over Tuft's committee work, sorted all their tenants out and made a plan to leave.'

'It's just so strange,' Paddy said. 'I agree it looks that way, Finnie, but it's a really strange way to go about whatever it is they were trying to do.'

'I'm going to check with their gardener too,' I said. 'See if they paid him off. I don't suppose you know who it is, do you, Shannon?'

'It's a van with a green lawn on the side. Striped green, you know?'

'It just makes no sense,' Paddy said. 'What's the point of installing a new partner in a firm he's leaving behind? If he's going to Brazil because he can't be forced out again, what's the point of hanging on to the firm at all? We can't pay him over there.'

I wished I could send him a signal to dial it down a bit. He was only running with what I had started, but he didn't know the Dudgeons and he should have been able to cope with them doing something surprising. In fact, he should be annoyed with his new boss for leaving him in the lurch rather

149

than mystified and disbelieving, like Shannon and Mr Sloan were – after all, they had known Lovatt for months and years.

'Maybe the choice of Brazil's got nothing to do with extradition,' I said. 'Maybe it's just a good place to hide.'

'Hide from what?' Paddy said. 'He's a good man who does good work, like Shannon said. And Tuft's a fairy godmother who helps him.'

'Everyone's got dark places,' I said. 'Paddy, I don't know how much you know about why Lovatt specialised in adoption law, but Sonsie on the church committee didn't hang back.'

Paddy was nodding. 'I heard,' he said softly. 'Julie told me. But that makes it even harder to believe. After all he'd suffered, he'd be the last . . .'

'I wouldn't be so sure,' said Shannon. She waited until both of us were looking at her – gazing at our reflections in her mirror shades – before she went on. 'Finnie, you asked me if I was looking for my birth family. Well, the truth is I looked for my mother first but she had died. So now I'm looking for my brother. Or, at least, I'm trying to find out what happened to him. And I'm here in Simmerton because I think what happened to him was Lovatt Dudgeon.'

Chapter 16

Shannon lifted her glasses and scrubbed at her eyes. She looked at Paddy and me, her face so naked and the pain written on it so clear, I felt my eyes fill too.

'Come back inside,' I'd said. 'Have a brandy.'

She took her hat off as well once she'd sat down, and let her head rest against the high back of our sofa, her inky black hair stark against its pale grey. I put a glass in her hand and she smiled a faint thanks and raised it to her lips. After three long sips, she put her cap and glasses back on, leaned forward and banged the glass down on the coffee-table.

'Right,' she said. 'Of course I've got no proof. Or, at least, I didn't think I had any proof. If they've scarpered that's pretty suspicious, isn't it?'

'What is it you think he did?' I said.

'We're twins, you see,' Shannon said, as if she was answering me. 'Not identical twins, obviously, being a boy and a girl. But twins. Albino twins. Our mum gave us up for adoption when we were five.'

'Why?' said Paddy. 'Do you know?'

Shannon put her head on one side. I couldn't see her eyes but I could imagine the look she was giving him. 'My brother's sight was even worse than mine,' she said. 'He was registered legally blind and it's no joke bringing up a disabled child. And albinism, you know. Keeping out of the sun all the time. Never being able to go on holiday anywhere hot, never being able to go on a picnic or have a day at the beach, never being able to . . . And two of us.'

'But *you*'re not blind,' I said. I didn't have children but I couldn't see myself bringing a kid up until it was five, then sending it away over a bit of sunblock.

'That was a kindness,' Shannon said. 'We were supposed to go together. To the same family. Only it didn't work out that way. I went to my mum on my own. And my brother went somewhere else.'

'Couldn't your birth mum have stipulated?' I said.

'She did,' said Shannon. 'She thought she had. Like I said, she was dead before I started looking. She died not long after the adoption. In a car crash. But her sister told me Sean and me were supposed to go together.'

'Sean and Shannon,' I said, smiling.

'Yeah, like bloody goldfish. Anyway,' she went on, after draining the dregs of her brandy and shaking her head as Paddy raised the bottle, 'I thought it would be pretty easy to find him. The albino online boards, for one thing. It's a small club, except in Tanzania. There are loads of Tanzanian albinos. Did you know that? And then there's the RNIB too. I reckoned if I kept up to date with every little corner of the internet he'd pop up sooner or later. But he never did. I'm nearly forty now and I've been searching for Sean for over twenty years.'

'Where does Lovatt come in?' Paddy said gently.

'I shouldn't know this,' Shannon said. 'I only know it because someone made a mistake. I think because we were twins. Same birth date and same initials? At least once in the process of our birth mum giving us up and our new mums taking us on, the papers got crossed. I got a bit of Sean's documentation that I should never have seen. It wasn't much. Just one of the eleventy billion forms that need to be signed to give a kid to a different family. And I recognised two things. A phone number that matched the phone number on some of my papers. And a signature. I'd never have been able to decipher the signature if I hadn't seen it somewhere else as well, this time over a typed name.'

'Lovatt Dudgeon?' I said.

'Lovatt Dudgeon,' said Shannon. 'And the phone number was for St Angela's. It was just starting out then and the number changed after a few years but the Mitchell Library keeps all the old phone books in the reference stacks and I found it.'

'So Lovatt Dudgeon handled your brother's adoption,' said Paddy. 'St Angela's did. That's not really very surprising, is it? If your brother had a disability. Two disabilities? Is it two?'

'Opinions differ,' Shannon said.

'But the lawyer for the adoption can't have been the one that decided to split you up, could he?' Paddy said. 'Surely. He'd just have done whatever it was he had to do.'

'Well, he did something,' Shannon said. 'He did something wrong or crooked or, at least, he didn't want it getting out. And I know that because of what he did when I found him. Just over a year ago. I've changed my mind. I will take a drop more.'

Paddy splashed a healthy measure into her glass and she put a deep dent in it before she spoke again.

'I found out he'd moved to Simmerton,' she said. 'And I came down to confront him. I made an appointment and went into the office. I led up to it gently but in the end I asked him straight.'

'And?' I said.

'And he did everything by the book. Lots of sympathy but absolutely rigid confidentiality. Wouldn't entertain the idea of opening a file. Wouldn't confirm or deny anything. Not even whether my brother had found a permanent place, if he had gone into the care system, nothing. By. The. Book.'

'So?' said Paddy. But I knew more was coming.

'And then,' said Shannon, 'he started asking me about my situation and future plans. I was drifting and I didn't lie about that. And somehow, before I knew where I was, a cottage was available at a very reasonable price. Beyond reasonable, really. And Lovatt told me he had a business opportunity tailor-made for me. He had a clinic-quality SAD light that I could have for a song.'

'And you think that's a guilty conscience?' said Paddy.

'Don't you?' said Shannon.

Of course he didn't. Or, at least, he couldn't admit it. Because her story was our story: too good to be true.

'Amends, at least,' Shannon said. 'Bribery, if you're a cynic. And definitely he wanted me to be here where he could keep an eye on me. It was that cottage and that cottage alone. Bairnspairt. No cash alternative.'

'And your other business?'

'That didn't need any start-up,' Shannon said. 'It grew out of my lurking online looking for Sean. I've got a video channel.'

'Uh-huh,' I said.

'Oh, my God!' said Shannon. 'You're as bad as Mr Sloan. I'm not a prozzie. Listen, when Sean was a toddler he was obsessed with this set of plastic barrels that nested inside each other. He used to line them up in order of size, then put them together. He liked the clicking noise they made. He would hold them up to his ear and listen to it. He took those barrels with him when he left. So I found a set of them on eBay. You can find anything on eBay if you look every day. I got a set of them and put them up for resale and kept rejecting the offers, waiting for an offer to come in from a Sean one day. And I made a video of them too, setting them out and putting them together, A good mic to pick up the sound of the click.

'It was just one of the nets I cast to catch him. I made videos about all kinds of things I thought might interest him. You know, as far as I could guess when I hadn't seen him since he was tiny. All politics from the National Front to the SWP. Everything Scottish. All sports. All music styles. Made sure my face was in them all and I always used my own name. Shannon Shine. But it was the plastic barrels that took off.'

I had dug my phone out of my pocket and was googling. 'Here it is,' I said. 'Clicking Barrels by Shannon Shine. Eh? It's got half a million hits.'

'Yeah, you should see my "tidying the button box" video,' Shannon said. 'That's my best one. I sold ad space to a commercial film distributor for that one.'

I was watching it now. Shannon sat behind a table wearing her mirror shades, slowly stirring a pile of buttons and moving them into rows according to size and colour. 'I don't get it,' I said.

'I don't get it either,' said Shannon. 'I don't get the vids of girls pretending to clean your ears out, but it's big business.'

'And Mr and Mrs Sloan reckon it's kinky, do they?' I said, half wondering if I didn't agree with them.

'Not Mrs,' said Shannon. 'She's okay when you get past the doorman. Wait, no, that's not fair. She's pretty much a recluse and he takes good care of her.'

'I thought she was just under the weather today,' I said. 'Well, and Monday, actually.'

'And every other day,' Shannon said. 'The only thing that changes is the excuse. She hasn't been over the door once while I've been here. Poor old soul. Lovatt and Tuft go in and play mah jongg with them some nights, especially in the winter when there's less for Mr Sloan to do in the garden. They were there on Sunday. And I drop in when he's out of the way. But no one else ever sees her.'

'We're drifting off-topic a bit,' Paddy said. It was his lawyer's brain. He was like a border collie, hunting down the thread of a conversation and nosing it back into place.

'The point's made,' Shannon said. 'Lovatt's got something in his past somewhere that he doesn't want anyone getting too close to and I think it concerns my brother. Him taking off for Brazil just makes me even more certain.'

I looked at Paddy and he looked at me. Lovatt being dead removed the last whisker of doubt surely.

'Well, Shannon,' Paddy said, 'I'm bound by the same ethical and professional rules as Lovatt was.' Shannon's shoulders slumped. She hadn't noticed the *was* instead of *is*. At least I hoped not. 'But,' Paddy went on, 'there's one difference. I'm adopted. I don't think anyone who's not adopted can really . . .' He smiled at me. 'Sorry, Finnie. I don't mean to shut you out,

156

but it's true.' I smiled back. 'So, as I say, I can't break the rules. But I can bend them as far as they'll go. Lovatt was probably trying his hardest to keep everything quiet. I'll be trying as hard as I can to lift the lid.'

'Thank you,' Shannon said. 'Really. Seriously. Thank you. I've been on my own with this for so long.'

'You're very brave,' I said. I didn't know if Shannon would be the sort who'd blossom under flattery or if it would shut her down.

'Brave?' she said. 'How?'

'Weren't you frightened?' Paddy said. *He* understood what I was getting at. He had read me. But he had used the wrong tense again. I flashed my eyes at him.

'Wasn't I frightened of what?' said Shannon, not understanding.

'Weren't you frightened to move so close to their house, in such a quiet spot?' I said. 'Aren't you frightened still?' Paddy flinched, finally twigging that he'd slipped up. 'If you think Lovatt's got a secret, aren't you scared he'll do you harm?'

Shannon shrugged. 'Should have been,' she said. 'Probably. But I was too excited, thinking I might find Sean again after all these years. I was thrilled to get the chance to be right here on the spot, nose to the ground and all that. I thought I could volunteer at St Angela's, have a snoop around if I got the chance.'

'And did you?' Paddy said. 'Did you find anything out?'

'I wish I'd known St Angela's was all the way up in Stirling,' Shannon said. 'I found *that* out.'

'Oh!' I said. '*That*'s why you joined the church fundraising committee. It was nothing to do with my brilliant cheerleading for practical Christianity.'

157

'No,' said Shannon. 'It was neither. It was learning Tuft was out of the picture. I thought I could nip in and no one would stop me.'

'*Did* you know that Tuft was out of the picture?' I said.

'On holiday, I mean,' said Shannon. 'Or so we thought then.'

'Only,' I said, 'I sort of got the impression that you'd found out she'd gone after you got there. Didn't Sonsie and Adam tell you?'

'No, I got it on the grapevine,' Shannon said. 'Simmerton jungle drums. You'll soon find out.' Then she lifted her sunglasses and put her hands over her eyes. 'What a day. My head's banging. I'm not used to after-lunch brandy.'

So we waved her off, standing side by side on the doorstep.

As soon as she was out of earshot, Paddy spoke. 'Thank God she's gone. Finnie, there's something else I needed to tell you that I couldn't say in front of her. You need to brace yourself. Maybe you should sit down.'

'Just say it,' I told him.

'It's three things,' Paddy said. 'I'll tell you. And see if you come to the same conclusion as me.'

'Okay.'

He took my hand and started walking. But we were headed the wrong way. We'd be going round the house widdershins. I turned and started moving in the other direction. When he caught up with me, he began.

'The time stamp on the fax is too late for Lovatt or Tuft to have sent it.' I felt the blood drain out of my face. 'I got Julie to fish the papers back out of the file today. I told her I wanted to reread them, but I really only wanted to see what time they'd come through. It was quarter to eleven.'

'Quarter to eleven,' I said. 'Could he have scheduled it in advance? Can you do that with faxes?'

'I don't think so,' Paddy said. We were at the back door now. 'And here's the second thing. The fax didn't come from Widdershins. It was a different machine. Julie didn't notice – why would she? – because it was headed stationery. But I noticed. It was a different fax number from all the stuff he sent through to me before I got down here.'

I screwed up my eyes trying to make sense of it.

'And the final thing,' Paddy said.

'What?' I opened my eyes again.

'The thing that explains why, if he was sending a fax, he didn't just send an extra page with the news about the Brazil trip. Julie said this morning he usually scrawled a note and faxed it. He'd always do that before he'd type an email, especially on his phone. But he didn't.'

'And why's that?' We were back round the front.

'Because Julie and Abby both know his writing.'

My mouth was dry. I tried to lick my lips but my tongue dragged on them. 'The messages were sent after he died,' I said. 'They were sent from a different machine and typing an email was out of character?'

'Yep,' Paddy said. 'So you see, don't you?' I nodded. 'We said the fax and email were meant to buy time. But it wasn't Lovatt buying it. Or Tuft. And what's the only reason someone else would buy time?'

For a long empty moment we stared at one another. We both knew. We couldn't face knowing but we couldn't keep pretending. At last, Paddy started moving again. I fell in beside him.

'They didn't kill each other.' He said it, but it could just as easily have been me.

I squeezed my eyes tight shut again and this time the scene was playing behind them. 'No,' I said. 'Of course they didn't. He couldn't have killed her with that knife in his back. I knew that. So he must have died second. I really did know that. But he can't have died second. It's all wrong.'

'What?' Paddy said. 'What's wrong?'

'It's the cuts,' I said, as we turned the corner to the darkest side. 'I've been dreaming about them.' Paddy was breathless, his steps faltering. 'Those gashes all over her hands. All those stabs and slices. Those God-awful *cuts*.' He slumped back, as if someone had shoved him, and leaned against the wall, his breaths tearing at him. 'They must have come first, see? She couldn't have driven that knife into his back so deep with her hands slashed to ribbons, could she?'

'*That's* what's been eating at you?' Paddy said. His breath had started up again, too fast now. And he was walking faster too, back towards the light, such as it was, at the front of the lodge.

'Yes, and I didn't know why. The blood's so thick it's black on his jacket. It's from his heart. She couldn't do that, with those hands.'

'She probably couldn't do that even without any nicks and scratches on her hands.'

'They're not nicks and scratches,' I said. 'They're deep, deep cuts. Didn't you *look*, Paddy? Didn't you *see*?'

He shook his head. 'No. I saw nothing and neither did you. We have to forget. Someone killed them. We don't know who and we don't know why. But we're safe. By some bloody miracle, we're safe. God, when I think of us traipsing back up there and walking in. The blood was still running!'

'Who do you think put my bag out in the hall?' I said, suddenly struck by it.

'*Don't* think about it,' Paddy said. 'If . . . whoever it was . . . knew we'd been up there, they'd have done for us too. No one knows we saw them. We have to forget we saw them. We have to forget everything.'

He took a deep breath, so deep it put white lines down the sides of his nostrils. Then he blew it out through pursed lips, like he was smoking, and heaved in another one. 'Come on, Finnie,' he said, in a creaking gasp, not using the breath on the words. I gulped a lungful of my own and this time we blew out together.

'Let's go round one more time,' I said. 'For luck.'

'They've gone away unexpectedly,' said Paddy, setting off. 'They'll be back in three weeks. Okay?'

'And that's when I'll meet them for the first time,' I said. 'These two strangers who're nothing to me.'

'Meanwhile we just act normal. Act like two people starting a new life together. In a new place. Making friends and doing our jobs. Act normal and get ready to act surprised when someone, like you said, when someone finds them.'

'And then even more surprised when the police solve the case,' I said. 'Eventually.'

'Right,' said Paddy.

I could do that. There was no reason not to make friends with the people I'd met. It was none of them, after all. Mr Sloan wouldn't make himself homeless. Him and his poor wife. Julie and Abby wouldn't risk their jobs. No one at the church had a motive. When it all came out, it would be someone we didn't know.

We were back at the front door. 'Paddy?' I said. 'Who do you think—'

'No!' he said, harsher than I'd ever heard him. 'God's sake,

161

Finnie. We breathed it away. We went three times round in the magic direction. Let it work!'

'I'm sorry, I'm sorry,' I said.

'I *don't* think,' Paddy said. He was nearly hissing. 'And you shouldn't either. If you think about it you'll ask questions and then we won't be safe. Forget it. Turn your mind away from it and unknow it.'

I couldn't. I didn't believe in magic. 'Shannon,' I said. 'It was Shannon. She didn't hear on any "jungle drums" that the Dudgeons had gone. She knew they were "gone" because she killed them.'

'Where's *this* coming from?' Abruptly, almost roughly, Paddy pulled me inside and closed the door.

'She just said it. She thinks Lovatt Dudgeon's withholding—'

Paddy put his arms round me and drew me towards him. 'If she thought someone knew where her brother was she might kidnap him and put thumbscrews on him until he gave up the secret but she'd never – no adopted kid would ever – kill him and let him take his secrets to the grave. No way.'

'Sorry,' I said. I hated Paddy explaining her to me. Like I was the outsider. 'Sorry,' I said again. 'Okay, I'll forget. I'll unknow. I'll breathe myself to shreds. I'll wear a path round the house. It won't be too long now anyway.'

And so it was Shannon's brother who tiptoed into my dreams that night. He peered out from a quilt-tent shrouding a plant on the Widdershins terrace, ghostly white and pink-eyed with long yellow teeth that stuck straight down, like a rabbit's. I watched him scrabble the window open and slip inside, up

162

and over the sill, like a four-legged creature instead of a boy. And the noise he made, once inside, was a woodland shriek. The sound of trapped panic. I fumbled at the window as the trapped boy squealed and scuffled, stuck in there, the air turning rank with the stink of his desperation. So much blood. Black as sin and reeking. My mum and dad were swimming in it, coming down through the hills to save me.

Thursday

Chapter 17

I dabbed concealer on the shadows under my eyes, smeared blusher on my white cheeks, and tried to shake the dream off me. A nice neutral reading for the school assembly was what I planned. A nice neutral easing into my new role in my new place. I'd toyed with the Good Samaritan. But when I thought of the words 'and stripped him naked and wounded him and left him for dead', all I could see was Lovatt Dudgeon in the bright kitchen, still clothed, it was true, but wounded and left there. So I plumped for my favourite, these days. It's topical, popular, uncontroversial unless you're a total git: the sojourner at the gate. Or 'stranger', as the modern Bible would have it. The 'alien' is what American churches say, but that's a bit on the nose, even for me.

An hour later, looking out over a sea of bent heads, I felt my throat start to tighten around the words I was reading. 'And if a stranger comes within your gates you will not reject him. The stranger at your gate will be as one born among you and you will love him as you love your own family.'

As I spoke, an idea began to whisper itself to me, like another voice inside my head, drowning my own. I fell silent, listening. I even closed my eyes, to see if I could tune in any better. When I opened them again, none of the students were scrolling or tapping at their phones. Every face was turned up towards me. I felt a flush begin to creep up from under my collar.

'That got your attention!' I said, too brightly. 'Here I am, a stranger among you! And it's not *me* telling you you need to treat me like a lifelong friend, like a member of the family. It's *God* telling you.'

Someone smothered a giggle. A teacher shushed them. I'd saved it. I hiked in a sharp breath and smiled. 'Of course He's not talking about a new deacon at your school assembly, is He? Who's He talking about? Who is it we need to open our arms to?'

'Hearts fans,' shouted a boy in a Hibs scarf. 'Forget it!'

I kept smiling through another giggle and another shushing. I looked around the room, waiting for a more sensible answer.

'Like homeless and that?' came a voice from the back. 'Instead of moving them on kind of thing?'

'Definitely,' I said. 'Who else?'

'Immigrants,' said someone off to the side. There was a rustle of whispers.

'Refugees!' Now they had it.

'Foster kids?'

'Gypsies!'

'Visitors from outer space!'

A teacher turned as if to hand out a scolding for that one, but the kid turned to me, eyes wide and hands out, beseeching. 'Eh, no, miss? If space aliens came we'd need to be nice to them. Eh, no?'

'Absolutely,' I said. 'Imagine how scared they'd be. Let's have a hymn now, so if they land their spaceship on the roof they'll know we're friendly.'

The teachers were glowering, but I didn't care. The kids loved me. And the singing gave me time to ponder what that little voice had been whispering. There's almost as much in the Bible about kindness to strangers as there is about murder. It used to puzzle me, till Jed in the first parish pointed out that it's pretty easy not to murder people day-to-day and much harder to be open-hearted to weirdos. Lovatt should have tried harder to act like everyone else – who need to be told. He shouldn't have given Paddy a partnership and me a deaconship and both of us a cottage. He was even more reckless, giving Shannon a house and all that expensive equipment. And the Sloans were set for life. It made me wonder about the family with the skateboards. Were they lucky winners in Lovatt and Tuft's big giveaway too?

I wasn't going against what I'd agreed with Paddy. I wasn't going to investigate. I was going to leave it. Like we said. I was just thinking. There was no harm in that.

It was eleven o'clock as I turned the corner onto the high street. I stopped at the coffee shop at the top of the town. It was what passed for a hipster joint in Simmerton, with an espresso machine, muffins instead of scones.

'Am I too late for elevenses?' I said, backing into Dudgeon, Dudgeon and Lamb minutes later with a cardboard tray. Paddy was missing, as I'd expected, but the other two were there, Abby in her office with the door ajar and Julie behind the front desk at her screen.

'Lifesaver, you are,' Julie said. 'The coffee machine here

makes pigswill. I have to burst my diet every day with Irn Bru to take the taste away.'

I put the tray down and let a small avalanche of sweeteners fall out of my sleeve onto the table.

'Two lattes, one caff, one decaf,' I said. 'One Americano, one flat white. I'm not fussed so I'll have whatever's left.'

'Paddy's not here, you know,' said Julie. She snatched up the Americano as I knew she would. She hadn't got that figure chugging lattes.

'What are you buttering us up for?' said Abby, coming to the door of her office as I pulled the bag of muffins from my backpack and ripped it open to make a plate.

'Not buttering,' I said. 'More like seeking comfort from familiar faces. I just did the school assembly. Feral, they were.'

'Wee toerags,' said Julie. 'Mind you, we tormented the minister something chronic in my day too.'

'And mine,' I admitted. 'So, Paddy told me you reckon the Dudgeons are a goner. Not just on holiday.' I still wasn't breaking my deal with him. I was just chatting. It would be weirder if I didn't. If whoever it was – and I still couldn't stop asking myself who'd put my bag on the hallstand – if they saw me being silent, like I was hiding something, they'd start to wonder what and why. 'Has anyone told them along at the church?' I went on, trying to sound casual. 'Or will St Angela's do that?'

'I suppose it'll get out soon enough,' Abby said. She had tipped three sachets of brown sugar into one of the lattes and taken the chocolate-chip muffin. That explained her pasty complexion, I thought, then caught myself. I was too young to turn into my granny just yet.

'That's where Paddy's gone right now,' Abby said. 'St Angie's. To see if anyone up there can shed any light on it all.'

'And you're absolutely sure?' I said. 'Maybe Lovatt just switched to more favourable terms for Pad to give him a nice surprise. It seems weird to me but then I don't know him. Is that what he's like?'

'It's not just Paddy,' Julie said. 'Lovatt's done a lot of clearing up and setting to rights on the quiet over the last few months. Things he'd definitely need to do if he was clearing out. Things he'd never do if he was staying put.'

'Even getting Paddy in as a third partner, to be honest,' Abby said. She caught my look. 'No, it's not sour grapes because he didn't wait till I was ready, then hand the practice to me. Just that there's not really enough work for two active partners and a trainee.'

'We reckoned it was a first step to him retiring, didn't we?' Julie said.

Abby, chewing a mouthful of muffin, nodded glumly. She took a swig of coffee to wash it down and said, 'This is going to cause a stink. St Angela's would be totally justified in deciding they want another firm looking after them.'

I tried to look sympathetic, but I probably failed because, if St Angela's decided they wanted to look elsewhere, I might lose my job too. I knew we couldn't stay but you never want a decision like that to be mutual.

'But *is* that what he's like?' I said. 'Reckless? Incautious?'

'He's a lawyer,' Julie said. 'What do you think?' She threw a cheeky look at Abby as she spoke.

I tried a different approach to the same spot. 'Has he ever done anything that explains why he would do this now? What's he running away from?'

171

'To Brazil?' said Abby. 'The long arm of the law. Must be. We're toast once everyone knows.'

'So,' I said carefully, 'are you going through everything trying to find out where the irregularity is? The mistake he might have made. It must be professional, right? Embezzled funds, kickbacks from the planning department.'

'I've done nothing but snoop in his private papers and records all morning,' said Julie. 'I can't see anything. Lovatt was the king of "reply to all". If anything he was *too* open.'

'Maybe Paddy'll find something,' I said.

'I can't believe there'll be "irregularities" up there,' said Julie. She finished her coffee and dabbed her lips with a folded napkin. 'I remember the beginning of St Angela's. I remember Lovatt when his wife and children died. I worked for him up in Edinburgh, you know. He was broken. A broken man. And then this one adoption he just happened to be handling fell through and he couldn't move on. He sat in his office with his hands spread on his empty desk and just stared into space. It was like . . . he couldn't save his own kids but he couldn't stand by and see another wee tot suffer. So then he looked at the record of the adoption agencies – the local authority and the privates – placing children like the one his client wanted to adopt, and at last he started to come back to life. It fired him up, you know. He was full of ideas, dashing off letters left, right and centre. He was himself again.'

'But is it possible that – all fired up like that – he made a mistake and it's come back to bite him?'

'A mistake like what?' Abby said.

'I don't know. Or maybe he cut corners, barged through red tape. What corners could a principled man cut – for the good of the children – that would get him into trouble if it came out?'

The two of them shared a troubled look, then shrugged. I had to take a step back if I wanted not to spook them. 'Or maybe it's Tuft,' I said. 'Maybe the irregularity is with the fundraising. That makes just as much sense, doesn't it? Maybe Lovatt's gone to be with her because *she* had to run.'

'I tell you one thing,' said Julie. 'They didn't have money worries. I've just been looking at the tenancy agreements for the cottages this morning and they were only asking a pittance.' She gave me a quick glance. 'If that.'

'Let's go back to Lovatt,' I said. 'I'm just kicking ideas around. What sort of thing could go wrong in an adoption and then come to light? Because here's what I'm thinking: say a parent gives a kid up on some condition or other but no one who wants to adopt meets that condition, so Lovatt fudged it. Everyone's happy. Only when the kids get to eighteen and find their birth parents, it all hits the fan.'

'Illegal adoptions?' said Abby. 'St Angela's kids aren't really the kids that illegal adopters go after. You know? It's healthy white infants that get smuggled and sold to the highest bidders. Not . . . I know it sounds terrible but it's true. Look.'

She stood up and rummaged on the reception desk for a remote. She pointed it at the screen where the photos of houses for sale were fading in and out to the fake *Twin Peaks* soundtrack. She clicked the remote and the slideshow changed. Gone were the houses, and in their place were portraits of children. Some had breathing tubes taped to their cheeks, a few were strapped into full-support chairs, others were lying on mats, but all were grinning and some had been caught mid-guffaw, mouths wide and eyes dancing. The soundtrack was a cacophony of giggles and shrieks of delight.

'Okay,' I said. 'Oh, God, look at them! Okay, so not illegal adoptions, but like I was saying. Cut corners? Irregularities? Say there was a sibling group that was supposed to stay together and he split them. Or say a family got a kid and handed it back and that was kept from the birth family. Something like that. Is that possible?'

'It's possible,' said Abby. 'Anything's possible. But if that had happened the injured parties wouldn't be secretly blackmailing Lovatt. They'd be shouting it from the rooftops. For the compensation.'

I nodded but I wasn't really listening. I was trying to block out her voice because the germ of an idea was trying to take root in my head. Something someone had just said. Only all the words following on were washing it away.

'Anyway,' said Julie, 'I still don't think it's St Angela's where something's wrong, if something's really wrong.'

'Exactly,' I said, taking the plunge. '*If* something's really wrong. How can we be sure Lovatt didn't just have a big clear-up for Paddy coming, then whisk Tuft off on a surprise trip? He might come back in three weeks' time and laugh at all the fuss. How can we tell for sure?' No one answered. 'I don't suppose this "extreme openness" extends to personal finances, does it?' I said.

'How d'you mean?' said Abby.

'Well, if you knew his passwords for his personal bank account or credit card, you'd be able to find out if he booked return tickets. Or how long he arranged accommodation for. Or something.'

174

I knew I was shocking them but it was deliberate. I wanted to say outrageous things so that when I dialled back to my real idea it would seem mild in comparison.

Because I *couldn't* keep the pact with Paddy. Three weeks of this would kill me. And I thought he was wrong to assume we were safe, just because nothing had happened yet. The sooner the bodies were found and the investigation started, the sooner we could admit we were scared, lock our doors, buy extra bolts, stop pretending life was normal.

'Or does anyone have a key for their house?' I said, offhand, like it had just occurred to me. 'Does anyone go in to feed the cat or water the plants? Surely you'd be able to tell if they've gone on a trip or for keeps.'

'Popping in at the house is better than hacking into his credit card,' Abby said. She turned to Julie. 'What do you think?'

Julie twisted her mouth to the side and screwed up her nose. 'I know this is funny,' she said, 'because *we*'ve known each other for years and he's brand-new. But technically he's the boss, so I think we should ask Paddy. There's a key in a fake pebble by the front door, but let's ask Paddy. If he says okay, okay. Okay?'

Abby nodded and shifted onto one buttock to fish out her phone. She had him on speed dial already.

I couldn't hear his side of the conversation but Abby was a good relayer. She gave us the thumbs-up and a grin, then an elaborate frown as she turned the thumb sideways.

'Are you sure?' she said. 'Of course, of course. But ... No, of course.'

We were all silent by the time she hung up, even paler than her pasty usual and swallowing hard.

'What, for God's sake?' Julie said.

'St Angela's is winding up,' Abby said. 'Winding down. The staff's down to one and *she*'s been on notice for six weeks. There haven't been any new files opened for over a year. Henry, a year past October was the last one. They thought we knew.'

'Simmerton Kirk definitely doesn't know,' I said. 'I wouldn't have a job if Simmerton Kirk knew. And I won't have a job once they find out.' I had thought Paddy was nuts, Tuesday morning, talking like we could stay on. But here I was, two days later, mourning it.

'Join the club,' said Abby. She put down a half-eaten second muffin, looking a bit sick. 'Disruption halfway through training's a big blot.'

'What did he say about going to snoop round the house?' I said.

Abby blinked. 'Oh! He said go for it. He said if we can prove Lovatt and Tuft have hooked it we can call the police and then – like you were saying, Finnie – if there is an irregularity somewhere, the cops'll sniff it out. Something here stinks to high heaven, doesn't it? I still can't quite wrap my head round it but my nose is sold.'

I tried to smile at her, thinking I couldn't let her walk into that kitchen, also that I didn't know how to stop what I had started. 'What if they're . . . there?' I said.

'What – like faking a holiday to get a bit of peace, you mean?' said Julie. 'I've been tempted to do that. Much cheaper, but it hurts people's feelings if they find out.'

'I don't know what I mean,' I said. 'It's just that they're elderly and they're missing and if it was just one of them I'd be scared they'd taken a tumble and were lying there.'

176

Abby stared at me.

'Hazard of the job,' I said. 'I've gone into some bad flats once the neighbours got worried.'

Abby grimaced but Julie sniffed. 'No need to worry about me,' she said. 'I was on the volunteer fire brigade for ten years after they opened it up to women. The sights I've seen!'

'Oh, Julie's got a world-famous gag reflex,' said Abby. ''Member when that mouse drowned in the toilet over the Christmas break and wouldn't flush?'

'Anyway,' Julie said, 'it's *not* just one of them. It's an empty house. No gagging, guaranteed.'

'So are you both going?' I said.

'Best had,' Abby said. 'We need to witness each other.'

'Can I come?' I found myself asking. 'I know I'm not part of the firm but I'm sort of connected one way and another.' I *couldn't* let them walk into that house, into that room, into that hellhole. If I went with them I could maybe try to soften it for them somehow.

'Paddy suggested it,' Abby said, with a smile.

That troubled me but I put it out of my head. Something lay ahead and it was going to take all my courage to get to the far side of it.

'No time like the present,' Julie said. 'We could stop for a spot of lunch after. The church café does tomato and roasted garlic soup on a Thursday.'

I gave Julie a tight smile and hoped my face wasn't turning white. The gashes on her hands as if she was holding bundles of red twigs. The knife bisecting his back, like the body of a butterfly between those spreading black wings.

Besides, Abby was shaking her head. 'I can't,' she said. 'I've got a meeting to go over a power of attorney. Poor old

177

Mrs—' She flicked a glance at me and swallowed the indiscretion. 'And I think I'd rather do it after work. On our own time? So it's not so . . .'

'After dark!' said Julie, flashing her eyes. 'Full-face balaclavas. Synchronised watches.'

'I'll come back at five,' I said. 'Take it from there, eh?' Julie gave me a sharp look, hearing the break in my voice, but she said nothing.

Chapter 18

I wanted some time for myself anyway, to do what Jed in that first parish called a 'wide-mesh trawl'. The more I thought about *whoever it was*, possibly still right here, hiding in plain sight, noticing who was acting normal and who was troubled, the more I wanted to do exactly what I would be doing if we hadn't gone to Widdershins on Monday night. Or hadn't gone back, anyway. It would keep me safe. And it was a cover story too. My cloak of innocence for after tonight, when the bodies were found and the questions started.

Jed was the kind of minister who downloaded sermons off the internet, changed enough words so he wouldn't get sued and never thought twice about it. Sunday was his day off. The other six days, he was out on the streets of his beat – lifts and walkways mostly – offering an ear, a shoulder, a fag, a bit of cash or a quiet pint to anyone who looked like they needed it and didn't tell him to eff off when they saw the collar. He picked up good stuff at charity shops and kept it all in his car with the back seat flat, in case someone he dropped in on said the kids were missing school because of shoes or trousers. He trained me and I was a good disciple, a true convert to his methods, including the wide-mesh trawl. I'd spent four years sitting at bus stops, going into spit-and-sawdust beer shops at opening time, dropping in at corner shops for a chat. It wouldn't work in Simmerton, though. There *were* no spit-and-sawdust pubs in this kind of town. They all had blackboards outside with the daily menu specials. And the bus stops were empty.

Still, starting at Dudgeon, Dudgeon and Lamb, I worked my way up one side of the high street and down the other. I introduced myself to the girls on the till at the independent grocer and deli. Students, I reckoned, with long blonde ponytails and coloured braces. The folk in the post office, a pair of Adam and Sonsie lookalikes. The family butcher, three red-faced brothers in blue hats. A cobbler, for the love of God! An actual living, breathing shoe-mender, standing there in his brown apron, busy extending the lives of hand-stitched Simmerton brogues by another five years. They were polite and uninterested. Soul-crushing, really. What was I *doing* there?

It was the atheist candle-maker who broke me. I knew as soon as the shop door dinged and she raised her head. The wide-eyed look couldn't hide the burst of panic, then the disdain settling in at its back.

'Hiya,' I said, weaving between the stands of hand-made greetings cards and little books of proverbs to where she stood behind the counter, her handiwork ranged behind her. 'I'm Finnie Lamb. I'm new down at Simmerton Kirk. I'm a deacon. I'm just saying hello to everyone.'

'Oh, well, I'm not one of your flock,' the woman said.

'Right. Well, like I said, I'm just saying hello. I'm not taking a register or anything. Are you the Mo? Of Mo's Handmade Candles?'

'Yes, but I'm not interested.'

'In candles?' I said. 'That must make life a bit of a drag.'

Her eyes flashed. 'In organised religion.'

'Ah,' I said. 'Well – again – I was just saying hello but I'll let you get on with making these beautiful candles and I'll get on with helping people who haven't paid their lecky and might actually need one when their power's cut off.'

She opened her mouth but nothing came out.

'No offence,' I said. 'And I hope there's none taken.'

'What did you say your name was?' she said. She was struggling with a feather-topped pen, trying to click out the nib so she could make a note of what had just pissed her off so mightily.

'Finnie Lamb,' I said. 'Tell me, though, before I leave you to it, would you be willing to donate any of your merchandise to St Angela's? For our next silent auction maybe?'

'What's St Angela's?' she said. 'Why should I support a wealthy girls' school shored up by Vatican gold?'

'Vatican gold?' I said. 'I wouldn't be so quick to dismiss it if I was you. Say what you like about the papes, they do buy a lot of candles. I'll keep you in mind, eh?'

'No point,' she said. 'I've never heard of St Angela's and I'm not going to shovel my hard-earned money into some shady religious operation sending Bibles to perfectly happy little Paraguayan children, ruining indigenous culture.'

'I think you might have turned over two pages at once there. Who mentioned Paraguay?'

'I saw a poster outside the church.'

'And,' I added, '*hard-earned*?' I gave a final look around her shelves and left.

There was a little snicket beside Mo's Candles, leading to the back lanes. It was narrow and dark and, after less than a week in Simmerton, I had turned into the kind of creature that thought darkness pressing in all around offered comfort. I went a few feet up it and leaned against the cold bricks of the wall, cursing myself.

I dug my phone out of my bag and hit speed dial two.

'Doyle's House of Damnation and Delight,' said my dad's voice. 'Whassup, chicken?'

'Hiya,' I said, feeling better already. 'I've just done something really stupid. I got in a fight with Richard Dawkins's evil twin.'

'Ah, sod him.'

'Her.'

'Sod her. Dozy bitch. Forget her. Go and look her up on her cloud in a hundred years and blow her a raspberry.'

I laughed. 'How's Mam?'

'Ah, she's grand. She'll be fine for Saturday.'

We both left a moment of silence, knowing what he meant and knowing it didn't need to be said. My mum was trying to drop her sedation and raise her anti-anxiety meds, hoping to hit the sweet spot on Saturday morning where she'd be able to enjoy the day without being overwhelmed or getting manic.

'Give her a hug from me,' I said. 'Unless I can have a quick word.'

'Best not.' Then he got the chuckle back in his voice. 'Tell us more about this atheist.'

'She's got a candle shop.' His snort gave me a lift. 'And she won't donate money to any good cause that might have a Bible knocking around it.'

'Typical!'

'I was a real cow to her, though. I used St Angela's – the adoption folk, you know? – to score a cheap point. Poor wee mites. It's closing down.'

'Ah, well, now,' my dad said. 'If you were still the daughter I raised you could go and confess your sins. But as things stand –'

'Sod off –'

'– way to talk to your father. How's Paddy?'

'He's fine,' I said. 'Bit more in at the deep end than he expected. But, as I say, St Angie's closing will probably lighten his load. Unless we can fundraise like crazy, which we can't if I keep alienating donors.'

'Maybe it's a good thing,' my dad said. 'Don't quote me to the Pope if he texts you, but if there's not enough special-needs kiddies needing a home to keep a charity open, that's an improvement.'

'So you've heard of it anyway,' I said. It was bothering me that Waxy Mo, who worked up the street from Simmerton Kirk, didn't have clue about its main charity effort. No wonder it was folding.

'I've heard of it because you told me about it. Dozy mare.'

'I love you,' I said.

'Well, there's a coincidence,' he said. 'I love you too. Now, go and bug someone else. It's paying your rent and keeping you out the bookie's.'

'See you Saturday,' I said. 'Is Elayne giving you gyp?'

'Nothing I can't handle.'

'Hug Mam.'

'Hug Paddy.'

I clicked the phone off and put it away. And I left the utter blackness of the little close for the regular dimness of the high street, thinking – stupidly – it was the candle-maker, or Paddy's mum and her shenanigans, or maybe even my own mum that was bothering me.

For the rest of the trip round the burghers of Simmerton, as I waited for five o'clock to come round, I kept my head down. Or, at least, my lip buttoned. And when good works didn't shift the guilty feeling from the pit of my belly, I tried phoning Elayne.

I was in a wee tearoom down at the bottom of the street, where the buildings were beginning to peter out and the trees starting to close in. The woman behind the counter had called me 'Sister' and given me a free scone with my Earl Grey. I was among friends. Slightly confused friends, but friends. No one was at any of the other tables, so late in the day in the pits of winter. The owner was through the back loading a dishwasher.

'Hello?' Elayne's voice was worried from the off, suspecting a cold-caller.

'It's Finnie,' I said, thinking if she'd put her specs on she'd know that from the ID.

'Is something wrong?'

I let the sigh out silently, with my mouth wide. 'No, I'm just phoning to say how much we're looking forward to seeing you on Saturday. Just checking it's all okay.'

'It would be much easier if Paddy would come and get me instead of bothering Eric,' Elayne said. She meant it too. It would strike her as much easier for Paddy to drive two hours instead of my dad going three minutes out of his way.

'Eric's all set,' I said. 'Looking forward to seeing you too. Listen, Elayne, can you do me a favour?' Oh, I was an expert.

'Of course, dear,' she said. I could hear her voice changing as the idea that I needed something only she could provide began to sink in.

'Will you be anywhere near a Marks & Sparks before Saturday?' It was fifty-five per cent likely to work. Elayne was a true believer in Marks & Spencer. But she knew I wasn't. It would delight her if a week in the sticks had converted me. So long as she didn't see through the ruse and so long as she didn't remember that my dad would be driving past a huge edge-of-town on his way.

'I could get the bus down tonight,' she said. 'Late-night opening. I'll have a coffee. What are you after?'

'A tub of those Rocky Road bites?' I said. 'And one of the caramel wafer bites if it's not too much to carry.'

'You don't need to go buying cakes,' Elayne said. 'I can bake and bring a tin down with me.'

'Wow,' I said. 'That would be even better. If you've got time.'

'I'll make a coffee and walnut cake.'

'You're too good to me,' I said. 'Don't tell my mum you've got it in the car. She'll be in the tin before you're over the bypass.'

Elayne chuckled. I could hear the happiness. Now she'd definitely come and she'd take the lift too, although she'd nag Paddy to take her back at night. I'd need to make sure he was over the limit at dinner. She'd never want a lift from me.

Then I ruined it.

'And how's Paddy?' she asked.

'He's fine,' I said. 'He's off on a jaunt today. Up in Stirling.'

The line went dead, as if we'd been cut off. I knew we hadn't. I knew she was thinking that driving from Simmerton to Stirling would have taken Paddy within two miles of the turn-off to Stenhouse where she lived. Yet he hadn't told her, he hadn't stopped in on the way there and he hadn't warned her he might be stopping in on the way back.

'Oh, damn it!' I said. 'I wasn't supposed to tell you. He was going to surprise you. But I've ruined that anyway, haven't I? Asking you to bob down to Marks for me. You might have missed him.'

Now I'd have to text Paddy and tell him he had to go to his mum's on the way home.

'You're surely not jealous, are you?' Elayne was saying, sounding happy again. She had, as quick as that, decided I'd tried to stop Paddy seeing her by cooking up a story about wanting Rocky Roads. I couldn't imagine living inside Elayne's head and was glad I didn't have to. 'I'd better run,' she added. She'd be making dinner for him now, hoping to send him back to me too full to tackle whatever slop I would put in front of him.

I wish I could say it didn't give me a little flip when I saw, minutes later, out on the street, that Paddy was back in Simmerton already. He was flying along, his jacket flapping and his tie over his shoulder. He had two briefcases in his hands, neither of them his, both of them bulging, and he was running like a bank robber, like a convict on a prison break. Running for his life, as if all the hounds of Hell were after him.

Chapter 19

'Paddy!' It was too loud to shout in the street, in a small town. But then that was too fast to run. And I'd made him stop, at least. He'd stopped as if I'd shot him. I took darting looks all around as I loped up to him. *Whoever it was* would know something was wrong, if they were watching.

'Have you been?' he hissed at me, as I caught up with him outside the office door. 'Out to the house? To Widdershins?'

'I'm just on my way to scoop up the girls and go now,' I said. 'Tell me what's wrong. But calm down. People are staring.' I didn't know that for sure but I could feel eyes on me and, as I spoke, Abby was nosing a little blue car out of the carriage arch at the side of Dudgeon's, slowing to cross the pavement. She wound her window down as Julie stepped out the front door and locked it.

'Paddy?' Julie said. 'More trouble?'

'Get in,' Paddy said. His voice was grim. 'Finnie, get in.'

As he bundled me into the back seat, I mouthed, 'What's *wrong*?' to him again, but he shook his head.

'Are you coming with us?' said Julie, sliding in beside me.

'Let's just get away from here,' Paddy said. He clambered into the front seat beside Abby, clutching the two briefcases like lifebelts.

'Paddy, what is *wrong*?' I asked a third time.

'Where to?' said Abby, before he could answer me.

'Go to our house,' said Paddy. 'The gate lodge. I don't want any of this within a mile of our offices.'

'What's "this"?' said Julie. 'Something you found at St Angela's?'

'Something I didn't find at St Angela's,' Paddy said. 'A dog that didn't bark.'

'So . . . paperwork?' I said, sitting back as my breath left me. 'Irregularity?'

Paddy looked at me out of the corner of his eye but said nothing.

I could feel Julie's antennae quivering so hard the tension filled the whole of the car and I was sick with it before we were out of the town and onto the cut. The fug of Julie's nicotine and the perfume she used to mask it was bad enough, the stale smell of Abby's bad suit didn't help, but the sweet-sour reek of Paddy's panic was worst of all. I'd never smelt anything like it before, except with my mum on the worst night of her worst crash when she ran with sweat and trembled.

'Are you okay?' Abby asked him at one point, but he laughed and then was silent. We were all silent until we got there.

'Come in, come in,' I said. It was starting to spit with rain. 'I'll put the kettle on.'

Paddy carried the two bulging briefcases inside and dumped them on the coffee-table in the living room, then fetched the brandy bottle and four tumblers and set them down with a rap on the hearthstone.

'For later,' he said. 'Abby, dig into that lot and tell me what you think.'

'Oh, for God's sake, Pad,' I said. 'Just tell us.'

'I want a second opinion,' said Paddy. 'I went in cold this morning. I want to know if a second pair of eyes comes to the same conclusion.'

'Is this some kind of test?' Abby said. 'See if I'm up to snuff? Lovatt never sets me tests.'

'Just see if you feel the same about your dearest darling Lovatt after you've read that,' said Paddy.

'With you all standing over me, drumming your fingers?' Abby said.

'Look,' I said, probably too loudly, 'Abby, why don't you go through to the bedroom. You can spread all the stuff out. I'll bring you a cuppa. And then Paddy can tell Julie and me what the hell's going on before one of us bursts.'

'I'll second that,' Julie said. 'I'll carry one of the cases through for you.' Even at a moment like this, if there was a neb at our bedroom going, Julie didn't want to miss it. I rolled my eyes at Paddy and got a ghost of a smile in return before the shutters came down again.

Five minutes later, we were all settled, Abby propped up on the bed, fanned folders and printouts all around her, a cup of tea and a plate of biscuits on my bedside table for her.

Julie and I were on the couch and Paddy was standing in front of the unlit fire, chewing his lip, getting his thoughts in order. I twitched the throw off the sofa back and offered it to Julie. Our Edinburgh flat had been as draughty and cold as Edinburgh flats usually are, so maybe it was dread, or maybe it was the darkness, this all-day darkness that I'd never get used to, but the cold of the house was getting into my bones, and Julie's bones were so near the surface, she must have been freezing.

'I don't know where to start,' Paddy said.

'Just start!' I yelped at him.

'Right,' he said. 'Right. Well, okay. I found out who the board of directors of St Angela's are. That was the first thing.'

'And?' said Julie. 'So?'

'Tuft Dudgeon is the finance director,' Paddy said.

'No, she's not,' Julie said. 'She can't be.'

'And Lovatt is the chief,' Paddy said.

'He can't be!' Julie said. 'He's the lawyer. He can't be on the board too.'

'Abby's looking at the articles right now,' Paddy said.

And at exactly that moment we all heard Abby's voice, muffled by the two closed doors but clear enough. 'Holy shit!'

I laughed but Julie's face fell. 'I've never heard Abby say worse than "bum" in three years,' she said.

'And the rest of the board are . . . Well, who knows?' Paddy said. 'Maybe they picked them out of the phone book and maybe they found the names on gravestones, but they don't exist. That's what I'm actually trying to tell you. St Angela's doesn't exist.'

'Doesn't . . .?' I said. 'So what has Simmerton Kirk been raising money for?'

'Of course it exists,' said Julie. 'We've had summer gala days and Christmas treats. We've seen the kids' videos. What are you talking about?'

'There might have been gala days,' Paddy said, 'and there might have been Christmas treats, but whoever the kids at them were, they weren't adopted through St Angela's Agency.'

'No, of course not,' Julie said. 'They've all got very complicated health needs. And they live all over the country.'

'You mean it's a scam? It's a front? They've been embezzling all the money and now they've . . . scarpered?' I managed to say, as Paddy's eyes flashed. *Ended it all*, was what I had nearly blurted out. *Been caught and punished*, was what I really thought.

'But this is ridiculous,' Julie said. 'Why would they have company papers if it was all a scam? What is it that Abby's reading?'

'Oh, the evaluations are all real,' Paddy said. 'The home checks and psychological studies, the police checks on prospective parents. They're all real. But there are no kids. There are no adoptions. There's something very strange going on that I don't understand. I hope Abby does.'

'Paddy,' Julie said slowly, as if she was talking to a drunk, 'we have a slide show of kids running on a loop in our offices.'

'A slide show that we got from St Angela's,' said Paddy. 'Which doesn't exist. And I want to go back to something else you just said. About the parents being all over the country. That's true. They were in Scotland to start with. All of their evaluations are done in Edinburgh or Glasgow but none of them live here now. They're in Somerset and Lincolnshire. They're in Wales and the Isle of Man. Some are in Southern Ireland or scattered around the EU. There are eighty-four families that have supposedly been paired with a special-needs kid through St Angela's and every single one of them has moved a long way from where they were when the adoption started.'

'That makes no sense,' I said. 'That's the very time when you need to be near your family, isn't it? Your mum and any random aunties? Adopting a disabled child must be hard even with all the help in the world. Why would they move away?'

'Aren't people's names in the files?' Julie said. 'Can't we just phone them up and ask them who handled their adoption? It's obvious something's going on, but we can come at it from the other end.'

'I tried,' Paddy said. Before he could say more, the door opened. Abby was standing there with a sheet of paper in her hand. It fluttered because she was shaking.

'I don't get it,' she said. 'What does this mean? It all looks normal and proper, everything above board, except the names of the board directors. There's no way Lovatt can serve on the board and Tuft shouldn't be fundraising if she's their finance officer. But never mind that. I don't understand why everything just stops. All the pre-adoption stuff looks fine and then it all just ... stops. They all ... disappear off the radar.'

'We were just saying,' Julie said. 'We need to start at the other end. With the parents.'

'And *I* was saying I tried,' Paddy said. 'That's what I was doing all morning, as soon as I realised something was seriously wrong. I picked the most unusual names and tried to find numbers for them. And when that didn't pan out I tried to find Facebook pages or Twitter accounts. Instagram. Then I looked for them on the forums they might have joined. Cerebral palsy, muscular dystrophy, whatever. Couldn't find a single one. Eighty-four families and not a single member of a single one has a personal or professional website, a social-media account, or a mention in the press. They don't exist. St Angela's doesn't exist. And I have no idea why not.'

Abby came in and sat down in the armchair. 'What will we do? Call the police?'

'We were going to the house to make sure they'd really skipped,' said Julie. 'Will we still do that?'

Paddy looked at me, waiting for me to weigh in. Something was bothering me. Something he'd just said had snagged on a little nick in my mind somewhere. I stared at him, trying to bring it to the surface. Social media? Was that it?

'None of them moved to Brazil?' I said. But that wasn't it either.

Then it came to me in a rush. Muscular dystrophy and cerebral palsy. The online forums. That really *was* a good place to look for someone who'd been missing for years.

'One of them's real,' I said. 'There was at least one adoption through St Angela's years ago. Two, actually.'

'Shannon!' said Paddy. 'Finnie, get her on the phone.'

'I already am,' I said, dialling her number and trying to think what to say.

I hung up before I had punched in all the numbers, though. 'I'll go along and tell her to her face,' I said. 'We can't just summon her, like a witness for the prosecution. This is real for Shannon. This is potentially very real. Paddy, tell them while I'm getting her.'

I unhooked his waterproof coat from its peg and shoved my feet in my big socks into his wellies. Then I left, pulling the door closed behind me. It was true what I had said about Shannon. If the story of St Angela's was chapter after chapter of adoptions that hadn't happened and children who'd disappeared forever, then the lead she believed she had on finding her brother had just evaporated.

The rain was getting determined now. I put my hood up, my head down, my hands deep in Paddy's coat pockets, and scurried out between the gateposts and along the puddling lane to Shannon's cottage. It was wetter than you'd think it could get when there were trees so close on either side. Shouldn't they give some protection? Or did the rain collect on their branches and funnel down even harder into the gap between them? It felt that way: a curtain of rain I had to push my way through, only to find another wave of it and another. I blew upwards to get rid of the droplet on the end of my nose.

There were so many different kinds of cold in Simmerton. There was the middle-of-the-night bone-chilling cold, when Paddy's muttering disturbed me and getting up for a pee was such a torture, getting back into bed so luxurious. Then there was the crisp morning chill that felt as refreshing as splashing your face. This soaking, seeping cold was something else. It was airless and lifeless, making me fight for each breath, as though I was gulping something heavier than oxygen down into me and pushing it out again. And all the smells of the forest seemed to grow plump on this dead seeping cold: the wet earth; the sharp stink of pine; the bad-breath belch of everything slowly breaking down under there in the dark of the trees. My stomach rolled. Mushrooms, Shannon had said. Bags of rotting leaves, Mr Sloan had said. Don't ask, Paddy had said. Don't make me tell you.

I heard the dogs before I saw them, high-pitched yips and busy panting. Mr Sloan was just closing his front door, juggling the keys, the leads and the poo bags. Making a proper job of it too, turning the mortis lock and trying the handle to check it was locked.

'Hiya,' I called. 'They keep you at it, don't they?'

The terriers nearly pulled him off his feet trying to get to me.

'Best thing about owning a dog,' he said. 'Gets you out of the house twice a day, come rain or shine. Where are you off to?'

'Just being neighbourly,' I said. 'Going to pop in on—'

'You can't come in here,' he told me, his voice rising. 'Myna's making jam. She can't be disturbed when she's got jam boiling.'

'Her ankle's all better then?' I said.

'Even I'm banished on jam days,' he said. 'My, but it's worth it. Rhubarb and ginger from our own rhubarb. I'll drop you in a pot when it's labelled up.'

'Lovely,' I said. 'Doesn't she mind being locked in?'

'She doesn't like to be disturbed when I'm not there,' he said. 'So don't you go thinking—'

'It's Shannon's I'm headed for,' I said. 'Have a nice walk.'

'That I will,' he said, though he still looked rattled.

'Did you catch the gardener up at Widdershins?' I asked. 'You were going to see if he knew about this Brazil trip.'

'I'll need to get on,' was all the answer I got. 'Bracken here's got her legs crossed and I don't like them going in the garden. If you'll excuse me.'

I let him go and watched him until the dark swallowed his pale anorak and the two little straw-coloured blobs of dog. I hoped it really was Mrs Sloan's choice to live as quietly as she did.

But I needed to forget Mrs Sloan and think about Shannon. *She* was definitely in. The old windows had steamed up with condensation and the lamplight behind them was a bleary glow. The chimney was smoking too, the rain turning the sweet smell of burning wood into something rank.

She answered the door before I'd even knocked. 'Saw you coming,' she said. 'Come in, come in. Take that wet coat off.' She sniffed and swallowed. I didn't know if she had a cold or had been crying: those sunglasses hid so much.

I sniffed too, coming from the soaking cold into the fug of the woodstove. The incense was even stronger, and the curry smell was sweeter, with something eggy underneath it. But it faded when we were in the living room with the door closed. Shannon sat down and picked up the lumpy knitting on the round needle. It was six inches longer than it had been yesterday and I thought what a cosy life it was, living in this snug little cottage, with the radio burbling and her knitting. She should have a cat. Or a couple of dogs, like Mr Sloan, as well as her chickens. Something to curl up with that she didn't kill for the pot. Her couch was clear today, the bedding folded neatly on a stool in the corner. I had a flush of guilt for embarrassing her and spoiling such a harmless little treat as a duvet and DVD habit.

'Well?' she said.

I hadn't realised how long I'd been sitting there in silence. When I started speaking, what came out was as big a surprise to me as it was to Shannon. 'Paddy was adopted out of the care system, like I told you. And he kept it quiet. So did his mum. And then he got this partnership pretty young. Too young, if we're honest. And too easily, after kind of a rough patch. Then I got offered this job. That was a bit of a turn-up too. Like you said. Remember? That deacons were usually in troubled parishes. Not places like Simmerton. So, when I tell you what I'm going to tell you, don't think I'm not involved in it somehow. I'm not meddling in your business. Or not yours alone. It's my business too.'

'Have you found something out?' Shannon said. 'About Sean.'

'Indirectly. Just listen and then you tell me.'

I relayed everything Paddy had discovered, and what Abby made of it. Shannon did listen. She took her glasses off once and wiped her eyes, but she listened without interrupting.

'What's so special about us two, then?' she said, when I had finished. 'If most of the adoptions fell through before the placements were complete, how come I got my lovely mum and my happy home? What's it all about, Finnie? Do you see what the pattern is? Because I'm damn sure I don't.'

I shook my head. 'We're going to have to hand it all over to the cops anyway.'

'No!' said Shannon. 'Won't that mean Dudgeon, Dudgeon and Lamb closes down?'

'Probably,' I said.

'So Paddy loses his job?'

'Yep, and my job's a goner anyway.'

'Don't you want to try to . . . weather it?' she said.

I stared. Wouldn't she crawl over hot coals to get answers? Why would two strangers' jobs count in her reckoning?

'Anyway, is it definitely a police matter?' she said.

So that was the problem, was it? Shannon didn't think her life would stand up to official scrutiny. I could hardly judge her for that.

'I don't know,' I said. 'There's corporate irregularity going on, if nothing else. St Angela's is as bent as a three-pound note, obviously. And if we can prove that Lovatt and Tuft have gone for good—' I stopped myself. It's unsettling the way the stories we tell ourselves take hold. I was halfway to believing what everyone else believed, forgetting what I'd seen with my own eyes. 'If they've really gone,' I went on, 'the cops will be able to start looking at the financial irregularities too.'

'You think Tuft embezzled all the funds that were raised?'

'They can't have charged the adopters,' I said, 'can they? Not if they never handed over any kids.'

'I don't know,' Shannon said. 'Maybe the fee's for hours of work, regardless of outcome. Like a private detective.'

'But if it's a charity, do they actually charge at all?'

'I don't know that either,' she said. She was silent for a moment. 'What's it all *about*?' she went on at last. 'Most scams, you can see what the scam is. What's the scam here? What's the point?'

I shook my head. 'It's got to be something to do with what happened to Lovatt's family,' I said. 'It's too much of a coincidence that someone loses his kids like that because of a parent that can't deal with her health problems and theirs, then spends the rest of his life helping kids with serious health conditions find new parents. Or pretending to.'

'I suppose,' said Shannon. Then she stopped talking and gave me a look I couldn't have fathomed with a week to ponder it. 'Don't laugh,' she said.

'Unlikely.'

'And don't tell anyone I said it.'

I flicked my dog-collar. The starch made a stiff ping and she smiled.

'That's definitely what happened?' she said. 'It was definitely Lovatt's ex-wife – whatever her name was – who killed the kids and herself, and not that Lovatt killed all of them?'

Immediately, I could feel the pull of it. *Whoever it was* had had a motive, and revenge is as good a motive as any. But what about the decades in between?

That was bothering Shannon too. 'If we're right, though,' she said, 'we're saying he atoned all these years by running an adoption agency.'

'Fake adoption agency,' I said. 'Which makes no sense.' I wished it did because the other idea tugging me towards it was worse by far. 'There's another possibility,' I went on at last. 'But I don't want to talk about it.'

Shannon quirked her head, considering me. When the idea hit her, her mouth fell open a little and her lip trembled. 'You mean,' she said, in a small voice, 'he started out by killing his wife and children because they had Huntington's and got a . . . taste for it?'

'That's what I mean,' I said. 'Angel of Death. If you were that kind of monster, getting access to children no one wan—' I couldn't say it. 'Well, setting up a fake adoption agency would be a good first step.'

'But it's not possible.' Shannon's voice was so soft now I was basically lip-reading.

'No,' I said, feeling the relief flood through me and leave me tingling. 'Of course it's not. There has to be a plainer answer. That's why I came to you. Because you don't fit any of the worst patterns, do you? Lovatt did the legal work for your adoption and here you are.'

'But it would explain something.' She was on her feet,

stowing her knitting in a bag by her chair and kicking off her slippers. 'It would explain why they've scarpered.'

I nodded. It would explain why *whoever it was* had hated Lovatt and Tuft enough to kill them too. We needed to have their bodies discovered, get the police onto this and all of it would unravel. And when *whoever it was* was found – if it was the relative of some lost child – they'd probably get a therapist, a bit of community service and a round of applause. I know that's what I'd vote for if I was on the jury.

I was deep in this daydream when Shannon dropped the bomb. She was pulling on her boots and winding one of her long scarves round her neck, changing her indoor cap for a waterproof hat with a brim all round.

'I can think of an even better way to connect his own kids dying with all those other ones,' she said. 'Better than the Angel of Death thing.'

'What?'

'He got rid of his ex-wife and two kids that were doomed to Huntington's?'

'The story is she killed herself and them.'

'Bear with me. So he sets up an adoption agency to place children who're hard to find homes for. Disabled children. Unwanted children. They go through all the motions and . . . he sounds the parents out.'

'Sounds them out about what?' I said, even though deep down I thought I knew.

'A permanent solution,' Shannon said.

'No,' I said. 'No one would do that. No one would even think that in their darkest moment.'

'You sure?' Her mirror lenses showed my face to me,

owlish and stupid-looking. 'You telling me you've never seen anything in your life that rotten?'

My head was starting to pound. I'd seen something only days ago that was worse than I could fathom but violence is quick. What Shannon was hinting at, with a half-smile on her face, was slow and careful and had to be impossible.

'What about the parents who said no?' I asked, hating how desperate my voice sounded. 'Some of them would be bound to say no.'

Shannon was nodding, the smile spreading across her face. 'Early on, I'm sure. While they were finding their way. Then they'd get a feel for it, don't you think?'

'But Paddy didn't find *anyone*.'

'From the early years – when more kids really did get adopted – there's more chance of the names having changed. Divorces, deaths, kids renamed in their new families. It would be easy for a few successful cases to slip through Paddy's search. And then later on, when Lovatt and Tuft got better at identifying clients who'd be interested in their service – their *real* service, I mean, not the cover story – of course there aren't any records. Of course those people changed their names.'

I closed my eyes, sick and dizzy just from the thought of it. I could remember Tuft saying how she approved of the morning-after pill, but not of scans and testing. I'd thought she meant that Lovatt's children had deserved a life. Maybe she meant their supply was drying up. She couldn't, though. No one could. It was unthinkable.

'Why are you grinning?' I said, when I finally opened my eyes again

'Because here I am,' said Shannon. 'Even if it's true, here I am. Living, breathing proof that my birth mother said no to

201

Lovatt's offer. And that means Sean is still alive.' I tried to smile back at her. 'Are you okay?' she asked me.

I hadn't realised I was rubbing my temples. 'Just a headache,' I said. 'I need some fresh air maybe.'

I stood up and started buttoning myself back in, pulling my hood down close around my face, to scurry the few hundred yards to the lodge. Then I did what I had done the last time. Confused by the nooks and crannies of that cluttered little cottage, with its draped curtains, I went to the wrong door. I swear it was an accident. But I saw the flash in Shannon's eyes, as I turned the handle.

'It's locked,' she said. 'Lot of expensive equipment.'

'For your online video-streaming business,' I said.

'Look, I know we've been thrown together,' Shannon said, 'but when you get right down to it, I barely know you.'

'Hey!' I said, hands up and stepping back. 'Don't let the dog-collar fool you. I don't care what you're doing in there. I've got bigger things to worry about than anything behind that door.'

Chapter 20

We were silent on the way back. The rain hammered down, relentless, loud on the hood of Paddy's coat. It was running down the backs of the sleeves too and getting into the pockets. I could feel the trickles of cold on my knuckles and dug my hands deeper into the nests of receipts and tickets and rewrapped gum shoved in there. Every coat and jacket Paddy owned, trousers too and the door pockets of the car, his briefcase, his bedside table, everywhere he went there was a flotsam and jetsam of ring pulls and wrappers, tangerine skins and price stickers. I felt a helpless wave of love for him as I took my left hand out of the pocket to push the front door open and saw a little white plastic net dangling from my hand, snagged on my engagement ring. I plucked it off and dropped it into the junk-mail bin by the coat pegs.

'Come in, come in,' I said, taking Shannon's coat and rubbing her arms, halfway to a hug but partly because of the miserable weather. 'Come in and sit down.'

I could tell from their faces that Paddy had filled them in. Julie had that soupy look some women get whenever they hear a sob story. It didn't sit well with her over-plucked eyebrows and her drawstring mouth. And Abby was straining, like one of Mr Sloan's little dogs, so eager to start interrogating this new witness. She might only be a trainee but she was a born lawyer. She was just like Paddy, who used to reduce me to tears arguing about whatever there was to argue about. He had probably taught me to tussle with agnostics better than any theological training I'd ever get. I went over to him, hugged him hard and dropped a kiss on his head.

'So, you're a genuine St Angela's client?' Abby said. Shannon nodded. 'And has Finnie told you you might be the only one?' Another, smaller, nod. 'Would you be willing to let us see your paperwork, if you've got it? Compare it with all the other records we've found?'

'What will that prove?' Shannon said.

'Clutching at straws,' Abby admitted.

'Look, we've come up with an idea,' I said. 'It's a horrible idea, just to warn you, but it might explain things. Here goes. Did Lovatt's first wife – what was her name? – really kill herself and the kids or did Lovatt do it and get away with it?'

There was a moment of silence all round.

'Denise,' said Julie. 'No, he definitely didn't do it.'

Shannon slumped. Paddy had shoved a mug of tea into her hands and she bent her head and sipped at it.

'You're sure?' I said.

'Positive,' said Julie. 'No question. They were on the rocks by that time. Because Denise had had them tested – completely illegally – and Lovatt couldn't forgive her for it. But when she killed them he was out of the country, precisely so there was no chance he could find out and stop her.'

'He was out of the country?' I said, feeling the theory collapse.

'He was on holiday,' said Julie. 'He had gone off on a trip to cheer himself up. He was losing his wife and he was scared he'd lose his kids. There's always some stupid judge'll give custody to the mother.'

'Not that mother!' Paddy said.

'Things we've seen,' said Julie, darkly. 'So he went off on a treat. Who could blame him?'

'The papers blamed him,' Abby said. 'He showed me the clippings one time. The tabloids had a field day.'

'Where was he?' I asked. I knew how the gutter press liked to twist things.

'He was on the Orient Express,' Julie said.

'You're kidding!' said Shannon.

'It had been a pipe-dream ever since he was a little boy.' Julie sounded defensive.

'But could it be any fishier?' said Shannon. 'He went on a trip on a train that's like a flipping code-word for getting away with murder.'

But that wasn't what was bothering me. What *was* bothering me? There was a faint memory of something I'd seen or something someone had said. A trace so faint it faded before I could grasp it. For some reason, the slide show from Dudgeon, Dudgeon and Lamb came into my mind, the endless loop of pictures, each bleaching out as the next filled in, changing, changing, as if you were travelling past them on a journey. But the wisp of thought was gone.

'What *was* your idea?' Paddy said. 'Just out of interest.'

I shook my head. 'It wasn't very realistic, even if we accepted Lovatt as a murderer. It's not worth airing, if he's definitely not. Look, we need – someone needs – to go up to the house and see if we can get solid proof that they've scarpered. Then we need to phone the cops and get this show on the road.'

'I'm ready,' Julie said.

Paddy was shaking his head and I was sure his face had drained of some colour. *No*, he was telling me. *No*. He couldn't walk into that kitchen again. He was safe, because I couldn't make him.

'What exactly is it you expect to find?' said Abby.

'Emptied wardrobes,' I said. 'Shredded papers. Fridge turned off and propped open, I don't know, but there's got to be a difference between a house you've walked away from for three weeks and a house you've left for ever.'

Abby was nodding. 'Okay. Will you come along, Finnie? Like you said. I'd be happier if there was a witness from outside the firm.'

'Even if I'm married to the junior – only – partner?'

'You caught me,' Abby said, and her sallow cheeks were faintly pink for a moment. 'I think you being a deacon'll make it look less dodgy that we're breaking into our boss's house.'

'Shannon,' I said, 'will you stay here with Paddy or can we drop you back at your place?'

Shannon shook her head and took another sip of tea. 'I'll stay.'

It was raining even harder now. Little floods were coursing and chuckling down each side of the drive to pool between the gateposts, and when we looked past the flashing wiper blades, the veils of rain falling between the black trees looked too solid to push through. Abby put her headlights on full beam and crawled along, hunched forward in her seat.

'I've been to the house before, Finnie,' Julie was saying. 'Plenty of times. Lovatt and Tuft always ask the staff round at Christmas and again in the summer. But it's a thought to go in uninvited and start poking around. What if we're wrong?'

'And they come back from Brazil and report you for housebreaking?' said Abby. 'That's why there's three of us, backing each other up. We can say we were worried.'

'If you thought the email was dodgy, you'd be worried,' I said.

'Dodgy how?' said Abby.

I'd slipped up. The email was dodgy as hell, but I wasn't supposed to know that.

'Maybe there's an alarm set,' I said, 'and it'll be out of our hands as soon as we open the front door. If it's linked to the police station, we won't even have to call them.'

That distracted them from my gaffe about the email, but Abby laughed it off. 'Tuft and Lovatt aren't the burglar-alarm sort,' she said. 'They're the spare-key-in-a-fake-stone sort.'

'But they're not *that* sort!' Julie said. She had rubbed a clear patch in the condensation in the passenger-side window and she was pointing at the house as we drew up on the flooded gravel, feeling the tyres wedge into the sludge as the car stopped. 'The storm door's open to the vestibule. There's no way they'd have left the house like that for three weeks, never mind for good.'

'Of course they didn't,' Abby said. 'They're back. Or they haven't actually left yet. The lights are on, so there's definitely someone in there. Let's go.' She had switched off the engine but now she started it up again and threw the car into reverse.

'Maybe it's a house-sitter,' I said. 'We could knock and ask what they know.'

'I can't see Lovatt and Tuft using a house-sitter,' said Julie, 'even if the holiday story *is* true. And if they've done a runner they're hardly going to have someone in there.'

'Or what day does the cleaner come?' I said. I was getting desperate. As much as I dreaded walking into the air of that house after three days, and as much as I dreaded the sight lying beyond that kitchen island, at least once I'd faced the worst, it would be over. I would be able to stop thinking about them: her dull eyes and slashed palms, the slump of his chest over her body and that black butterfly. Once someone knew, it would stop. I could open my eyes and forget this dark prayer of memories, each point – eyes, hands, mouth, back – like a bead on a poisonous rosary.

'They haven't got a cleaner,' Julie said. 'Tuft's a bit of a stickler when it comes to housework – isn't that right, Abby? Wouldn't trust a cleaner to do it right.'

'Look, I'll go on my own,' I said, as Abby swung round to point the car back down the drive. 'I'll go and knock and see if anyone answers. They can't sack anyone for that.' Then I was out and splashing across the gravel before they could stop me.

I couldn't help breathing in deep, to see if any of the smell that must have been filling the house, like a cloud of mustard gas, had seeped out around the edges of that stained-glass vestibule door. All I could smell was the rain, sharp with pine and soft with rot, but vegetative rot – mushrooms and mould. Not the sick sweetness of meat beginning to bloom and slough.

I leaned forward and pressed the doorbell. I heard it inside the house and a helpless picture filled my head of Tuft's clouded eyes blinking and her curled hand coming round to shake Lovatt's stiff shoulder. Her mouth moved around the shrinking cake of blood that filled it as she whispered, 'There's someone at the door.' Then Lovatt, creaking and groaning, with the knife blade screeching against his vertebrae as he moved, would pull himself up to his feet and begin to walk, hair falling in hanks from his decaying scalp and bursts of gas popping from his joints as he moved them. He was coming my way.

'Well?'

I screamed and turned to shove away whatever horror had sidled up behind me. Julie went sprawling backwards, clutching at the ivy to stay on her feet.

'Jesus Christ,' she said. 'What the *hell*?'

'What's wrong?' Abby called over from the car.

'What was *that*?' said Julie.

'I'm sorry,' I said. 'I'm really sorry. I can't hear a thing with this hood up and I was concentrating on whether there was any noise inside. I think I heard something in there.'

Abby had joined us now. She went straight past me into the vestibule and turned. 'What happened?'

'I thought I heard a noise inside the house,' I said. 'But I rang and no one answered.'

'Ring again,' said Julie. And this time we all stood with our heads cocked, waiting. The silence was broken only by the rain drilling on the roof, blatting on the car, pattering on the ivy leaves all round the door.

Abby banged on the wooden transom between the stained-glass panels and we waited again.

'Oh, stuff this,' Julie said. 'There's something not right. Lights on, door open?' She was rummaging at the roots of the ivy plant to one side of the door among some lichened old curling stones and drying pot plants. 'I'm getting the spare key.'

'Try it first,' I said to Abby. 'You never know.'

I took a deep breath and held it as Abby reached out and pushed the handle down. She started back in surprise as the door clicked and swung open.

'Oh, God,' said Julie. '*That*'s not right. That's not right at *all*.'

'Okay, now we're on solid legal ground,' Abby said. 'We knew they were away, we came up the drive, saw lights on, saw the door open, tried the handle and found it unlocked. Anyone would be worried about this, wouldn't they?'

She had opened the door wide and was looking either way, with her head inside and her feet still on the vestibule tiles.

Julie, close behind her, leaned over her shoulder and shouted, 'Anyone at home?'

I was as far back as I could get on the step without being out in the rain. I waited for one of them to react, but Abby stepped onto the parquet floor of the hall and Julie followed her. Neither of them sniffed or gagged or said anything, except when Abby turned to me and asked, 'You coming?'

The hood pulled close around my ears seemed to make my pulse thump so loudly I thought each beat must be visible. My breath hissed through my teeth, shaky with sobs. But I stepped forward. I closed my mouth and breathed in deeply.

There was nothing. The air inside Widdershins smelt like polish and dust, faintly of wood smoke, faintly of cooking, of coffee, of a woman's perfume, of soap set out in dishes, and of softener used on clothes. It smelt of nothing.

'Where will we start?' Julie said. 'I could go through the wardrobes.' She was moving towards the stairs.

'I'll start in Lovatt's desk in his study,' said Abby.

'What about me?' My voice had lost all its volume, all its power. It was just a breath leaking out of my open mouth.

'God, I really did give you a turn, didn't I?' Julie said. 'You're still waxy.' She rummaged in a side pocket of her handbag. 'Suck a sweetie,' she said, holding out a wrapped toffee. I took it and smiled thanks, but I held it in my fist. I'd retch if I tried to eat it and my hands would shake getting the wrapper off.

'You could look through the household papers,' Abby said to me. 'See if there's anything.'

'And where would the household papers be?' I asked, sure that I knew.

'In the kitchen, at a guess,' said Abby. 'Down that long passageway.'

It seemed longer than ever, telescoping as I looked towards the half-open kitchen door. I breathed again. How was it possible that the stink had come and gone already? Even a mouse took longer than three days to desiccate.

I shivered. And then I thought I knew. It was January and they were hardy country folk. The house was cold and ventilated and it hadn't started yet. The changes hadn't begun. When I opened the door it would be the same sight that had been living behind my eyes since Monday. There would be nothing worse, because nothing different.

I pushed the door and entered, my eyes flicking to the island, to the one smear of red on the rim of the hob.

It wasn't there.

I gazed at the long, unbroken, reflected shine on the white ceramic. Could a mouse, could a rat, have licked it away? Would a mouse, would a rat, bother with a smear of dried blood when such a feast lay on the floor?

211

Could enough rats have eaten everything before it started to rot, before the stink began? And – everything eaten, the clothes tunnelled hollow and the bones stripped clean – would a rat, would a mouse, lick up even that one last smear?

Scared to lift my feet in case my balance deserted me, I shuffled to the end of the island and, holding on as the room began to spin around my fading consciousness, I leaned and looked and saw.

Tuft and Lovatt Dudgeon were gone.

Friday

Chapter 21

The Reverend Robert Waugh would have made a good headmaster in a black-and-white film. *The Winslow Boy*, was it? *Mr Chips*? He was looking at me over his glasses, his fingers steepled and pressed against his lips, nearly managing to hide his shock under a performance of disapproval.

'And how did you come to be in possession of this knowledge before me?' he said.

'Paddy went up there yesterday to . . . I don't know why, actually, but he found it winding down. Packing confidential papers, shredding the rest. Shutting up shop. They were down to a skeleton staff anyway, apparently. And yesterday the office manager was finishing off.'

'And your husband just went ahead and told you all of this?'

'I think it was probably part of why we got the jobs, don't you? A matched pair to pool our resources and work harder for St Angela's together than any other two people could work apart.'

'You *work*,' said Waugh, 'for Simmerton Kirk.'

'Good to know,' I said. 'Here was me thinking my job might be on a shoogly nail now. I suppose the fundraising machine can just redirect itself. How do we decide where, though? If I get a vote I'd say keep it more local.'

'We can take care of all of these questions when Mrs Dudgeon returns from her unexpected holiday.'

'Yeah, about that,' I said. 'That's something else, Robert. I don't think that's going to be happening.'

'What?'

'Tuft coming back.'

'What do you mean?'

'Look, I only came in to soften the blow a bit. I'll leave it to the experts to tell you the details.'

'What experts?'

'The police are here to interview you. They're just outside.' He blinked at me. 'So, I'll show them in, will I? And crack on? I've got plenty to do in my safe-as-houses job today.'

I didn't know why I was antagonising him. Except that I was sure my job was a goner, no matter what he said. I stood up and opened the door, letting him see the uniformed copper who was waiting to talk to him.

Give him his due, he still managed to ask me: 'Are you ill, Finnie? You seem out of sorts this morning. Off-kilter. Did you have a late night?'

He was asking me if I was drunk and I didn't blame him. I could feel myself sliding towards some kind of meltdown and I didn't much care. Yesterday, at Widdershins, staring down at the clean kitchen floor, my headache had vanished, like a flicked switch. The tension of the past four days, all the fear, all the dread, had flooded up and over and left me reeling.

By the time Abby and Julie came back, I had managed to drag a chair out from under the table and sink into it, but that was all.

'Well, that's a turn-up,' Julie said. 'Are you okay?'

'No,' I said. 'What turn-up?'

She was so full of her discoveries, she sailed on regardless. 'They've definitely not taken all their stuff with them. I don't think they've taken *any* of their stuff with them.'

'They might have bought all new holiday clobber,' I said. I was staring at the floor as if I might see an outline, or a smudge of blood, but there was nothing.

'I went into the bathroom and they haven't taken their prescription bottles. Folk that age – even if they're healthy – they're always on a few pills.'

'They might have counted out three weeks' worth,' I said. 'Taken it in daily dispensers.'

Abby had been listening but she cut in now. 'They've fled. Left everything at their backs. The desk's like the *Mary Celeste*. Unpaid bills. Uncashed cheques. A road-tax form that needs seen to.'

'If they've fled to a country with no extradition,' Julie said, 'why would they care about road tax?'

'You didn't let me finish. They've left credit cards –'

'They've probably got new ones.'

'– and they've left about ten thousand pounds' worth of cash.'

That shut Julie up. She turned my way. 'What did you find, Finnie?' she asked. 'And what did you say was wrong with you?'

Abby looked at me properly for the first time then and frowned.

'Stop me if this is a daft idea,' I said, 'but do you think they're okay? I'm worried that they're not on holiday in Brazil, or even gone to live in Brazil. I'm worried that two people in trouble have disappeared and the things they've wound up – the partnership in the firm and St Angela's – are the things that need to be wound up for other people's sake. And the things they haven't bothered with – bills and car tax – are the things that only concern them. I'm worried most of all, if I'm honest, that they've gone somewhere you don't need money.'

Julie sat down opposite me and stared. 'You think they're dead?'

I nodded. 'I think the whole thing – whatever the hell it was – got too much for them and they decided to end it all. They stopped St Angela's and basically handed over the law firm to Paddy and then they just—'

'Why would that be, then?' said Abby. 'Don't look at me like that. I'm not jealous. I just wonder why they didn't wind up Dudgeon, Dudgeon and Lamb as well?'

'Because it's legitimate?' said Julie. 'Unlike St Angela's.'

I didn't answer.

'Wouldn't they have left a note?' Julie went on.

'There's nothing in the study,' Abby said.

I stood up and walked over to the little household desk that was fitted into an alcove beyond the table. The desk I was supposed to be searching anyway. It was as neat and orderly as everything else in Tuft Dudgeon's life. A monthly planner covered the entire surface and I could see various appointments and reminders written in the pretty but illegible hand of an elderly lady. The entries carried on past today, on into the year. They were lighter as the weeks went by but they were there.

218

'I don't think it was a joint decision,' I said. 'Not if this is Tuft's writing on the calendar.'

Abby came over and looked. 'It is,' she said. 'But that's Lovatt's there.'

She was pointing at the corkboard on the wall behind the desk. It was perfectly clear, except for a single white envelope, pinned by one corner. 'To Whom It May Concern' was written on it in a spidery hand.

'It concerns all of us,' Julie said. She reached between Abby's shoulder and mine and plucked the envelope. Then she shoved her thumb under the flap and rucked it open.

'Should we . . . fingerpri—' I said, but Julie was already speaking.

'"Friends and colleagues. It would be redundant to say by the time you read this we will be dead. We tried to remedy the great sadness of my past with good works and we have failed. We have hidden that failure for too long and, heartsick and bone weary, we now choose to depart this cold world rather than see out the sorry dregs of our burdensome lives. Forgive us. L and T."'

'Is that all?' Abby said, but Julie was turning the top sheet over to read a second page.

'This is his will,' she said, and her eyes grew round.

'Read it,' I said. 'What does it say?'

'"My dear wife having predeceased me, I, Lovatt Dudgeon, being of sound mind, voluntarily bequeath all my worldly possessions, including the Dudgeon family estate and the law firm of Dudgeon, Dudgeon and Lamb to Pascal David Fleming and his issue born and yet to be born, in perpetuity."'

I felt my throat close.

'Who the hell's that?' said Abby. 'Did he get it witnessed? God, don't tell me Tuft witnessed it, did she?'

'No,' said Julie, squinting at the paper in her hands. 'It was witnessed by a Josephine Mary Doyle.'

'Who the hell's *that*?' said Abby. 'Julie, have you ever heard of a Josephine Doyle?'

They didn't ask me, newcomer that I was.

Julie was reading the top sheet again. 'What does it mean "redundant"?' she said. 'How could it be redundant to say you were dead?'

'Maybe,' I said carefully, 'they never dreamed we would come snooping. Maybe they thought their bodies would be found before anyone came into the house.'

Julie clicked her fingers. 'That's it,' she said. 'That's right. Oh, my God, though. Where *are* the bodies? Where are they that they thought they'd surely be found?'

I shrugged. 'Search me,' I said steadily. 'I don't know the area and I don't know where they'd be likely to go. Favourite picnic spot? Favourite walk, maybe? If their car's gone, maybe they went and parked somewhere quiet and fed a pipe in the window.'

Julie put her hands up to her mouth and pressed them in hard. Her eyes were wide and shone with unshed tears.

'Oh, God,' she said. 'Oh, my God, that's awful.'

It was. It was so awful it stopped her thinking about who Pascal and Josephine might be.

They were fizzing all the way back down the drive, dead set on dialling 999 to get the cops out searching for two bodies. But Paddy was their boss and they'd both lose their jobs if things went toes up at the firm. So when he read over the note and the will, managing not to react to 'Pascal' and 'Josephine', then said he wanted to think it over before he did anything, they took it. Grudgingly, but they took it.

Once they were gone, we sat and stared at each other. Where to start?

'What happened to Shannon?' I said at last.

'She had a booking for her SAD light,' Paddy said. 'Her phone dinged and she took off.'

'Sure it was for the SAD light?' Then I shook my head at his frown. 'Not important. So. You see what that note means, don't you? If that's Lovatt's writing, it makes it look as if they really did kill themselves.' *Whoever it was* was no one and we were safe again.

'She stabbed him and then he stabbed her,' Paddy said. 'Back to what we thought.'

'But why all those gashes on her hands? If she agreed to it?'

'Lost her nerve?'

'But she got it back, didn't she? To put the knife in him like that?'

'What an absolutely unbelievably horrible way to kill yourself,' Paddy said. 'Why make it look like murder when you're leaving a suicide note anyway?'

'And you see what "redundant" means, don't you? They were supposed to be right there on the floor in the same room as the note. No one was supposed to move them. Who the hell moved them and didn't raise the alarm?'

Paddy shrugged miserably.

'Oh, God, Paddy. When you went back to get the Christmas cactus, why couldn't you have had a look round and noticed the envelope?'

'Yeah,' he said. 'What the hell are we going to do?'

I stared at him. I had no idea. I just wanted to curl up in a ball and pull a duvet over my head. I smiled at him instead. 'Fancy a cheese toastie, an orange and a cup of cocoa?' I said. It was our code for wanting to run away. I teased Paddy about how he could always get a day off work by giving himself a migraine when I had to go to all the bother of acting. He usually smiled and sometimes even laughed. This time he did neither. His cheeks flushed slightly and he leaped up to fetch a cup of tea.

Watching his back through the two open doors, as he filled the kettle and gathered cups, I could feel an idea chasing around the back corners of my mind.

'Why would a lawyer leave a will that's so full of holes?' I asked, when he came back a few minutes later, pushing a mug into my hands.

'Holes?' said Paddy. 'I take it Julie and Abby didn't twig who "Josephine Doyle" is, by the way?'

'They didn't,' I said. 'No one down here knows I sometimes use my maiden name and they probably think Finnie's short for Frances.'

'And Paddy for Patrick,' he said. 'But what "holes"?'

'Are you kidding? For one, Tuft didn't pre-decease him, so there's that.'

'But we're not supposed to know that,' said Paddy. 'If we hadn't seen them minutes after they died we wouldn't.'

I frowned at him. 'What difference would it make when we saw them?' I said. 'What are you talking about?'

'Eh?' he said. 'Look, never mind that. What are the other holes?'

'I didn't witness it,' I said. 'It's not legal, because however they got something that looks like my signature on that piece of paper, I did not witness Lovatt's will.'

'Unless you did,' Paddy said. 'It must have been among the papers you signed after dinner on Monday night.'

'But I didn't witness Lovatt *signing*,' I said. 'You just went. "Paw-print, Finn!" and I wrote my name.'

'You're the only one who knows that.'

'And anyway,' I said, 'what's the point, when he got *your* name wrong?'

'He didn't get my name wrong,' Paddy said. His breathing was too fast and he wasn't sitting still. He was bouncing in his chair and his elbows were flapping in the strange way they sometimes do when he's in some kind of turmoil. It's not exactly a tic, but I always wondered if it was some faint ghost of something like epilepsy. Or related to the migraines anyway. 'He got my name right. He must have had to dig deep to find it. And he wouldn't have done all that if the will wasn't watertight.'

'Dig deep? What's "Fleming"?' I said. 'Your birth name? Doesn't adoption wipe that out?'

'What?' said Paddy. 'Yes, of course it does. Fleming's my mum. She uses her married name – you know what she's like – so I use it too. But she was born Elayne Fleming and so, adopting me after her divorce, I'm Paddy Fleming. Technically.'

Even in the middle of everything, I felt a shift inside me. 'How did I not know your name?' I said. 'On our marriage certificate, you're Lamb. Is *that* legal?

'Are we married, you're asking?' Paddy said. 'Of course we are! But speaking of legal, we can defend this will, Finnie. We can fight for what Lovatt wanted to give me.'

'Paddy, we can't,' I told him. 'If you benefit they're going to have a good hard look at you as the potential killer. And we were *there*. And then we went back in and then *you* went back in again. And we were so stupid – this only just occurred to me, but it's true. We wiped the prints from when we went back, but not from when we sat and ate dinner. Do you see?'

'But you've been back in today,' said Paddy.

'What about you?'

'I wiped round when I went back for the cactus,' he said. 'Round the chair where I sat. Round the drinks tray in the dining room.'

I stared at him. 'Is that why you wanted me to go with Julie and Abby?' I said.

'What?'

'Doesn't matter. Look, Paddy . . . Really think about it. If you try to benefit from that will we're going to end up getting done for murder. I think you should put in your notice and I will too and we'll just go.'

'What the hell are you talking about?' Paddy said. 'We own that gorgeous house now. We own this house! And the cottages. And the firm!' He was getting wild, a sheen of sweat on his brow and a glitter in his eyes I couldn't remember ever seeing before.

'Pad, Pad,' I said, putting a hand on his nearest arm. 'The will's no good. I didn't witness it. Even if we get round the wrong name, you won't inherit anything. So it's not worth raising suspicions.'

'Suspicions of what?' he said. 'They killed themselves. We thought that all along and we just decided it again!'

'Not all along,' I said. 'Only until whoever it was sent a fax and an email after the Dudgeons were dead. And now someone's moved the bodies too. It's time to face facts.'

'What facts?'

'He had a knife in his back! Who does that?' I screwed up my eyes as the gauze began to fall again. I knew I was whimpering and I couldn't help it. That black stain spreading around the knife handle – why was that the sharpest image of all? It wasn't, for all the horror, Tuft's open mouth or clouded eyes. It wasn't the bright creases of blood drying in her gashed hands. It wasn't the hideous jauntiness of that pleated skirt swinging up at the side. It was the black butterfly. I started talking again just to make the picture go away.

'Whoever it was held a knife to Tuft's throat and told that poor old man what to write in the suicide note,' I said.

'And he loved his wife so much he did it,' said Paddy.

'Then whoever it was killed them both anyway.'

'And pinned the note to a corkboard with a will leaving everything to me in the same envelo— Why are you looking at me like that?'

I blinked. I hadn't known it was showing on my face. 'Was it you?' I found myself saying. 'Did you move them when you went to get the cactus? Is that why you wouldn't talk about it?'

'Move them where?' Paddy said. 'You think maybe they're in the shed out the back? Go and look. You think they're in the boot of the car? We better not do a big shop, eh?'

'Don't,' I said. 'Stop it. Don't be so horrible.'

'*Me* horrible? Where's this coming from?'

'How did you know the note was pinned to a corkboard?'

Paddy blinked too. 'You told me.'

'I don't think I did.'

'Someone told me. You or Julie or Abby. Someone definitely mentioned it. I think.' He shrugged. 'Or maybe it's just because there's a pinhole in one corner and I assumed.

What does it matter? Finnie, seriously. Why are you looking at me like that?'

'Because,' I said, 'you're the most honest person I know.'

His face clouded over.

'I thought it was funny when you wangled us moving here,' I said. 'You were so bad at pretending you hadn't seen the house already. And you mucked up saying you'd been there for lunch. I thought it was sweet. Like a puppy barking at a mirror. Because you're the most honest person I've ever met.'

'I am,' he said. 'I'd never hide anything from you.'

'Except three years on an oil rig to pay off a loan to cover up—'

'Not to cover up,' he said. 'To make good. That's what *turned* me honest. Like your thing turned you . . . What? Serious? Moral?'

'Right,' I said. But something else was troubling me. With a flash that seemed so real I closed my eyes against it, I was on my feet and through to the hall. I fished in the bin by the coat pegs, scrabbling past the junk mail until I found the little white plastic net.

'What are you doing?' Paddy said, standing half hidden behind the living-room door.

'Babybel!' I said, shaking it in his face. 'And orange peel. I thought it was kids. I was even kind of tickled, to think this was such a nice place to stay that the kids put their crap in a bin instead of dropping it in the verge. But it was you, wasn't it? You gave yourself a migraine so – so that you'd . . . What?'

Paddy was staring at me with the two yellow lines down his cheeks that he gets when his blood sugar drops. 'So that I wouldn't have to go and pretend to check up on them,' he said. 'I bottled out. I couldn't face it. Yes, I gave myself a migraine. Then, by the time Julie found the email saying they'd gone off on holiday, it was too late. I even went and stuck my fingers down my throat. Have you ever puked up soft cheese and Twixes? Well, don't bother.'

'But then you went back anyway,' I said. 'Two days later. When it was going to be even worse.'

'Yeah,' Paddy said. His colour was coming back again. And it shouldn't have been. If he was thinking about what he'd seen in that kitchen, he should be going yellow all over and heaving.

'They were already gone, weren't they?' I said.

'Yeah.'

'And you saw the note. On the corkboard.'

He closed his eyes and said nothing.

'What's going on, Paddy?' I asked him.

His eyes flew open again. 'I don't know. I honestly do not know.'

And I smiled, as if I believed him. I didn't remind him that two minutes ago he'd looked me right in the eye and told me he'd 'never hide anything from' me when he was hiding three things right that minute.

I didn't say a word. I managed to keep smiling as long as he was looking at me. But something changed that day. It was like I stepped off the seesaw of our marriage. I left him on the other end and I didn't care whether he was in the air or grounded. The next day when I sat in Waugh's office getting scolded like a schoolgirl, trying to get my head round what the hell was happening in our wonderful new life in this sweet little town, I was working alone.

Chapter 22

'Was that the police going into Robert's office?' Sonsie had turned the sign to 'Closed' at the charity shop and was right behind me, actually nudging my back with the soft woolly domes of her gravity-defying bosom. I took a step away but she followed me, bumping up against me like a little water-buffalo. Some really truly round women have no clue where their bodies end, as if they're only responsible for the core area and there's disputed territory at the edges where it's up to you to maintain the border.

'Yep,' I said.

'What's happened?'

I'd heard people say their heads were fizzing before that day. Clients at a low ebb, neighbours at my mum's bit, loads of my dad's relations when things got out of hand with partners, ex-partners, officials, kids, pals, texts, calls and the telly blaring. But until that moment, standing in the dark hall of the church, halfway between the shop and Waugh's office, I had never felt it for myself.

'Lovatt and Tuft Dudgeon are dead,' I said. 'I need to sit down, Sonsie. I need to go and sit in the quiet awhile.'

I blundered through the doors at the back of the aisle and slipped into one of the elders' seats in the last pew. But, of course, she followed me.

'Was it a plane crash? I never heard on the news. Or was it a hold-up? South America, you know what they say.'

'They never got to South America,' I said. 'I don't think they were ever *going* to South America. They just said that so no one would look for them for a while.'

'Suicide?' Sonsie breathed. Perched on the edge of a seat, she had no lap at all. Her stomach bulged forward all the way – it wasn't far – to her knees, but that didn't stop her grabbing one of my hands in both of hers and holding it in that non-existent lap, pressed against her belly, with the underside of her bosom brushing my knuckles.

'Suicide,' I said, lying in a church. 'At least, there was a note. Lovatt left a note and his will. But there's no sign of the bodies. So the police are searching.'

'Searching the *church*?' The organ was right above us and it chimed in tune with her sudden shriek.

'No, no, I don't think so. They're talking to Robert because Tuft worked here. Volunteered here anyway. They'll probably want to talk to you too. They might even want to talk to me. Because of Paddy. Even though I never met them.'

Was I really going to lie to the cops?

'But they can't be dead,' Sonsie said. 'They would never kill themselves. They didn't believe in it. Tuft volunteered at the Samaritans. Saturday nights, no less – a right rough lot you get when the pubs close. And she didn't believe in suicide, or capital punishment. Not even war. We had some falling-outs when it was Kosovo. Well, discussions, I suppose you'd say.'

I found myself squeezing Sonsie's hand.

'She wasn't depressed either,' Sonsie said. 'She was looking forward to meeting you. She said on Monday she was going to stop in at the gate lodge on the way home and try to get you up to Widdershins for dinner.'

'Did she?' I said. 'Did she really?' I hoped Sonsie didn't notice my hand turning slick as she held it. She did notice. She let it go and wiped hers on the bulge of her tweedy thigh. But she didn't register. She was still lost in denial of Tuft's suicide.

'They were good neighbours,' I said. 'Planning to have us round, playing mah jongg with the Sloans. Strange how Mr Sloan never said that, though. He told me on Monday his wife had a tummy bug.'

Sonsie searched my face, hers drawn up with anxiety. 'Tummy bug?' she said. 'So, could it be natural causes? Have they both taken ill and slipped away? They're not as young as they were and there's not a picking on either of them.'

'But there was a note,' I told her again, gently. 'He left a note.'

She sat back, her feet lifting off the floor and swinging. I bent to put a hassock under them and she rewarded me with a distracted smile. 'Well,' she said, 'he hadn't his troubles to seek. Like I told you. With his first wife. His family. But he'd turned it all to the good. St Angela's. All those happy children. All those years of good work. What's suddenly gone wrong now?'

St Angela's, I thought, nodding. His first wife and his family. All those years of what looked so very much like good work. All those pictures looping to make a slide show in the offices of Dudgeon, Dudgeon and Lamb. 'How did Simmerton Kirk get involved with St Angela's?' I said. 'It never struck me before, but if their offices are in Stirling, why wasn't it a Stirling church that stepped in?'

Sonsie frowned. 'Why would we mind where the office was?' she said. 'The children were from all over, the parents too. We sponsor a school in Paraguay. We've got a twin parish in Seoul. What's Stirling?'

'Right,' I said. 'Right. I wonder if it was awkward for them – St Angela's – to have the lawyer and the fundraisers away down here instead of on the spot. Did you ever have to do any traipsing up and down?'

'Me?' said Sonsie. 'I'm a humble worker-bee.'

'Or Robert. Or Adam. Ignore me. I'm just . . . typical new broom! Carping about something that's been working smoothly for years.' But still I couldn't help poking at it, sore-tooth style. 'I suppose I just wonder why Lovatt didn't settle in Stirling when he left Edinburgh. Unless Dudgeon and Dudgeon came first and the St Angela's connection was second.'

'What?' She shook her head, as if getting rid of a gnat. 'What does that have to do with this now?'

'Right,' I said again. 'They came down here to be close to where Denise and the children are buried – is that right? To be close to the old homestead, even though it's burned down? Jerusalem?'

'I don't know where they're buried,' Sonsie said. 'I don't even know *if* they're buried. Or they might be cremated and scattered somewhere lovely. That's what Adam and I have said for when we go. I wonder if Tuft and Lovatt have left word. Will the funeral be soon or are the police going to stall everything while they . . . What is it they're doing?'

'The funeral?' I said. 'Well, they'd have to find the bodies first. They've got no idea what happened to them.'

Sonsie pressed her hands to her mouth again and this time tears formed and splashed down. 'I can't believe it,' she mumbled, through her fingers. 'Tuft would never. She would never! She used to rant about it to me - people throwing themselves off bridges and putting the lifeboat crew in danger, hanging themselves for their families to find and never sleep easy again. She would never.'

'As far as that goes, she hasn't,' I said. 'Maybe that's the whole point. Maybe they'll never turn up. Sorry!' Sonsie had moaned in distress at that thought. 'The cops've barely started searching yet. They'll turn up. They will. And they'll get a proper send-off. Soon. I'm sure of it.'

'Are you?' said Sonsie. 'Too sure to pray?'

I smiled at her and we both turned to face the front. She bent her head, but I stared at the altar. I don't know if you'd call what I did praying, exactly. It felt more like letting my mind drift. So much had happened since Monday night that I didn't understand. There was a murderer walking around, for one thing. And all the mess of St Angela's. The mystery of why Paddy and I were here in the first place. Whatever was going on with Shannon. But the thing my mind kept drifting back to was – *where are they*?

I must have been praying after all. When my prayer was answered, so clearly and so quickly, the sound of my gasp echoed round the empty church and set the organ pipes humming again.

'What?' said Sonsie, looking up.

I was already sliding round her and out of the pew. 'I forgot something I'm supposed to do,' I said. Lying in church again. 'I'll find Adam and send him in to you, will I?'

'He's golfing,' Sonsie said. She patted herself where her waist should have been. 'I could ring him, though. Robert hates us using our phones in here, but—'

'Time like this,' I said, as Sonsie ripped a mobile phone from a Velcro fastening under her jumper. 'Go for it. Will you be okay till he gets here?'

'I'll pray a bit more,' Sonsie said, jabbing buttons. 'You go on, Finnie. I'll sit here and have another wee pray.'

Paddy was out of my way in his office, dealing with a pair of coppers of his own. I had the car keys in my bag and, thanks to the landscape of the Simmer Valley, with its one road and its two cuts, I was pretty sure I could find my way where I wanted to go. And even if I was wrong, it was a chance of some silence, some solitude, to let the fizzing stop and wait in hope for calm, for clarity, and for answers.

It had been a beautiful morning, the ribbon of sky above our rooftops a pale opalescent blue and a dazzle behind the waving tree tips, showing where the sun was still shining. Up out of this black valley and its cuts there were hills where sheep felt warmth on their thick winter backs. There was light drenching the ground and throwing shadows. Somewhere away to the north my dad would be tutting and shutting the blinds to get the glare off the news.

But clouds had gathered and thickened by the time I left Sonsie in the church, and I started the wipers along with the engine, the headlights too, and I felt my heart slump in my chest as I realised they really were lighting my way as well as making my little car brighter. As I swung onto the east back road and headed up out of the town, I even tried the full beams.

'It's bloody one o'clock!' I said. 'This place is a joke!'

But I wasn't laughing. Little courtyard developments had been squeezed into the valley floor at the south-west corner on the way to Widdershins. Neat pairs of semis and clutches of townhouses, with patios and a bit of parking, were tucked into the steep lanes. But up this way, there was just one row of grey cottages that used to be sweet shops and smithies and along the back of them ran the slimmest of passages to let folk in and out their back doors. Then the hill started to rise, behind retaining walls that bulged and crumbled, flakes of whitewash lying on the ground and moss filling the cracks. Then, at the end of the row, abruptly, Simmerton gave up. The pavement stopped and the bracken-covered bank came right down to meet the yellow paint at the edge of a single-track lane.

'The cut,' I said. 'The road to Jerusalem.' I shivered, and turned the wipers up a notch.

If I thought the lane to Widdershins and our gate lodge was dreich, this knocked it into a coal bucket. Shannon had said Bairnspairt Cottage was in the quarry, but I reckoned whoever had built the country seat of the Dudgeons had blasted out this cut too. It couldn't be natural, surely. On either side of the roadway, there were slate walls, great slabs of rock with seams of quartz shining in the rain. They loomed jaggedly up over the roof of the car, seeping rusty water that gathered and ran down in streams. At the top, the knuckles of the pine roots looked like the claws of gigantic birds, perched there. I turned the radio on, for a bit of cheer, but of course there was no reception.

And even when a clearing opened up on my left side – a verge and a drystone wall with what I thought might be a meadow lying beyond it – it turned out to be a graveyard, the entry still padlocked shut although one of the gateposts had crumbled badly enough to leave the gates buckling as they twisted round the chain that joined them.

I drove on. '"Last night I dreamed I went to Manderley again",' I said to myself. 'Then how does it go? Gates rusted shut, drive choked with weeds, bushes and trees rampaging. Three out of three.'

I was at the entrance to Jerusalem House now. I knew because the gateposts were the same as ours and, just like ours, the name on them was wrong. 'Giro' said one and 'Solem' the other.

'Oh!' I said. *Giro solem* – following the sun – had changed to Jerusalem, like Widow's Portion turning into Widdershins. I still didn't understand Widdershins. Going round a church anti-clockwise was bad luck and an ill omen for a house. There was no 'turning to the sun' at Jerusalem either. This cut faced due north. They'd get a noonday blast at midsummer and the rest of the year they'd spend in shadow.

I shook my head to get the nonsense out. Who were 'they', with their unlucky houses and strange nicknames? Why did they bother me? Well, I knew that, at least. 'They' were that poor woman and her diagnosis. 'They' were her children, sentenced by their father's selfish decision to leave them and their mother's disastrous decision to test them.

I wondered if she'd even got a therapist to talk things over with. Posh Scots thirty years back, it was unlikely. Then I wondered if she'd ever considered just moving. Getting the kids out of this open-air dungeon into a nice bright villa somewhere fun. Not Edinburgh. Somewhere she could have fallen apart without everyone getting a cat's-bum mouth and calling her 'hysterical' behind her back. Brighton, I thought. If only the story of Lovatt Dudgeon was that his first wife lived in Brighton with her care team and her grown-up kids. A few grandchildren around who wouldn't mind that she was slow and shaky because they'd never known her any other way. Then – and I was sure of this – Lovatt and Tuft would still be alive.

But would Paddy be the newest partner at Dudgeon, Dudgeon and Lamb? Would I be here in Simmerton, working as a deacon for a church that raised funds and didn't ask where the money went? No way.

And that, I thought, as I nosed into this dead end, feeling it close and darken around me until I couldn't see anything except the white fuzz of raindrops in my headlights, would be fine by me. I wished I had said to my mum and dad that I'd go to them tomorrow instead of them coming down here to me. I wanted more than anything to be on the seventeenth floor, in the block of flats where I'd been born. If Denise Dudgeon could have moved in next door she might have been fine.

'Best-kept secret in the city,' my dad used to say, waving a lordly arm at the view spread out below us, whenever he was on the balcony having the fag my mum knew about, and sharing it with me, which she didn't. 'If them in their leafy suburbs knew what we've got up here, Finnie, they'd have it off us.' He leaned his elbows on the rail and feasted his eyes. I loved the view too, but it was my dad I was watching. He traced the arterial routes down to the city centre, to where church spires and grand bank buildings began, then the castle on its rock and the sleeping giant of Arthur's Seat, and beyond even that, the glinting ribbon of the Forth and the green hills of Fife. 'We're rich, Finn,' he always said to me.

It was his sanctuary, out there on that balcony: drinking in the view, feasting on the light, watching the clouds scud for hours across that massive sky, getting friendly with pigeons and starlings. It nourished him and got him ready to open the sliding door into the living room and deal with my mum again.

The dream faded as the cut opened out like the top of a keyhole. Suddenly, there was Jerusalem House, a skeleton now, no roof and no glass, its stones still blackened decades later because they'd never been cleaned. There was no way the woman who had lived in this house would ever get into the lifts at our flats with her shopping or dry her wash on the balcony. It was enormous. I had known it was going be quite a pile because Widdershins was big enough to be a hotel and dower houses were where unwanted mothers-in-law were shunted off to, but Jerusalem House was so big and grand – and so over-the-top ornate – I was surprised I hadn't heard of it. I was surprised some trust hadn't bought it and put the roof back on, opened it up for weddings or something, charged entry.

I trundled round one side of the pond that split the drive and stopped, staring up the front steps at an arched doorway. There were still urns on either side, and when I got out and walked up there, I could see there was still soil in the urns. There would have been flowers here the day she gave her kids their last warm drink and cuddled them down in their beds.

The front door was gone, replaced by a sheet of warped hardboard with a danger notice nailed onto it. It had been undisturbed for years, like the hardboard over the windows to either side. Anyway, they were narrow and stone-mullioned. It might have been possible to wriggle through one but stuffing a pair of corpses in would have been hard work. I stepped down and started walking to the right to take a turn around the place and check for signs of entry.

But I stopped before I'd reached the first corner. I was going widdershins. And even though it was a load of old rubbish and I didn't believe in bad luck, I turned and walked towards the other corner, to go round Jerusalem.

I didn't even know what made me so sure they were here. And the echo of that time I'd gone round the side of the dower house to look in the kitchen window was a bit too clear as I paced along the weedy gravel and turned the corner to see another terrace, another low stone wall, more urns, a dry fountain and three sets of French windows, boarded up, with a danger notice insolently bright on each one.

I walked to the far edge of the terrace and looked back at the place. This was a . . . an orangery, I think you'd call it. All those windows, for one thing, and there was nothing above it except a walkway built on its flat roof. The upstairs windows were set well back. There was no way in. I pushed myself up off the balustrade and took the second corner.

Round here was heartbreaking. It was that much more obvious that this wasn't an ancient ruin, sacked in some ancient tribal scuffle. There were coal sheds and an outside toilet with no door but still with a chipped, seatless bog and a white sink on iron legs, a plug chain still wound round one of the stumps where a tap had been looted and carried off. That was the only open doorway; the house itself was shut fast. There were bars on some of the windows so they hadn't been boarded up and were broken now. I switched on my torch app and shone it in, seeing here and there the pattern of a tiled floor under landslides of fallen plaster. Craning in past the shards in the window frame, I saw a room absolutely intact, slate shelves and a strange dull-metal finish to its walls.

Around the third corner was a stableyard, a high wall blocking the view of it from the downstairs windows of the house. This hadn't burned, thank God. Or maybe they didn't have horses in these loose boxes thirty years ago. But Sonsie had said Denise wore riding boots in town and I imagined plump little ponies, one for the girl and one for the boy, and something massive and glamorous that Mummy took out cantering on her private road. Up and down the cut. I imagined the poor creatures rolling their eyes and kicking at their stable doors as the light and heat of the fire reached them. As the noise reached them. Fires big enough to destroy a house like Jerusalem are deafening.

Even though the stable hadn't burned, it was ruined. The roofs had fallen in and the thin brick walls were wavering outwards in some places, stove in at others. Probably some wee scallies had been and nicked the lead the same time they took the taps from the outside kludgy and that was the start of it. Roof leaking, the timbers would rot and the rain would get into the walls. Thirty years was plenty time for the place to come this close to total destruction. This close but not close enough. The stable door held when I tried it. Anyway, the weeds and rotten leaves showed no one had opened it recently.

Why did he leave them? I came back round to the front and got into my car, turning on the engine and the heater. He must have known how low she was. Why did he go off on a treat on the Orient Express and leave her to cope? It was so ostentatious. Much more in her face than a plane to a beach. It bothered me.

'Never know now,' I told myself, looking in the rear-view mirror before I shifted gear. I was distracted by the sight of myself. The soft, soaking rain had beaded on my hair and on my eyebrows. It had wrecked my mascara, putting new streaky grey stains under my eyes on top of the dark grey smudges that always started creeping out by lunchtime. I lifted up to see the rest of my face. Rain had beaded on the down that was starting to thicken on my cheeks and my lip. I was turning into my mother. I was so busy worrying about getting my dad's eyebags that I hadn't seen my mum's moustache coming for me. I swiped the beads away with my knuckle and then dried my face, much wetter for the swiping, with my scarf. Stupid fleece scarf. Absolutely useless for absorbing moisture.

I had chased away a thought there, freaking out about the old Freddie Mercury I was getting. I stared at myself and tried to catch it again. Inheritance? Mother and father? But as I stared, that same vision came crashing back again: the blood in the cuts and the blood in the butterfly. I drove away.

Chapter 23

There was a very different view on the way back down the cut towards the town. Light beckoned and the lane widened. I felt my shoulders drop, even though I hadn't realised I'd raised them. It was strange how the architect, away back whenever, hadn't tried to make the approach more welcoming. Why not set the house in the light? Or maybe Jerusalem was sanctuary. Maybe the first owner, the one who had made the decisions, took comfort at the drawing in, the way my mum took comfort from seventeen floors and the fact that she knew who was on either side, and no one else ever got off the lift to come and bother her. Maybe Mrs Sloan loved *her* life too, with her husband covering for her and the Dudgeons popping in to play mah jongg. Maybe Shannon and I could learn the game and take over. If we were staying.

I almost missed the clue, so busy thinking about the life to come for Paddy and me in Simmerton. If there was any chance Lovatt's will would hold. If I could bring myself to lie about witnessing it. If I even wanted to try.

I was past the graveyard before it registered. I stopped and slowly reversed up beyond the entrance again to take a second look at what I hadn't seen on my way north. The gates were mangled and twisted around where the chain held them together, but they hadn't been like that for long years, as I'd thought looking at them from the other direction. Facing this way, I could see a brand new scar, pale and sharp, in the mossy stone of the southern gatepost. I switched off the engine and climbed out, swishing through the long grass of the verge in what I was sure were someone's footprints. Yes, a clump of moss had definitely been scraped off by the sharp edge of the gate as it pivoted. It was sitting on the wet grass, like a pom-pom. And the gate *had* pivoted. There was a mark in the grass, the outline of the top edge, yet that top edge was now three feet in the air. I put my foot on it to bring it back down, like a seesaw, and watched it settle back into the dent of dead grass where it belonged.

Steadying myself with my arms out, I stepped up until I was balanced on the wonky slope, feeling the hard rods of the individual railings bite into my insteps. I stretched up as tall as I could make myself. I had no doubt about what I would see.

Mostly what I saw was brownish grass, too long and already showing the hand of winter even with the worst months still to go. I saw fallen headstones and a few weathered but still standing. I saw empty flower stands and paths so thickly overgrown they were just dents in the weeds.

Then, at the back where the trees overhung the wall, I saw something that didn't belong. It might have been a bundle of rags if this was the city where some poor soul spent nights in the lee of a graveyard wall and left all his stuff there during the day. But I thought I recognised the blue colour. It hadn't looked bright in the kitchen on Monday night but it stood out here against the grey, even if the pleats were crushed and gone. And I definitely recognised the flash of white, actually rather yellow in the wet. A rigid shampoo and set that had made me think of the Queen.

I stepped down and went to lean against the car until my legs stopped shaking. I had found them. I felt a bubble of hysteria start to rise in me. The bodies were in the graveyard. Who would ever have thought of looking for them there?

By habit, I checked my phone but there was still no signal, no chance of summoning reinforcements. Either I had to leave them there while I went for help or I had to be brave enough to climb over that broken gate and face this alone.

Taking the deep breaths I needed to steel myself, I thought at least there'd be no smell. And perhaps all this rain would have rinsed the blood off their skin, cleaned out the gashes on her hands, even washed away that black butterfly on Lovatt's back, spreading the blood and rainwater mixture over the cloth until it was gone.

Why did that thought snag at me as it passed, bringing back the memory of my own face in the driving mirror with the smudges and stains of mascara?

I wiped the rain from my face with the sides of my hands and started to scale the gate, edging forward gingerly. I was ready for it to pivot when I got halfway and pivot it did. I skidded down the far side and landed on the wet grass, going over on my ankle but still standing.

I couldn't see the bright bundle from here, what with the gravestones. My impression that most of them had fallen was wrong. Now I was in here, peering around and between them, they were a pretty efficient blind. But I knew where I was headed and I set off with my face up and my shoulders back.

Then I saw it. My steps faltered and I half turned to run. Something had moved over there. Something less than a flash but definitely more than just the smirring down of the rain. Something brown over there by the back wall had, I was sure of it, moved. Animals, was my first thought. A fox or a rat, feasting on an unexpected treat, loath to leave it but keeping an ear cocked for me coming closer.

Even though I'm not squeamish exactly, I couldn't face a fox or a rat busy with the bodies. I knew I couldn't. And yet I couldn't let it carry on, could I? If I made a loud enough noise to scare the creature off, then covered their faces – could I bear to get close enough to cover their faces? – maybe it would be frightened enough to stay away until I was back with police and an ambulance. I didn't have to go all the way to the station. I would drive to the top of the high street where the reception kicked in, then come back and guard them.

I flexed my muscles, ready to run up, shouting, scaring it away, whatever it was. Then I'd chuck my jacket over one face and my cardie over the other – I began wriggling out of them in preparation – and I'd leg it back to the gate, up and over—

I froze. Half in and half out of my cardie, my jacket bunched between my knees to keep it off the wet ground, I stopped dead. That gate was up at the outside and down at the inside when I arrived. It hadn't tipped back the other way. Whoever had got in by scaling it and waiting for it to overbalance, just like I had, was still in here.

Sidling as quietly as I could, I edged behind a tall grave-stone to my left and crouched to make sure the top of my head wasn't showing. Still no signal on my phone. I jammed it back into my trouser pocket. The sensible thing to do was leave as quietly as I could and drive away. But then whoever it was – *whoever it was!* – would hear the car starting.

My stomach rose. Whoever it was must have heard the car *stopping*. Whoever it was would be an idiot if they weren't moving through this graveyard – stone to stone – right now, to get a look at me and assess the threat.

I whipped my head up and saw nothing on either side but wet granite and dead grass blurred by the rain. One cautious step forward and I still saw nothing. Two more steps brought me close enough to the nearest fallen headstone to pick up a chunk that had broken off it; a good jagged chunk the size of a tennis ball. I gripped it tight in my right hand and selected another one. It was too big really, about the size of a cauliflower, but my left hand was useless for throwing anyway. It didn't matter. I could make some noise with it, make them look the other way and then I had a chance with my right. I peered round the side of a tall obelisk that was blocking my view. Seeing nothing, feeling stupid, like a spy in a kids' cartoon, but not stupid enough to make me do it differently, I advanced in a zigzag, stone to stone to stone, flitting across the open spaces and stopping to breathe whenever I was hidden. I kept shooting glances back towards the gate, in case whoever it was had circled the outside and was creeping up behind me, but I saw nothing.

And as I drew closer and closer, into the shadow of the trees overhanging the far wall, holding my breath and moving silently through the curtain of rain, I began to hear something.

Someone was crying, sobbing their guts out in dry, aching hitches as if they'd been at it for hours. I straightened up and walked out into the open beyond the last row of headstones.

It wasn't Tuft and Lovatt lying there. It wasn't their killer, lurking. It was Shannon. She was huddled into the rain shadow of the wall, with her hands over her head, weeping helplessly. The blue was her anorak, not Tuft's pleated skirt, and the white wasn't Tuft's old lady hair. It was Shannon's white blonde. The wig was missing.

'Hey,' I said.

She jerked her head up. Her sunglasses were off too, as well as her hat, and she squinted as she looked at me.

'What's wrong?' I said. 'What are you doing here? How did you get here?'

Shannon was staring at the rocks in my hands. 'What am *I* doing here?' she said.

I let them drop onto the grass and wiped my palms on my jeans. 'I saw someone. I was scared. What are you *doing* here?'

That just made her cry again. She rolled until she was leaning against the base of the wall and stretched her legs out in front of her.

'Okay, me first,' I said, going over and letting myself drop down at her side. The trees above us were a good umbrella. It was earthy and chilly there but we weren't getting dripped on. 'I wanted to see the house,' I said. 'I wondered if Lovatt and Tuft might have gone back there. Killed themselves there, you know? Since that was where it all started. That's like the source of all the . . . Well, not really. I mean, from Denise Dudgeon's point of view all those years ago, the source of all the misery was her, wasn't it? Her genes.'

'That's not how it is, though,' Shannon said. She sniffed. Snorted, really, after all that sobbing. 'I should know.'

'How d'you mean?'

She heaved a big breath and blew it out again. Then she put her sunglasses on. 'Same as how everyone thinks their baby is beautiful. Even their dog. Those yappy wee rats Mr Sloan dotes on. The thing about a genetic disorder is, if you wish it away the person you love wouldn't be the person you love.'

'I see. I think. But would that occur to anyone? I mean, apart from scientists.'

'Absolutely,' Shannon said. 'We spend a lot of time thinking about genes, people like me. I used to think all those sparks and blobs behind my eyes when I shut them *were* my genes. Or maybe my chromosomes.'

I said nothing. I'd give anything to see the red sparks and blobs of my own eyelids whenever I closed my eyes. Her hands. His back.

'That's why I don't believe it,' Shannon was saying. 'I don't believe Denise Dudgeon, all those years ago, killed her children.'

'Me neither,' I said. 'From what Sonsie said about her. Striding around in riding boots. Stiff upper lip. Don't frighten the horses.'

'That's right,' said Shannon. 'That type. Living round here, you can hardly avoid them.'

'So what *are* you doing here?' I said.

'Same as you,' said Shannon. She wiped her eyes and put her sunglasses on. 'Looking for the bodies. I thought they might have killed themselves here. Beside the graves.'

'But how did you know Denise and her children were buried here? I know Sonsie didn't tell you, because she doesn't know where they're buried or even if they're buried. So how come you do?'

'I saw them when I came on a walk after I first moved here,' Shannon told me. 'I always go for a walk round the graveyard when I'm in a new place. Don't look at me like that. Loads of people do it.'

'I'm not looking at you.' She was right. It was one of my mum's favourite outings when she still went out: a trip to a nice busy cemetery with new stones to look at, messages on wreaths to read if she was lucky. 'But if you've seen them before why were you crying?'

Shannon turned her face. I couldn't see myself as clearly in the black lenses she wore outside, but clearly enough to know I looked like Alice Cooper. I wiped my eyes with my shirt cuff. 'Why was I crying, looking at the graves of two murdered children?' Shannon said. 'What kind of question is that?'

'What kind of answer is that? I'm not buying it. Two poor wee dead mites might make you shed a tear but you were honking like a hung-over goose. What gives?'

She turned away again. 'Just . . . facing facts. At last. My brother's gone. He's as gone as all these people who're buried here. The letters are so faded on their stones you can't read them any more and no one's picked up the ones that have toppled over. There's no flowers. It's like you said. They're forgotten. They're really, really dead now that no one remembers them. And when I looked at Denise's grave and the kids', it was like they're forgotten too, now that Lovatt's gone. There's no one.'

'There's probably cousins,' I said. 'Tuft's family won't remember them, of course, because they were dead before

248

Tuft and Lovatt ever met, but there's bound to be Dudgeon connections somewhere.' I fell silent. If there were Dudgeon connections, they'd be coming out of the woodwork as soon as the police found the bodies or the fiscal decided, with or without them, that the suicide note was for real.

No way that will in Lovatt's shaky handwriting, with the stupid mistake about Paddy's name and my bogus signature, would stand. When was I even supposed to have witnessed it?

Well, Monday night, clearly. They were supposed to have been found dead in their kitchen when someone wondered where they'd got to, and then the will would be discovered with the suicide note and we'd freely admit we were round there for dinner and I'd probably say I had witnessed him signing something. Probably. If a house and four cottages and a law firm were hanging on it, I probably would have.

But then we went back for my bag. And someone moved the bodies and sent an email saying they were in Brazil and the whole stupid plan went off the rails.

'Finnie?' Shannon said, and I could tell from her tone it wasn't the first time. 'Do you?'

'What? Sorry, what?'

'Do you want to see them?'

I knew my eyes widened. I couldn't see Shannon's but her glasses shifted on her cheeks as if, behind them, her eyes had widened too. 'See them?' I repeated.

'The gravestones.' She paused. 'Of course.'

'And then I'll give you a lift home,' I said. 'I want to speak to Mrs Sloan. She spent Sunday night with them. *Not* the gravestones. With Tuft and Lovatt, I mean.'

Shannon pulled herself up and put out a hand for me. 'Where's your coat?' she said.

249

I didn't want to tell her about my plan to cover the faces of two corpses with my own clothes, then frighten a fox too badly for it to nose them aside. It would sound crazy now. I just trotted over and picked it up, the graveyard feeling half the size now I wasn't flitting about like the Pink Panther. 'Where are you?' I called, when I had draped it over my shoulders. It was too sodden to be worth putting it on properly. I saw her hand, in its knitted mitten, waving over the gravestones off to the north.

The stones were as low-key as it was possible to get. No outpouring of emotion for Lovatt Dudgeon. They were just three small slabs about the size of an open book and propped up at an angle like that too. One said 'My wife Denise, 1951-1985' and the other two only 'Vanessa 1979-1985' and 'Simon 1980-1985'.

'God, that's terrible,' I said.

'She was only six,' Shannon said. 'Or seven, depending on her birth date. He wasn't even that.'

'Yeah, they're pretty vague, aren't they?' I said. I stared at them, wondering what was bothering me. Was it the lack of any message of love? Well, maybe it was difficult to decide what to write in such strange circumstances. It wasn't so very long since Denise Dudgeon wouldn't have been let inside the graveyard wall, murderer that she was. Allegedly.

'I know what it is!' I said. 'You told me you'd found them when you came for a walk here, right? How did you know who they were, from just the first names?'

'I heard the story,' Shannon said. 'I put it together.'

'You heard the story before you came for the walk?' I said. 'Someone got off the mark quick, didn't they? If a walk in the graveyard's your first stop in a new place.' I was keeping it light-sounding, teasing her, really. But the truth was, it

250

troubled me. Anything that seemed the least bit off was troubling me now.

'What are you getting at?' Shannon said.

'Me? Nothing. Only when Sonsie told *me* the story yesterday it seemed like it was news to you too. And it wasn't.'

'But I always do that,' she said. 'I hate when I'm telling a story, or even a joke, and someone says they've heard it before. Don't you?'

We faced off for a second or two, then she turned away and headed for the gate.

Getting over it turned us into sisters again. I balanced on it and gave her a hand up, then we clutched each other, edging forward until it tipped down and deposited us back on the verge. We didn't actually speak until we were in the car, though, heater blasting and windows steaming from how sopping wet we both were.

'That wasn't strictly true,' Shannon said, as I got going. 'I didn't hear the story before I saw the graves. I just remembered the graves. Looking for Sean all these years, more and more sure he's gone, I suppose I just always notice when children die.'

'Well, you would,' I said. 'Yeah. Sorry.' We were nearly out of the cut now. I could see light ahead and the whitewashed side wall of the first cottage. 'Let me make it up to you. Paddy's mum and my lot are coming down for lunch tomorrow. Join us! We want them all to get to know our new home and our new friends.'

'I don't want to muscle in on a family party,' Shannon said. She leaned forward and cleared her side of the windscreen with her sleeve. I had both blowers going up my side for safety's sake.

'Believe me,' I said, 'this family party needs all the dilution it can get. I might ask the Sloans too. Mr Sloan and Paddy's mum would get on like a house on fire.'

'Mrs Sloan won't come,' said Shannon.

'It's just along the road,' I said. 'I'm going to try. My mum's got a few . . . what would you call them? . . . too. So that's something I'm good at dealing with, because I've had to be. Even if I suck at understanding adoption.' Shannon was silent. 'Or not. I'm not trying to offload my dirty work onto you.'

She didn't say another word until I had the car on the verge at her garden gate and switched off the engine.

'I'd love to come,' she said. 'Love to. I'll be there.'

Then she scuttled off, leaving me tingling as I watched her go.

Saturday

Chapter 24

'Who's the six?' Paddy said, when I dumped the cutlery on the table for him to arrange. I always get something wrong that bugs Elayne: knives inside out or butter plates too near the wine glasses. Some crap like that.

'Yeah,' I said. 'Well, I asked Shannon.'

'What? *Why?*' Paddy was polishing the knives on his shirt tail. He had pulled a nice shirt out from deep in the ironing basket and pressed it himself. I was too tired to iron. The dreams were exhausting me more than sleeplessness could ever do. Last night it was a graveyard, of course. Underwater, as if a hurricane had washed a tidal wave up the valley and it had settled there. I was trying to dig someone up, someone I cared about, although I couldn't say who it was or how I knew him. I was scrabbling at the mud of his grave, knowing that the train was coming, the train was coming, and I couldn't leave him there.

Paddy had left the board up and I couldn't decide if it was a hint to me to iron a dress or if he was just too tired to put it away. He'd had a rough night too. 'Too dark! Too dark!' I'd heard him when I got up at four to change my sweaty nightie and wipe my face with a cold cloth. My dress was under an apron anyway, I told myself, and the kitchen was already steamed up enough to make any wrinkles drop out of it. Just because it was Saturday and not Sunday didn't mean I could get away with a nice loaf and a trawl of the Simmerton deli counter. If Elayne was coming for lunch, that meant potatoes peeled, meat roasted and a gravy boat warming.

'You're lucky it's just Shannon,' I said. 'I asked the Sloans too but they said no.'

Mr Sloan had stared at me as if I'd suggested a bunk-up. He'd come to the door in a pair of carpet slippers, a shirt and tie under his Fair Isle jumper.

'Nothing fancy,' I said. 'Just Paddy and me, our parents and Shannon. I haven't met next door yet, so I can't ask them.'

'What makes you think you can ask us?' Mr Sloan had seemed so fit and efficient out on his drive tending his bonfire, walking his dogs. Now he was hesitant and doddery, and his eyes were wet-looking as he dithered on his doorstep, opening and closing his mouth.

'Why not?' I said. 'My mum and dad and Paddy's mum will want to meet our new neighbours. And I'd like the chance to chat to you and Mrs Sloan.'

'Chat to Mrs Sloan?' he said, with a quick glance over his shoulder. 'What about? I can tell you about the bin days and the buses. Or Robert Waugh can. At the church. He's your boss. It's him that's brought you in here among us. Ask *him*.'

'Not bins,' I said. He took a step back as a squall of rain somehow found enough open air between the pine trees to get up a bit of speed and lash the backs of my legs and my sodden anorak. Mr Sloan looked down at the drops of water spattering the mat just inside his door. 'Can I come in?' I added.

'In?' he said. 'In here? No. Sorry, dear. No, it's not suitable today. Mrs Sloan has a terrible headache and she's lying down.'

'What a rotten run of luck she's having. But no wonder she's got a headache. You must have heard what's happened. Haven't you? Have the police been here yet?'

He mouthed the word but hearing it had knocked all the breath out of him and there was no sound.

'*Haven't* you heard?' I said. I wondered how old he was and how his heart was. It was something I thought about with my mum and dad. It's all very well for one out of a pair to retire from the world but it needs the other to be a rock. 'It's Lovatt and Tuft,' I said. 'They've . . . well, they've died.'

'Died?' said Mr Sloan. 'No, they've not died. They've gone on holiday. You've picked up the jaggy end of the shark there.' He blinked at me, satisfied that he'd set his world to rights again. 'I know what'll have happened,' he went on. 'Someone's said, "They've gone," and you've jumped to the wrong conclusion. Quite a big jump, if you don't mind me saying so.'

'No,' I said. I pressed forward a bit, truly not trying to muscle my way in, just that I was getting soaked. 'They've committed suicide, Mr Sloan. I'm really sorry to be the one to break the news. But it's true. They left a note. They left their will. They've wound up their affairs and they've – like you said, but there's no mistake – they've gone.'

His chest was rising and falling at quite a clip now and I thought there was a hitch in it too. He glanced behind himself again, at the living room and then up the stairs. 'You better come in,' he said. 'Come away in.'

He didn't ask for my coat and that surprised me. He was the sort. I wouldn't have been stunned if he'd made me take my shoes off, but he just pointed the way and shut the door at my back.

The living room was set up for a sweet little life. I recognised all the signs. A jigsaw on a trolley, a budgie cage, two armchairs with footstools and reading lamps. A collection of videos, DVDs and crossword books on a tall pine bookcase against the back wall. There was an orchid on the side table by the smaller armchair. But, for all that, it was a closed life that was lived there. The air was stale, and worse than stale, really. There was a taint in this snug little house that stirred unpleasant memories. I swallowed hard as Mr Sloan let himself drop into the bigger chair and waved me towards the couch. I sat back but immediately wriggled forward again as I felt my wet clothes stick to me.

'Does anyone come to give Mrs Sloan communion?' I said. 'If she doesn't manage out to the services.'

'Doesn't manage?' he said. 'It's only a headache. What are you making such a fuss over?'

'My mum's very shy too,' I said. '*She* doesn't go about. It's a big thing for her to be coming down here tomorrow, actually. I think maybe she'd like to meet your wife. You know, meet another lady about her age who likes to keep quiet too.'

'Who's been saying this?' Mr Sloan demanded, sitting forward. 'Is it that nasty piece at the end?' At least he had admitted Shannon's existence. 'Look, never mind silly gossip. People should mind their own. Tell me what happened to the Dudgeons. Who found them? Was it you?'

'Well, that's the trouble. Part of it anyway. No one's found them yet, as far as I know. Or they hadn't found them earlier this morning.'

'Well, there you are.'

'But they're looking. And they're definitely going to want to talk to your wife and you. You might be close to the last ones who saw them. To talk to properly, instead of just in passing.'

'Us?' he said. 'Me? Who's told you that?'

'Sonsie,' I said. I dug down deep, deep, deep for the name and managed to find it. 'Sonia Webb. Tuft told her that you all had a game of mah jongg on Sunday. Although you didn't mention it to me, did you? Wednesday, was it? When we walked up the drive.'

'Oh, yes,' he said. He looked up at the ceiling. 'I forgot about that. The days run together when you're retired. Well, they were neither up nor down on Sunday night. They said nothing about anything to either Mrs Sloan or me. The police have got no reason to come pestering us. Either of us. I'm busy with my garden.'

'In January?' I said. 'Burning more . . . whatever it was you were burning?'

'Leaves,' he said. 'Plenty to do whatever the month. In a tidy garden.'

'It's just routine,' I said. 'They'll need to talk to everyone who knew them. Especially if they still haven't found the bodies.' I was leaving a wet print on the wooden arm of the sofa from my sleeve. I put my hands in my lap. 'They'll be asking everyone. Colleagues, committee members. Other friends. You are friends, aren't you? Were friends?'

'They were very good to us years ago,' Mr Sloan said. 'When Myna had a wee bit of trouble. They were kind. And then they changed our lease, like I told you. I suppose you might say we're friends.'

'So can you think where they would go? A special place?'

'And if I could, you'd pass it on to the coppers and stop them bothering Mrs Sloan and me?'

I opened my mouth to tell him no way, then reconsidered. I was the deacon of his church and I had a stake in his well-being. 'I'll try,' I said. 'If they find them there's maybe no reason for the cops to bother anyone.'

My guilt leaped at the breath he let out and the way he sat back in his chair, passing a hand over his brow. 'Thank you, dear.'

'I wish you'd come along and say hello to my dad tomorrow,' I said. 'Never mind the rest of them. Or my dad could come along and have a wee cup of tea with you. He'll be sick of the wittering before we're halfway through dinner anyway. He really does understand, Mr Sloan. Look, I don't want to upset you. If you want to say stomach bug, twisted ankle, making jam, headache, you just go ahead and say it. Whatever works. But it's a stressful role being a carer and my dad's been doing it a lot of years. He could help you.'

'They're not in their house then, I take it? The Dudgeons.' He was ignoring me.

'They're not,' I said. 'And they're not over at Jerusalem or in the old graveyard either.'

'The church?' he said. 'The offices. Dudgeon and Dudgeon.'

'They've been checked,' I said. 'And no one would do that in a church anyway, would they?'

'Is the car there?' Mr Sloan said. I shrugged. 'It'll be in the garage, like mine. Not like that lot next door. Garage full of junk and cars parked on the grass. It would make you weep.'

He tutted, distracted by his annoyance. Then he seemed to remember why he was thinking about cars. 'Because if they've flung themselves in the sea then they're in the sea, aren't they? If they've flung themselves in a river it's the same do. If they've booked into a wee hotel somewhere and taken a lot of pills, the hotel staff'll know soon enough.'

This was going nowhere. There was no overlap between the places a couple would drive on a suicide bid and the places a third party would dump their corpses. They could be absolutely anywhere in the country. They could be on the Continent if someone had enough bottle to get on a ferry with two corpses in the boot of a car or under the bunks in a camper van.

'So there's nowhere nearby that's like a significant spot for them?' I said. 'Somewhere they'd go to spend their last moments? A picnic spot? Or somewhere they'd scattered ashes in the past?'

'Ashes?' said Mr Sloan. 'What ashes?'

'A pet, I was thinking,' I said. 'But any ashes. I'm clutching at straws, if I'm honest.'

'I don't hold with that,' Mr Sloan said. 'Scattered ashes! What's wrong with a decent plot in a cemetery? It's done till now. It'll do me.'

'Some people find it morbid,' I said, 'to think of a body mouldering on and on.' The image came as a shock to me. Not the tableau in the kitchen and not that flash of blue and white in the rain of the graveyard. This time the vision was Lovatt and Tuft in ash, as if a clear cast of their two bodies had been made – pleated skirt, patched jacket, knife blade and all – like a vessel, and inside this vessel ashes swirled. The ashes were gritty. They scraped against the inner wall of the see-through shape, always moving, like when Paddy used grains of rice to clean the red wine stains from a carafe, swishing it and swishing it until the water clouded pink. 'But each to their own,' I added, hoping that, if we kept talking, the image would loosen its grip on me.

'Exactly,' he said. 'If you're harming no one.' He clapped his hands on his knees and smiled at me. 'Well, if we're done . . .'

'Could I use your toilet?' I said.

'You're yards from home,' he said, seeing through me. Because, of course, I wanted to introduce myself to Mrs Sloan. Maybe Tuft had said something to her it would help to know.

'You're right,' I said. 'I don't play mah jongg, Mr Sloan, but I'm a fiend at cribbage. Or Scrabble even. It's not a good idea to let your wife withdraw any further.' I held up my hand as he started to talk over me. 'I wish you'd let me send my dad down for a word,' I said. 'But I'm not going to nag.'

'Bit late,' he said.

'Do you think she'll be okay?' I said, going through to the little hall and dropping my voice. There was no sound from upstairs. Despite the two armchairs and the jigsaw table I thought Mrs Sloan must live up there. The stale smell – worse than stale – was coming down the stairs from the landing.

'Will who be okay?' he said. He had positioned himself across the bottom of the staircase as if I was just going to burst up there and blat the door open, shove pastoral care down her neck in a raid.

'Your wife,' I said. 'How's she going to take it that her friend is gone?'

Mr Sloan stared at me for two blinks before he licked his

lips and spoke. 'You leave her to me. I'll take care of her. I'll not upset her.'

'Of course,' I said.

Outside on the doorstep, when I shivered, it wasn't just my damp clothes and the cold air with the soak of rain through it. I walked down the path, then looked back at the house, at the upstairs window, lamplight behind net curtains. A shadow moved but I couldn't tell if it was Mr Sloan or his wife watching me go.

'So at least we've escaped that,' I said to Paddy the next day. I had taken the Christmas cactus away, but the truth was, there was nowhere else to put it and nothing else we could use as a centrepiece, so I replaced it as Paddy polished glasses, three at each place. My dad would have trouble not mocking that.

'God, yes, Mrs Sloan and your mum, like a pair of bookends,' Paddy said. 'Might have been a bit much for any party to rise above. It's not exactly a sure thing as it is.'

'I'm worried about her,' I said. 'Not my mum. I'm worried it's not Mrs Sloan's choice to live shut in there. I'm a bit worried that he's got her that way. Like boiling a frog.'

'Ask the rev,' Paddy said. He hadn't heard the way Tuft talked about Robert Waugh, calling him a chocolate teapot and hinting that his laziness – or maybe it was just golf – suited her. That hadn't struck me too hard on Monday night, but I wondered now what it was she needed him not to see.

'Could do,' I said.

'But she looked okay to me,' said Paddy. 'She was out in the front garden yesterday when I was on the way to work. Just putting something in the wheelie but she waved and said hello.'

'Well, you're honoured,' I said. 'I was sitting in her living room and she never came to say hello to me.'

'Make the gravy,' said Paddy. 'Plenty time for Mrs Sloan another day.'

'Bisto, or port and cornflour?'

We both laughed. It was impossible to please both sets of parents. I'd always thought, as long as Paddy and me were united, we'd muddle through the middle of them all. I didn't know what I thought now.

Chapter 25

The meat had shrunk to the size of a brick, which was bad. Elayne would move chewed-up gobs of it to the side of her plate under cover of her hand and give me sad smiles. And my mum, looking at the chewed-up gobs of meat on Elayne's plate, would push hers away completely. Then my dad would clap my mum's dinner between two bits of bread and scarf it down once he'd finished wiping his own plate, and Elayne's mouth would purse so hard it practically disappeared, for all the world as if she hadn't started it, pretending she couldn't swallow my food.

There was an upside. All the juice that poured out as the joint shrank would make both sorts of gravy. And it would drive Elayne spare to be served the gravy she wanted instead of getting to complain.

I divided it into two jugs, making sure to put all the fat in hers. Sometimes when she ate a lot of fat she got evil wind by mid-afternoon and watching her clench and squirm was like a cabaret. I was raking through a cupboard for the Bisto, asking myself how kitchen cupboards could get so chaotic so quickly, when the knock came at the door.

It wasn't crazy early for Shannon, but that was a copper's knock.

'Come in!' I sang out and, as the door swept open on the squall and bluster outside, suddenly there they were, two of them, enormous in their yellow jackets, jostling for space in the little hallway. 'Have you found them?' I said. 'Have they turned up?'

'Mrs Lamb?' said one of them. 'Mr Lamb?'

Paddy was leaning in the living-room doorway with the tea towel over his shoulder.

'We've put out an alert for them,' one of the coppers said. Paddy had passed him the tea towel to wipe his face, which was streaming with rain. He ran it over his stubbled head too.

'You mean you think they're alive?' I said. 'In spite of the note and the will?'

Paddy said nothing.

The cop shook his head. 'Their car's in the garage up there. Their passports are there. Their cards. Phones haven't been used since that last email on Monday.' He gave Paddy the cop smile that spells trouble. '*You* phoned the house late on Monday, sir. That's why we're here. We wanted to ask you about that.'

'Me?' said Paddy. 'I don't think so.'

I felt as if I'd been turned to stone. That was right. Paddy had dialled the number, hadn't he? In the middle of the first storm of it all, when we didn't know what to do and every minute made it too late to do anything, he had dialled the number and heard Lovatt's voice on the answerphone and he'd hung up again in panic and misery.

'Was it a long call?' Paddy was saying. 'I honestly have no

memory of it. Finnie, can you remember what we were doing on Monday night? What sort of time?'

'We were unpacking,' I said, hoping my voice sounded even halfway normal. 'Could it have been when you found your charger at last and plugged your phone in?'

'It was eighteen seconds long,' said the cop. He finished with the tea towel, folded it and put it under his arm while he looked in his wee notebook.

'There you go, then,' Paddy said. 'Bum dial, probably. So what now?' I wondered if they'd resent it, him sounding like it was time to move on, or if they'd assume it was just a lawyer thinking about settling the estate, executing the will.

'Search me,' said the other cop, taking the tea towel and wiping his glasses before putting them back on.

'It's not illegal to kill yourself,' his colleague said. 'Much as we sometimes wish it was.'

'You do?' I agreed – but, then, I would.

'When you've scraped some twat off a railway line and interviewed the train driver,' he said, 'or tried to get emergency counselling in her native language for some poor cow of a Polish chambermaid who's just found some other twat.'

'Right,' I said. I grinned at him. If this was a typical Simmerton polis, I could enjoy liaising. If we weathered it. If we stayed. If there was even still a 'we'. 'Sonsie – Sonia Webb – reckons Tuft thinks that too, you know.'

'Did you get anywhere with the note and the will?' Paddy said.

'Until we find bodies, we're hanging fire,' said the speccy cop. 'Why?'

'Just wondered if you'd started searching for the beneficiaries yet,' he said. 'And what about . . . I mean, has anyone said anything about St Angela's?'

'What's this?' said the baldy cop.

I hesitated. How did he not know? Then I realised that if anyone was going to tell the police about wrongdoing at the adoption agency it would have been Paddy, and there was no way Paddy would have opened his gob. Since he'd read that fake will, he'd lost his mind.

'Mr Waugh didn't say anything?' I asked the cops. 'St Angela's is the charity Tuft raised funds for and Lovatt acted as lawyer for. And – actually – we found out that the Dudgeons are CEO and finance bod for it, too, and the rest of the board are ghosts. We think it was a scam.'

'Makes sense,' said Speccy. 'We were wondering what they had to run away from, however it is they've run. A long con's exactly the sort of thing that makes folk consider suicide. Surprised you never mentioned any of this, Mr Lamb.'

Paddy was staring at me as if I'd stripped to my knickers and given them a lap dance.

'I'm still going through the papers,' he said, in a strangled sort of voice. 'I'll need to get some advice from the Law Society about what to do with them. I can't just turn over confidential documents, but Finnie's right. There's a lot of irregularities need looked into.'

'Confidentiality doesn't trump criminal investigation,' said Baldy. 'Have you got these papers here? We can take them away with us and hand them over to Financial.' He was patting his jacket pockets. 'Got any evidence receipts on you?' he asked his partner.

'In the car,' Speccy said, jerking his head.

'They're at my work,' said Paddy, which was a total lie. Both bulging briefcases were right there beside the couch where he'd put them when we cleared off the table to set it and I knew he was working not to glance at them. His face was frozen and his eyes, trained on the cops' faces, were beady. But either they couldn't read him because they didn't know him, like I did, or they couldn't read him because they weren't detectives. For one reason or another they bought it.

'No point getting you to open the office on a Saturday when you're obviously busy,' Baldy said. 'Someone'll drop round on Monday morning. None of this is going anywhere, is it?'

'No,' Paddy said. 'And anyway, from what I've seen, there's no criminality. My wife should have picked a better word than "scam". There's certainly no embezzlement.' I started to protest and managed to bite my lip, ending up letting out no more than a squeak. 'If I come across anything that hints at where they might have gone, to do whatever they did, I'll get straight back to you.'

The coppers seemed to be satisfied with that. They put their hats back on, Velcroed their hi-vis jackets shut and went on their way.

'What the hell, Paddy?' I said, as soon as the door was shut behind them.

'Sorry,' he said. 'Contradicting you in front of them. I know.'

'Not that!' I said. 'Who cares? I meant what the hell are you doing lying to the police? They'll see for themselves on Monday when you hand the stuff over.'

'But it's true,' he said. 'I was up last night going through it all again. It didn't make sense to me that they would be so careful in some ways – faxing through my forms, getting your signature on the will – and so reckless in others. Why make sure and have an heir if your estate'll be frozen and all your assets confiscated for financial wrongdoing?'

'And?' I said. The two lots of gravy were cooling and congealing and the clock was against us. 'What did you find? Why didn't you wake me?'

'Small print,' he said, ignoring the other question. 'The logos and banners were all St Angela's.' He went over to the couch and started scrabbling through some of the files in one of the briefcases. 'Look.' He held an elderly deed-of-covenant certificate. It was a photocopy of a photocopy, the print thick and fluffy, ghosts of paperclips and staples visible in the top corner. 'See what I mean. This is all headed up in the name of St Angela's, but the small print lays out a commitment to donate' – he squinted at the form – 'no less than eighty-six per cent, after admin costs, to a charity supporting adoption and fostering in Scotland or overseas. Which is what they did. St Andrew's usually and one or two others. It's all above board, Finnie. Not just deeds of covenant. The receipts, the accounts, any wee contracts they had to draw up for liability and all that. The whole bit. And they managed more than eighty-six per cent most years. Especially recently, when all the admin was done online with downloadable forms.'

'*When* did you see all this?' I said, heading back to the kitchen. I wanted to shake him, but I had to keep on with getting the table ready.

'Last night, like I said. I sat up.'

'And why didn't Abby notice it?' I walked back through to the living room with the salt and pepper to put near my dad's place. He'd douse everything before he took a bite but, to spare my feelings, he'd choke half of it down before he asked for ketchup.

'I think she was the same as me. The shock of the news stopped her scrutinising the documents as thoroughly as she should.'

'Right,' I said. 'Right, of course. So what does it mean? Is it an answer to anything? Because it strikes me as just another layer of mystery.'

'How?'

'Embezzlement makes sense!' I said. 'Stealing money and then hopping it to Brazil, or stealing money and then killing yourself when it all catches up with you. Both of those make a horrible kind of sense. But this is crazy.'

'But that's good.'

'How is "crazy" good?'

'*Because* it doesn't make any sense. It raises so many questions. And, as long as there are questions to be answered, there's a chance the answers will make everything clear. Everything.' He was sounding manic again. 'And there's something else.'

I waited.

'Like I said, I was going through papers last night. Papers I hadn't looked at for years. Adoption papers.' He waited, staring hard at me.

'Wait,' I said. '*Your* adoption papers?'

'I found them years back and made copies. The name didn't mean anything then, of course, but it jumped out at me this time. Do you see?'

I had to swallow before I could speak. 'St Angela's handled your adoption?'

He smiled at me but I couldn't smile back. My head was swimming. 'It's nearly lunchtime,' I said.

'Yeah, sorry. We'd better get on with—'

271

'Paddy!' My voice was a shriek. 'I'm not talking about the bloody gravy. How could you find that out last night and not tell me till now?'

'Sorry,' he said, so calm I wanted to scream. 'I shouldn't have waited. But now you know, what do you think?'

'Okay,' I said, heading back to the kitchen because, despite what I'd shrieked at him, I needed to crack on. And all of this would be easier to say if I wasn't looking him in the eye. 'So this couple met after one of them had lived through a massive tragedy: the death of his wife and their two little children. They moved to the town where the deaths occurred and set their lives up *as if* they were dedicated to preventing any such thing ever happening again. They've spent the whole twenty-five years they've been married fundraising for *real* adoption charities – except in a pretty underhand way – and pretending to take care of the legal side of a *fake* adoption charity that they're using as cover. Except that this fake adoption service has actually overseen at least three adoptions: Shannon's and Sean's. And then yours. Sean disappeared. Shannon tracked Lovatt down and was more or less given a house. You were headhunted to join his practice. Your wife was headhunted to join the fundraising organisation. The Dudgeons immediately kill themselves, making it look like murder and putting us in line for a major inheritance, except that the will is a piece of crap. The fake charity is wound up. The new partner is given free rein. Oh, and maybe they didn't kill themselves because someone's moved the bodies and said they've gone to Brazil.'

'There's two things wrong with your round-up,' Paddy said. He was taking plates out of the cupboard to warm in the oven. If we gave Elayne a cold dinner plate she wouldn't even get as far as chewing her meat and spitting it out again. She'd just push wrinkles into her congealing gravy and shudder.

'Oh?' I thought I'd done a good job.

'One: the will's only a piece of crap if you won't confirm that you witnessed it.'

'Wrong,' I said. 'You can't confirm a lie, Paddy. You can only shore up a lie with another lie.'

'And that's your problem, is it? So holier-than-thou all of a sudden?'

'No,' I said. 'Look, I can't suddenly say I witnessed the signature of someone I've been going around saying I've never met. The plan went wrong, Paddy. I get that it's infuriating, when you can see a good wedge slipping through your fingers, but the plan went wrong. We weren't supposed to go back. We weren't supposed to see them. And they weren't supposed to be moved. Obviously I was meant to go to work on Tuesday morning saying we'd been round there for dinner and signed a lot of papers and then when the will was found . . . Bob's your uncle.'

'Only you forgot your bloody bag!'

'What?' I was staring at him. 'That was an accident. Because I'd had some wine and I had things to carry.'

'And then you had to go snooping inside the house!'

'I was worried about them!' I said. 'There had been those noises of someone crashing around in the trees.'

'It was a deer.'

'It had a torch!' I shouted. 'I was worried because all the lights were on and the door was open but they weren't answering the bell. Oh, no! That's my dad's car.'

We had both heard the growl of his engine as he pulled up and we both saw the sweep of his headlights across the front windows.

'I'm sorry, I'm sorry,' Paddy said. He sounded like a kid who'd broken an ornament. 'I'm sorry I blamed you. I just don't know what to do.'

'Really?' I said, going to the front door. 'It seems fairly obvious to me.' I threw it wide and opened the golf umbrella that was sitting on the step. 'Shannon's mum and birth mum are both dead. Her brother's missing. She was a kid. You were a baby. Lovatt's dead. Tuft's dead. There's only one person left who could answer any of our questions about adopting through St Angela's.' I stepped down and held the umbrella up as the passenger door of my dad's car opened. 'Elayne! Welcome! Come away in out of this weather. I've got something I want to ask you.'

Chapter 26

But my own mum distracted me. It was easier when I lived with her and saw her every day. Back then it only hit me hard very occasionally, when I dreamed of her old self, her foul-mouthed, sharp-witted bossy old self, sparring with my dad and keeping all of us in line, then woke up to the reality of her slumped, grey and slow, in her dressing-gown by the window with her sippy-cup of warm tea. When I moved out, only visiting once a week, sometimes I'd forget how she was and I'd find myself in the lift on the way up scraping the picture of her out of my head to ditch it, forcing the truth in so my face didn't fall when I saw her. And if I managed to fix a vision of her at her very worst – dirty hair, dead eyes, clumsy fingers – I might even be cheered to see her if it was a good day, if she raised a hand to wave and smiled at me. Now, seeing her after two weeks when I'd had so much to think about and she'd hardly crossed my mind, I knew my face fell and I had to blink tears away.

Paddy took his mum inside and I waited while my dad undid her seatbelt and held his hands out for her. She emerged from the back seat as though from hibernation, creaking and blinking, and she tottered a bit to get her footing.

'Mammy!' I said, surging forward and wrapping my arms round her. 'Thanks for coming down. You've no idea how much it means to me. How are you doing? Do you need a wee lie-down?'

My dad was beaming, standing with his hand under her elbow, and when I drew back I saw why. She was stiff from the journey but she was having a *spectacular* day. Her eyes were twinkling and her mouth was steady. 'No, I'm fine, Finnie doll,' she said. 'I dozed in the car. What with the soundtrack.'

I laughed and squeezed her. If she was bitching up Elayne she really was on top form.

'So this is it, is it?' my dad said, coming in for a hug and kissing me just in front of my ear, like he always does, leaving it ringing. 'What's it like in daylight?'

'God, I know,' I said. 'I think I'm getting rickets after a week. Come on in and get settled.'

My dad opened the boot to unload all the gifts he'd brought as I ushered my mum inside.

Elayne was already installed on the end of the couch with her slippers on and her bag tucked down by her feet.

'Come and sit by me, Mary,' she said. 'Get yourself warmed through. I had to have the car cold in case I turned queasy.' It was a habit of Elayne's to give a lot of information about her digestive system. And her menopause.

'Oh, I think I'll stick to the kitchen, see if Finnie needs a hand,' my mum said. She took her coat off and hung it up. Elayne's eyes narrowed as she saw my mum take her fag packet and lighter out of a pocket. She sniffed the air, her nostrils pinching.

'There's a shed, Mam,' I said. 'Just out the back. I'll show you.'

My dad was unloading carrier bags onto the worktops, shoving aside the things I'd placed where I needed them. 'Turnips,' he said, dumping a muddy load of them, the size of footballs, in the sink. 'Brilliant turnips this year.'

'Lovely,' I said. 'Still at the allotments, then?' He shared one with a couple of pals. I think it was just a way to get a break from my mum. They spent more time sitting in the potting shed with the racing papers than they did digging and weeding but this harvest was undeniable and there was no way he'd bought such misshapen turnips in a shop.

'Well, it's a break for him,' my mum said. 'I don't mind.' She had propped herself in the kitchen doorway, blowing the smoke out into the rain and ignoring the fact that most of it curled in again. 'Ashtray, Finn?'

I gave her a saucer and watched as she flicked ash onto the step anyway.

'So how are you doing?' I said, as my dad went through to show Paddy the bottle of homebrew he'd brought with him. 'You seem well.'

'I am,' my mum said. 'I think I'm turning the corner. I'm feeling better than I have for years.'

I was stripping the green bits off a cauliflower and breaking it up and I bit my tongue to keep from answering. It took years for that first black cloud to lift off her. Whether it was her hormones changing, or the doctors finally getting her prescription right, or maybe just time doing what people are always saying time does best, when I left home she was having good days and bad days. Good weeks sometimes. We'd all take those days back now. Because after them came the time when the cloud lifted enough, lightened enough, for her to get ambitious. She started beating herself up about how long she'd been down. She read some guff about positive-thinking and pomegranate juice and start mucking about with the fabulous, miracle, genius pills that had saved her life and brought her back to us. That first crash was worse than the darkest days after the miscarriage. She was completely gone, my dad on compassionate leave, a nurse coming in to bathe her. She even went into the Royal Ed for a bit. They got her drugs balanced and she came out, shaken, grateful and living each day. None of us ever dreamed it would happen again. Now we didn't dare to dream it would ever stop. And this – her saying she'd turned a corner, better than she'd felt for years – was how it started every time.

'I'll just see if Elayne needs anything,' I said. I ignored my mum's look, not really an eye-roll. It wouldn't even register as a look to anyone who didn't know her as well as I did. To me, it spoke volumes: one mum chumming along out in the kitchen and the other sitting like the Queen of Sheba on the couch waiting to be run about after.

'Sherry, Elayne?' I said. She had that pinched expression on her face because Paddy and my dad were off somewhere and she'd been left sitting on her own.

She looked at her watch and one of her eyebrows lifted.

'Wee glass of sherry and a bit of shortbread at half eleven,' I said. 'Nothing wrong with that.'

'You didn't need to go making shortbread,' she said. Cow. 'Oh, that reminds me.' She leaned over to the side and had a rootle in her handbag, sitting tidily by her side. 'Rocky Road bites and caramel wafer bites, you said?'

'Lovely,' I said. 'What do I owe you?'

She muttered and fluttered but she took the receipt out of her bag and slipped it into my hand. And when she saw the shop-bought shortbread she was right back to her sunny mood again, thinking how embarrassed I must be. None of it was conscious, I was sure. And it didn't even bug me any more. I thought eventually, as the years rolled by, it would make me love her.

My mum joined us just as I was prising the cork out of the sherry bottle. 'Not for me, sweetheart,' she said. 'Not with my medicine. One of the reasons I'm looking forward to ditching it.'

'Nice wee set-up,' my dad said, easing himself into the middle seat of the couch and making Elayne's mouth purse up again. 'As long as they don't work you to a standstill. What like's the boss, Paddy?'

Here it was then, already. I had hoped to have the starter down them and the main course served before we got into it. Paddy drained his sherry glass. It was tiny, one of the set his mum had given us for an engagement present. I was such a crawler.

'Well,' he began. We had discussed how to broach it. 'It's all been a bit fraught, to be honest. It turns out it wasn't just chance that got me this partnership right here and right now. The managing partner had a pretty specific reason for installing me. It's quite a tale.'

Elayne put her bit of shortbread down on the tea plate she'd insisted on – my mum held hers in her hand and my dad had put his on his trouser knee. My heart flooded with love for them both. 'Why shouldn't you get a partnership?' she said. 'It's no more than you deserve.'

'Thanks, Mum,' said Paddy. He sat down backwards on

279

one of the dining chairs and leaned his elbows on its top spur. 'But it was more than that. It turned out the partner and his wife – she was a partner too – wanted to hand the business over.'

I was staring at Paddy. This wasn't at all what we had decided. He was starting at the wrong end.

'Hand it over? For free?' my mum said. She really was better if she was materialistic again. When she started haggling in the hospice shop I'd know she was out from under.

'And then they . . . went away,' Paddy said.

'Went away?' Elayne said. 'When?'

'Monday,' said Paddy. 'My first day. As soon as I had signed the papers of partnership.'

'*What?*' Elayne said. 'That's terrible. What a trick to pull on you. Getting you down here and then leaving you high and dry. What a rotten thing to do.'

'Not exactly,' Paddy said. 'They've passed ownership of the firm to me. Passed ownership of quite a lot of stuff, actually.'

Both my dad and Elayne perked up at that. My mum was quivering like a deer in a clearing.

'But there's a problem,' I said. 'Questions, Elayne. About Lovatt Dudgeon.'

Elayne, brushing shortbread crumbs out of the openwork stitches that decorated the neck of her jumper, froze suddenly, so that she looked as though she'd put a hand to her throat in shock.

'What's this?' my dad asked.

'The law firm specialises in adoption,' Paddy said. 'Like the church where Finnie's the deacon does too. Special adoptions.'

'Special how?' said my dad.

'So I caught their attention, I suppose,' Paddy said, ignoring him. He was back on script. 'Mum?'

Elayne was looking sick. She drained her sherry glass and set it down with a little rattle on the side table. 'Dudgeon,' she said faintly. She had been gripping the arm of the couch. She let go now, leaving a dark mark from her sweaty palm.

'Are you all right, Elayne?' my mum said. If things had been different my heart would have soared to hear her taking an interest in someone else that way.

'Fine,' Elayne said, then ruined it by jumping, like an electric shock, at the sound of our doorbell.

'You get Jehovah's Witless all the way out here?' my dad said.

'It'll be Shannon,' I said. 'A neighbour. She's joining us.'

'Who?' said Elayne. 'I thought it was just family. This is no time to be having strangers in.'

'She's not a stranger,' I said. 'She's involved. She's adopted too. And it was Lovatt Dudgeon that did *her* adoption. She's part of this. Whatever this is.'

'Lovatt Dudgeon,' Elayne repeated. Her face really had paled. Her make-up was standing out, swipes of pinkish-orange all around her jaw line. 'Is he coming too?'

'Like we said, he went away,' Paddy told her. He flicked a glance at me.

'He died,' I said. 'And – Dad, this is for you – no funny comments when Shannon comes in, okay? She's sensitive about her looks. Her condition. Actually, I'm not sure it's a condition. Her looks.'

'What's wrong with her?' my dad said. 'Is she one of these transpeople that are all over the place, these days?'

'Shut up!' I said, going to answer the door. I didn't know for sure if Shannon *was* sensitive about her looks. The hats and shades were functional. 'Shannon!' I sang out, opening the door wide and giving her a smile. 'Welcome. Come through and meet everyone.'

She wasn't wearing the wig today. Her hair was still the bright platinum sheet I had seen through the rain at the graveyard. And, as she came into the living room, she took her glasses off too, to polish the steam away.

'Oh, my God.' The voice sounded so strange, guttural and wavery, I didn't know who had spoken. My mum was smiling at Shannon and looking around as if to work out where the newcomer could be squeezed into a seat. My dad was as bright-eyed as a blackbird, holding in all his wisecracks for once, since I had warned him. Paddy was staring down at his lap. It must have been Elayne. And, as if to confirm it, as Shannon put her shades back on and came forward to greet everyone, Elayne closed her eyes and slithered off the couch, boneless as an eel, to lie in a dead faint on the floor.

Chapter 27

'Mum!' Paddy was on his knees at her side, patting her cheek. Slapping it, really. Her eyes fluttered open and she put up a hand to stop him.

'You should have said if you were feeling ropy,' my dad said. 'Finnie, have you got a drop of port and brandy for her?'

'Maybe I better go,' Shannon said.

'No,' I said. 'You stay put.'

'Upsy-daisy,' said my mum as, between them, she and my dad hoisted Elayne back onto the couch.

'Do you want to go to the out-of-hours, Elayne?' my mum said. 'Where's the nearest out-of-hours to here, though, Finn? Is it away back to A and E at the Infirmary?'

'I'm fine,' Elayne said. 'I'm not ill. I don't need a doctor.' She looked over at Paddy. 'I'll take that port and brandy, though. That's good for shock.'

It was me who went to get it and my dad followed me through to the kitchen, whispering fiercely. 'You get on at me for being loud,' he said, 'but I've never passed out from some poor soul looking a bit strange. What the hell's her problem?'

'It wasn't Shannon,' I said. 'God's sake, Dad. It was all that stuff about adoption suddenly coming out. You know she never talks about it.' I ripped a sheet off the kitchen roll and wiped my forehead. It was searing hot from the oven being turned right up to roast the potatoes.

'You're wrong,' my dad said. 'She took one look at your friend there and she was done for.'

Elayne was halfway through a fairytale, for Shannon's benefit, that she'd fainted from hearing so baldly that Paddy's boss had passed away. She gave me a pointed look as she said it was the sort of news that should be softened and led up to.

'Sorry,' I said. 'But the truth is Lovatt and his wife both died on Monday. They left a suicide note.'

'And a will,' Paddy said, defying me to argue.

'Of sorts,' I said. 'They did their best to wind up their affairs. I'll give you that much.'

'But they took their secrets to the grave,' said Shannon. I thought maybe Elayne paled again, but she was only midway through the gargantuan glassful I'd poured her and took another pull at it.

'Did they, though?' Paddy said. 'I wouldn't be so sure. I reckon the secrets are there to be uncovered.'

'Dinner's ready,' I said, 'if you'll all come to the table.'

'And let's not talk about suicide,' said my mum. 'Not while we're eating.'

'It's that or worse,' I told her. 'It could be murder.'

'It wasn't murder,' Paddy said. 'They left a note.'

'Shhh,' said my mum. 'I'm feeling better but not better enough for this, Finnie doll. And Elayne's still looking peaky.'

So we got through the soup on how much of a difference it makes when you grill the tomatoes first.

'No hardship if the oven's on anyway for a joint,' my mum said. 'This is lovely. And garlic bread!'

I beamed and felt my eyes fill. Hearing her voice with a touch of enthusiasm in it, knowing she could taste her food, even if we knew it would overbalance soon, was nearly as big a joy for us as it was for her.

'I'll have a plain cracker instead of garlic bread, if you've got one,' Elayne said. 'The soup's rich enough without a lot of butter as well.'

Paddy went through to the kitchen and came back with a packet of oatcakes. Wrong on two counts, I thought, as he put them down.

'Have you forgotten about my diverticulosis?' Elayne said. 'And have you run out of plates?'

But Paddy had had enough. He sat down without going in search of a third option. 'Finnie's cooked half a stone of spuds,' he said. 'You can fill up on the next course.'

It was when I was clearing the soup plates, my dad opening red wine and my mum having another fag at the open back door, that I heard Shannon speaking.

'So Paddy tells me you adopted him, Elayne. Did he tell you I'm adopted too? I was one of the very few children handled by Lovatt Dudgeon's pet project, St Angela's. It didn't take off the way he expected it to. But, give him his due, he didn't flog it. He was just as happy to support the other agencies. Isn't that right, Paddy?'

There was silence from the other room. I went through with the meat platter, plenty of Yorkshire puddings and roast potatoes around the edge trying to disguise the niggardly size of the roast itself.

'There's been some shrinkage,' I said. 'I won't judge you if you go out for chips.'

'There would have been plenty for the family,' Elayne said.

I had never heard her abandon passive aggression for good old-fashioned aggressive aggression before and I couldn't think of a damn thing to say. I went scurrying back for the veg dishes.

'Cut it out, Mum,' Paddy said. 'Shannon's a guest here, same as you. Don't be such a bag.'

'Jesus!' my mum said softly, stubbing out her fag and shutting the kitchen door. 'Not like your Paddy to talk to Bootface like that, is it?' She went back through, not wanting to miss anything.

My dad had got the cork out at last. He looked at me over the top of the open bottle. 'What's going on, chicken?' he said.

'I don't know,' I said. 'But it's long past time to get it all out on the table and sort it through.'

I put down the veg, the two gravy boats, the ketchup for my dad. And then they all just sat there with empty plates. Paddy spoke first.

'I think my adoption's dodgy,' he said. He was looking at Shannon.

'Dodgy how?' said Elayne. I couldn't quite believe she was sitting there taking this. I would have expected her to set off in the rain in her slippers, assuming Paddy would come after her in the car, full of apologies. But, then, after a sherry, a port and brandy and some white wine with her soup, and the way she was glugging into her first glass of red, maybe her sensibilities were blunted.

'It was the best thing that ever happened to me,' she was saying. 'I was happily married for ten years and then I nursed my poor Eddy through a long illness. It wasn't until after his chemo we ever thought to be tested, in case he was . . .'

'Firing—' my dad began, but stopped at a matching pair of looks from my mum and me.

'And it turned out it was me,' Elayne said. 'It was me. And I didn't see him for dust.'

'Scumbag!' Shannon said. 'He left you?'

'He still sends a Christmas card,' she said. 'Or his wife does. A photo of their children and grandchildren.'

'Tosser!' said Shannon.

'It was a nurse at the . . . at the . . . at the mental-health clinic who told me I could still have a little baby all of my own, even without him.'

Paddy and I were staring golf balls at each other. If Elayne Lamb was admitting to mental-health issues, we were right through the looking glass. She took another slug of wine and went on, 'Of course, she was just trying to cheer me up, that nurse. A woman the age I was then, all on her own, was never going to get a tiny healthy baby.'

'But you did,' I said.

'No, she didn't,' Paddy said. 'I was nearly school age.'

'What?' I said, looking between him and Elayne. 'I've seen all your photos. Newborn.'

Elayne shot a look at Paddy, but he was staring straight ahead and refused to meet her eye. 'Not with me in them,' she said. Her voice shook. 'If you think about it, Finnie. I'm not in any of the pictures, am I?'

I couldn't have sworn to it either way. 'But that's surely just because you took them,' I said. Elayne was shaking her head, a sad smile on her lips. 'So Paddy wasn't a baby?' I was still half asking, still unbelieving.

'I didn't care about a baby,' said Elayne. 'I wanted a child – I could still hope for a *child*. Especially if I was willing to take one that was a bit—'

'Squashed,' said my dad. 'Like the cheap cakes at the City Bakery. Bashed bargains, we call them.'

'Chrissake, Eric,' Paddy said. 'Go on, Mum.'

'And Lovatt Dudgeon helped me,' Elayne said. She didn't blink at Paddy's language. We were through the looking glass and down the rabbit hole.

'So, you just happened to approach St Angela's?' I said. 'What took you to them instead of one of the other agencies? The bigger ones.'

'No, it wasn't like that. I met Lovatt through his wife. She and I were very pally at one time.'

'You were?' I said. 'How?' It made no sense to me that Denise Dudgeon, horsy countrywoman, could have run across Elayne Lamb, suburban housewife, who rode nothing but her knitting machine.

'At the hospital,' Elayne said, 'if you must know.'

'The hospital?' I said. 'When your husband was ill and she was ill?' If Elayne had poured her heart out to Lovatt in the waiting room when Eddy was in the midst of his chemo and Denise Dudgeon was in the midst of whatever treatment they give you for Huntington's, that could make a lasting bond. If Lovatt remembered the sadness of the woman, aching for a child, he might seek her out when St Angela's was getting off the ground.

'No, Finnie,' Elayne said, sounding like her usual snippy self, which was comforting in a way. 'The psychiatric hospital. How many times are you going to make me say it? I was there and she was there. It's a bond.'

I reached over and took her hand in mine, squeezing it and wrinkling my nose at her. Of course Denise Dudgeon would have tried some counselling or therapy or something before she decided it was all a bust and killed herself. And Elayne was there trying to recover from the tosser behaviour of scumbag Eddy.

I still couldn't work out the timeline, though. If Lovatt Dudgeon only got interested in second chances for children after his wife killed his own, how could a woman *she* met before her final descent be in touch with *him*? If it had been Simmerton, it would be different. But the Dudgeons lived in Edinburgh then. Or did they? They owned Jerusalem House and Denise died there.

'Where was the clinic?' I said. 'In town or down here?'

'Why would it be down here?' said Elayne. 'But no, it wasn't in the city. It was a private clinic, out in East Lothian, if you must know, because I didn't want to run into anyone I knew. Neighbours or that. So I used to get the train down the coast and go to a wee clinic there. I sometimes think the journey, sitting looking out the train window at the sea view, was what did me most good, not the endless yak-yak-yakking once I got there.'

She sounded like herself again. With one last squeeze I let her hand go. 'Look, let's eat,' I said. 'By all means, keeping talking but let's eat too, eh?'

'Don't need to tell me twice,' my dad said, digging into the potatoes. 'So this St Angela's,' he went on, 'it was an agency that dealt with . . .' I was glaring at him and he came through for once in his clueless life '. . . special-needs children? Why was Paddy on their books? Elayne, do you know?'

'Don't mind me,' Paddy said.

289

'It might not have been anything to do with the child himself,' I said. 'It might have been that Paddy's birth parents wanted to deal with St Angela's for some reason. Maybe they knew Lovatt.'

'That's it,' Elayne said. 'It came from the birth parents. It was a surprise to me. A gift from the gods.' She had put the smallest amount of everything on her plate that you could put on your plate and still claim to be eating a meal. One potato, one floret of cauliflower, a slice of beef where the knife had gone off-course and shaved a thin sliver, like a nail paring.

'So you adopted Paddy through St Angela's when it was brand-new,' Shannon said. 'I wonder how many of us actually passed through its hands. That's at least three now, including me and my brother, if we're right about him.'

'You and your brother weren't adopted together?' my mum said. 'That's not nice, lovey. That's a shame.'

'Sibling groups are harder to find homes for than single children,' Shannon said.

'Is that right?' my mum said. 'I'd have thought a wee perfect family, a boy and girl, would be just what anyone wanted. Wouldn't you, Elayne?'

She hadn't eaten a bite of her midget dinner. She hadn't even picked up her fork. She was sitting back with her hands in her lap. 'I'm very happy with just my Paddy,' she said. Her voice was shaking.

'You didn't want a girl too? To dress and spoil?' My mum smiled at me. 'Not that this one let me dress her. She had that pudding-bowl haircut when she was six and there's never been a ribbon or a bobble since. Now, if *you*'d been mine, Shannon – with all that lovely long hair!'

'Well,' Shannon said, 'perfect wasn't really the word for Sean and me. My brother's got more severe ocular albinism than me. He was pretty well blind. I've been lucky really.'

'When . . .?' Elayne said, before her dry voice gave out. She took a small sip of water and tried again. 'When was your adoption?'

'Me?' said Shannon. 'Why? I mean, it was nineteen eighty-six.'

'That was earlier than I thought St Angela's started up,' I said. 'That was really soon after the Dudgeons died.'

'After the *Dudgeons* died?' Elayne said. 'What do you mean? They died last week, you said. What are you talking about?'

'Elayne, didn't you know?' I said. 'Your friend – Mrs Dudgeon. She killed herself and her two little children. Years ago. Just before St Angela's started. Right before. It's hard to believe Lovatt was in a fit state to do anything except grieve, actually.'

'They were definitely up and running, though,' Paddy said. 'I was adopted in 'eighty-six too.'

'A woman killed herself and her children?' my mum said. 'As long as I live I can't believe the wickedness of this world. Let's go to church tomorrow, Eric, eh?'

My dad nodded absently. He wasn't really listening. 'Elayne?' he said. Elayne had bowed her head. As we watched, a couple of tears fell and splashed into her lap. 'Are you okay?'

'I would have done anything,' she said, 'for a baby. For a child. I would have been happy with a boy and a girl. I didn't care if they had . . . problems. But he told me – the lawyer did, Mr Dudgeon – that the boy and the girl had to go to separate homes. I was going to get the boy but I couldn't get the girl too.'

291

The five of us were like statues, sitting watching her, listening to it all coming out, beginning to see what she was trying to tell us. The food lay forgotten.

'I'm sorry,' she said. 'I'm sorry. I didn't know. I didn't know. I went through the process. All the visits, all the assessments. References. There was a little boy and a little girl. I didn't mind which one came to me. I wanted both. I couldn't have both, though. And I never understood how they picked me for the boy and someone else for the girl, but they did. I thought I was getting a little boy with visual impairment and some other special needs. And then the news came that the little boy I was getting was perfect. No health issues, no concerns. He was perfect. He was you, Paddy. He was you.'

My mum was the only one who hadn't cottoned on. Her meds make her dozy. It's hard to blame her for always wanting off them, really.

'So there was a boy and girl killed by their own mammy,' she said, trying to get things straight in her head. 'And there was a boy and girl, not perfect but precious, adopted out to separate homes?'

'No,' I said. 'There was a little girl with a faulty gene. She was killed. And a little boy who was lucky. Adopted. Spared.'

'And a little girl adopted out too,' said my mum, smiling at Shannon. 'And what about the other little boy?'

She was the only one who seemed surprised when Shannon let out a howl of pain from the pit of her belly, pushed away from the table and ran out into the rain.

Chapter 28

I was right behind her. She had left her hat and her coat hanging in our house and her hair was soaked into rat's tails before she was halfway home, darkening to a nasty nicotine yellow-grey and bouncing on her back, as if it was whipping her.

'Shannon!' I shouted. 'Shannon, wait.'

'Jaysis, feck!' The cry came from behind me. It was my dad, splashing shin deep in a puddle at the side of the track just outside the Sloans' gate.

'Dad,' I said, wheeling round and stopping. 'Go in there. It's a Mr Sloan and his wife. She's got some of the same problems Mam does. And he's not coping. I told him you might stop in today. Go and talk to him.'

'What are you on about?' my dad said. 'We're in the middle of something here, girl. That kid – where's she gone? That kid's just found out she's busted, hasn't she? She's tracked down the people who killed her brother and now she's done for them. Why the hell on earth would I go visiting?'

'Because he knows something,' I said. 'He had a bonfire the morning after the deaths. He said it was leaves. But there's no leaves to burn in January. And he acted like Shannon didn't exist. They all did. And I couldn't work out why. And— Oh, God, Dad, I think the bodies are in his house. Upstairs in his house. There was a smell I couldn't place. But I know what it was now. It was like that badger under the caravan at Whitley Bay that summer.'

My dad took a step back, blanching. His hair was plastered to his head and the rain had made him ruddy, but the memory of that badger turned him pale again.

'I think they're wrapped,' I said. 'In fact they must be because of the blood. They'll be wrapped in plastic. Sealed, you know? It'll be faint. But I know what it was. Who could forget it?'

'Blood?' said my dad. 'How do you know there was blood? I thought nobody had seen them.'

'Just— Look,' I said, 'just go and keep him talking. Or get Paddy to talk to him.'

'Elayne needs Paddy,' Dad said.

'So go!' I was shouting. 'He's an old man and I think he's ready to give in. The tension must be killing him. I need to talk to Shannon.'

I left him standing there but, by the time I was throwing myself in the gate at Bairnspairt, he was disappearing up the path towards the Sloans' front door.

'Shannon!' I shouted, hammering on the door. 'Let me in. If you don't let me in this minute, I'll dial 999.' I tried the door handle and nearly overbalanced as the door gave and I fell into the little hallway. The fug of incense was missing today and the cottage seemed cold and damp. She had opened her windows at the tops despite the weather. 'Shannon?' I looked into the living room, then the kitchen. She was nowhere to be seen. She wasn't in the bright room with the SAD light either. I went to the last door, her private room, and knocked. Then I tried it and, feeling the lock give, pushed it open.

My heartbeats were bulging up into my throat, but behind that door there was nothing worse than Shannon's bedroom. She was curled up on her bed under that same duvet from the couch, her face turned into her pillow, sobbing deep and hard. On the far side of the room a curved computer desk was set up with three monitors and a keyboard, a fan at one side to cool the air when all the machines were whirring. Why had she feared me seeing this? I wondered. Maybe it was just her sanctum. Or maybe it was the photographs by her bed. Little white-haired boys in sunglasses and baseball caps. They weren't Sean. She couldn't really have photos of Sean, could she? Maybe she was embarrassed that she'd printed out stock pictures and framed them.

'Hey,' I said, going over and sitting down beside her. The mattress dipped under my weight and rolled her closer to me. 'Don't cry like that. You'll make yourself sick.'

'He's dead,' Shannon moaned, turning towards me and letting me put my arms round her. 'I thought he was. I knew he was, deep down. I kept hoping but I knew. I knew yesterday. That's why I went to the graveyard.'

'Yes,' I said. 'I think so. I think it was Lovatt that tested the children, not Denise. *He* tested ... What were their names?'

'Vanessa, Simon,' Shannon said. She had stopped gulping

quite so badly now. She sat up and rested against the bedhead, sniffing and wiping her nose with the heel of her hand.

'Right. Vanessa and Simon.'

'She was positive and he was negative.'

'Yeah,' I said. 'Lovatt needed a plan to get rid of Denise and little Vanessa and keep Simon.'

'The worthwhile child,' Shannon said. 'The perfect child.' She was crying again, tears coursing down her cheeks, her eyes red and sore-looking.

'So he set himself up as an adoption lawyer and he found a woman – a total stranger – who wanted a child. She was happy to adopt a child with some special needs. But when she heard that the little boy she was getting was perfect she was happy then too.'

'He switched them,' Shannon said. 'He killed my brother along with his wife and child. That's right, isn't it? That's what happened. Criss-cross. He switched them.'

'Except he didn't. He was on the Orient Express. Like it was some kind of joke! He went on the bloody Orient Express to alibi himself. I knew there was something dodgy the first time I heard it.'

'Do you mean maybe Sean's not dead?' Shannon said. The light in her eyes was painful to see. 'But someone has to be in that grave, Finnie. Simon Dudgeon's little grave. You think there's a lot of paperwork for an adoption, you should see a death.'

'No, I'm sorry,' I said softly. 'He is dead. I just don't think Lovatt killed him. Because of the alibi. The train.' There it was again. A flicker of something just out of my view. Even what Shannon had just said – criss-cross – was making me twitchy. Shannon saw the thoughts flit across my face and leaned closer, still hoping. I shut my eyes. 'I'm sorry,' I said, trying to let her down gently.

'It's okay,' she said. 'I told you I know. I've known for years. It's just this last couple of days has been hard, guessing where he died and when. And why. And then Paddy's mum hammered in the last nail there.' She scrubbed at her face. 'But never mind that. I've got the rest of my life to grieve. If it's right enough – what you're saying – that it wasn't Lovatt, maybe whoever it was is still alive to get arrested and convicted and do hard time. So, you were saying . . . alibi?'

'Alibi,' I agreed. 'Lovatt's alibi for the time his family died. It's off. I know it is. Something's been bothering me about it since I first heard the story.'

'It's pretty elaborate,' Shannon said. 'But maybe he loves trains and doesn't read detective fiction. Maybe it never occurred to him that it would ring all the wrong alarm bells for some people. People who couldn't care less about trains.'

'Trains,' I said.

'What about them?'

'Oh, buggeration!' I put my head in my hands and squeezed my eyes shut. 'It's something to do with trains. It's . . .'

'What?'

'Shhh,' I said. 'It's just out of reach. It's just on the tip of—' I sat up. 'I've got it.'

Shannon was staring at me.

'Okay, I need to admit something first, though,' I said. 'I met Lovatt and Tuft. On the night they died. I met them.'

'I know,' Shannon said. 'I mean, I thought so. You spoke as if you had.'

'And Tuft said it took Lovatt just a few months from meeting her to proposing. Twenty-five years ago. And she also said that they met at North Berwick at Christmas time, just before the old station was pulled down and it all went automatic. She said Lovatt's mother was pissed off about the station. And I've got a hunch. Maybe a memory. Google it for me, will you?'

Shannon was scrambling off her bed almost before the words were out of my mouth. She woke one of her monitors and typed something very fast into the browser.

'That's right,' she said. 'North Berwick station. Closed down and demolished. Oh, wait – in nineteen eighty-five. That's not twenty-five years ago. That's over *thirty* years ago.'

The click as everything fell into place was so clear I swear I could hear it happening.

'Nineteen eighty-five,' I said. 'When Lovatt met Tuft and proposed. And Paddy's mum went to a private clinic in East Lothian, a lovely train journey along the coast. What do you bet it was Berwick she was going to? Tuft Dudgeon's home town. What do you bet when Lovatt and Tuft went looking for a vulnerable woman, unconnected to them, who would bring up Simon and ask no questions, they found her at a mental-health clinic in Berwick? The "Mrs Dudgeon" Elayne got to know was Mrs Dudgeon-in-waiting. And I think *she* took care of turning her intended into a widower, while he was off constructing an alibi for himself. On that bloody stupid train.'

I tilted to the side so I could get my phone out of my back pocket. I dialled Paddy.

'Hi,' I said. 'How's your mum? How's mine? Shannon's fine. *He*'s okay. He's talking to Mr Sloan. Listen, ask Elayne to

298

describe Mrs Dudgeon. I know it's years since she saw her but it was an intense experience. She should remember.'

There was a succession of muffled noises while Paddy relayed the question and then passed over the phone.

'Finnie?' Elayne said. 'Why do you want to know? She looked just normal. We weren't raving maniacs.'

'Did she have long red hair?' I said.

'No, she had a shampoo and set,' said Elayne. 'Lots of women did back then. I did, if it comes to it.'

'Thanks,' I said. I hung up the phone. She had still had her shampoo and set last Monday, the little kiss curls at her temples soaked in spilled blood, her face as grey as her hair had turned in the thirty-odd years since Elayne had met her. I squeezed my eyes shut. The picture was back. Her open mouth and her slashed hands and the hump of his chest and the black butterfly spreading its wings on either side of the knife handle. I almost hoped they really were in Mr Sloan's cottage, wrapped in plastic. I wanted to see them now. Anything to take that vision away.

'Can you face coming back to mine again?' I asked Shannon. 'You don't have to but we need to talk this out – Paddy and I have got a lot to come clean about – and then we need to decide what to do.'

'You think *you've* got a lot to come clean about!' She pushed herself up off her bed and wriggled her shoulders. 'I'll come but not in these wet clothes.' She peeled her top off, revealing skin so white it was luminous in the low light. She looked like a Botticelli – I think I mean Botticelli – so rounded and smooth, no sign of muscles underneath that pale flesh. Then she shrugged on a new jumper and twisted her hair up into a topknot. She put on a pair of sunglasses that were sitting on her bedside table and smiled a brave smile, not quite steady, at me.

We huddled under a shared umbrella back out in the rain. It hammered like fists on the taut nylon, dropping like marbles on the sagging quilts over the banana plants, like snare drum brushes as it hit the waxy cabbage leaves.

Outside the gate, my dad was standing. He was quite still, not even bowing his head against the downpour. It ran over his glasses and behind them too. He blinked when he saw me.

'I . . .' he said. 'I didn't know what to do, Finn. I don't know what to do.'

'Are they in there?' I said.

'What's this?' said Shannon.

'I think he's got the Dudgeons in there,' I told her.

'No, no, he hasn't,' my dad said. 'Poor auld sowel. He doesn't know a thing about *that* anyway.'

'So what's up?' I said.

'She's dead,' my dad said. 'His wife's dead.'

'Mrs Sloan died?' Shannon cried out. 'When?'

'Years back,' my dad said. 'It looks like years ago.'

'That can't be right,' I said.

'I just saw it with my own eyes, Finnie,' my dad said. 'She's a skeleton. It's the bonfires, like you said. He scrapes . . . And then he burns . . .'

'But . . .' I didn't know why it was troubling me so much but before I could catch the thought, another one struck me. 'So *that*'s the deal he had with the Dudgeons, is it? They pretend they're seeing Mrs Sloan regularly for mah jongg nights and he does whatever it is he does for them. Keeps whatever secret it is he keeps for them.'

'It's not just me, then,' Shannon said.

'Or me and Paddy either,' I said. 'Oh, God, let's go and talk about it inside, eh?'

As we splashed our way back along the lane to the gates and the lodge, I could feel the eyes upon me from the upstairs windows: Mr Sloan hovering behind his net curtains, watching us walk away.

Sunday

Chapter 29

I woke at six the next morning after a dreamless night. It was still dark – of course it was! – and the room was cold outside the covers. Actually, the room was pretty cold inside the covers because we'd given our top quilt to Paddy's mum, on the couch. My mum and dad had gone along to Shannon's to her fold-out sofa-bed to save her being alone. I lay beside Paddy, listening to him muttering, 'Too dark, it's too dark.' When that stopped, I listened to the silence. The rain had let up and the wind had stilled. If any creatures were moving about the forest, they were tiny ones or they were tiptoeing. I told myself Simmerton – its newsagents opening soon for rolls and papers, its garage open now for fags and juice and ten-pound pay-outs off last night's lottery – was a five-minute drive away, or a ten-minute walk up and over the steps. We weren't marooned here. We weren't stranded.

But all I could think of was the thin thread of the road slicing through miles of black trees, the two cuts on either side, the burned shell of Jerusalem and the graveyard up one,

Widdershins and the Bairnspairt down the other – death and death and more death all around.

'You okay?' came Paddy's gravel voice.

'No,' I said. 'You?'

'No.'

'But I need to get on with it anyway. Why did I agree to preach today?' It was a stupid question. Why wouldn't I have agreed to contribute a sermon on my first Sunday in my new parish, as a way to say hello to my new community, as a fresh step in my new life, my bright future?

'I might not make it,' Paddy said. 'My head's killing me.'

'Hangover or migraine?' I said, as if it made a difference.

'We'll see,' he said. He was quiet for such a long time I thought he was sleeping again. 'We're finished, aren't we? You and me.'

'I don't know,' I said. 'Maybe.'

'Was it the will?'

'The will was the last straw,' I said. 'Caring so much about money, Paddy. About *things*. But giving yourself a migraine to avoid looking at the bodies?'

'I had a good reason for that,' said Paddy. 'A reason, anyway.'

'Go on,' I said. 'If you've still got something to say. Only I thought we'd said everything last night. That was the point, wasn't it?'

'I wanted you to identify them because you're a deacon so you're . . .'

'Above reproach?'

'Further above reproach than a slimy lawyer who's going to win big from the deaths anyway.'

'But you hadn't seen the will then,' I said. 'Wait, but you

knew about the partnership papers. Hang on, no. You found out about the partnership papers same time you found out they'd "gone to Brazil", right? And by then you knew you weren't going to have to go into the house and see the bodies. Right? Paddy, right?'

'I saw the signed papers first.'

'Faxed papers first, then cheese and chocolate, then the email. Like that?'

'Shhh,' Paddy said. 'Don't talk about food.'

He never did have a stomach for boozing.

We hadn't meant to get drunk last night. None of us. My dad had meant to drive home, take Elayne home. My mum didn't even have her morning pills with her and I was worried about how she'd be through the day, even though I knew it took longer than that for her dose to dip.

But we'd got a head start at lunch and then my dad had needed a wee something for the shock of 'meeting' Mrs Sloan. Shannon needed something to calm her nerves. I needed something too. And when you put a bottle of whisky on a coffee-table with six people sitting round it, six Scots with a nip of Irish anyway, it's a done deal.

'Why aren't we going to the polis?' my mum said.

'Because we need to get it straight first,' said Paddy. 'I need to know where my mum stands. Legally.'

'Get it straight?' said Shannon. 'Where do we start?'

'How about with a prayer?' It's not often I play the God card, but this was a very strange day.

'How about with an agreement?' my dad said. 'Nobody here killed anyone, right?' Nods all round. 'And nobody here covered up for a killer, right?' More nods after a few glances to check that everyone else was nodding. 'Right, then. We go forward on that basis. If we all agree.' I smiled at my mum. It was years ago my dad was made redundant, but he had snapped back into shop-steward mode as if he'd never been away.

'What about Mr Sloan?' I said. 'Are you calling the cops on him?'

'Who's Mr Sloan?' Elayne said. '*Sloan?*'

'Not today,' my dad said. 'Not on a Saturday teatime, to get him slung in the cells with a lot of drunks after the football. It's waited this long. It can wait till tomorrow.'

'Right,' I said. 'Right-oh. That's nothing to do with this anyway.' But even as I spoke I could feel a wriggling inside me, a worm of doubt burrowing into my gut. There was something about the idea of Mr Sloan, loving his wife too much to let her go, hanging on and hanging on to the scraps that were left: washing her clothes and pegging them out, talking about her to neighbours. I couldn't work out why it was bothering me. But I needed to pay attention to what was happening here in my own house. My dad was handing round the whisky glasses. Paddy was speaking.

'So the adoption – my adoption – wasn't legal?' he said.

'I'm your mum,' said Elayne, miserably.

'Of course you are,' said Paddy. 'Of course you are.'

'I didn't know.' She turned to Shannon, pleading. I always wanted to shake Elayne when she turned on the 'poor wee me' routine, but Shannon was twice the woman I was, clearly.

'Don't upset yourself,' she said. 'You were happy to take a little boy with a visual impairment and other issues, weren't you? That's what you said. You'd have taken both of us, you said.'

'I would,' Elayne said. 'I really would. Not that – I mean, your mum, the woman who brought you up, wouldn't be without you.'

'She died,' said Shannon.

Elayne shuffled forward so she could reach Shannon's hand and squeeze it. 'I'm sorry,' she said. 'I'm sorry for all of it. I don't know why they picked on me.'

'If it wasn't you it would have been someone else,' I said. 'I think Tuft Dudgeon – she wasn't Tuft Dudgeon yet, because Denise was still alive, but anyway – was on the hunt for someone. She was at the clinic specifically on the look-out for someone who would go along with their plan. You were perfect, Elayne, because you were trusting and innocent and you wanted a child. You've got nothing to be sorry for, you see?'

'Why didn't they get someone who'd do it with her eyes open?' Elayne said. 'For pay?'

'Maybe they would have, if they hadn't found you,' I said. 'But they'd always have worried, wouldn't they? They'd always have had to keep paying.'

I saw her eyes flash at the same exact second the light came on for me.

'Sloan!' she said. 'Myna Sloan. She was there at the same time. She was older than me, going through the change. They do say if you're aching for a baby of your own, the change can be rough.'

'That's right,' I said. 'That's what Mr Sloan had on the Dudgeons. They tried there first! Lord above.' But even as the light-bulb came on and burned away inside my head, making sense of things, I knew that wasn't what had really been tugging at me.

'So,' my dad said. 'Lovatt Dudgeon – bloody stupid name – wanted rid of his wife and daughter and wanted to keep his son safe. Even if it meant he'd never see the lad again.'

'Why not just kill his wife and daughter and make it look like suicide?' I said. 'And then he'd have kept his son safe and with him all these years. He did stay away, didn't he, Elayne? He didn't visit Paddy? He didn't have contact. Sorry! I'm sorry! I know, I know.'

'Nothing!' Elayne said. 'There was nothing. I never saw hide nor hair of either of them again. He was my little boy and that was that. That was all, Finnie. I wish you'd believe me.'

'Except there was the money,' Paddy said. 'There was the money, Mum. Come on, eh?'

I nodded. As soon as he'd mentioned the missing money and the loan and the oil rig on Monday night, the thought had struck me that he'd always had too much. I was used to everyone having more money than me so I didn't question it, but he should have come out of a law degree with some student debt. It was even longer than an ordinary degree and I knew he'd had a little hatchback car while he was at uni. There were photos of him on trips with the orienteering club. And he hadn't worked in the holidays: there were photos of him backpacking and scuba-diving and all that. I thought he was so glamorous when we first met. Me, who'd gone on school field trips to the country park in wellies because I didn't have anything else except trainers, and we'd been told not to wear them.

'I had a benefactor,' Elayne said. I could tell it was killing her. 'I thought it was the birth family. I thought maybe they'd found out where Paddy had gone.'

'It *was* the birth family,' I said. 'The birth father, anyway. Lovatt.'

'He had a heart,' Shannon said. 'Not *her*. She was just a brain. Like a calculator. She was the one that cottoned on to me. She had me taped as soon as I got here. Day one.'

'Do you think you can tell us?' I said. 'I know it must be painful, but like my dad said . . . If we agree?'

'Wait, though.' That was my mum. 'Finnie doll, I think I know why they hatched this mad plan instead of doing what you said.' She shook her head, as if she was literally trying to drive out the fug of her meds and the booze she'd chased them down with. 'Because if a wife and kid with Huntington's just conveniently die and the dad swans off with the healthy son and gets married again? People would talk, wouldn't they? Folk would wonder. I know I would. But the way he did it – never having any more kids after that, marrying a woman too old to give him any, dedicating his life to helping other children like his own? He's untouchable. I bet no one ever dreamed he was anything less than an angel.'

'And then suddenly after years of getting away with it, they kill themselves,' I said. 'They just up and kill themselves.'

'Exactly,' my mum said. 'That's what I mean.'

My dad nodded. 'What changed?' he said. 'Mary, you've nailed it. *What changed?* Paddy, how did you come across the job advert?'

'It was in my inbox,' Paddy said. 'Someone emailed it to me.'

'So *you* didn't find *them*,' my dad went on. 'You didn't close in on them and frighten them. You weren't a threat to them.'

'All they would need to do was not give me the job,' Paddy said. 'I would have shrugged and moved on to the next one.'

'No, son,' my dad said, the choice of word hitting all of us with a clang. He licked his lips before going on. '*They* sent the advert to you. They must have decided to bow out and pass everything on to you. But why?'

'Health again, maybe,' Elayne said. 'A bad diagnosis.'

'I think,' said Shannon, 'it might have been me. If we're really talking in confidence. When I first got here, I had made an appointment to see Lovatt and I took all the paperwork from my adoption, all the correspondence from my mum – my mum that brought me up, I mean – and from my birth mum. I marched in there and started asking about Sean. I showed them how hard I'd tried to find him. I even asked if there was any way the lawyer who'd handled it away back then would be able to find out, for sure, if he had died. I asked if Lovatt could help me find out if Sean had died.'

'Jaysis,' my dad said. 'If we're right about all of this, love, you're bloody lucky it's them that's dead and not you.'

'They seemed sympathetic,' Shannon said. 'They wanted to help me. They offered me such a fantastic deal on the cottage I couldn't say no. But it backfired. The house was supposed to sweeten me up and shut me down but it just made me more suspicious.'

'They wanted you close,' I said. 'Like the Sloans. Where they could keep an eye on you. Maybe they were looking for leverage on you too. Something they could hold over you, like they held Mrs Sloan over that poor old man.'

'There's nothing to find,' Shannon said. 'I've never had so much as a parking ticket. Because I can't drive. I suppose they could have threatened me with taking the cottage back.'

'Could they?' I said.

Shannon smiled. 'No. I'd have slept in a hedge to get the

truth.' Then her face fell. 'What I can't forgive,' she said, 'and I'll never forgive, is why they took their secrets with them. Why – if they were dying – couldn't they leave a letter for me? Why couldn't they tell me if he suffered at the end? Why couldn't they just tell me he *didn't* suffer at the end? I'd have believed them. Why didn't they leave a letter for me?'

I flashed a look at Paddy, but he didn't get what I was trying to say. Were we sure they hadn't? There was nothing in the kitchen desk, the place I'd checked. But he had searched the office and Abby had searched Lovatt's study. Would a letter to a neighbour have struck them as important? Or might there still be some comfort for Shannon hidden somewhere? Then another thought struck me. What made her so sure there wasn't?

I glanced back at her. She was flame-faced and looking down at her lap.

'Were you in the house?' I said.

She raised her head, showing me my own face reflected in her mirror shades.

'My house?' she said. 'When?'

I didn't push it.

'So they killed themselves,' my dad said, heaving a sigh and filling his glass. 'Another suicide.'

'Except the first one wasn't,' my mum said. 'In nineteen eighty-five. It was murder.'

'And the second one wasn't either,' I said. 'Or not entirely. One of them wanted to die and decided to take the other down. But which one was it? Did she kill him or did he kill her?'

'You tell us, Finnie,' said my dad. 'You saw them after they died. What did the corpses tell *you*?'

'*What?*' Paddy said, jerking in his seat. 'Why did you say that?'

'The time's past for secrets,' I said. 'Between us anyway – we agreed that much. What did they tell me? That he died second with a knife in his back. But she couldn't do it with her hands cut to shreds. I keep thinking about it, dreaming about it. Can't stop seeing it and I don't know why.'

'And can't go back for another look either,' my dad said. 'Because even if it was just between the two of them when they died, someone else got involved for sure afterwards. Right?'

'Right,' I said.

'Who except a killer would have moved them?' my dad said.

'Right,' I said again.

For a moment we were silent. Then my mum said what we were all thinking. 'Where are they?'

Chapter 30

I was getting too old to drink that much, I thought, looking at myself in the cruel side-light hitting the bathroom mirror in what passed for dawn. I remembered when pallor and dark eyes were just a Gothic touch. Today I looked washed up. I looked seedy. A black cassock and the harsh white slash of the dog-collar did me no favours either. I put some blusher on my cheeks but that only made the rest of me look greyer so I swiped a fistful of bog roll and scrubbed it off again.

I could tell from the commotion outside the bathroom door that my dad had arrived, revelling in his hangover as ever.

'Mouth like a junkie's carpet,' he was saying, as I sidled into the kitchen. 'Bacon roll, Finn?' He had the frying pan out and buttered rolls lying open on plates.

'Go on, then,' I said. 'What time did you pack it in? I never heard Paddy hitting the mattress.' I had gone to bed as soon as we'd made our decision.

My dad nodded and groaned. 'God knows. I was bladdered. We wrote everything down, though. Here was me ripping the piss out of your boy for taking notes, but he's right. He's not wrong.'

'And?' I said. I had half an ear cocked for what my mum was saying to Elayne in the living room, the timbre of her voice, the depth of the dips and the height of the peaks in her intonation. Her voice flattening out was an early sign of her beginning to sink again. But there was nothing of that about her this morning. She was clucking over it all like a flustered chicken. And Elayne, answering, warbled like a pigeon. They were both fine.

'And,' my dad said, 'Paddy reckons that this Lovatt – his father! You can't get your brainbox round it, can you? – played a canny hand. St Angela's was as bent as a seven-bob bit but he never kept a penny of the takings. All handed over fair and square. So none of Paddy's inheritance is tainted. It's not the proceeds of crime. And it really is his inheritance too.'

'Are you sure?' I said. 'Is Paddy sure?'

'Yep,' said my dad. 'It's Paddy's – inherited from Denise, his mother.'

'What about Tuft?' I said.

'Nope,' said my dad. 'Lovatt never owned it – can't benefit from a crime you committed – so he couldn't leave it to his second wife, even if she did outlive him by a minute or two.'

'So what was the point of the fake will?' I asked. Then I answered myself: 'So Paddy could get it without the story coming out.'

'Bingo,' said my dad. 'Nice as ninepence.'

'Yeah,' I said. 'Pretty neat.'

'You don't sound happy,' my dad said. 'I mean, I know it's a lot to take – it's like something off the telly – but if your life's going to turn into a soap, better *Dynasty* than *EastEnders*, eh?'

I said nothing.

'You can sell it all if it's too tainted.'

'The problem is, Dad, it's tainted for me but not for Paddy. He's okay. He didn't even seem bothered about what Elayne was going through.'

My dad grunted, hunched over the frying pan, pushing the bacon around. 'Aye,' he said quietly, after a bit of thinking time, 'you've got a point. I was as bad, off my head on that homebrew and thinking it was just a puzzle. Just a . . . Like a game. I never thought of Elayne.'

'She's your daughter's mother-in-law,' I said. 'You can forgive yourself. But she's his *mum*. And it's not just that.' I was whispering now, hoping, between the clucking and cooing in the living room and the hot fat spitting in the frying pan, Paddy wouldn't hear me. 'Why's he not freaking out? Or why's he not catatonic? Why's he so on top of it all? Checking out his financial situation and feeling pleased about it? It's not right, Dad.'

'Trained mind?' my dad said. 'What's that thing they say about surgeons?'

'Compartmentalisation. But why's he not worried about who moved the bodies? Someone moved them. Someone sent an email to buy a bit of time. That someone might even have killed both the Dudgeons. Paddy should be scared he's next. Shouldn't he? How can a job and a bit of money, even a few cottages . . . How can they even register?'

My dad turned to face me, and all the bravado of how much he loved a crippling hangover was gone now. He looked old and ill and more troubled than I had ever seen him.

'We agreed to leave it,' he said.

317

I nodded. We had. Every one of us. To save Elayne a bashing in the tabloids, to save Shannon more pain, to save Julie and Abby's jobs, to make sure Mr Sloan had privacy while Social Services did what they had to do, we had agreed. I'd say I witnessed the will and we'd all take the true history of Sean and Simon to our graves.

'You don't suspect him, do you, Finn?' my dad said. 'Of moving the corpses?'

'All I'm saying is we're not at the bottom of this and Paddy doesn't care.'

I saw a movement in the doorway and the skin on my neck shrank, pulling my shoulders up and freezing them. Turning, ready to face him if I had to, all my breath rushed out of me again in a gust of relief as I saw it was Shannon. And that very fact brought tears to my eyes. To be so relieved it was this woman I hardly knew, instead of the man I'd thought I knew better than I knew myself.

'There she is!' my dad said. 'That's a rare comfy sofa-bed you've got along the road. I slept like a slug. Zed beds we crashed on when we were young and daft and couldn't afford a taxi? They'd cripple you. And a nice fierce shower too. I'm halfway to fixed. Couple of bacon butties . . .'

'How did *you* sleep?' I said. Shannon was so white she looked blue, but it might have been the cold light and her dark clothes, the fact that she had her black wig on again.

'I dozed a bit towards morning,' she said. 'Dreamed of Sean, of course. But a different dream from usual. The start of the process, probably.' She took a shuddering breath in and caught her lip. Then she sniffed deeply and shook her head. 'I'm not going to cry today. Don't know what I *am* going to do. But no crying.'

'Come to church,' I said. 'I'm preaching a sermon. You can give me a star-rating after.'

'I'm not really—' Shannon began.

'Have a bit of a sing-song,' I said. 'It's like going to *Mamma Mia*. Or *The Rocky Horror Picture Show*.'

'Maybe,' Shannon said. 'Is there any quiet time?'

'That's Quakers,' I told her.

'Because you're right,' Shannon said. 'There's a bit of this that's still out of sight, isn't there? There's something missing. I can't help thinking if I just sat and thought for long enough it would come into view. Like . . .'

'A magic eye picture,' I said. 'Yeah, me too.'

'That's what yesterday was supposed to be,' my dad said. 'We maybe overdid the refreshments, mind you.' He was lifting bacon rashers from the pan now and folding them onto the rolls. 'Here you go, girls. Bacon butties coming your way, ladies,' he called through to my mum and Elayne. 'Paddy?' he added, raising his eyebrows at me.

'Migraine,' I said. 'Let him sleep on.'

I didn't want him in the pew, watching me. I didn't want him in the church. I didn't trust that he had a right to be there, in God's house, in good faith. You had to hand it to the Prods, I supposed. If you couldn't play the old confession card, that was a hell of a good reason to keep your nose clean and make sure you never needed to.

The church was packed. Of course it was. There was a new deacon – a slip of a girl, at that – and there was a scandal the like of which Simmerton hadn't seen for decades to be picked over. Tuft and Lovatt had disappeared. Out of the world or out of the country, either way it was another delicious chapter in the tragic lives of the Dudgeon family. It would keep the parish going through more than that morning's service. The book clubs, darts nights, keep-fit classes and indoor-bowling fixtures would have perfect attendance for a while yet before everyone was done with the post-mortems.

Robert Waugh, as I'd suspected, was one of those ministers at his best on a Sunday morning, belting out benedictions and intimations, like a true vicar of the Old Testament God. I wondered if he had offered this sermon to me purely so I would make him look even better. He introduced me after the first hymn and prayer and I ascended the short flight of steps to the pulpit, tasting bitter adrenalin and feeling my hands prick with a sweat I couldn't have said was hangover or nerves.

My mum and dad were smiling up at me. Paddy's mum gave me a wary look then glanced away. Julie put her thumbs up and winked. I couldn't see Abby. Maybe she wasn't a churchgoer or maybe she'd faded into the background in her Sunday best, same as weekdays. I recognised one of the butcher brothers, a barista from the good coffee shop and the Webbs, of course, in the front row.

'I'm going to read today,' I began, 'from one John, chapter one, verses five, six and seven. "Now this is the message that we have heard from Him and proclaim to you: God is light and in Him there is no darkness at all. If we say "we have fellowship with Him" while we continue to walk in darkness, we lie and do not act in truth. But if we walk in light as He is in the light, then we have fellowship with one another, and the blood of His Son Jesus cleanses us of all sin."'

I'd been pleased with myself coming up with this passage to hang my debut sermon on, thinking the people of

Simmerton would like nothing better than to focus on light and hope at the deepest days of their dark winter. But as I looked out across the pews, I saw a few disappointed faces, even a couple of raised eyebrows and twisted mouths, and I wondered if maybe every guest who hit this pulpit had the same brainwave and they were sick of it. Maybe it was rude for newcomers to mention it, like a great big birthmark on someone else's baby.

I really wished I hadn't started thinking of babies. I could see Shannon sitting there right at the back. But I'm not experienced enough to switch sermons on the run and I couldn't drum up something to comfort her instead of this clueless riff on light and darkness, reminding her of her condition and her brother's. The throw of the genetic dice that sealed his fate.

'No need of UV rays . . .' I was saying, ' . . . warmth of the Simmerton welcome, bright smiles of my new neighbours . . .' I thought of Mr Sloan. I saw the congregation shuffling its feet with a cacophony of gritty, scraping noises. Of course they all knew that two of our neighbours had died as soon as we arrived. If they'd known – or even dreamed – what else those neighbours had done, pretending a child was dead when it was living . . .

My brain ran up against this fact like a brick wall and stalled. My mouth kept talking. I had practised the sermon enough times for it to pour out of me. But all of my mind was elsewhere now. They had both conspired once before to pretend that a person was dead. They had pretended little Simon was dead. They went as far as to substitute another child's body and bury it.

And what was happening this time? Paddy and I had seen

two bodies and then they had disappeared. Someone had sent an email from a dead man's phone. No one could work out who had moved the bodies or where they'd been put or who had sent the email or why.

But what, I was suddenly asking myself, what if the same thing had happened again? What if they *weren't* dead? What if Tuft, lying there with blood glossy in her mouth and bright in her cuts . . . What if Lovatt, slumped over her with that knife sliced into his back and the bloom of that black butterfly . . . What if, once we had seen them, they got up and walked away? Flew to Brazil, safe from Shannon, safe from everyone. Scot free.

Maybe *that* was why the tableau had kept pulsing in my head, filling my dreams, pounding at me to pay attention. Some bit of my brain knew some bit of that picture was wrong.

I was still talking, about light and hope, about truth and clarity, and I was still thinking: we were always supposed to go back and see them. That wasn't a slip. It was part of the plan. I wasn't supposed to forget my bag. No one could have made me do that. It was the signed papers we were supposed to go back for, the papers Paddy thought he had, that Lovatt must have taken back from him. The bag was just an unexpected bonus.

But, then, why the hell did they send the email about going on holiday? That made no sense at all. Less than putting the bag out on the hallstand.

I drove my mind away from it all and back to the pulpit, back to the words I was speaking, back to the upturned faces of the Simmerton churchgoers. I was horrified to realise that they were speaking too. We were halfway through praying

322

together in chorus, without a word of it – my direct address to God! – having glanced against any particle of my brain.

'Forgive us our trespasses,' I said, hoping they wouldn't hear my voice change, 'as we forgive those who trespass against us. And lead us not into temptation but deliver us from evil. Amen.'

The congregation kept muttering and started shuffling again but I didn't even register the dissonance until Robert Waugh, taking over again from behind the lectern, made some snippy little dig about the many paths to God.

I had said the Our Father of my childhood instead of the Lord's Prayer as approved by my current bosses.

It was the least of my worries today.

Chapter 31

'They'll put it down to nerves,' my dad said, tucking me under his armpit and shaking me after I had finished saying goodbye to the parishioners, filing out with their dead eyes and their pursed mouths. 'It's nothing. They loved you. You were fantastic up there. End of the pier. Céline Dion at Caesar's Palace.'

'For God's sake,' I said, and went to the vestry to take off my robes and get my anorak. Robert Waugh was in his office but he didn't want to speak to me any more than I wanted to speak to him. I nipped in and out like a rat terrier and left by the side door.

My dad was still there, standing with Shannon. 'Don't get rid of me that easy!' he said.

'Okay, okay,' I said. 'Thank you. You're right. My first outing was a triumph. You happy?'

'Me? I'm always happy,' he said. It was true.

'But *I* need a bit of time,' I told him. 'I need a walk on my own, then I'll be happy too. I won't be long.'

'We're all going for a pub lunch,' my dad said. 'Elayne,

your mum, Paddy, if we can rouse him. You in, Shannon? Where's got decent beer and a roast dinner?'

'Text me where you are,' I said, beginning to walk away. 'I'll join you, honest, Dad. I just need some alone time.'

'You'll be okay?' he called after me. 'Lot of funny stuff going on round here, Finnie. I could come with you.'

I flapped a hand at him and walked on. The funny stuff was all in Brazil, I was nearly certain. Simmerton was back to its quiet life again. Simmerton, Jerusalem and Widdershins – the sliver of valley and its two needle-thin cuts – had had their adventures and now they could settle back into obscurity. I just needed to work out whether I could settle into obscurity along with them. Or if I had to keep at it, like a loose tooth, until that last niggling question was answered. Did I have to keep picking at the threads of that squeak-tight knot until it loosened and I could smooth the strands and follow them, all the way from Denise Dudgeon's genetic black luck to Paddy's future as my husband, the father of my – maybe, who knew? – children and my safe place in this harsh world?

The rain, for a mercy, had stopped. The strip of sky above the trees was like the inside of a mussel shell, that shape cupped over me, those bands of blue and grey criss-crossing me. I walked with my head tipped back, drinking it in and feeling my worst fears shrink down until they were spiders instead of monsters: bad enough but nothing I couldn't stamp on.

Trouble was, there was nowhere to walk. If I circled the town I'd meet my parishioners, maybe even my family, and if I headed out at the south end I'd end up at home. So I found myself walking where I'd driven on Friday. Up the east cut past the graveyard towards that blackened, shuttered house.

I would walk round it just once, clockwise, like an act of faith that somewhere outside this valley the sun really was still rising, crossing the wide sky and setting again. Then, whether or not I had come to any conclusions, I would join my family and eat. I would even ask for a doggy bag for Paddy.

Maybe in spring there would be wild garlic up here, I tried to tell myself, as I left the last of the cottages behind me and slipped into the cut. Primroses, bluebells, orchids. Maybe in summer there would be wild raspberries and families with buckets out picking them, coming back in autumn for the brambles, making jelly and winning rosettes at the village show.

'Right, Finnie,' I said. 'And the men'll be whistling and the women'll tie scarves over their hair and the kids'll play Pooh-sticks because you've left the city and moved to nineteen fifty.'

That strip of sky was beginning to make me feel dizzy, so I lowered my head and faced where I was going, passing the graveyard, with its mangled gate, passing the mossy and mouldering gateposts, picking my way through the tall weeds and saplings sprouting in the rotting drive, until once again the house was before me and then beside me and then behind me as I circled it and took the last corner to turn for home.

Then stopped.

Something had changed.

I retraced my steps to the back of the house again, to where the store rooms and sculleries dribbled out into lean-tos and sheds. There, beside one of the many iron-barred windows, the board across a doorway was broken. It had been pulled free and had split in a ragged diagonal, then been propped back in place.

I knew better but the habit was ingrained. I plucked out my phone and looked for a signal. I was tugging at the bottom half of the broken board before I'd got the bleep and the frowny face. I flipped my phone to torch and faced it away from me.

Behind the board, when I stooped to see, there was a plain corridor of white walls and stone floor, doors along its length and a staircase rising up at its far end.

'Hello?' I shouted. 'Is anyone in there?' I put one foot inside and tested the floor. It felt solid enough.

Of course I shouldn't go in. I wasn't a moron. But I told myself if a homeless member of the Simmerton community had moved in here, he – probably he – was just the person a deacon needed to meet.

Assuring myself it was nothing sinister, telling myself that the door first closed then open in Shannon's cottage was nothing to worry me, I slipped inside and started walking.

The fire hadn't reached down here to the back basement. The rooms off the corridor were empty but intact, nothing more than the odd sheet of yellowed newspaper on the dusty floors. The staircase I had seen at the far end was a different story. Halfway up to the first landing the paint on the stone steps turned black and crackled and the walls darkened to a blistered brown. But the steps *were* stone. I tried the first, then the second and, listening closely for warning creaks, I climbed them.

Decades after the fire, the dead air on the main floor was still kippered, smoke and rot in equal doses turning my stomach. I stood at the head of the stairs and played my torch around. The floor of this hall was – I thought – marble. I could see faint traces of squares and little diamonds under a thick layer of greasy dust. There was another staircase opposite me, with a splayed bottom step and a newel post with a bulbous, carved base. The top of the post was burned to a jagged spear of charcoal and the steps above that one grand, sweeping riser were missing. There was a sagging landing banister twenty feet above that showed where the staircase had once arrived on the upper floor, but stair, floor and rooms had all burned away. The interior of the house above the ground was simply – and obscenely somehow – gone.

It couldn't be safe for anyone to be holed up in there.

'Hello?' I shouted again, and thought I heard scuffling. It was a small scuffling. But, I supposed, it might have been someone's boot heels scraping on the floor if he had been startled awake by some daft woman shouting.

'I didn't mean to scare you,' I called to him, willing him to exist. 'Are you okay?' Now there was silence, but I played my light over the floor towards where that scuffle had come from and I was sure I could see . . . not footprints exactly, but some kind of disturbance in the layer of dirt. I walked over, headed for an archway, its doors long gone.

There was something in there, I thought, standing on the threshold. But either this room was cavernous or my phone was starting to lose juice because the light, so sharp at my feet, only just picked out the shapes I was peering at.

'*Are* you okay?' I said. Whoever it was was on the floor and he didn't smell too good. I took a deep breath and started making my way over. I had thought my days of homeless drunks who'd pissed and puked and never changed their clothes were over when I took this job but I wasn't complaining. I didn't have 'WWJD' tattooed inside my wrist for nothing. And I knew the answer this time. He'd wash their feet.

'Are you awake?' I said, halfway there. I clicked my phone off and clicked it on again but the light was the same smeared and feeble yellow. 'Don't get a fright,' I said, stepping softer. I lifted my phone and closed my eyes, so's I'd have a better view when I opened them.

I got one good look before my phone went black as I dropped it, shrieking.

The rat I had startled, shouting from the hallway, was a bold one. It had come back. It was sitting on Tuft's chest gnawing at the ropy skin of her neck. And she was watching it. Her yellow eyes were turned down towards her body, bulging as if with outrage.

Lovatt lay beside her on his back. The knife must be gone. The knife was gone and his face was gone too. It was slashed to . . . they weren't ribbons. They looked like entrails: lumpy and ragged, hanging down the sides of his head and jumbled at the base of his throat. I whimpered as I realised the blob of gristle nestled above his collar was his nose.

I turned away, then whipped back again, hearing the claws of that plucky little rat click on the floor, slow but determined, as it inched back towards the feast.

'No!' I shouted, and stamped my feet, feeling my phone crunch under my heel. 'Stop it! Go away!' I shrieked, as loud as I could. I heard the rat's claws as it fled.

'It's okay,' I said. 'It's okay, Finnie. Mortal remains can't harm you. They have gone to God. They've gone home to God.' I was sure they had, no matter what doctrine I was going by. This was no suicide. That spindly old lady couldn't have done that to Lovatt's face and there was no way on Earth or in Heaven anyone could do it to himself. Someone had killed them both, and by the grace of God, they were with

329

Him now. There was nothing in this house for me to fear. Not even the rat, God's creature, living his allotted life, a part of God's plan.

Finally, I had talked myself into moving. I knew the floor was solid behind me. I would find my way. I turned and, with my arms straight out in front, I searched for the open archway.

How could I be lost inside a room with just one door? It was large and I was moving slowly, but it seemed like half an hour I spent edging forward, feeling empty air with my waving arms, before I grazed my knuckles on a wall and began to feel my way around it.

It had to be here somewhere, that yawning empty opening where the double doors had burned out. Unless – this stopped me – unless I had walked straight through it already and was edging my way to the stairs right now, about to plummet down them and lie there until someone else saw the ragged board and found us all.

'Dear Lord, hear my prayer,' I said. 'Please help me to . . .' My mind ran dry and my voice petered out. 'Oh, sod it!' I said, so loud it rang above me. 'Hail Mary, full of grace. Our Lord is with thee. Blessed art thou among women, and blessed is the fruit of thy womb, Jesus. Holy Mary, Mother of God, pray for us sinners, now and at the hour of our death. Amen. Hail Mary, full of grace. Our Lord is with thee . . .'

It took two and half to find the doorway. It took the other half and three more before I hit the back wall of the hallway and inched my way round in the pitch black to the stair head. Then, hugging the blistered wall, I slid down the stairs on my bottom to the long corridor with the stone floor and the faint light through the broken board far ahead of me.

I ran down the drive, down the cut, past the graveyard and banged on the door of the first cottage I came to.

'What on earth?' Sonsie Webb answered it in her slippers with a folded newspaper under her arm. 'Finnie, where have you been? Are you all right? You're filthy.'

'Phone,' I managed to mumble before I grabbed Sonsie by both her hands and used the resistance of her solid little round body as a counter-weight to stop me sliding too fast to the floor.

Chapter 32

I was done with secrets. Really done this time. When the police arrived at Sonsie and Adam's house – Speccy and Baldy, I was glad to see – I told them everything.

Starting with what was lying on the floor of that huge empty room at Jerusalem.

'Yes, dead,' I said. 'Very, very dead. And no bloody way it's suicide. Lovatt's cut to ribbons.'

'Drink your tea, dear,' Adam Webb said. He had tried to get a nip of whisky down me but my hangover was still raging so he'd settled for sweet, milky tea.

'Look,' I said. 'I don't know everything, but I know this. They died in the kitchen at their house. I saw them there. I know! I know! Charge me with it, if you like, but just listen. Then they spent a few days at Bairnspairt – Shannon Mack's cottage. They were in her bedroom. She burned incense but it was still pretty bad. They left there yesterday to go where they are now. But Shannon can't have taken them because she can't drive.'

'Hasn't got a licence, you mean,' said Speccy, grimly.

'No,' I said. 'Can't drive. Bad eyesight and, anyway, no car. There's no way she would have set off up that dark road in the low light. I don't know who moved them but it wasn't Shannon. I don't know why she agreed to have them in her house. Or who she agreed *with*. Paddy.' I blurted it out. 'Oh, bugger it all to Hell, it's my husband, Paddy. It must be. He must have known. He's Lovatt Dudgeon's son.'

'Your husband?' said Baldy, and shared a look with his partner. 'Have you had a fight, hen? Have you been under any strain lately?'

'Look,' I said, struggling up from where I was reclining on the couch with a pillow under my knees. Sonsie had manhandled me into position, then put such a heavy quilt over me I felt trapped. 'I know this sounds absolutely bloody mental. I'm sorry. But my husband, who goes by the name Paddy Lamb, is actually Simon Dudgeon. And the little boy in Simon Dudgeon's grave is really a child called Sean Mack. Lovatt and Tuft killed him.'

The two police pulled back and shared another look.

'I know!' I said. 'But you don't need to believe me. You can check the DNA. You can test Paddy. And you can test the little boy if you disinter his remains. It's all true.'

'Right,' said Baldy. 'Well, I know I shouldn't say it, but when you've spent days looking for bodies it's nice to find out for sure that they're really dead.' He tapped his teeth with the pencil he had pulled out to make notes with, notes he hadn't taken because he didn't believe anything I'd said. 'So who sent the email saying they were in Brazil, then?'

'I have no idea,' I said. 'Sorry. No clue.'

'CID's problem,' Speccy said. 'And they're going to want to talk to you, hen. *We* need to get on with recovering those bodies. Get a team in. Get a doc in. Disturb the fiscal on a Sunday.'

'Yes,' I said. 'There's a rat eating her neck.'

That got them moving.

'Can we drop you at home?' said Baldy. 'Not leave you here swearing your head off and mucking up the upholstery?'

'My family's at the pub,' I said. 'With Shannon.' Although I didn't know which pub because the text telling me was in my crunched phone on the floor up there.

'I don't think—' Baldy began.

'Me neither,' I said. 'I need to go home and talk to Paddy in peace. Find out what he's got to say for himself.'

We were halfway there, right through the town and up the Widdershins cut, when I had to ask them to pull over so I could puke in the verge.

'Sorry,' I said, when I got back in. 'It's not even the bodies. I was hammered last night. I've been feeling like shit all day.'

'Don't apologise,' said Speccy. 'Anyone that gets out this car *before* they start throwing up is ahead of the game. You're a lady.'

'I've never heard anyone in a cassock swear so much, except an Irish priest, though,' said Baldy. 'You've changed my mind about the Church of Scotland today. I thought youse were all like the Webbs there.'

'The Webbs are okay,' I said. 'I'm a bad example.'

Then we were swinging into the Widdershins gate and I scrambled out.

'Don't go anywhere,' Baldy said, before he slid his window up and made the tight turn to drive away. I trotted after him and banged on the roof. The window slid down again.

'Mr Sloan,' I said. 'He needs a Social visit when you get a minute, by the way.'

'Oh?' said Speccy. 'Why are you telling us and not the local authority?'

'Trust me. Send a family liaison officer round tomorrow.'

Then they were gone.

Paddy was in the living room and I could tell from his face it was a hangover, not a migraine.

'How did it go?'

I blinked a couple of times, winding back through this nightmare day. 'Oh! The sermon? Not great but it doesn't matter.'

'Not great how?'

'I was distracted by the sudden thought that Tuft and Lovatt weren't dead.' I waved his objections away. 'So I went for a walk to try to think it through and . . . Prepare yourself for a shock, Paddy. I found them.'

Paddy stared at me. 'Alive?' he said at last.

'You know they're not alive,' I said. 'You need to stop trying to fool me. I've already called the police to go and see to the bodies and I told them – the police – what happened on Monday night. I didn't tell them you went back, but only because I forgot. I'm not covering for you any more. I'm done. I'm out. If that means we're over, we're over.'

'Where's everyone else?' Paddy said. 'Have they gone back to Edinburgh?'

'Are you trying to work out if you'll be interrupted while you finish me off too?' I was almost completely kidding. 'Well, I'm sorry, but they're out for lunch in a pub in town there. With Shannon. So I wouldn't.'

'You don't think much of me, do you?' Paddy said.

335

'I think you're lying to me. I just don't know what about.'

'I could swear on a Bible,' Paddy said, looking around as if he expected to see one.

'I bet you could,' I said. 'Are you working with Shannon?'

'Shannon? I met her less than a week ago.'

'Mr Sloan? It's his area of expertise after all.'

'Finnie, what are you talking about? I moved here for a good job. A great job. And not a bad job for you. Okay, I got talked into living in this cottage and I steamrollered you. But when we got here last Saturday it was to start a new life together, you and me. It went off the deep end pretty fast and I've been clinging on by my fingernails ever since. It would have been good to think you were in it with me. I shouldn't have crapped out of seeing the bodies on Tuesday. I know I should have told you they'd gone when I went back for that bloody cactus. I get all that. I really do. I shouldn't have been so fired up by the will. I get that too. I disappointed you. And – at least – I should have thought about my mum instead of myself when everything started coming out yesterday.'

It was the first thing he'd said that really meant something to me.

'But I *didn't* know he was my dad and I *didn't* know he was going to kill himself. Honestly, Finnie. I swear I didn't know.'

'He didn't kill himself,' I said.

'Jesus! Why nitpick now? I didn't know Tuft was going to kill him and then herself. Is that better?'

'No one killed themselves. And neither one of them killed the other. Tuft couldn't have done what was done to Lovatt's body. And he couldn't have done it to himself.' I squeezed my eyes shut but the tears seeped out anyway. Had I really wanted to find them at the graveyard? Had I really wanted to see them again to drive away the vision in the kitchen? If I could get that vision back now I'd be happy for the rest of my life. The black butterfly on Lovatt's back instead of the octopus jumble of his face? The blood in her mouth instead of the rat on her throat?

'*He* couldn't have done it to himself,' Paddy said. 'But she could have. Of course she could. A sharp enough knife, and if she was lucky and didn't hit a rib. Why not?'

'I'm not talking about what killed him,' I said. 'I'm talking about what was done to his body. His face was slashed. So much hatred it must have taken.'

'Sounds like a wife to me,' Paddy said. 'Don't look at me like that. That's what they say. It's only crimes of passion that make people try to obliterate each other. Hit jobs are clean kills.'

He was talking as if this was a movie, some designer-violence fantasy.

And he was wrong too. 'Setting fire to people is a pretty good way to obliterate them,' I said. 'And that wasn't passion.'

A look of such pain crossed Paddy's face then, the like of which I had never seen, and he caught his breath in a sob. 'That wasn't to obliterate them,' he said. 'He loved them. His wife and his little girl. He wanted to save them pain. He must have killed them painlessly. I need to believe that, Finnie. The fire was to hide the fact that the boy wasn't me.'

'Right,' I said. 'Right enough. The little boy wasn't you.'

Then a shiver passed over me, as if I'd been doused in ice water. I'd made a mistake earlier when my mind had spun away from my words during the sermon. 'We lie and do not act in truth,' I said.

'What?' Paddy frowned at me.

But I didn't answer. I was thinking better now – clearer and sharper – and finally it all made sense. Lovatt hadn't just pretended once before that someone alive was dead. He had switched a body. One boy for another. *Now* I knew why that image from the kitchen wouldn't leave me. The bright red cuts in her hands and the knife in his back.

'The black butterfly,' I said.

'What?' said Paddy.

He'd done it again. That old man had his face cut to ribbons not out of hate, not from passion, but to hide his features in gore so dreadful no one would look for long. He was the same age and height and weight as Lovatt Dudgeon and he was wearing Lovatt Dudgeon's clothes. No one – not cops, not lawyers, not friends and neighbours – *no one* would doubt who it was. No one would call for forensics to prove it. The fiscal would save the public purse the price of a postmortem. But Lovatt Dudgeon – just like Simon all those years ago – was gone.

Chapter 33

I was waiting in Shannon's cottage when my dad's car slowed at her gate. She came trotting up the path through a fresh shower of rain and let herself in. It was four o'clock and black as hate outside. I was sitting in the shadows and I spoke before she saw me.

'How did he persuade you?'

She started and, when she turned, she was trembling.

'How did Lovatt Dudgeon persuade you to hide the bodies in here until the police were finished searching?' I said.

'He didn't,' Shannon said. She came and sat in the opposite armchair, the other side of the cold fireplace. Rain was dropping on the ash in the grate, and the air was rank with the smell of it. 'Of course he didn't. He couldn't have. I would never.'

'Shannon, I know it was you. Jesus, I accused Paddy! I suspected my own husband. But I know it was you.'

'Wait,' said Shannon. 'Yes, that's not what I mean. I'm not denying it. I'm saying I couldn't have been leaned on to hide bodies,' she said. 'Bodies plural. I thought I was agreeing to one body. Tuft's body. I was going to keep it here until the cops had found her suicide note and then he was going to take it away.'

'Lovatt.'

'Who else?'

'Why?' I said.

'Because she killed his wife and daughter. That's what he said to me. *She* masterminded it. He didn't know. That's what he told me. He didn't work out what had happened until I contacted him and asked about Sean. And he wanted revenge on her.'

'He . . . What? He heard you out and then he suddenly had this incredible revelation about his current wife killing his first wife?'

'And daughter. And stealing his son. It sounds mad now, but I believed him.'

'Why wouldn't Tuft just kill both children?' I said. 'Why keep Simon alive and turn him into Paddy and give him to Elayne?'

'Insurance,' said Shannon. 'So if Lovatt ever busted her she'd have a hold over him.'

'But he organised the adoption,' I said.

'Unless she could forge his signature.'

'And he gave Paddy a job.'

'Unless she persuaded him.'

'And why was it important for the body to be hidden for a while? Why move it here and then move it on?'

'He said the murder would be harder to solve if it wasn't found straight away. And also if it turned up somewhere the police thought they'd checked, they'd be on the defensive and less likely to make trouble.'

'Right,' I said. 'Right. So . . . what happened? What went wrong?'

'I peeked,' Shannon said. 'I opened the door.'

'Jesus. When?'

'Monday night. Because one of their phones rang. I thought *her* phone was ringing – because I thought she was alone in there. So I went in. And there were two of them. Tuft and . . . I thought it was Lovatt. I thought he'd pulled a double-cross on me. Landing me with two bodies so I'd go to jail for murdering them.'

'But that's crazy,' I said.

Shannon held up a hand and went on. 'The phone was in Lovatt's pocket. I stopped it ringing – it was just a junk call – and I used it to email the office and tell them the story about Brazil. That's where he'd told me he was going. I was so scared, Finnie. I didn't know what to do. So I bought some time, sending that email so no one would look for them. Then I went up and faxed the papers. Like Lovatt had told me to.'

'How long did it take you to realise?'

'I woke up in the middle of Monday night and it was like someone had whispered it in my ear,' Shannon said. 'If that's Lovatt . . .?'

'Who moved the corpses.'

'Exactly. I realised the old man – his face, Finnie!'

'I've seen it.'

'I realised he was a decoy. Lovatt had lied about the plan. The story was never "Tuft killed herself because her husband left her". The story was "Two old people killed themselves".'

'And that got you thinking?'

'Slowly. Very slowly, I pieced it together. You helped.

341

Telling me Paddy had been enticed down here, had been given a partnership, was Lovatt's heir. He was the right age.'

'And you worked out that Lovatt's plan was to install Paddy, fake his own death and hook it?'

'You're quick,' said Shannon. 'It took me days to get there. But eventually I got there.'

'By Friday,' I said. 'That's why you went to Simon Dudgeon's grave.'

'To see Sean at last after all these years,' she said. 'Yes. And while I was there, he moved them again. Two more bodies in Jerusalem House.'

'He was taking a hell of a chance,' I said.

'Not really. Paddy wouldn't open his gob, would he? Mr Sloan would hardly. I couldn't.'

'What about the family in the other house?' I said. 'What are they called? McGann?'

'Mann,' said Shannon. 'That house has been empty for years. Those bikes never move. There's weeds in the sandpit and dead leaves in the trampoline. Didn't you notice?'

I shuddered. 'That's beyond creepy,' I said. 'What's the point of that, then?'

'I don't know. Maybe they kept it in case they needed to buy off someone else, like they bought off Mr Sloan and you two. And me.'

'The thing is,' I said, 'he must know we saw the bodies. He must have been in Widdershins on Monday night when we went back. It was minutes later. He must have realised we might crack.'

'He's pretty good at judging what people will hide,' Shannon said. 'He's never called it wrong before now.'

'But *why*?' I said. 'Where did it all start? Was Denise

Dudgeon even ill? Did she actually have Huntington's? Was little Vanessa really tested? Or did Lovatt just want rid of them? Was he just a monster? A monster who met another monster.'

'He *is* a monster,' Shannon said. 'He might have tricked Tuft the same way he tricked me. Maybe she found out on Monday night that her life was a lie. Maybe she had a split-second as the knife went in.'

We had been ignoring the sirens. Two police cars had flashed past, headed for the gate lodge and Widdershins' drive. Now one came back the other way and stopped outside.

'They've probably come for poor old Mr Sloan,' said Shannon, but I didn't think so and something about her saying it bothered me.

'Why would Lovatt think I'd keep the secret?' I asked her, as the police-car door slammed shut outside.

'Didn't you?'

'But how did *he* know? It was such a fluke. Yes, Paddy and I were in too deep before we'd taken a single step, but how did he *know*? And why didn't he lock the door?'

'Ninety-nine people out of a hundred finding their bag in the vestibule nice and handy would have left it at that. But you had to go and be the one.'

'That's me,' I said. 'Hang on, though. How did you know where my handbag was?'

'You told us all yesterday.'

I nodded. She was probably right and, anyway, that wasn't what was bothering me. 'I think the cops are coming here,' I said. 'Not to the Sloans. The Sloans,' I repeated. Was *that* it?

Right enough, a plain-clothes cop was walking up Shannon's path, talking into his phone.

'I can't face them,' Shannon said. 'Go and let him in, Finnie. I just can't face it.'

'Wait!' I said. 'I knew something was wrong when my dad told me how long she'd been dead. Shannon, you said you'd *met* Mrs Sloan.'

But she was hurrying into the kitchen and didn't answer me. I went to the door.

'Miss Mack?' the cop said. He had a plastic folder held over his head to keep the rain off him.

'No,' I said. 'She's in the—' My voice died in my throat as, at the same split second I saw down the path into the back of the cop car and Paddy sitting there, I heard Shannon's kitchen door bang.

'She's getting away!' I pulled myself out of the way of the cop, fitter than he looked as he raced through the house and out again, yelling for his partner.

The passenger side of the police car flew open and another man in plain clothes skidded and scrambled up the path and round the side of the cottage.

I walked down, slowly, in the rain, and bent to look in at him. He was handcuffed to a bar that ran along the back of the front seats.

We stared at each other a good while. We said plenty in that silence, as the rain washed my head, cleared my mind.

'You said you saw Mrs Sloan putting her bins out,' I said. 'That wasn't true. None of it's true.'

'He did offer me a partnership,' Paddy said. 'That's true. Only I said I wouldn't take on St Angela's so he started winding it down.'

'St Angela's is legit?'

'Of course it's legit! This isn't the Wild West. How could someone fake an adoption agency?'

I took a step to steady myself. 'Did Shannon have a brother?'

'Shannon's got two brothers. They live near her parents.'

'But neither one of them is poor Sean, with his bad eyes and his clicking barrels.'

'No.'

'So the whole thing about her twin and the adoption ... nothing's true? Her Scandinavian mum and the poetry. None of it?

'I don't know if her mum writes poetry,' Paddy said. 'Could do. They're not close.'

'Did Lovatt kill his family?' I said. I had to put a hand against the car for support.

'Don't be stupid. Denise killed herself and the kids. Because of the Huntington's.'

'And what about what your mum said? About the clinic and the little boy?'

'She'd say anything for me.'

'But *she* said she'd met Myna Sloan too!'

'Shannon worked everything in,' said Paddy.

'And she fainted! Your mum did. Yesterday.'

'She bottled it when Shannon walked in. You think she's scared of you, Finnie? She's petrified of Shannon.'

'She's right to be,' I said. 'And I don't really scare her, do I? Lying to me scared her. The thought of me seeing through her scared her.'

He was barely listening. He had a dreamy look on his face, thinking about Shannon. It was a look I knew. I'd just never known what put it there.

'You didn't act as if you'd just met her, you know.' He shrugged. 'On Wednesday. At lunchtime. When you started talking about our rent and your partnership in front of her.'

'You didn't twig,' he said.

'So what's the truth? How did you get the job? Why did he make you a partner? And what about my job?'

'Oh, I *am* his kid,' Paddy said. 'That's true. My mum used to work in his office in Edinburgh.'

'So she's really your mum?'

'Yep.'

'She took your baby pictures?'

'Yep. One of them's in the same living room, Finnie.'

'So,' I said. I was feeling a bit steadier now. I stood up straight again. 'You and your girlfriend, Shannon, killed your boss and his wife so that you'd inherit his firm and his estate? And you cooked up a story so . . . insane that no one would question it? Is that it?'

'*You* bought it, didn't you? A deacon of the kirk, no less. You swallowed it whole.'

'I thought I'd caught them out,' I said. 'Tuft and Lovatt. I thought I'd caught them lying about when they met.'

Paddy's head jerked up.

'She said twenty-five years ago when Berwick station went automatic,' I said. 'But that was over thirty years back. Shannon checked it.'

'Oh, *Shannon* checked?' said Paddy.

'Right,' I said. 'Idiot. She must have been lying. Only . . . why would she lie about that?'

'For fun,' Paddy said. 'For the hell of it. Or maybe he did meet Tuft before Denise and the kids died. Maybe he did

346

dump his family for wifie-poo number two. Tuft didn't have to live in a semi, knitting for cash, did she?'

I nodded. 'I'm still trying to get my head round it,' I said. 'Brazil? Sean Mack? Simon Dudgeon? St Angela's? It was all . . . a dust storm?'

'And the papers I doctored to show to Abby and the signed documents I left behind so we'd have a reason to go back up there. Then you left your bag, which was even better.'

'You're a good actor,' I said. 'I didn't know that about you, but you fooled me over the fax and the email.' His face showed a flicker. 'What?' I said. 'Weren't you acting?'

'She kept changing things. The papers were supposed to be there. The bodies weren't supposed to move. She wasn't even supposed to be on the drive on Monday night. In the trees. All that planning and then she kept changing things.'

'Why?' I said.

Paddy shrugged, his face drawn up in the creases and puckers that were bound to bring on a migraine. Then he laughed again. 'For the joy of it,' he said. 'Same as how she added all the mad extras, like that barrel video. Mind you, she was right – she showed it to you. And you bought it.'

'Why *did* she move the bodies?' I said.

'I don't know!' That had rattled him, but he recovered. 'She'll have had a good reason. She always does.'

'Because no one would do *that* for fun, would they?' He didn't answer. 'Maybe,' I went on, 'she made all the changes so you'd make mistakes. So you'd end up where you are.'

'What?' said Paddy. Even now, sitting in the back of a police car, he couldn't see past her. 'No, this wasn't part of the plan, Finn. And we really did plan. We planned longer than you'd believe.'

'Try me,' I said. 'Tell me how long. You knew about me, didn't you? About the car crash, the jail time. And me a deacon.'

'Of course I did. And I knew how ashamed of it you were.'

'I was selected? I was a stooge?'

'Well, put it this way. I thought it would come in handy. And it did.'

'And I take it the oil rig and all that was a load of crap? The old lady client who died? The loan?'

Paddy's face snapped shut. 'No,' he said. 'That was true. I went to my father – my own bloody father – to help me straighten it out and he did. He gave me the loan and then he told me I had to pay it back. The rig was his idea. It was quick money and it sure as hell felt like prison. He didn't need the cash, you know. He just wanted me to learn a lesson. So I decided I'd teach him one instead. I had already started planning it that night I met you.'

'And then you were going to offload me?'

'Except I didn't have to,' Paddy said. 'You were just about to leave me of your own accord, weren't you?'

'Clever,' I said.

'Shannon's a genius,' said Paddy. 'Sloan's secret gave us part of the idea too. Creepy necro Mr Sloan. Shannon just folded it into everything else.'

'But I don't understand why Lovatt and Tuft covered for Mr Sloan if he had nothing on them,' I said.

'They didn't!' said Paddy. 'They didn't know Mrs Sloan was lying up there. Only Shannon knew that.'

'But they said they played mah jongg with her. Sonsie told me they were there on Sunday night.' I screwed my face up with the effort of remembering. We were sitting in the back pew of the church, Sonsie and me. 'No!' I said. '*I* told *her*. But who told *me*?' Paddy said it in chorus with me as I remembered.

'Shannon.'

Then he went on, 'If you just say things straight out to people who trust you, nine times out of ten they'll swallow it. She taught me that.'

'Oh, Paddy,' I said. 'She didn't half.'

'What?' he asked me, still not seeing.

'Why did they give her a cottage?' I said.

'They didn't! She paid the going rate. Of course, Lovatt regretted it when she started tightening the screws.'

'Why did they pretend she didn't exist?'

'What?'

'They said there were two houses when there's three. What do you mean "screws"?'

'She pretended she suspected him of killing his children. He was terrified of her.'

'He was right as well,' I said. 'You're the one who got her wrong, Paddy. You're handcuffed in a cop car and she's on the run. Do you really think she'll stick with you, back up your version, if they catch her?'

'Course she will,' he said.

'You still think you're in this with her?'

He was shaking but it might have been the cold. I was shaking too. 'We're a team. I'm the money and she's the brains. Some of it went right over your head, you know.'

'I don't think so,' I said. 'If you mean the butterfly?'

'What butterfly?'

'The black butterfly on Lovatt's back. The blood should have been red. *All* the blood should have been red. The black stain on his back was supposed to make me think *that* blood

349

was old, right? Make me think that old man was longer dead than Lovatt Dudgeon could have been. Then we'd "work out" that the old man wasn't Lovatt after all.'

'Oh, you caught that, did you? Why did you never ask what I was saying? In my sleep.'

'Too dark?'

'You were supposed to ask me. And I would "think about it a while" and "realise".'

'And I'd be convinced because it would explain why I couldn't stop thinking about it either. The black butterfly.'

'Too dark!' said Paddy. 'She's a genius. She can act, forge handwriting and signatures, spin so many different tales no one even knows where to start unravelling them.'

'She's very resourceful,' I said. As I watched, a pale blue people carrier came along the road and pulled in at the Manns' house. A woman stepped down and looked back along the lane to where the cop car sat with its doors open, and a girl in a dog-collar stood by it in the pouring rain. Then she opened the back doors and shooed a gaggle of teenagers into the house ahead of her. I raised a hand to wave but, as you would, she ignored me.

'Trouble is, Paddy,' I added, 'she's completely insane. And she's ruined your life. Too dark is about right.'

I could hear my dad's car coming. I saw his headlamps picking out raindrops as he came swinging round the corner. I left Paddy sitting there and walked towards the light.

After

I'm a connoisseur of crematoriums now. This one at Warriston is my fourth since January. Mrs Sloan was first, in the small service room at Mortonhall, with only seven of us there. Robert Waugh came through with a eulogy and an address I couldn't have landed on if I'd had five years to get ready. I've felt different about him since that day. He can golf all he wants as long as he's there to pick up the reins anytime we're cremating a six-year-old corpse with her husband watching, a police officer on either side of him in the front row.

He didn't do time for it, poor old Mr Sloan. He got probation and counselling. Which didn't work. He's feeble now, stays inside. He's let the garden go to pot.

Then there was Tuft and Lovatt, after the inquiry. They were done together at Dumfries. 'A beautiful crem,' Sonsie Webb told me. And so it was, all blond wood and abstract stained-glass windows. That was packed, of course. All of Simmerton was there. All of the old St Angela's staff and a good lot of Edinburgh solicitors too. And press, naturally. Oh, the press. *Valley of Death!* they settled on, as the story got going. And they found the worst, darkest, dreariest winter pictures, the gate lodge looking like a mausoleum and the drive so sinister as it slunk away.

The cameras were right up in our faces as we arrived. They called us by name. Called *me* by name.

'Finnie!'

'Over here, Finn!'

I put my head down and scuttled in with my dad on one side and Robert Waugh on the other. My mum wasn't well enough that day.

It had started to die down by then, until Tuft and Lovatt's funeral kicked it up again. Because, of course, no one believed I knew nothing. Well, no one ever does. I didn't believe the wives of all those monsters knew nothing either, when it was just a gruesome story in the tabloids: Sonia Sutcliffe, Primrose Shipman. Only the combination of me coming clean about that Monday night and both Paddy and Shannon telling the cops – taking such delight in telling the cops – how they'd fooled me put me in the clear.

I assumed I'd lose my job anyway, but I was wrong there. The Church stood by me. It took some time for me to work out why and it hurt a bit, for a while.

But I was getting harder to hurt by then, to be honest. When Paddy killed himself, on remand in his cell, I thought my heart would stop. It didn't feel like something breaking. It felt like something freezing. Calcifying. As if I could go and stand on a headland with my arms up and be a landmark, but I'd never laugh or sing or hug again. The only thing that bucked me out of my petrified grief was the thought of Elayne. I went to the house. Robert drove; I wasn't safe behind the wheel just then. But she refused to see me. And in six months she's kept refusing. But I'll get her in the end. No one could resist the gift I'm going to give her. She just needs time, because she loved him so. He really *was* loved. He was loved by all three of us.

They were worried about Shannon after she found out he'd gone. She was on suicide watch for eight weeks. She was in hospital. She's back in her cell now. There's only one women's prison in Scotland so I know exactly what she's going through every day. I can picture it clearly. Sometimes I wonder if she's in the same cell I was in. Except it wouldn't really be the same cell, would it? Not if you're looking at it as your home for life. I'll ask her, when I go to visit. Which I will. Which I'll have to.

Because Shannon wants me to be the guardian of her baby, when it's born, come September. Elayne fought it and Shannon's mum, that poor woman, fought it too, but it's Shannon's choice as long as I agree. And I agreed. I talked to Robert, got his permission to refuse – 'Good God in Heaven, Finnie, you're only human!' he'd said – then found myself agreeing anyway. At least this way the poor wee thing gets all of us. Shannon's mum would never have let Elayne within a mile. And vice versa. But I want both grannies on Team Baby. It's going to need all the help it can get, with that start in life. And no matter what Robert says I reckon it's my duty. There's a reason they call a new baby 'the little stranger'.

I keep calling it 'poor' but it's not. It's the rightful heir. I get nothing. Paddy didn't use his real name when he 'married' me so we were never really married. That was supposed to make it easier for him to walk away with Shannon.

But the baby's a different story. Jerusalem, Widdershins, the Bairnspairt, the gate lodge, the cottages. And all those trees. It was Lovatt's so now it belongs to his grandchild, with me as trustee till it's twenty-one. An heir in utero was a nice big mess for the lawyers but, thanks to the 'yet to be born' clause in Lovatt's will, and the fact that there were no Dudgeon cousins after all, no one's arguing.

And since there's no way I could stay in any of those places, not one single night, I'm happy to let the Church do whatever it wants with them. A halfway house, a children's retreat, a camp-ground for Scouts and Guides down from Glasgow. It'll take some fundraising but the sites are free. In a few years, I'll have a better think about it. Not yet, not now.

The Manns have left. They couldn't get away quick enough. But I'm letting Mr Sloan stay on. Simmerton's the only place he'll ever feel at home. Still close to Myna. Julie pops in on him. Abby's gone back to Edinburgh to finish her training but Julie started at the health club, which suits her down to the ground, except she's had to pretend she's stopped smoking. She nags me to join whenever I see her.

I'll have plenty to keep me busy without a treadmill. Part-time deacon-work and a new baby and looking after Sonsie, who was so good, looking after me. I lean forward to see if I can glimpse her face, in the front row, but her head's down and her hat brim hides it. Poor Sonsie. Adam Webb was sitting at the breakfast table, reading out the headlines to her, when a thunderclap of a heart attack came. Sometimes it's hard to see God's plan. Sometimes I'm sure there's no plan at all. But I'll keep checking.

Acknowledgements

I would like to thank:

Lisa Moylett, Zoe Apostolides, Elena Langtry and all at CMM Literary Agency; Nettie Finn, April Osborn, Kelley Ragland, Sarah Schoof, Sarah Grill, Allison Ziegler and all at Minotaur; Krystyna Green, Rebecca Sheppard, Beth Wright, Hazel Orme, Kate Truman and all at Little, Brown; the librarians and booksellers, reviewers and bloggers, posters and tweeters, and all who make this so much less a solitary job day by day; and my dear, patient friends and ever-growing family in the US and UK.

Simmerton is fictional. No character, house, business or charitable organisation in the book is based on any real individual, property or operation.